891.73 G195 Ksm65sc1
Garshin, V. M.
The signal, and other stories.

AAP-0650
060101 000

0 0003 0206752 0

Johnson State College

DATE DUE

PRINTED IN U.S.A.

BCL

THE SIGNAL
AND OTHER STORIES

THE SIGNAL
AND OTHER STORIES

TRANSLATED FROM
THE RUSSIAN OF
WSEWOLOD MIKHAILOVICH GARSHIN
By ROWLAND SMITH

Short Story Index Reprint Series

 BOOKS FOR LIBRARIES PRESS
FREEPORT, NEW YORK

John Dewey Library
Johnson State College
Johnson, Vermont

First Published 1915
Reprinted 1971

INTERNATIONAL STANDARD BOOK NUMBER:
0-8369-3941-7

LIBRARY OF CONGRESS CATALOG CARD NUMBER:
77-163027

PRINTED IN THE UNITED STATES OF AMERICA

PREFACE

It has been said that to know the literature of a country is to know its people, and to know a people is to appreciate them. The wealth of the Russian language, its nuance of expression, its bewildering detail and plentiful use of diminutives, makes its translation into equivalent English especially difficult. But I trust, nevertheless, that this volume of short stories, translations from the Russian, may assist in promoting knowledge in England of Russia and Russians.

Nowhere is there more genuine hospitality than in Russia, and in no other country is there greater or more general kindliness of feeling.

TRANSLATOR.

GARSHIN

(1855–1888)

Wsewolod Michailovich Garshin, the " melancholiac," as he is sometimes called, was of good family. He was born in February, 1855. In appearance of a Southern type, he was nice-looking, and possessed a sweetness of disposition and a temperament sympathetic to a degree unusual in a man. His early life was spent on the family estate with his parents, his father having retired from the army in 1858. When nine years old, he was placed at school in St. Petersburg. His original intention of becoming a doctor was frustrated by the issue at that time of a Government regulation making a University course obligatory on all wishing to take up medicine. He early showed an abnormal nervousness, and in 1872, when only seventeen years old, was temporarily placed under restraint. Recovering his sanity in 1873, and having completed his school course, he entered the Institute of Mining Engineers in 1874. In 1876 the Russo-Turkish War broke out. Although the horrors of war affected him very deeply, Garshin considered it his bounden duty to take an active share in the campaign, and enlisted at Kishineff as a private in an infantry regiment of the line. He displayed great gallantry in action, was wounded in the leg, and invalided home. From this time his mind became periodically unhinged, and it was immediately preceding one of these attacks that he wrote " A Night," which bears unmistakable evidence of a disordered brain. Finally, in 1887, in an access of physical and mental agony, he succeeded in eluding those who were watching by his bedside, and threw himself down a flight of stone steps which formed the staircase leading to his apartment. He inflicted grave injuries to himself, and added to his mental trouble by brooding over the state of mind which had led him to commit such an act. He was shortly afterwards transferred to a hospital for better treatment, where he expired in April, 1888, at the early age of thirty-three, in the presence of some of his always numerous friends and a devoted wife.

An added interest is given to his stories (he only wrote some twenty in all), from the fact that the majority of them possess a groundwork of truth, and embody personal ideas and experiences, or those of friends and acquaintances.

GLOSSARY

Alesha, an intimate form of Alexander. See Names.

Arshin, equals 2½ feet (approximately).

Baba, a peasant woman (old).

Barin, Sir or Master } Words used by servants or the lower
Barinia, Ma'am or Mistress } classes when addressing superiors.

Chinovnik, the generic name of all officials, but more usually applied to the smaller class of Government officials. Is often used in contempt.

Dessiatine, equals 2·70 acres.

Droshky, a small open four-wheeled hackney-carriage.

Dvornik, a yard porter. Each house has one or more dvorniks, whose duties are to cut and carry firewood, etc. They are also responsible for the cleanliness of the street and pavement immediately adjoining the house, and must assist the police.

Dvu-grivennik, a silver coin of the value and size of sixpence.

Euprakseiushka, a character in early Russian history.

Fortochka, a framed pane of glass in a window. It is on hinges, and can be opened for ventilation purposes when the window itself is hermetically sealed up for the winter.

Gorodovoi, a policeman.

Ilia Murometz, a character in early Russian history.

Ispravnik, a provincial police officer.

Izvoschik, a cabman; used indifferently to mean the man or his conveyance.

Kaftan, a three-quarters length overcoat, usually of leather lined with sheepskin.

Koliaska. See Droshky.

Kopeck, a copper coin of the size and value of a farthing.

Krasnoe Solnishko (beautiful sun), a famous early ruler of Russia, and the first of them to embrace Christianity.

Lineika, a four-wheeled conveyance usually seating ten or twelve persons who ride back to back as in an Irish car.

x GLOSSARY

Masha, an intimate form of Maria or Mary. See Names.

Mateik, the name of an artist.

Miatel, a blizzard.

Miekoff, an action in the last Polish Rebellion.

Moujik, a Russian peasant (man). Often used to mean a boor or uncouth person.

Nada, Nadia, intimate forms of Nadejda. See Names.

Names. Every Orthodox Russian has but one Christian name and a patronymic in addition to his surname, which last is not used in conversation. In the case of a man, the patronymic is formed by adding -ovich to his father's name, or -ovna in the case of a woman. Thus, a man christened Ivan whose father bore the same name would be known as Ivan Ivanovich. Similarly, a woman christened Olga whose father's name was Ivan would be known as Olga Ivanovna. In addition to the above there are variations of the Christian name used only by relatives and intimate friends, such as Vasia or Vassenka, intimate forms of Vassilli, Nada or Nadia, intimate forms of Nadejda. Thus, a man whose full name was Simon Ivanovich Spiridoff might be addressed as such, or Simon Spiridoff, or as Simon Ivanovich, or Simon Ivanich, or Senia, or Senichka, dependent on the relations between the two persons.

Opatoff, an action in the last Polish Rebellion.

Pechenegs, a tribe of Turkish origin which early settled itself in Russia.

Poltinik, a silver coin of the value and size of a shilling.

Pood, equals 36 pounds avoirdupois.

Pristaff, a police superintendent.

Prorub, a hole cut out in the ice.

Rouble, a silver coin of the value and size of a florin.

Russ, the ancient name of Russia.

Sajene, equals 7 English feet.

Samovar, a tea-urn in which the water is boiled and kept hot by charcoal.

Sasha, an intimate form of Alexander or Alexandra. See Names.

Semiradski, a Russian artist.

Senia, Senichka, intimate forms of Simon or Simeon. See Names.

Shuba, a fur-lined overcoat of full length.

Sonia, an intimate form of Sophia. See Names.

Sotnia, a squadron of cavalry (applied to Cossack troops only).

Traktir, a humble kind of eating-house frequented by the working classes.

CONTENTS

		PAGE
I.	THE SIGNAL	1
II.	FOUR DAYS	13
III.	AN INCIDENT	27
IV.	COWARD	47
V.	THE MEETING	72
VI.	A NIGHT	95
VII.	A TOAD AND A ROSE	116
VIII.	ATTALEA PRINCEPS	124
IX.	"MAKE-BELIEVE"	133
X.	OFFICER AND SOLDIER-SERVANT	139
XI.	NADEJDA NICOLAIEVNA	156
XII.	THE SCARLET BLOSSOM	230
XIII.	THE BEARS	249
XIV.	THE FROG WHO TRAVELLED	270
XV.	A VERY SHORT ROMANCE	276
XVI.	FROM THE REMINISCENCES OF PRIVATE IVANOFF	282
XVII.	THE ACTION AT AISLAR	339

THE SIGNAL
AND OTHER STORIES

I

THE SIGNAL

SIMON IVANOFF was a linesman on the railway. From his hut it was twenty versts to the nearest station on one side, and ten versts on the other. Last year, about four versts away, a spinning-mill had opened, and its tall chimney stood out darkly against the forest, but except for the huts of other linesmen there was no living soul nearer him.

Simon Ivanoff's health had broken down generally. Nine years ago he had been at the war and had acted as servant to an officer, with whom he served right through the campaign. He had starved, been roasted by the sun, had frozen, and had made marches of forty and fifty versts in the heat and frost. He had been under fire, but, thank God! no bullet had touched him. Once his regiment had been in the first line. For a whole week there had been skirmishes with the Turks; the Russian and Turkish firing-lines had been separated only by a deep strath, and from morn till eve they kept up a continuous cross-fire. Simon's officer had also been in the firing-line, and three times a day Simon took him a steaming samovar and his dinner from the regimental kitchen in the ravine. As he went with the samovar along the open, bullets hummed about him, and snapped viciously against the stones in a manner terrifying to Simon, who used to cry, but still kept on. The officers were very pleased with him, because there was always hot tea for them. He returned from the campaign whole, but with rheumatism in his hands and feet. He had experienced no little sorrow since then. He arrived home to find his father, an old man, had died; his little four-year-old son also dead (his throat), so there only remained Simon and his wife. They could not do much. It was difficult to plough with swollen hands and feet. They could no longer stay in their own village, and they started off to seek fortune in new places. Simon and his wife stayed for a short time on the line, in Cherson and in Donschina, but nowhere found luck. Then the wife went out to service, and Simon, as formerly, travelled about. Once he happened to travel on an engine, and at one of the stations he saw the station-master, whose face seemed familiar to him. Simon looked at the station-master and the station-master at Simon, and they recognized each other. He had been an officer of Simon's regiment.

"You are Ivanoff?" he said.

"Exactly, Your Excellency; that's me."

"How have you got here?"

Simon told him all.

"Where are you off to?"

"I cannot tell you, sir."

"You idiot! How 'can't' you tell me?"

"Quite true, Your Excellency, because there is nowhere to go. I must look for work, sir."

The station-master looked at him, thought a bit, and said: "Look here, friend, stay here a bit at the station. You are married, I think. Where is your wife?"

"Yes, Your Excellency, I am married. My wife is at Kursk, in service with a merchant."

"Well, write to your wife to come here. I will give you a free pass for her. We have a linesman's hut

THE SIGNAL

empty. I will speak to the District Chief on your behalf."

"I shall be very grateful, Your Excellency," replied Simon.

He stayed at the station, helped in the kitchen of the station-master, cut fire-wood, kept the yard clean, and swept the platform. In a fortnight's time his wife arrived, and Simon went on a hand-trolley to his hut. The hut was a new one and warm, with as much wood as he wanted. There was a little vegetable garden, the legacy of former linesmen, and there was about half a dessiatine of ploughed land on either side of the railway embankment. Simon was rejoiced. He began to think of doing some farming, of purchasing a cow and horse.

He was given all necessary stores—a green flag, a red flag, lanterns, a horn, hammer, screw-wrench for the nuts, a crow-bar, spade, broom, bolts, and nails; they gave him two books of regulations, and a time-table of the trains. At first Simon could not sleep at night, and learnt the whole time-table by heart. Two hours before a train was due he would go round his section, sit on the bench at his hut, and look and listen whether the rails were trembling or the rumble of the train could be heard. He even learned the regulations by heart, although he could only read by spelling out each word.

It was summer; the work was not heavy; there was no snow to clear away, and the trains on that line are infrequent. Simon used to go over his verst twice a day, examine and screw up nuts here and there, keep the bed level, look at the water-pipes, and then go home to his own affairs. There was only one drawback—*i.e.*, whatever he wished to do he had first to obtain permission of the Traffic Inspector. Simon and his wife even began to get bored.

Two months passed, and Simon began to make the acquaintance of his neighbours, the other linesmen on either side of him. One was a very old man, whom the authorities were always meaning to relieve. He scarcely moved out of his hut. His wife used to do all his work. The other linesman nearer the station was a young man, thin, but muscular. He and Simon met for the first time on the line midway between the huts. Simon took off his hat and bowed. " Good health to you, neighbour," he said.

The neighbour glanced askance at him. " How do you do ?" he replied ; then turned around and made off.

Later the wives met. Simon's wife passed the time of day with her neighbour, but she also did not say much and went off.

On one occasion Simon said to her : " Young woman, your husband is not very talkative."

The woman said nothing at first, then replied : " But what is there for him to talk with you about ? Everyone has his own business. Go your way, and God be with you."

However, after another month or so they became acquainted. Simon would go with Vassili along the line, sit on the edge of a pipe, smoke, and talk of life. Vassili, for the most part, kept silent, but Simon talked of his village, and of the campaign through which he had passed.

" I have had no little sorrow in my day," he would say ; " and goodness knows I have not lived long. God has not given me happiness, but what He may give, so will it be. That's so, friend Vassili Stepanich."

Vassili Stepanich knocked out the ashes of his pipe against a rail, stood up, and said : " It is not luck which follows us in life, but human beings. There is no wild beast on this earth more ferocious, cruel, and evil than man. Wolf does not eat wolf, but a man will readily devour man."

" Come, friend, don't say that ; a wolf eats wolf."

" The words came into my mind and I said it. All the same, there is nothing more cruel than man. If it were not for his wickedness and greed it would be possible to

THE SIGNAL

live. Everybody tries to sting you to the quick, to bite and devour you."

Simon pondered a bit. "I don't know, brother," he said; "perhaps it is as you say, and perhaps it is God's will."

"And perhaps, then," said Vassili, "it is waste of time for me to talk with you. To put everything unpleasant on God, and sit and suffer, means, brother, being not a man but an animal. That's what I have to say." And he turned and went off without saying good-bye.

Simon also got up. "Neighbour," he called, "why do you lose your temper?" But his neighbour did not look round, and went on.

Simon gazed after him until Vassili was lost to sight in the cutting at the turn. He went home and said to his wife: "Well, Arina, our neighbour is a wicked person, not a man."

However, they did not quarrel. They met again, and, as formerly, discussed the same old topics.

"Ah, friend, if it were not for men we should not be sitting, you and I, in these huts," said Vassili, on one occasion.

"And what about the huts? . . . not so bad; it is possible to live in them."

"Possible to live in them, indeed! . . . Eh! You! . . . You have lived long and learned little, looked at much and seen little. What sort of life is there for a poor man in a hut here or there. These cannibals are devouring you. They are extracting all your life-blood, and when you become old, they will throw you out just as they do with husks they feed pigs on. What pay do you get?"

"Not much, Vassili Stepanich—twelve roubles."

"And I, thirteen and a half roubles. Allow me to ask you why? By the regulations the Company should give us fifteen roubles a month with firing and lighting. Who decides that you should have twelve roubles, or I thirteen and a half? Ask yourself! . . . And you say it is possible to live! You understand it is not a question of one and a half roubles or three roubles—even if they paid us each the whole fifteen roubles. I was at the station last month. The Director passed through, so I saw him . . . I had that honour. . . . He had a separate carriage, came out and stood on the platform, stood. . . . Yes, I shall not stay here long; I shall go, anywhere, follow my nose."

"But where will you go, Stepanich? One does not seek good from good. Here you have a house, warmth, a little piece of land. Your wife is a worker . . ."

"Land! You should look at my piece of land. Not a twig on it—nothing. I had planted some cabbages in the spring, just when the Traffic Inspector came along. He said: 'What is this? Why have you not reported this? Why have you done this without permission? Dig them up, roots and all.' He was drunk. Another time he would not have said a word, but this time it got into his head . . . three roubles fine! . . ."

Vassili kept silent for a while, pulling at his pipe, then added quietly: " A little more and I should have done for him."

"But, neighbour, you are hot-tempered."

"No, I am not hot-tempered, but I tell the truth and think. Yes, he will still get a bloody nose from me. I will complain to the District Chief. We will see then!" And he did complain.

Once the District Chief came along to inspect the line. Three days later important personages were coming from St. Petersburg, were to pass over the line. They were conducting an inquiry, so that previous to their journey it was necessary to put everything in order. Ballast was laid down, the bed was levelled, the sleepers carefully examined, spikes driven in a bit, nuts screwed up, posts painted, and orders were given for yellow sand to be sprinkled at the level crossings. The woman at the

THE SIGNAL

neighbouring hut turned her old man out to weed. Simon worked for a whole week. He put everything in order, mended his kaftan, cleaned and polished his brass plate with a piece of brick until it fairly shone. Vassili also worked hard. The District Chief arrived on a trolley, four men worked the handles, the levers making the six wheels hum. The trolley travelled at twenty versts an hour, but the wheels squeaked. It reached Simon's hut, and he ran out and reported in soldierly fashion. All appeared to be in repair.

"Have you been long here?" inquired the Chief.

"Since the second of May, Your Excellency."

"All right. Thank you. And who is at hut No. 164?"

The Traffic Inspector (he was travelling with the Chief on the trolley) replied: "Vassili Spiridoff."

"Spiridoff. Spiridoff.... Ah! is he the man against whom you made a note last year?"

"The same."

"Well, we will see Vassili Spiridoff. Go on!" The workmen laid to the handles, and the trolley got under way. Simon watched it, and thought, "Well, there will be trouble between them and my neighbour."

About two hours later he started on his round. He saw someone coming along the line from the cutting. Something white showed on his head. Simon began to look more attentively. It was Vassili; he had a stick in his hand, a small bundle on his shoulder, and his cheek was bound up in a handkerchief.

"Where are you off to, neighbour?" cried Simon.

Vassili came quite close. He was very pale, white as chalk, and his eyes had a wild look. Almost choking, he muttered: "To the town—to Moscow—to the Head Office."

"Head Office? Ah, you are going, I suppose, to complain. Give it up! Vassili Stepanich, forget it...."

"No, mate, I will not forget. It is too late. See! He struck me in the face, drew blood. So long as I live I will not forget.... I will not leave it like this! ..."

Simon took him by the hand. "Give it up, Stepanich. I am advising you truly. You will not better things...."

"Better things! I know myself that I shall not do better. You spoke truly about Fate. Better for myself not to do it, but one must stand up for the right, mate."

"But tell me, how did it all happen?"

"How? ... He examined everything, got down from the trolley, looked into the hut. I knew beforehand that he would be strict, and so put everything into proper order as it should be. He was just going when I made my complaint. He immediately cried out: 'Here,' he said, 'is a Government inquiry coming, and you make a complaint about a vegetable garden. Here,' he said, 'are Privy Councillors coming, and you come worrying about cabbages! ...' I lost patience and said something—not very much, but it offended him, and he struck me in the face ... and I stood still; I did nothing, just as if it was in the proper order of things. They went off; I came to myself, washed my face, and left."

"And what about the hut?"

"The wife has stayed. She will look after things all right. Never mind about their roads."

Vassili got up and collected himself. "Good-bye, Ivanoff.... I do not know whether I shall get anyone at the Office to hear me."

"Surely you are not going to walk?"

"At the station I will try to get on a goods-train, and to-morrow I shall be in Moscow."

The neighbours bade each other farewell. Vassili was absent for some time. His wife worked for him night and day. She never slept, and wore herself out waiting for her husband. On the third day the commission arrived. An engine, luggage-van, and two first-class saloons; but Vassili was still away. Simon saw the wife on the fourth day. Her face was swollen from crying and her eyes were red.

"Has your husband returned?" he asked. But the woman only made a gesture with her hands, and without saying a word went her way.

*   *   *   *   *

Simon had learnt when still a lad to make flutes out of a kind of reed. He used to burn out the heart of the stalk, make holes where necessary, drill them, make a mouthpiece at one end, and tune them so well that it was possible to play almost anything you wanted on them. He made a number of them in his spare time, and sent them by his friends amongst the guards on the goods-trains to the bazaar in the town. He got two kopecks apiece for them. On the day following the visit of the commission he left his wife at home to meet the six o'clock train, and, taking a knife, started off to the forest to cut some sticks. He went to the end of his section—at this point the line makes a sharp turn—went down the embankment, and went into the wood under the mountain. About half a verst away there was a big marsh, around which there grew splendid bushes out of which to make his flutes. He cut a whole bundle of sticks and started back home. As he went through the wood the sun was already getting low, and in the dead stillness only the twittering of the birds was audible, and the crackle of the dead wood under his feet. As Simon walked along rapidly and easily he fancied he heard the clang of iron striking iron, and he redoubled his pace. There was no repair going on in his section at this time. What did it mean? he wondered. Coming out on to the fringe of the wood, the railway embankment stood high before him; on the top of it a man was squatting on the bed of the line busily engaged in something. Simon commenced to crawl up quietly towards him. He thought that it was someone after the nuts which secure the rails. He watched, and a man got up, holding a crow-bar in his hand. He had loosened a rail with it, so that it would move to one side. A mist came before Simon's eyes; he wanted to cry out, but could not. It was Vassili! . . . Simon scrambled up the bank as Vassili with crow-bar and wrench slid headlong down the other side.

"Vassili Stepanich! For the love.... Old friend! Come back! Give me the crow-bar. We will put the rail back; no one will know. Come back! Save your soul from this sin!"

Vassili did not look back, but disappeared into the wood.

Simon stood before the rail which had been torn up. He threw down his bundle of sticks. A train was due; not a goods-train, but a passenger-train. And he had nothing with which to stop it, no flag. He could not replace the rail and could not drive in the spikes with his bare hands. It was necessary to run, absolutely necessary to run to the hut for some tools. " God help me!" he murmured.

Simon started running towards his hut. He was out of breath, but still ran, falling every now and then. He had cleared the forest; there only remained another hundred sajenes to the hut, not more, when he heard the distant hooter of the factory sound—six o'clock! In two minutes' time No. 7 train was due. " Oh, Lord! Have pity on innocent souls!" In his mind Simon saw the engine strike against the loosened rail with its left wheel, shiver, careen, tear up and splinter the sleepers— and just there, there was a curve and the embankment eleven sajenes high, down which the engine would topple—and the third-class carriages would be packed . . . little children. . . . They are all sitting in the train now not dreaming of any danger. " Oh, Lord! Tell me what to do! . . . No, it is not possible to run to the hut and get back in time."

THE SIGNAL

Simon did not run on to the hut, but turned back and ran faster than before. He was running almost mechanically, blindly; he did not know himself what was to happen. He ran as far as the rail which had been pulled up; his sticks were lying in a heap. He bent down, seized one without knowing why, and ran on farther. It seemed to him that the train was already coming. He heard the distant whistle; he heard the quiet, even tremor of the rails; but his strength was exhausted, he could run no farther, and came to a halt about one hundred sajenes from the awful spot. Then an idea came into his head, literally like a ray of light. Pulling off his cap, he took out of it a cotton scarf, drew his knife out of the upper part of his boot, and crossed himself, muttering, " God bless me !"

He buried the knife into his left arm above the elbow ; the blood spurted out, flowing in a hot stream. In this he soaked his scarf, smoothed it out, tied it to the stick and hung out his red flag.

He stood waving his flag. The train was already in sight. The driver will not see him—will come close up, and a heavy train cannot be pulled up in a hundred sajenes.

And the blood kept on flowing. Simon kept pressing the sides of the wound together wanting to close it, but the blood did not diminish. Evidently he had cut his arm very deeply. His head commenced to swim, black spots began to dance before his eyes, and then it became dark. There was a ringing in his ears. He could not see the train or hear the noise. Only one thought possessed him. " I shall not be able to keep standing up. I shall fall and drop the flag ; the train will pass over me. . . . Help me, oh Lord ! . . ."

All became quite black before him, his mind became a blank, and he dropped the flag ; but the blood-stained banner did not fall to the ground. A hand seized it and held it high to meet the approaching train. The engine-driver saw it, shut the regulator, and reversed steam. The train came to a standstill.

People jumped out of the carriages and collected in a crowd. Looking, they saw a man lying senseless on the footway, drenched in blood, and another man standing beside him with a blood-stained rag on a stick.

Vassili looked around at all; then, lowering his head, said : " Bind me ; I have pulled up a rail!"

II

FOUR DAYS

I REMEMBER how we rushed through the wood; how the leaves and twigs came fluttering and twisting down on us as the humming bullets cut their way through the thick foliage. I remember how, as we pushed through the thick and prickly undergrowth, the firing became hotter and the fringe of the wood became alive with little spurts of flame which flashed redly from all points. I remember how Sedoroff, a recruit of No. 1 Company (How had he got into our firing-line? flashed through my mind), suddenly sat down, and without saying a word gazed at me with big startled eyes as a little stream of blood commenced to trickle from his mouth. Yes, I remember it well. I remember also how, just as we were on the very edge of the wood, I first saw *him* in the thick bushes. He was a huge and bulky Turk, but I ran straight at him although I am small and weak. There was a deafening noise; something enormous seemed to flash past me, making my ears ring. He has fired at me, I thought. I remember how with a scream of fear he pressed himself backwards into a thick and prickly bush, although he could easily have gone round it, but he could remember nothing from fright, and strove instead to push his way into its prickly branches.

With a blow I disarmed him, and lunged with my bayonet. There was an indrawn sob and a piteous groan. Then I rushed on. We cheered as we went forward, some falling, some firing. I remember I fired several times. We were already out of the wood into the open. Suddenly the cheers became a long loud roar, and we all rushed forward. That is, the line did, but not I, because I stayed behind. Something strange seemed to have happened, and then, stranger still, everything disappeared, all the cries and firing died away. I could hear nothing, and saw only something blue, which must have been the sky. Then it, too, disappeared.

* * * * *

I was never in such a strange position. I am lying apparently on my stomach, and can see in front of me only a little clod of earth, a few blades of grass, up one of which an ant is climbing head downwards, and some little mounds of dust, last year's dead grass. This is my whole world, and I can only see with one eye because the other one is being pressed by something hard ; it must be the bough against which my head is resting. It is dreadfully awkward, and I absolutely cannot understand why, when I want to, I cannot move. And so the time passes—I hear the chirrup of grasshoppers, the humming of bees—nothing more. At last I make an effort, free my right arm from under my body, and, resting both hands on the ground, I try to kneel.

Something sharp goes like lightning right through my body from my knees to my chest, from my chest up to my head ; and again I fall, again darkness, again a blank.

* * * * *

I am awake, but why do I see stars shining brightly in the black-blue of a Bulgarian night ? Surely I am in a tent ? Then why have I crawled out of it ? I make a movement, and feel an excruciating pain in my legs. Ah, now I understand. I have been wounded. Dangerously ? I catch hold of my leg where it is hurting. Both right and left legs are covered with clotted blood. When I touch them with my hands the pain is worse. It is like toothache, a throbbing, sickening pain. There is a singing

FOUR DAYS

in my ears and my head feels leaden. Vaguely I understand that I have been wounded in both legs. But why have they not picked me up? The Turks cannot have beaten us! I commence, confusedly at first, then more clearly, to remember what happened, and come to the conclusion that we were far from being defeated. Because I fell (this, by the way, I do not remember, but I do remember how they all rushed forward, and that I could not, and saw nothing but blue) on the field on the hill, and that was the field to which our little officer had pointed and said, " Children, we must get there !" So of course we had not been beaten. But why, then, have they not picked me up? Surely here in this field—open ground—everything is visible. Besides which, I cannot be the only one lying here. The firing was too hot. I must turn my head and look. I can do this more easily now, because when I came to my senses and was able to see only grass and that ant climbing with its head downwards I tried to raise myself, and when I fell again it was not into the old position, but on to my back. That is why I can see the stars.

I try to raise myself into a sitting position. It is difficult when both legs are shot through. Several times I almost give it up in despair, but at last, with tears in my eyes from the awful pain, I succeed.

Above me—a scrap of black-blue sky in which a big star is burning and several smaller ones. Around me something dark and tall—bushes! I am amongst the bushes! They have missed me! I feel how the very roots of my hair move as I realize this. But how did I get into the bushes when they hit me in the open? When I was wounded I must have crawled here without remembering it, owing to the pain; only it is odd that *now* I cannot stir, but *then* was able to drag myself to these bushes. Perhaps I had only been hit once then, and the second bullet caught me here. There are pinkish stains around me. . . .

The big star has begun to pale, and the smaller stars have disappeared. It is the moon rising. How pretty it must be at home now! . . . Strange noises keep reaching me as if somebody was groaning. Yes, they are groans. Is it somebody else, also forgotten, lying near me with legs shot through or a bullet in his stomach? No, the groans are so close, whilst there is no one, it seems, near me. . . . It cannot be?—yes, it is I who am groaning and making these pitiful noises. . . . Surely it is not so painful really? I suppose it must be, only I do not understand why I am in such pain because my head is leaden and everything seems misty. Better lie down again and sleep, sleep. . . . Only, shall I ever awake again? Anyhow, it does not matter.

Just as I commence to lie down a broad pale gleam of moonlight clearly shows up the place where I am lying, and I see something dark and big on the ground about five paces from me. Something glistens on it in the moonlight. Is it buttons or equipment? Is it a corpse or somebody wounded?

Never mind, I will lie down. . . .

No! impossible! Our men cannot have gone. They are here; they have driven out the Turks and are campnig on the position. Then why no voices? no crackling of camp-fires? Probably I am so weak I cannot hear. Of course they must be here.

"Help! help! help!"

The wild, maddened, hoarse cries are wrung from me, but there is no answer. Loudly they resound in the night air, but everything else remains silent. Only the grasshoppers keep up their chirruping. The moon is looking down at me with a pitying gaze.

If he was somebody wounded my shouts would have roused him. It is a corpse. One of us or a Turk? But is it not all the same? And sleep is closing my fevered eyelids.

*   *   *   *   *

FOUR DAYS

I am lying with closed eyes, although I woke up long ago. I do not want to open them because through the closed lids I can feel the sun, and if I open my eyes the sun will scorch them. Besides, better not to move. . . . Yesterday (I suppose it was yesterday) they wounded me . . . a whole day has gone past, others will pass by, and I shall die. It is all the same. Better not to move. If only I could stop my brain working! But nothing will stop it. Ideas, recollections, thoughts come crowding in. However, all this is not for long, the end will soon come. There will be just a few lines in the newspapers that our losses were insignificant :—wounded . . . so many ; killed—one, Private Ivanoff—no, the names of the men are not given, they simply say killed . . . one. One private, as if it were one dog.

All the details of an incident which happened long ago flash to my mind. By the way, how long ago all my life seems—I mean that life when I was not lying here with my legs shot through. . . .

I was going along the street when I was stopped by a crowd which had gathered and was silently gazing at something white covered with blood lying on the roadway whining piteously—a little dog which had been run over by a tramcar. It was dying, as I am now. A dvornik pushed his way through the crowd, picked it up by the back of the neck, and carried it away, and the crowd dispersed. Will anyone take me away? No . . . you will lie here and die. And how good is life! How happy I was that day! I went along as if intoxicated. Recollections! do not torture me! Leave me alone with this present torture, then at least I cannot involuntarily make comparisons. Oh, this longing for home! It is worse than wounds.

However, it is getting hot. The sun is scorching me. I open my eyes and see the same bushes, the same sky, only by daylight . . . and there is my neighbour. Yes, he is a Turk, a corpse. What a huge man! I recognize him as the same man I . . .

Before me lies a man whom I have killed. Why did I kill him ? He lies there dead and blood-stained. Why did Fate bring him here ? Who is he ? Perhaps he has ... as I have ... an old mother. She will sit long and alone in the evenings at the door of her miserable hut, gazing towards the north, for her darling son, her protector and breadwinner. And I ? I also—would that I could change places with him. He is happy. He hears nothing, feels nothing, no pain from wounds, no awful sickness, no thirst ... the bayonet went straight through his heart. There is a big black hole in his uniform with blood around it. *I did that!*

I did not want to do it. I wished no one harm when I volunteered. It somehow never entered my mind that I should have to kill people. I only thought of how I would expose my own breast to the bullets. I came ... and now ... fool ! fool !

And this unhappy fellah (he was in Egyptian uniform)—he is even less to blame than I. First of all they packed him with others like herrings in a barrel on board a steamer and brought him to Constantinople. He had never heard of Russia or Bulgaria. They ordered him to go, and he came. Had he refused they would have beaten him with sticks, or perhaps some Pascha would have put a bullet into him. He came here by long and difficult marches from Stamboul to Rustchuk. We attacked and he defended himself, but seeing that we terrible people cared not for his patent English rifle, but ever leapt forward, he became terror-stricken, and when he wanted to get away, someone, a little man whom he could have killed with one blow of his big black fist, jumped forward and plunged a bayonet into his heart.

Why is he to blame ?

And why am I to blame, even though I did kill him ? How am I to blame ? Why is this thirst torturing me ? Thirst ! Who knows what this word means ! Even when we came through Roumania, making forced marches

FOUR DAYS

of fifty versts in the terrific heat, even then I did not feel what I feel now. Oh, if only somebody would come along!

God! Yes—there must be something inside that huge water-bottle of his. But I have to get to it. What will it cost me? Never mind, I will get there.

I crawl, dragging my legs behind me. My arms have grown so weak that they can scarcely help me. It is only a few feet, but for me it is more . . . not more, but worse than tens of versts. Nevertheless, I must crawl there. My throat is burning—burning like fire. Yes, no doubt without water you will die sooner, but still perhaps . . .

And I crawl. My legs seem chained to the ground and every movement causes insufferable pain. I yell, yell, but all the same go on crawling. At last! Yes, there is water in the flask, and what a lot! More than half full. It will last me a long time . . . until I die!

You are saving my life, my victim!

I commenced to unfasten the water-bottle, leaning as I did so on one elbow, when, suddenly losing my balance, I fell face forward on to the body of my deliverer. Already it was becoming unpleasant.

* * * * *

I have drunk. The water was warm, but still unspoilt. Moreover, there is plenty. I shall live several days more. I remember having read in a book that a man can live without food for more than a week if only he has water, and in the same book I read an account of a man who committed suicide by starvation, but lived for ages before he died because he drank water.

But what if I do live another five or six days? What will come of it? Our men have gone. The Bulgarians have dispersed. There is no road near. I have to die, only instead of three days' agony I have given myself a week. Would it not be better to finish it now? Near my neighbour lies his rifle. I need only stretch out my hand—then a flash and the end. There are cartridges lying there. He had no time to use them all. Shall I end it, then? . . . or wait? Which? Deliverance? death? Wait until the Turks come and commence to tear the skin from my wounded legs? Better to finish it myself. No, there is no need to lose heart; I will struggle to the end, to the very last. If they find me I am saved. Perhaps the bones are not touched, they will cure me. I shall see home—mother—and Masha. . . . Oh merciful God! grant that they may never know the whole truth! Let them believe I was killed outright. What if they find out that I suffered for two, three, four days!

My head is spinning round, my journey to my neighbour has completely exhausted me. And this awful smell. How black he has become! What will he be like to-morrow or the day after? I am lying here now only because I have no strength left to drag myself away. I will rest a little and then crawl back to the old place; the wind, too, is blowing from there, and will carry this smell away from me.

I am lying absolutely worn out. The sun is burning my face and hands. There is no shelter. If only night (the second, I suppose) would come more quickly!

My thoughts are getting confused, and I am losing consciousness.

*   *   *   *   *

I must have had a long sleep, because when I awoke it was already night. All is as before, my wounds ache as before, and he is lying there as before, just as large and motionless as before.

I cannot help thinking of him. Surely it was not only that he should cease to live that I gave up all—that I have starved, have been frozen by the cold, tormented by the heat, and finally am lying here in this agony? Have I done anything of any use to my country except this murder?

Murder! murderer!—Who? I!

When I was fascinated by the idea of going to the war,

mother and Masha did not try to dissuade me, although they both cried bitterly. Blinded by the idea, I did not see those tears. I did not understand (now I do) what I was causing to those near me. But why think of it ? It will not recall the past. And in what a strange light my action appeared to many of my friends—" Well, madman ! interfering without knowing why !" How could they say this ? How can they reconcile such words with *their* ideas of heroism, patriotism, etc. ? Surely in *their* eyes I represented all those virtues ? And yet I am a " madman and monster " !

And so I go to Kishineff. There they load me up with a knapsack and all sorts of military paraphernalia. And I go with thousands, of whom some, like myself, are going voluntarily. The remainder would stay at home if allowed. However, they too, like us, will march thousands of versts and will fight also like us, or even better. They will do their duty notwithstanding that, if allowed, they would immediately give it up and go home.

A chilling early morning breeze has arisen. The bushes are moving, and a bird is sleepily fluttering its wings. The stars have faded away. The black-blue of the heavens has taken a greyish hue, and is covered with soft, feathery clouds. A raw half-mist is rising from the ground. The third day has arrived of my—what can I call it ? Life ? Agony ? The third. . . . How many still remain ? In any case not many. I have become very weak, and apparently cannot even get away from my neighbour. Before long I shall be like him, and then we will not be so unpleasing to each other.

I must have a drink. I will drink three times a day : in the morning, at midday, and in the evening.

* * * * *

The sun has risen. His huge disc, crimson as blood, is intersected by the black branches of the bushes. It looks as if it will be hot to-day. My neighbour ! what will you look like after this day is over ? Even now you are awful. Yes, he is awful. His hair has commenced to fall out. His skin, originally black, has become a greyish-yellow. His swollen face has become so tightly stretched that the skin has burst behind one ear. Large blisters like bladders have pushed their way out between the buttons which fasten the leggings around his swollen legs. And he himself looks a veritable mountain. What will the sun do to him to-day?

To lie so near is unbearable. I must crawl away from him at all costs. But can I? I can still raise my arm, open the water-bottle, and drink, but to move my own heavy helpless body? Nevertheless, I will move even if a little way only, if only half a pace an hour.

I have spent the whole morning moving. The pain was awful, but what is that to me now? I no longer remember, I cannot imagine what it feels like to be sound and well. I am accustomed to pain now. I have succeeded this morning in crawling back to my old place. But I have not enjoyed the fresh air for long,—that is, if there can be fresh air within six paces of a putrefying corpse. The wind has changed. It is so appalling that I am sick. The convulsions of an empty stomach cause me new tortures, and my whole inside seems to become twisted. But the awful poisoned air still fans me. In my despair I burst out crying.

   * * * * *

Absolutely worn out, I lie in a semi-stupor. . . . Suddenly—Is this the fantasy of a disordered imagination? It seems to me that . . . no . . . yes it is . . . voices! The sound of horses' hoofs and human voices. I almost cried out, but just stopped myself. And what if they are Turks? What then? Then to my present tortures will be added others far more awful, even to read of which in the newspapers makes one's hair stand on end. They will flay me alive and roast my wounded legs. It will be well if they do no more than this, for they have great inventive powers. Is it really better to end life in their hands than to die here? But if they are some of ours? You cursed bushes! Why have you surrounded me with so thick a hedge? I can see nothing through them. In one place only is there an opening like a little window between the branches which gives me a view away on to the open ground. Yes, there is the small stream from which we drank before the fight. And there is the huge block of sandstone like a little bridge across the stream. They are sure to come across it. The voices die away, I cannot hear what language they are speaking, even my hearing has become weak. My God! if they are ours—I will call to them. They should hear me even from there. It is better than risking falling into the clutches of Bashi-Bazouks. Why are they so long in coming? In the torments of expectancy I do not even notice the dreadful air, although it has in no way improved.

Then suddenly Cossacks appear crossing the stream. Blue uniforms, red-striped trousers, lances all. A half sotnia of them, and in front, on a magnificent horse, is a black-bearded officer. As soon as they are across the stream he turns in his saddle and gives the order, " Tro—t, march!"

" Stop! stop! For God's sake! Help! help!—Comrades!" I cry, but the trotting horses, rattling scabbards, and loud talking of the Cossacks drown my hoarse cries—and they do not hear me!

Oh, curses on it! Exhausted, I fall face forward on to the ground, and cry in convulsive sobs. The water, my salvation and my insurance against death, is pouring out from the flask, which I have overturned, but it is only when barely half a glassful remains and the rest is soaking into the dry thirsty soil that I notice that in my fall I had knocked over the water-bottle.

Shall I ever forget the awfulness of that moment, the numbness which came over me? I lay motionless with half-closed eyes. The wind kept constantly changing, and blew alternately fresh and clean or almost overpowered me. My neighbour had become too dreadful for words. Once when I opened my eyes to snatch a glance at him I was appalled. There was no longer a face. It had fallen away from the bone. The horrible grinning skull with its everlasting smile appeared too revolting, although (as a medical student) I have frequently handled them, but this corpse in uniform with its bright buttons made me shudder. " And this is war !" I reflected. " This corpse is its symbol !"

The sun is scorching and baking me as usual. My hands and face have long been all blisters. I have drunk all the water that was left. My thirst was so maddening that I decided to take just a sip, but swallowed all that was left at one gulp. Oh, why did I not call to the Cossacks when they were close to me? Even had they been Turks it would have been better. They would have tortured me for perhaps two or even three hours, but now I do not know how long I shall have to writhe and suffer here. Mother, darling mother, you would tear out your grey hair, you would beat your head against a wall and curse the day you bore me ... you would curse the world which has invented war for the torturing of men did you but know. Good-bye, mother dearest, and farewell, my sweetheart, Masha, my love. How, how bitter !

Again I see that little dog. The dvornik did not pity it, but knocked its head against the wall, and threw it (though still living) into a refuse pit in the courtyard of the house near by, where it lingered for a day. But I ... I am more unfortunate because I have already suffered three days. To-morrow will be the fourth day—then there will be a fifth, sixth.

Death, where art thou ? Come ! Take me !

But death does not come and does not take me. And I lie here under this awful sun, with not a drop of water to cool my burning throat and a corpse which is poisoning me. It has become quite decomposed, and is a seething

FOUR DAYS

mass. When nothing but the bones and uniform are left it will be my turn. I shall be like that.

The day passes and the night passes. No change. Another morn is arriving just the same, and yet another day will pass.

The rustling bushes seem to be murmuring, and whisper, " You will die ! You will die ! You will die !" " You will not see ! You will not see ! You will not see !" answer the bushes from the other side.

" No, you will not see them," says a loud voice near me. I give a shudder and at once come to myself. From out of the bushes the kindly blue eyes of Yakoff, our corporal, are looking at me.

" Spades here !" he cries. " Here are two more of theirs."

No spades are wanted, no need to bury me. I am alive —I try to cry out, but only a feeble groan comes from my parched lips.

" Merciful God ! Alive ! It is our Ivanoff ; he is alive ! Come here, mates, our barin is alive ! Call the doctor !" In a few moments they are rinsing my mouth with water, brandy and something. Then everything disappears.

The stretcher-bearers move with a gentle and measured swing which lulls me to rest. I awake, then lapse again into oblivion. My bandaged wounds are not hurting, and an inexpressible joyous feeling of comfort pervades my whole being.

" . . . Ha—alt ! Low—er !" and the " relief " take the place of their comrades in carrying the stretcher.

The N.C.O. in charge is Peter Ivanovich, a corporal of our company, and a tall, lanky, but very good fellow. He is so tall that looking towards him I gradually descry his head and shoulders and his long straggly beard, although four stalwart men are carrying the stretcher shoulder high.

" Peter Ivanovich," I whisper.

"What is it, old friend ?" and Peter Ivanovich bends over me.

"Peter Ivanovich, what did the doctor say to you? Shall I die soon?"

"But, Ivanoff, what are you talking about? Of course you will not die; no bones have been broken. My word, but you are lucky. Not a bone or an artery touched. But how have you lived these three and a half days? What had you to eat?"

"Nothing."

"And to drink?"

"I took the Turk's water-bottle. Peter Ivanovich, I cannot talk now—afterwards."

"All right, chum. Try and sleep now."

Again sleep—oblivion. . . .

When I awake again it is to find myself in the Divisional Hospital tent. Around me stand nurses and doctors, one of whom I recognize as a well-known St. Petersburg professor. He is leaning over me, his hands are bathed in blood. He does not examine my legs long, and turning towards me, he says: " God has been kind to you, young man. You will live. We have had to take one leg from you, but . . . well, that is nothing. Can you talk?" I am able to talk, and I tell him all that I have written here.

III

AN INCIDENT

I

How it has come about that I, who for almost two years have never thought seriously about anything, have suddenly commenced to reflect—I cannot understand. It cannot be that man who has set me thinking, because I so often meet with men of his type that I am accustomed to their sermonizing.

Yes, they almost all, with the exception of the absolutely hardened or really clever ones, invariably talk about matters which are of no use to them or even me. First they ask my name and my age; then in the majority of cases, with an air of concern, they begin to ask, " Is it impossible for you to give up such a life ?" At first this kind of thing used to upset me, but now I am accustomed to it. One becomes accustomed to a lot.

However, for the last fortnight, whenever I am quite alone and am not feeling gay—that is, not drunk (because can I really be merry except when drunk ?)—I begin to think. And, however much I do not wish to think, I cannot help it. I cannot get away from depressing thoughts. There is only one way of forgetting—to go out somewhere where there are plenty of people, where there is drunkenness and indecency. Then I too begin to drink and misbehave. My brain gets muddled, and I remember nothing. . . . Then it is—easier. But why is it that this never happened before ?—not from the very first day I bid good-bye to everything? For more than two years I have lived here in this beastly room, always spending the time in the same way, frequenting the various restaurants and dancing-saloons, and all the time, if it has not really been gay, I at least have not thought so. But now—it is quite, quite different.

How dull and stupid it all is! It is not because I go nowhere; I go nowhere simply because I don't want to. I entangled myself in this life, I know my own road. In a copy of an illustrated paper which one of my " friends " brings me whenever there is something " spicy " in it, I once saw a picture. In the centre there was a pretty little girl with a doll, and around her there were two rows of figures. On the one side above they went from the child to the little school-girl, then the modest young girl, afterwards the mother of a family, and finally an honoured, respected old woman. On the other side, below—was a shop-girl carrying a box, then me, me, and again me. First me—like I am now, second me—sweeping the streets with a broom, and third—the same—as an absolutely repulsive, loathsome old hag. However, I shall not let myself get to that stage. Another two or three years, if I can stand this life as long, and then into the canal. I can do this, I am not afraid.

But what a strange chap the man must be who drew this picture! Why does he take it for granted that a school-girl becomes a modest young lady, an honoured mother and grandmother? And I? I too can show off my French and German in the street! And I don't think I have forgotten how to paint or draw flowers, and I remember " Calipso ne pouvait se consoler du départe d'Ulysse." I remember Pushkin and Lermontoff, and all—all. And the examinations and that momentous, awful time when I became a fool, a silly fool, and listened to all the passionate, silly speeches of that conceited fop, and how stupidly I enjoyed it, and all the lies and filth in the " best society " from which I came into this, where

AN INCIDENT

I now make an idiot of myself with vodka.... Yes, now I have begun even to drink vodka. " Horreur !" my cousin, Olga Nicolaievna, would say.

Yes, and is it not in reality " horreur " ? But am I to blame in this matter ? If I—a seventeen-year-old girl, who for eight years had sat within four walls and had seen only other girls like myself and their different mammas—had not met my " friend," with his hair à la Capoul, but some other and good man—then it would all have been different.

But what an absurd idea ! Are there really any good people ? Have I ever met any since or before my downfall ? Can I believe that there are good people when of the scores I know there is not one whom I could not hate ! Can I believe that they exist when amongst those I meet are husbands of young wives, children (almost children—fourteen and fifteen years old) of " good family " ! old men, bald, paralytic, half dead ?

And finally, can I help hating and despising them, although I am myself a despicable and despised being, when amongst them are such persons as a certain young German with a monogram tattooed on his arm above the elbow ? He explained to me that it was the initials of his fiancée. " Jetzt aber bist du meine liebe, allerliebste Liebchen," said he, looking at me with oily eyes, and then read me verses from Heine, and unctuously explained that Heine was a great German poet, but that they had even greater poets in Germany—Goethe and Schiller—and that only such a great and gifted nation like the Germans could produce such poets.

How I longed to scratch his disgusting greasy face, with its white eyebrows and lashes ! But instead I gulped down the glass of port wine he had poured out for me and forgot all.

* * * * *

Why should I think of the future when I know it so well ? Why think of the past when there was nothing in it which could replace my present life? Yes, it is true. If I were asked to-day to return to those luxurious surroundings, to mingle amongst people with their beautifully dressed hair and elegant phrases, I would not! I should stay and die at my post....

Yes, I have my post! I, too, am wanted, am necessary. Not long ago a young man came to me who talked everlastingly, and recited me a whole page he had learnt by heart out of some book. "That is what our philosopher—a Russian philosopher—says," he explained. The philosopher said something very obscure but flattering for me to the effect that we are "the safety valves of public passions." . . . Disgusting words! The philosopher himself is no doubt a beast, but worst of all this boy who repeated it.

However, not long ago, this same idea came into my mind. I was up before a magistrate, who fined me fifteen roubles for obscenity in a public place.

As he read his decision whilst all stood, I thought to myself: "Why do all this public look at me with such contempt? Granted that I carry on an unclean, loathsome trade, a most contemptible calling—still, it is a calling! This judge also has a calling. And I think that we both..."

I don't think of anything, I am conscious only that I drink, that I remember nothing, and get muddled. Everything gets mixed up in my head—the disgusting saloon where I shall dance shamelessly to-night and this horrible room in which I can only live when I am drunk. My temples are throbbing, there is a ringing in my ears, everything is swimming in my head, and I am being carried away. I want to stop, to take hold of something, if only a straw, but there is nothing, not even a straw.

I lie! There is one! And not a straw, but something perhaps more hopeful. But I have sunk so low that I do not wish to stretch out my hand to seize this support.

* * * * *

AN INCIDENT

It happened, I think, about the end of August. I remember it was a glorious autumn evening. I was strolling in the Summer Garden, and there became acquainted with this " support." He did not appear to be anything extraordinary, excepting perhaps a certain good-natured talkativeness. He told me about almost all his affairs and friends. He was twenty-five, and his name was Ivan Ivanovich. As for the man himself, he was neither bad nor good. He chatted away with me as if I had been an old acquaintance, told me stories of his Chief, and pointed out to me any of those in his Department who happened to be in sight.

He left me, and I forgot all about him. About a month afterwards, however, he reappeared. He had grown thinner, and was moody and depressed. When he came in I was even a little frightened at the strange, forbidding-looking face.

"You don't remember me?"

At that moment I remembered him, and said so.

He blushed.

"I thought perhaps you did not remember me, because you see so many..."

The conversation stopped abruptly. We sat on the sofa, I in one corner and he in the other, as if he had come for the first time to pay a call, sitting bolt upright, holding his tall hat in his hand. We sat like this for quite a time. Then he got up and bowed.

"Good-bye, Nadejda Nicolaievna," he said with a sigh.

"How did you find out my name?" I exclaimed, flaring up. The name I went under was not Nadejda Nicolaievna, but Evgenia.

I shouted at Ivan Ivanovich so angrily that he became quite frightened.

"But I didn't mean any harm, Nadejda Nicolaievna.... I have never wished or done harm to anyone.... But I know Peter Vassilovich of the police, who told me all about you. I meant to call you Evgenia, but my tongue slipped, and I called you by your real name."

"And tell me why you have come here?"

He said nothing, and looked sorrowfully into my eyes.

"Why?" I repeated, getting more and more angry. "What interest do I possess for you? No, better not to come here. I will not start an acquaintanceship with you because I have no acquaintances. I know why you came! The policeman's story interested you. You thought—here is a rarity, an educated lady who has fallen into this kind of life. . . . You had visions of rescuing me? Clear out! I want nothing! Better to leave me to perish alone than . . ."

I chanced to glance at his face—and stopped. I saw that every word was striking him like a blow. He said nothing, but his look alone made me stop.

"Good-bye, Nadejda Nicolaievna," he said. "I am very sorry that I have hurt you and myself too. Good-bye."

He put out his hand (I could not but take it), and slowly went out of the room. I heard him go down the staircase, and saw through the window how, with bowed head, he went across the courtyard with the same slow and tottering gait. At the gate of the yard he turned round, glanced up at my window, and disappeared.

And it is this man who can be my "support." I have only to make a sign, and I can become a lawful wife. The lawful wife of a poor but well-born man, and can even become a poor but well-born mother, if only the Lord in His anger will yet send me a child.

II

To-day Evsei Evsevich spoke to me:

"You will listen to me, Ivan Ivanovich—what I, an old man, am going to say to you. You, my dear boy, have begun to behave stupidly. Take care that it does not reach the ears of the Chief!"

AN INCIDENT

He went on talking for a long time (trying to speak of the very essence of the matter by roundabout means) about the service, the respect due to rank, of our Chief, about myself, and finally began to talk about my misfortune. We were sitting in a traktir, where Nadejda Nicolaievna and her friends often came.

Evsei Evsevich had long ago noticed, and had long ago drawn from me a number of details. I could not hold my stupid tongue, and let it all out, and even almost cried.

Evsei Evsevich got angry.

" Bah! you old woman, you tender-hearted old woman! A young man, a good official, you have started all this nonsense for such rubbish! Have done with her! What have you to do with her? It would be all right if she were a respectable, decent girl; but for, if I may say so . . ."

Evsei Evsevich even spat.

After this incident he often returned to the subject (Evsei Evsevich was sincerely grieved about and for me), but he no longer stormed at me, because he saw that it annoyed me. At the same time, he could not contain himself for long, and although he would try at first to talk in a roundabout way on the subject, eventually he would come to the one conclusion that it was necessary to have done with it, etc.

And I, strictly speaking, agree with what he says every day to me. How many times have I also thought that it was necessary to have done with it. Yes, how many times! And how many times after such thoughts have I gone out of the house, and my feet have borne me to that street. . . . And here she comes, berouged, with pencilled eyebrows, in a velvet shuba, and a dainty sealskin cap, straight towards me, and I cross to the other side, so that she shall not notice that I am following her. She goes up to the corner, then turns back, impudently, brazenly looking at the passers-by, and sometimes talking with them. I follow behind her from the other side of the street, trying not to lose sight of her, and hopelessly I gaze at her little figure until some . . . blackguard goes up to her and speaks. She answers him, turns round, and goes with him . . . and I after them. If the road were strewn with sharp nails it could not be more painful for me. I go along hearing nothing, seeing nothing, except two figures. . . .

I do not look where I am going, and go along with my eyes starting out of my head, bumping against passers-by, and meeting in return with reproofs, abuse, and pushes. Once I knocked a child over. . . .

They turn to the right, then to the left, they go through the little door into the yard. She first, then he. Almost always out of some strange politeness he gives her the way. Then I follow. Opposite her two windows, so familiar to me, there stands a shed with a hayloft. There is a small flight of iron steps leading up to the hayloft, ending with a small landing devoid of any railing. I sit down on this landing and gaze at the lowered white blinds. . . .

To-day I was at my awful post, although there was a sharp frost. I became thoroughly benumbed. My feet lost all feeling, but still I stood there. Steam rose from my face, my moustaches and beard became frozen, my feet began to freeze. People kept passing through the courtyard, but did not notice me, and, talking loudly, used to pass by me. From the street came sounds of drunken singing (it was a gay street), interchange of abuse, the noise of the scrapers on the pavement as the dvorniks cleared it of snow. All these sounds rang in my ears, but I paid no attention to them or to the frost, which was biting my face and my benumbed legs. All this, the sounds, my feet, and the frost, seemed to be all far, far away from me. My legs were aching violently, but something inside me was aching even more violently. I have not the courage to go to her. Does she know that there is a man who would consider it happiness to sit with her in a room, and only look into her eyes, not even touching her hands? That there is a man who would hurl himself into the fire if it would help her to get out of the hell in which she lives, if she wanted to get out of it? But she does not wish. . . . And I, up to now, do not know why she does not wish. I cannot believe that she is spoilt to the very marrow of her bones. I cannot believe this because I know it is not so, because I know her, because I love her, love her.

* * * * *

A waiter went up to Ivan Ivanovich, who had placed his elbows on the table, and with his face buried in his arms, was shuddering from time to time, and touched him on the shoulder.

" Mr. Nikitin. You mustn't sit like this. . . . In front of everyone. . . . The proprietor will make a fuss. Mr. Nikitin! Please get up. You must not act like this here."

Ivan Ivanovich raised his head and looked at the waiter. He was not the least drunk, and the waiter understood this as soon as he saw his mournful face.

" It is nothing, Simon—nothing. Give me a bottle of vodka."

" What will you order with it?"

" What? A wineglass. And give me a big bottle. Here you are, pay for it all and take a couple of dvu-grivenniks for yourself. In an hour's time send me home in an izvoschik. Do you know where I live?"

" I know. . . . Only, sir, what does it all mean?"

He evidently could not understand. It was the first experience of the kind in all his long career.

" No, wait a bit; better for me to do it."

Ivan Ivanovich went out into the passage, put on his coat, and going out on to the street, turned in at a wine-vault in the low window of which, brilliantly lighted up by the gas-light, were bottles with various coloured labels, tastefully arranged in a layer of moss. A minute later he came out carrying two bottles, went to his lodging, which he had in some furnished rooms, and locked himself in.

III

I have again forgotten and again I am awake. Three weeks of incessant debauchery ! How do I stand it ? To-day my head, bones, every part of my body is aching. Remorse, boredom, fruitless and tormenting arguing ! If only someone would come !

* * * * *

As if in answer to my thought a ring at the door sounded. " Is Evgenia at home ?" " At home ; come in, please," I heard the voice of the cook reply. Uneven, hurried steps resounded along the corridor, the door flew open, and through it appeared Ivan Ivanovich.

He was not at all like the timid, bashful man who had come to see me two months ago. His hat was on the side of his head, he wore a bright-coloured tie, and a self-assured, insolent expression. His gait was staggering, and he smelt strongly of liquor.

* * * *

Nadejda Nicolaievna jumped up from her seat.

" How do you do ?" he began. " I have come to see you."

And he sat down on a chair near the door, without taking off his hat or overcoat. She said nothing and he said no more. Had he not been drunk she would have found something to say, but now she lost her presence of mind. Whilst she was thinking what to do, he again spoke.

" Nadia ! See, I have come. . . . I have the right !" he suddenly shouted out, and drew himself up to his full height. His hat fell off, and his black hair fell in disorder on to his face, his eyes blazed. His whole appearance expressed such delirium that for a moment Nadejda Nicolaievna was frightened.

She tried to speak tenderly with him.

AN INCIDENT

"Listen, Ivan Ivanovich, I shall be very pleased if you will come another time, only go home now. You have had too much to drink. Be a good fellow and go home. Come and see me when you are well."

"She is frightened," Ivan Ivanovich muttered half to himself, again sitting down on the chair—tamed! "But why are you hunting me away?" he broke out again fiercely. "Why? I began to drink through you; I used to be sober! Why do you draw me to you, tell me?"

He wept. Drunken tears stifled him, trickled down his face, falling into his mouth contorted with sobbing. He could scarcely speak.

"Another woman would consider it a piece of fortune to be taken out of this hell. I would slave for you like a bullock. You would live without care, quietly and honourably. Tell me, what have I done to merit your hatred?"

Nadejda Nicolaievna kept silent.

"Why are you silent?" he yelled. "Speak, say something!—anything you like, only say something. I am drunk—that's true. . . . I should not have come here if I were not. Do you know how afraid I am of you when I am sober? You can do what you like with me. Tell me to steal!—I'll steal. Tell me to kill—I'll kill. Do you know this? Of course you know! You are clever and see everything. If you do not know it . . . Nadia, Nadia, my heart's darling, pity me!"

And he threw himself on to his knees before her. But she sat motionless, resting against the wall, with her head thrown back and her hands behind her back. Her eyes were fixed on some far-away point. Did she see anything? Did she hear anything? What were her feelings at the sight of this man who had thrown himself at her feet and was imploring her love? Pity? Contempt? She wanted to pity him, but felt she could not. He only excited her aversion. And could he have excited any other feeling in this pitiful state ?—drunk, dirty, abjectly imploring ?

He had already for some days past given up going to his work. He drank every day. Finding consolation in drink, he began to follow the object of his passion less, and sat all the time at home drinking and trying to muster up courage to go to her and tell her *all*. What he would say to her he did not himself know. " I will tell her everything, open my soul," flashed through his fuddled head. At length he made up his mind, went and began to speak. Even through the mist of his drunkenness he realized that he was saying and doing things not at all calculated to inspire love towards him, but all the same, he went on speaking, feeling that with every word he was falling lower and lower, and drawing the noose tighter and tighter around his neck.

He spoke long and disjointedly. His speech became slower and slower, and finally his drunken, swollen eyelids closed, and with his head thrown back against the chair, he fell asleep.

Nadejda Nicolaievna remained in her former pose, vacantly gazing at the ceiling, drumming with her fingers on the wall-paper.

" Am I sorry for him ? No. What can I do for him ? Marry him ? Dare I ? Would it not be the same selling of myself ? Yes—no, it would be even worse !"

She did not know why it would be worse, but felt it.

" Now, I am at least frank. Anyone may strike me. Have I not suffered insults ? But then, how would I be better ? Would it not be the same depravity, only not less frank ? There he sits asleep, his head hanging backwards. Mouth open, face pale as death. His clothes are all stained. He must have fallen down somewhere. How heavily he is breathing . . . sometimes even snoring. . . . Yes, but this will all pass, and he will become once more a decent, self-respecting man. No, it isn't that. It seems to me that if I let this man get the upper hand of me he will torment me with recollections . . . and I could not endure it. No, I'll stay what I am. . . . Yes, it won't be for much longer."

She threw a shawl around her shoulders and left the room, slamming the door behind her. Ivan Ivanovich woke from the noise, looked around him with unmeaning eyes, and feeling it uncomfortable to sleep on a chair, with difficulty staggered to the bed, fell on to it, and dropped off into a dead sleep. He awoke with his head aching, but sober, late in the evening, and, seeing where he was, fled.

* * * * *

I left the house not knowing where I was going. The weather was bad. The day gloomy and dull. A wet snow was falling on my face and hands. It would have been much better to stay indoors, but could I sit there with him? He is going absolutely to ruin. What can I do to keep him? Can I change my relations towards him? My whole soul, my whole inner being revolts and burns at the thought. I do not myself know why I do not wish to take advantage of this opportunity to have done with this awful life, to rid myself of this nightmare. If I were to marry him? A new life, new hopes. . . . Surely the feeling of pity which I nevertheless have for him would turn to love?

But no! Now he is ready to lick my hand, but afterwards will trample me underfoot and say: "And you still oppose me, contemptible creature! You despised me!"

Would he say this? I think so.

There is one means of salvation for me, an excellent one, on which I have long made up my mind, and to which I expect I shall eventually have recourse. But I think it is still too soon. I am too young. I feel too much that I am alive. I want to live, to breathe, to feel, hear, see. I want to be able, even if rarely, to see the sky and the Neva.

Here is the Quay. On the one side enormous buildings, and on the other—the blackening, icebound Neva. The ice will soon move, and then the river will be blue. The park on the opposite side is becoming green. The islands, too, are becoming covered with foliage. Although it is a Petersburg spring, still, it is spring.

And suddenly I remembered my last happy spring. I was then a girl of seven years, and lived with my father and mother in the country in the steppe. They paid little heed to what I did, and I ran about where and as much as I chose. I remember in the beginning of March how the rivers rushed along the gullies, roaring with the melted snow, how the steppe became darker, how wonderful the air became, how moist and joyous. First the top of the mounds showed themselves with the short grass on them becoming green. Then afterwards the whole steppe became green, although drift snow still lay in the gullies and ravines. Rapidly, in a few days, literally as if they had sprung already freed from out of the earth, bunches of peonies grew up and on them, their gaudy bright crimson blooms. The larks began to sing.

Oh Lord! What have I done that even in this life I have been thrown into hell? Surely all that I go through is worse than any hell!

The stone steps lead straight down to a prorub. Something impelled me to go down these steps and look at the water. But is it too soon? Of course it is. I will wait a little.

All the same, it would be nice to stand on the slippery wet edge of the prorub. It would be so easy to slip in. It would only be cold. . . . One second—and I should float under the ice down the river. A mad beating of the ice above with hands, feet, head, face. It would be interesting to know if daylight is visible through the ice.

I stood motionless over the prorub, and so long that I had got to the state when one thinks of nothing.

AN INCIDENT

My feet had long been wet through, yet I did not move from the spot. It was not a cold wind, but it pierced right through me, so that I was shivering all over; but still I stood there. I do not know how long this would have lasted if somebody had not called out from the Quay:

"Heh, Madame! Lady!"

I did not turn round.

"Lady, please come back on to the pavement!"

Somebody behind me began to come down the steps. In addition to the shuffling of feet along the steps sprinkled with sand, I heard a sort of dull noise. I turned round. It was a gorodovoi, who had come down, and it was his sword I had heard. When he saw my face, the respectful expression on his face abruptly changed to one of coarse insolence. He came up to me and seized me by the shoulder.

"Get out of this, you! The likes of you are everywhere. You will be fool enough to throw yourself into the prorub, and then I shall lose my billet through you."

He knew by my face what I am.

IV

All is the same as before. It is not possible to be one minute alone without being seized with melancholy. What shall I do so as to forget?

Annushka has brought me a letter. From whom? It is so long since I had had a latter from anyone.

"Madame Nadedja Nicolaievna,

"Although I thoroughly understand that I am nothing to you, I nevertheless believe that you are a nice girl and will not want to offend me. For the first and last time I beg you to come and see me, as to-day is my

name-day. I have no relations, no friends. I implore you to come. I give you my word I will say nothing displeasing or offensive. Pity your devoted
"Ivan Nikitin.

" P.S.—I cannot think of my recent behaviour in your rooms without shame. Come to-day at six o'clock. I enclose my address.—I. N."

What does this mean? He has had the courage to write to me. There is something behind it all. What does he want to do with me? Shall I go or not?

It is difficult to decide—go or not? If he wants to lure me into a trap, either to kill me or . . . but if he kills me, all is ended.

I will go.

I will dress more plainly and modestly, wash the rouge and powder off my face. It will be more pleasing to him. I will do my hair more plainly. How my hair has fallen out! I did my hair, put on a black woollen dress, a black scarf, white collar and cuffs, and went to the glass to look at myself.

I almost cried out at seeing in it a woman not at all like the Evgenia who performs indecent dances so well at various cafés. It was not the impudent, berouged cocotte with smiling face, flash puffed-out chignon, and pencilled lashes. This draggled and suffering woman, pale-faced and melancholy-looking, with big black eyes and dark circles around them, is something quite new—it is not I. But perhaps it is I. And that Evgenia whom all see and know is something strange, mocking me, pressing me, killing me.

And I really cried. I cried long and bitterly. They have assured me since babyhood that one feels easier after crying, but this cannot be true for all, because I do not feel easier, but worse. Every sob hurts me, every tear is a bitter one. To those who have still some hope

AN INCIDENT

of peace and of being cured such tears perhaps give relief ; but what hope have I ?

I dried my tears and started off.

* * * * *

I found the address without any difficulty, and the Finnish maidservant showed me Ivan Ivanovich's door.

" May I come in ?"

There was a sound in the room of a drawer being hurriedly shut. " Come in !" Ivan Ivanovich called out quickly. I entered. He was sitting at a writing-table and was sealing an envelope. He did not seem even to be glad to see me.

" How do you do, Ivan Ivanovich ?" I said.

" How do you do, Nadejda Nicolaievna ?" he replied, rising and putting out his hand. A gleam of tenderness flashed across his face when I put out my hand, but disappeared immediately. He was serious and even severe. " Thank you for coming."

" Why did you ask me ?" I inquired.

" My goodness, surely you know what it means to me to see you ! But that is an unpleasant topic for you."

We sat down and kept silent. The Finn maid brought a samovar. Ivan Ivanovich gave me some tea and sugar. Then he placed some jam, biscuits, sweets, and half a bottle of wine on the table.

" Forgive me for this ' treat,' Nadejda Nicolaievna. Perhaps it is displeasing to you, but don't be angry. Be kind, make and pour out the tea. Eat something—there are the sweets and wine."

I began to do the duties of hostess, and he sat opposite me so that his face was in the shade, and began to gaze at me. I felt his eyes fixed steadily on me, and felt that I was getting red.

For a moment I raised my eyes, but dropped them again directly because he continued to look me straight in the face. What does it mean ? Surely the surroundings, the modest black dress, the absence of impudent people and stupid talk has not affected me so strongly that I have once more turned into a demure and confused girl, such as I was two years ago? I was annoyed, vexed with myself.

"Tell me, please, why are you poking your eyes out at me like that for?" I said, with an effort, but bravely.

Ivan Ivanovich jumped up and began to walk about the room.

"Nadejda Nicolaievna, don't be common. Be just for an hour as you were when you arrived."

"But I don't understand why you have sent for me. Surely not merely to sit and look at me and say nothing."

"Yes, Nadejda Nicolaievna, only for this. It at least does not give you any special annoyance, and it comforts me to look at you—for the last time. It was so good of you to come in that dress. I did not expect that, and I am still more grateful to you for it."

"But why for the last time, Ivan Ivanovich?"

"I am going away."

"Where?"

"Far away, Nadejda Nicolaievna. It is not my name-day at all to-day. I don't know why I wrote that. I simply wanted to see you once more. First, I meant to have gone out and waited until I met you, but afterwards I decided to beg you to come here. And you were good enough to come. God grant you happiness!"

"There is little happiness ahead for me, Ivan Ivanovich."

"Yes, that is true, for you there is little happiness. But you know better than I what is ahead of you. . . ." His voice trembled. "I am better off," he added, "because I am going away." And his voice trembled still more.

I began to feel inexpressibly sorry for him. Was it just all the bad I had felt against him? Why had I pushed him away so coarsely and harshly? But now it was already too late for regrets.

AN INCIDENT

I got up and began to put on my things. Ivan Ivanovich jumped up as if stung.

"You are going already?" he asked in an agitated voice.

"Yes, I must go...."

"You must?... Again there? Nadejda Nicolaievna! Yes, better for me to kill you at once!"

He said this in a whisper, having seized me by the arm and looking at me with a troubled expression in his dilated eyes.

"Is it better? Tell me!"

"But you know, Ivan Ivanovich, that you will go to Siberia for it. And I don't want that at all."

"To Siberia!... And is it only out of fear of Siberia that I cannot kill you?... No, that is not why.... I cannot kill you because... but how can I kill you? How can I kill you?" he murmured chokingly.... "I...."

And he seized me, lifted me up as if I had been a child, crushing me in his embrace, and raining kisses on my face, lips, eyes, and hair. Then, just as suddenly as this had all happened, he put me down and said quickly:

"Well, go! go!... Forgive me, but it is the first and last time. Don't be angry with me. Go, Nadejda Nicolaievna!"

"I am not angry, Ivan Ivanovich...."

"Go! Go! Thank you for coming."

He saw me to the door, and immediately afterwards locked it. I began to go down the staircase. I was feeling more depressed than before.

Let him go and forget me. I will stay and live out my time. Enough of sentimentality. I'll go home.

I quickened my pace, and began to think of what dress I should wear and where to go in the evening. And so my romance has ended, a momentary halt on the slippery path! Now I shall go on without let or hindrance ever lower and lower....

AN INCIDENT

But if he means to shoot himself now ! suddenly something cried out within me. I stopped as if transfixed. My eyes became dark, cold shivers ran down my back. I could not breathe. ... Yes, he is at this moment killing himself ! He slammed the drawer—he was looking at a revolver. He had written a letter. ... The last time. ... Run ! Perhaps I shall yet be in time. Oh God ! stop him ! God ! leave him for me !

A mortal strange fear seized me. I rushed back as if possessed, tearing my way through passers-by. I do not remember how I tore up the stairs. I only remember the vacant face of the Finn servant who let me in. I remember the long, dark corridor with its row of doors. I remember how I threw myself at his door ; but as I seized the handle a shot resounded from inside. People rushed out from all sides, everything swam around me, people, corridor, doors, walls. And I fell ... everything in my head also swam and disappeared. ...

IV

COWARD

The war is decidedly giving me no rest. I see clearly that it is dragging, and when it will end is very difficult to foretell. Our soldiers are as splendid as ever, but the enemy has proved far from being as weak as we thought, and now, four months from the declaration of war, no decisive success has been gained by our side. In the meanwhile every extra day claims its hundreds of victims. Is it my nerves which cause the telegrams merely stating the numbers of killed and wounded to affect me far more than those around me ? Somebody will calmly read out : " Our losses insignificant ; officers, wounded, so many, giving names ; rank and file, killed, 50 ; wounded, 100," and even rejoice that the numbers are so small; but to me the reading of such news immediately brings the whole bloody picture before my eyes. Fifty dead, one hundred maimed—this is " insignificant !" Why are we so horrified when the newspapers inform us of some murder where the victims are few ? Why does not the sight of corpses riddled with bullets lying on a battle-field strike us with the same horror as the interior of a house ransacked by murder ? Why does a catastrophe costing the lives of some scores of persons cause all Russia to cry out, whilst nobody pays any attention to advanced-guard skirmishes with " insignificant " losses, also of some scores of men ?

A few days ago Lvoff, a medical student and a friend of mine, with whom I often argue about the war, said to me: "Well, we shall see, my peaceful friend, what will become of your humanitarian convictions when you are called up and are obliged to fire at people."

"Me, Vassili Petrovich? They will not call me up. I am in the Militia Reserve."

"That may be, but if the war drags on it will affect the Militia as well. Do not be too sure about it. Your turn will come."

My heart seemed to contract. How was it that this thought had not come into my head before? Of course the Militia will be called up. There was nothing impossible in that. "If the war drags on," and it is sure to drag on. Even if this war does not last long it is all the same, some other war will commence. Why not have a war? Why not perform great exploits? It seems to me that the present war is only the forerunner of future wars from which I shall not escape, nor my little brother, nor even my sister's baby boy. And my turn will come very soon.

What will become of your " ego " ? Your whole being protests against the war, but nevertheless the war will compel you to shoulder a rifle, and go to die... and kill.... No, it is impossible! I am a quiet, kind-hearted young man who has up till now known only his books, the lecture-room, the family circle, and one or two close friends; who has dreamt in one or two years' time of beginning other work, the labour of love and of truth. I have been accustomed to regard this world objectively, accustomed to place it before me. I have imagined I understood all the evil in it, and so would be able to avoid this evil. But now I see my whole building of tranquillity destroyed, and I see myself automatically fitting on to my shoulders those same tatters, holes, and stains which I have hitherto only looked at. And no kind of development, no self-knowledge, no knowledge of the world, no kind of spiritual liberty will give me a pitiful physical liberty—the liberty to dispose of my own body.

* * * * *

Lvoff laughs when I begin to expound my views against the war to him.

"My dear old chap, look at things more simply, life will be easier then," says he. "Do you think that this carnage is to my taste? Apart from the fact that it will bring misfortune on all, it also affects me personally. It will not let me finish my studies. They will reduce the term of the courses, and send us out to cut off legs and arms. For all that I do not worry myself with fruitless reflections on the horrors of war, because, whatever I may think, I can do nothing to abolish it. Surely it is better not to think about it, but to mind one's own business? If they send us to treat the wounded, I shall go and do so. What is to be done in such a time as this? One must sacrifice oneself. By the way, do you know that Masha is going as a hospital nurse?"

"Not really?"

"The day before yesterday she made up her mind, and to-day has gone to practise bandaging. I did not try to dissuade her, but only asked her how she intends to arrange about her studies.

"'Afterwards,' she says... 'I will study afterwards if I am alive.' Never mind; let her go as a nurse. It will do her good."

"And what about Kuzma Thomich?"

"Kuzma says nothing, only he has become almost ferociously gloomy, and has quite given up studying. I am glad for his sake that my sister is going. He is simply wasting away, and is in torture. He follows her like her shadow and does nothing. Well—it is love!" and Vassili Petrovich shook his head. "He has rushed off now to escort her home, as if she has not always gone about alone!"

"It seems to me, Vassili Petrovich, that it is a pity he lives with you."

"Of course it is a pity, but who could have foreseen this? For myself and sister this lodging is too large. There was one room too many. Why not let it to a nice man? And a nice man took it and has fallen in love. And I am sorry, and it is sad for her. How is Kuzma beneath her? He is a kind, intelligent, good chap. But she literally does not seem to notice him. But now make yourself scarce. I have no time to waste. If you want to see my sister and Kuzma, wait in the dining-room. They will be back soon."

"No, Vassili Petrovich, I also have no time to spare. Good-bye."

I had only just got into the street when I saw Mary Petrovna and Kuzma. They were coming along without speaking. Mary Petrovna in front, with a determined, concentrated expression on her face, and Kuzma a little to one side behind her, literally not daring to walk alongside her, but from time to time casting a hurried glance towards her face. They passed by without seeing me.

* * * * *

I can do nothing and think of nothing. I have read the account of the third fight before Plevna. Twelve thousand casualties amongst the Russians and Roumanians alone!—without counting the Turks—twelve thousand!... These figures come before me in the form of an endless, drawn-out string of corpses lying side by side. If placed shoulder to shoulder they would form a road eight versts long.

"What is this?"

They tell me something about Skobeloff: that he hurled himself at some place, attacked something, took some fort, or they have taken it from him—I do not remember. In this awful affair I understand and see only one thing—a mountain of corpses serving as a pedestal for grandiose matters which will be inscribed on the pages of history. Perhaps it is necessary—I will not take it upon myself to judge, and I cannot. I am not arguing about the war, but regard it with a direct feeling aroused by the wholesale shedding of blood. The bullock before the eyes of which other bullocks are slaughtered probably experiences something similar. It does not understand why it is to be killed, and only gazes terrified, with starting eyes, at the blood, and bellows in a despairing, heart-rending manner.

* * * * *

Am I a coward or not?

To-day I was told that I am a coward. Certainly it was a very shallow-minded person who said so when I declared in her presence my unwillingness to go to the war, and expressed a fear that they will call me up to serve. Her opinion did not distress me, but raised the question—Am I really a coward? Perhaps all my aversion against what everyone else considers a great matter only arises from fear of my skin! Is it really worth while to worry about any one unimportant life in view of a great matter? And am I capable of subjecting my life to danger generally for the sake of any matter?

I did not occupy myself for any length of time with these questions. I recalled my whole life, all those occasions—truth to say, not many—on which I have been brought face to face with danger, and I could not charge myself with cowardice. I did not fear for my life then, and I do not now. Consequently it is not death which frightens me. . . .

Always fresh battles, fresh mortal suffering. After reading the papers I can do nothing. In books, instead of letters, I see prostrate rows of human beings. My pen seems a weapon inflicting black wounds on the white paper. If this goes much further it will become regular hallucinations. But now a new trouble has appeared which has somewhat taken me away from the everlasting oppressing thought.

Yesterday evening I went to the Lvoffs and found them at tea. The brother and sister were sitting at the table, but Kuzma was pacing quickly from corner to corner of the room, holding his hand to a swollen face tied up with a handkerchief.

"What is the matter?" I asked him.

He did not answer, but only made a gesture with his hand and continued his pacing.

"His teeth have been aching, and an enormous abscess has formed," said Mary Petrovna. "I begged him at the time to go and see a doctor, but he would not listen to me, and now see what it has come to."

"The doctor will be here directly. I went for him," said Vassili Petrovich.

"Very necessary," murmured Kuzma through his teeth.

"Of course, when it might easily turn into something most serious, and you still keep walking about, in spite of my entreaties to lie down. Do you know how this sometimes ends?"

"It is all the same how it ends," muttered Kuzma.

"Not at all, Kuzma Thomich," put in Mary Petrovna quietly. "Do not talk nonsense."

These words were sufficient to calm Kuzma. He even sat down at the table and asked for some tea. Mary Petrovna poured some out, and handed him the glass. When he took the glass from her hand his face took on a triumphant expression which was so incongruous with the comical appearance given him by his swollen cheek that I could not help smiling. Lvoff also laughed. Only Mary Petrovna looked seriously and compassionately at Kuzma.

The doctor arrived, a fresh-looking, ruddy-complexioned man with cheeks like rosy apples and a most cheery manner. But when he examined the patient's neck his usual cheery expression changed to one of some concern.

"Come along," said he, "let us go into your room. I must have a good look at you."

COWARD

I went after them to Kuzma's room. The doctor placed him on the bed and commenced to examine the upper portion of his chest, carefully tapping it with his fingers.

"H'm, you must lie quietly and not get up. Have you any friends who would give up some of their spare time for you?" inquired the doctor.

"I think so," replied Kuzma in a perplexed tone.

"I would ask them," said the doctor, turning politely to me, "to look after the patient from to-day, and if any new symptoms appear to come for me."

He left the room. Lvoff escorted him to the passage, where they talked for a long time in low tones about something, and I went to Mary Petrovna. She was sitting in a thoughtful pose, resting her head on one hand, and with the other was slowly stirring her tea.

"The doctor has ordered someone to watch Kuzma."

"Is there really any danger?" Mary Petrovna asked with alarm.

"Probably there is—otherwise, why should it be necessary to watch him? You will not refuse to look after him?"

"Of course not. I have not gone to the war, but yet must turn nurse. Let us go to him. It must be very dull for him to lie all alone."

Kuzma met us smiling, so far as his swollen cheek allowed him to do so.

"Thank you," he said, "and I was already beginning to think you had forgotten me."

"No, Kuzma Thomich, we will not forget you now. We must look after you. See what becomes of disobedience," said Mary Petrovna smilingly.

"And shall you—— ?" timidly asked Kuzma.

"Yes, yes, only you will have to obey me."

Kuzma closed his eyes and reddened with pleasure.

"Ah, yes," said he suddenly, turning to me. "Give me the looking-glass; it is lying on the table."

I gave him a small round looking-glass. Kuzma begged me to show him the light, and with the help of the glass he looked at the place. After this his face darkened, and, notwithstanding that we three tried to make him talk, he never uttered a word all the evening.

* * * * *

To-day they have told me that they will soon call up the Militia. I have expected it, and was not much surprised. I could get out of the fate I so fear. I could make use of certain influential friends, and stay in St. Petersburg at my post. They could "arrange" it for me, or send me as a clerk. But first I dislike resorting to such means, and second something vague and undefined within me is weighing up my position, and forbids me shirk the war. "It is not right," says a little voice inside me.

* * * * *

Something I never dreamt of has happened.

I went this morning to relieve Mary Petrovna in watching Kuzma. She met me at the door with tear-stained eyes, pale and worn out with a sleepless night.

"What is the matter, Mary Petrovna?"

"Hush!" she whispered. "Do you know all is ended?"

"What is ended? He is not dead?"

"No, no, not yet—but there is no possible hope. Both doctors—we called in another——" Tears prevented her from saying more.

"Come and look at him."

"You must first dry those tears and drink some water. You will quite upset him."

"It is all the same. Does not he know already! He knew yesterday when he asked for the glass. He would soon have been a doctor himself."

The heavy atmosphere of an operating theatre filled the room in which the sick man lay. His bed had been moved into the middle of the room. His long legs, huge body, and arms stretched by his sides, showed up clearly under the blanket. His eyes were closed, and he was breathing slowly and heavily. It seemed to me that he had grown thinner in one night. His face was sticky and moist, and had an unpleasant greenish tinge.

" What is the matter with him ?" I asked in a whisper.

" Let him tell you. You stay with him. I cannot."

She left the room, hiding her face in her hands and convulsed with the sobs she was trying to restrain, and I sat down near the bed and waited until he should awake. There was an oppressive stillness in the room. Only the rare, heavy breathing of the sick man was heard and the soft ticking of a watch lying on a little table near the bed. I looked at his face, which was scarcely recognizable. It was not that his features had changed so much, but that I saw an entirely new light in them. I had known Kuzma for a long time, and we were friends, although not on especially intimate terms. I had never been on such terms with him as now. I recalled his life, disappointments, and joys as if they had been my own. In his love for Mary Petrovna I had hitherto seen more of the comic side, but now I understood what torments this being must have experienced. Was he really in such danger ? I wondered. He cannot be. Surely a man cannot die from toothache ! Mary Petrovna is crying about him, but he will recover, and all will be well.

He opened his eyes and saw me. Without changing the expression on his face, he said slowly, pausing after each word :

" How do you do ?—See what—I am like.—The end has come. Has come so—stealthily, unexpectedly—it is stupid."

" Tell me, Kuzma, what is the matter with you ? Perhaps it is nothing like so bad as all that."

" Not so bad,—you say. No, no, old friend—it is very bad. I do not make mistakes on such a simple matter as this. Look !"

He slowly and mechanically turned down the blanket and unbuttoned his shirt. Commencing from the right side of his neck was a dark, unpleasant-looking patch, the size of one's hand, extending to his chest—gangrene.

* * * * *

For four days now by the sick man's bedside I have not closed my eyes, sitting first with Mary Petrovna and then with her brother. The patient appears to be barely living, yet life seems to be unwilling to leave his strong body. They have cut out the dead flesh, and the doctors have ordered us to wash the gaping wound left by the operation every two hours. Every two hours we two or three go to his bed, turn him over, raise his huge body, and wash the terrible wound with carbolic acid through a gutta-percha tube. It sprays the wound, and Kuzma sometimes finds strength even to smile because he explains " it tickles." As is the case with all persons who are rarely ill, he likes being nursed and tended like a child, and when Mary Petrovna takes in her hands what he calls " the reins of government "—that is, the gutta-percha tube—and begins to spray, he is especially pleased, and declares that no one can do this so skilfully as she, notwithstanding the fact that her trembling hands often cause the bed to be soaked with water.

How their relations have altered! Mary Petrovna, who had been something unattainable for him, on whom he had gazed and feared, who had never taken any notice of him, now nurses him tenderly, and often sits crying quietly by his bedside. And he calmly accepts it all as a matter of course, and talks to her as would a father to his little daughter.

Sometimes he suffers very much. His wound burns and fever racks him. . . . Then strange thoughts come into my brain. To me Kuzma seems one of those of whom there are tens of thousands mentioned in the reports. By his pain and sufferings I attempt to measure the evil caused by the war. How much suffering and

COWARD

anguish here in one room, on one bed—and yet all this is merely one drop in the sea of sorrow and agony being experienced by the enormous number of those whom they are sending forward only to lie on the field in heaps of dead or still groaning, blood-stained, plundered bodies.

I must ask Lvoff or Mary Petrovna to take my place, if only for a couple of hours, whilst I have a rest. I am utterly worn out from want of sleep and my depressing thoughts.

* * * * *

I was sleeping soundly, curled up on the little sofa, when I was awakened by someone touching my shoulder.

" Get up ! get up ! " said Mary Petrovna.

I jumped up instantly, without at first understanding anything. Mary Petrovna whispered something rapidly in a frightened manner to me.

" Spots ! new spots ! " I gathered at last.

" What spots, and where ? "

" Oh dear, dear ! he does not understand," she wailed. " New spots have appeared on Kuzma Thomich. I have already sent for the doctor."

" But perhaps it is nothing," said I, with the indifference of a just-awakened man.

" How nothing ? Look for yourself."

Kuzma was wrapped in a heavy, restless sleep. He kept tossing his head from side to side, and sometimes groaned deeply. His chest was bare, and I saw on it, an inch or so below the bandaged wound, two new little black spots. The gangrene had penetrated further under the skin, and spreading under it, had come to the surface in two places. Although before this I had little hope of his recovery, these new unmistakable symptoms of death made me turn pale.

Mary Petrovna sat in a corner of the room with her hands on her knees, and silently gazed at me with despairing eyes.

"You must not despair," I said to her. "The doctor will be here directly, and will examine him. Perhaps it is not yet all over, and perhaps we shall yet pull him round."

"No, he will die," she whispered.

"Well, if he dies," I answered, also quietly, "it will, of course, be a great grief to all of us, but you must not wear yourself out in this manner. You look half dead."

"You do not understand what tortures I suffer these days. I cannot myself explain why I did not love him, and even now do not love him, in the way he does me. But if he dies my heart will break. I shall always remember his steady, open glance, his persistent silence when near me, although he liked talking, and could talk well. I shall always reproach myself that I did not take pity on him, did not appreciate his cleverness, his love, his devotion. Perhaps this seems ridiculous to you, but the thought is a constant torture to me now that if I had loved him—we should have lived quite differently. All would have happened differently, and this awful and stupid business would not have happened. One thinks and thinks, excuses and justifies oneself, but all the time at the bottom of one's mind something keeps saying—Your fault, your fault, your fault!"

At that moment I glanced at the patient, fearing that our whispering would awaken him, and saw a change in his face. He had awaked, and was listening to what Mary Petrovna was saying, but did not wish to show he was. His lips trembled, his cheeks burned, his whole face was lighted up literally as if by the sun, just as a wet, sombre-looking field is brightened up when the clouds above it open and allow a ray of sunshine to peep through. He had evidently forgotten about his sickness and fear of death. Only one feeling filled him, and two tears trickled from his closed and trembling eyelids. Mary Petrovna looked at him for a second or two half-frightenedly, and then blushed. A soft expression flashed into her face, and, bending over the poor half-corpse, she kissed him.

Then he opened his eyes. " My God, how I do not want to die !" he murmured. And suddenly strange, quiet sobbing sounds filled the room—sounds quite new to me, who had never seen this man cry. I left the room, I was almost breaking down myself.

I also do not want to die, and all these thousands do not want to die. Kuzma at least has found consolation in his last moments—but there at the war ! Kuzma, for all his fear of death and his physical suffering, would scarcely change these present moments for any others of his life. No, it is not that at all ! Death will always be death, but to die amidst those near and dear to one, and falling into the mud and one's own blood, momentarily expecting someone will come up and finish you off, or that guns will ride over you and crush you like a worm.

* * * * *

" I tell you frankly," said the doctor to me in the passage, as he put on his shuba and galoshes, " that with similar cases in hospitals ninety-nine out of one hundred are fatal. I can only hope on the attentive nursing, the wonderful spirits of the patient, and his burning desire to recover."

" Every sick person longs to recover, doctor."

" Of course, but your friend has certain vivifying circumstances," said the doctor, with a smile. " And so this evening we shall operate again, and hope for the best."

He shook my hand, and went off on his rounds, leaving behind him the smell of his bearskin shuba. In the evening he came with his instruments.

" Perhaps you would like, my embryo colleague, to operate for practice," said he, turning to Lvoff. Lvoff nodded his head in assent, turned up his sleeves, and with a serious, gloomy expression on his face, began. I saw how he inserted some wonderful-looking, three-edged instrument into the wound, and saw how Kuzma, as the keen edge pierced his body, clutched the bedstead with his hands and clenched his teeth with the pain.

"Don't be an old woman," said Lvoff to him gruffly, placing a tampon into the new wound.

"Does it hurt very much?" asked Mary Petrovna tenderly.

"Not so very much, dearie, but I have grown weak, and am worn out."

They bandaged him, gave him some wine, and he calmed down. The doctor left, and I, with Mary Petrovna, began to put the room in order.

"Put the clothes right," murmured Kuzma in an even, dull voice. "There is a draught."

I commenced to readjust his pillows and bedclothes according to his directions, which he gave very irritably, declaring that somewhere about his left elbow there was a small opening through which the cold was coming, and begging me to tuck the clothes in better. I tried to do my best, but notwithstanding all my efforts Kuzma still felt a draught, now at his side, then by his feet.

"You are very awkward," he grumbled. "There is a draught again at my back. Let her." He glanced at Mary Petrovna, and then it became quite clear to me why I was unable to please him.

Mary Petrovna put down the medicine-glass which was in her hand and went to the bed. "Make you comfortable?" she said.

"Put the things right. That's right—and warm now."

He watched her whilst she settled the bedclothes, then closed his eyes, and, with a childishly happy expression on his worn face, dropped asleep.

"Are you going home?" asked Mary Petrovna.

"No, I have had a good sleep and can watch now, but if I am not wanted I will go."

"No, don't go, please. Let us have a little talk. My

brother is in his room all the time with his books, and it is so bitter, so depressing, to sit alone with the patient whilst he is sleeping and think of nothing but his death."

"You must be strong, Mary Petrovna; depressing thoughts and tears are strictly forbidden to hospital nurses."

"And I, too, will not cry when I am a nurse. Anyhow, it will not be so hard to nurse the wounded as one so near."

"Then in any case you are going?"

"Of course I am going. Whether he recovers or dies I am going. I have become so accustomed to the idea now that I cannot give it up. I want to do something good, something useful; I want to be able to remember good, bright days."

"Ah, Mary Petrovna, I am afraid you will not see much light at the war."

"Why? I shall work. But there is light for you. I should like even to take some part in the war."

"To take part in it! But surely, does it not inspire you with horror? What are you telling me?"

"I am telling—who told you that I love war? Only —how shall I tell you?—war—is an evil. Both you and I and very many others have this opinion. But it is inevitable. Whether you like it or do not like it makes no difference. There will be war, and if *you* do not go to fight they will take someone else, and, anyhow— mankind will be mutilated or tortured by its course. I am afraid you do not understand me, as I express myself badly. Listen! In my idea war is a *common* sorrow, a *common* suffering, and to avoid it is perhaps permissible, only such a course is not pleasing to me."

I kept silence. Mary Petrovna's words very clearly expressed my confused aversion to avoid the war. I myself have *felt* what she feels and thinks, only I have *thought* differently.

"You," she continued, "it seems, are all the time

thinking how you can remain here if they call you up for a soldier. My brother has spoken to me about it. You know I like you very much, and think you a nice man, but this trait in your character distresses me."

"What is to be done, Mary Petrovna? Different views. What shall I reply? Was it I who started the war?"

"Not you, or any of those who have died at it, or will die. They also would not have gone if they could have avoided it, but they cannot, and you can. They go to fight and you stay in St. Petersburg, alive, sound, and lucky, only because you have friends who would be sorry to send someone they know personally to the war. I will not take upon myself to judge—perhaps it is excusable, but I repeat, it distresses me."

She energetically shook her curly head and said no more.

*   *   *   *   *

At last it has come. To-day I put on a grey overcoat and have already tasted of the roots of military training—the manual. At the present moment there is ringing in my ears—" 'Tion! Form fours! Present arms!"

And I stood to attention, formed fours, and flourished my rifle. And after a short time, when I have mastered the intricacies of forming fours, they will tell me off to a draft, place us in railway waggons, transport us, and distribute us amongst the regiments to fill up the vacancies left by the killed. . . .

Well, it is all the same. It is all over. Now I do not belong to myself. I shall go with the stream. Now it is best not to think and not to judge, but to accept without criticism all the chances of life, and only cry out when in pain. . . .

They have quartered me in a wing of the barracks specially detailed for the " privileged " class recruits. This wing is distinguished in having beds instead of bunks for sleeping accommodation, nevertheless it is quite sufficiently dirty. It is very bad amongst the non-privileged recruits. They live—until told off to regiments—in a huge shed which was formerly a riding-school. Two rows of tents have been fixed up in it. Straw has been carted as far as the door, and the rest is left to the temporary inhabitants to fix themselves up as best they may. Along the passage going down the middle of the riding-school, formed by the two rows of tents, the snow and filth brought in every minute from outside by persons entering has mingled with the straw, and has formed an indescribable slush. Even on either side of this passage the straw is not overclean. Some hundreds of men are standing, sitting, or lying on this straw in groups, each representing some village contingent, the whole forming a veritable ethnographical exhibition. I searched for representatives from my district. The tall, awkward " little Russians " in new overcoats and caps lay in a huddled group, not saying a word. There were ten of them.

" Good-day, comrades."

" Good-day."

" Is it long since you left home ? "

" Two weeks. And who are you ? " asked one of them of me. I gave him my name, which was known to all of them, and this meeting with someone from their part brightened them up a little, and they became more communicative.

" Lonely ? " I asked.

" How not lonely ? "

" Where are you going ? "

" Who knows ! I suppose to kill the Turk."

" And do you want to go to the war ? "

" What are we going to do there ? "

I began to question them about our local town, and these recollections of home loosened their tongues. They commenced to tell me of a recent wedding for which a pair of bullocks had been sold, and how almost directly afterwards they had taken the young husband for a soldier. They told me about the pristaff—the devil stick in his throat!—the lack of land, and how in consequence of this some hundreds had decided to leave the village and go to the Amur. . . . The conversation was only of the past, no one referred to the future, to those hard times, dangers, and sufferings which awaited us all. No one took any interest in the Turks or Bulgars, or troubled himself about the question for which he was perhaps going to die.

A drunken young recruit of a local contingent, passing us, stopped at our group, and when I again began to talk of the war authoritatively said:

"This Turk must be wiped out."

"Must be?" I inquired, smiling involuntarily at the assurance of the decision.

"Of course, Barin, so that nothing shall remain of the unclean brute. Because through his mutinying how much suffering are we to undergo? Had he, for instance, kept quiet and behaved—I should be at home now with my parents and in a better state. But he is fractious, and there is grief for us. Be assured I am speaking the truth. Give me a cigarette, barin, please." And he suddenly stopped short, straightened himself in front of me, and put his hand to his cap.

I gave him a cigarette, said good-bye to my countrymen, and went back to barracks, as my leave was up.

"He is fractious, and there is grief for us," and his drunken voice rang in my ears. Short and vague, but at the same time it covers all there is to be said.

* * * * *

Heartsickness and depression reign at the Lvoffs. Kuzma is very bad, and although the wound is clean, has very high fever, delirium, and great pain. Both brother and sister remain with him all the time I am engaged in learning my work. Now, when they know I am going to the war, the sister has grown still more depressed, and her brother still more surly.

"Already in uniform?" he had muttered when I said "How do you do?" to him in his room, littered with books and reeking of smoke. "Oh, you people!"

"Why, Vassili Petrovich?"

"Because you will not let me study—that's why. And as there is no time, they will not let me finish my course, but will send me to the war, and there is so much I cannot learn, and then there are you and Kuzma."

"Well, Kuzma is dying, but what about me?"

"And are you not going to die? If they do not kill you, you will go out of your mind, or put a bullet through your head. I know you, and there are examples."

"What examples? Do you really know of any like that? Tell me, Vassili Petrovich?"

"Stop talking. Is it so necessary further to disillusionize you? It is bad for you. I know nothing. I was only talking."

But I was persistent, and then he told me of the example as follows:

"A wounded artillery officer told me," he commenced. "They had only just left Kishinieff, in April, directly after the declaration of war. The rain was unceasing, and the roads disappeared. Only a sea of mud remained into which the guns and baggage-train sank up to the axles. It became so bad that the horses could do nothing, so they hitched on drag-ropes with which the men pulled. The second half of the road was awful. We had twelve ridges to get over in seventeen versts, and the whole distance was a perfect quagmire. They got into it and stuck. The rain lashed them, and there was not a dry thread on any of them. They were half starving and completely worn out, but it was necessary to drag the guns along. Well, of course, the men pulled and pulled until they fell senseless, face downwards, into the mud. Finally it was impossible to move ahead, but all the same they continued to toil. It was awful, said the officer; it is dreadful to think of it. They had a young surgeon with them, a nervous fellow who wept, and exclaiming that he could not stand such a sight, said he would go on ahead, which he did. The soldiers cut down branches and made what was almost a raft, and finally succeeded in getting out of the bog. They dragged the battery on to the mountain, and there saw the surgeon hanging on a tree. There is the example. If the man could not stand even seeing such suffering, how will you be able to stand it?"

"Vassili Petrovich, is it not easier to bear torture than to hang oneself like the surgeon?"

"Well, I do not know. What is there good in the fact that they will harness you to a shaft?"

"Conscience will not prick me, Vassili Petrovich."

"Well, that is hair-splitting. Talk with my sister on that point—she is well up in such fine distinctions." Saying which he held out his hand and smilingly bade me good-bye.

"Where are you off to?"

"To the hospital."

I went into Kuzma's room. He was not asleep, and, as Mary Petrovna explained to me, felt better than usual. He had not yet seen me in uniform, and my appearance was an unpleasant surprise to him.

"Will they leave you here or send you to the army?" he asked.

"They will send me; surely you know?"

He was silent.

"I knew," he said after a pause, "but I had forgotten. I cannot remember or think of much these days. Well, go! It is necessary."

"And you, Kuzma Thomich, say this!"

"Why 'and I'? Is it not true what I say? What services have you rendered that you should be exempted? Go and die! There are people more necessary than you,

more hard-working than you, and they are going. . . .
Put my pillow right . . . that's better."

He spoke quietly but irritably, as if blaming someone for his illness.

"All this is true, Kuzma. But could I really not go? Could I really protest personally on my own behalf? If so, I should have stayed here without further talk; it would not be difficult to arrange. I am not doing this—they want me, and I am going. But at least they cannot prevent me from having my own opinion on this point."

Kuzma lay motionless with his eyes fixed on the ceiling, as if he had not heard me. Finally he slowly turned his head towards me.

"Do not take any notice of my words. I "—he murmured—" I am worn out and irritable, and really do not know why I tease people. I have already grown quarrelsome. I shall soon die; it is time."

"Enough, Kuzma; cheer up. The wound is clean and is healing, and everything is going on well. You must not talk of dying, but of living now."

Mary Petrovna looked at me with her large, sorrowful eyes, and I suddenly remembered how she had said to me two weeks ago: "No, he will not recover; he will die."

"And if I really do recover, it will be good," said Kuzma, smiling weakly. "They will send you to fight, and I, with Mary Petrovna, will come—she as a hospital nurse, and I as a surgeon. And I will look after you when you are wounded, as you are looking after me now."

"You will chatter, Kuzma," said Mary Petrovna. "It is bad for you to talk much, and it is time to begin tormenting you."

He resigned himself to us. We undressed him, took off the bandages, and commenced work on his huge and lacerated chest. When I directed the spray of water on the open places; on the collar-bone, which glistened like mother-of-pearl; on a vein which, clean and free, ran right throughout the wound, it was not like dressing a living person, but like working on some anatomical apparatus. I thought of other wounds, far more awful in nature, and overwhelmingly greater in numbers, inflicted, moreover, not by blind, unreasoning chance, but by the conscious acts of human beings.

*   *   *   *   *

I am not writing a word in this diary of all that is happening at home, and what I am going through there. The tears with which my mother meets me, the depressing silence accompanying my presence at the common table, the kindness of my brothers and sisters—all this is hard to witness and feel, but to write of it is harder still. When I think that in a week's time I must say good-bye to all that is dearest in the world, the tears rise to my throat.

*   *   *   *   *

At last the farewells. To-morrow morning, as soon as it is light, we are off by railway. They have allowed me to spend the last night at home, and I am sitting in my room alone for the last time. The last time! Does anyone know who has not experienced such a last time the whole misery of these two words? For the last time the family have separated, for the last time I have come into this little room, and am sitting at the table lighted by the familiar little lamp and littered with books and papers. For a whole month I have not touched them. For the last time I take the half-finished work into my hands. It has stopped short and lies dead, incomplete, senseless. Instead of finishing it I am going with thousands of others to the brink of the world because history has need of my physical strength. As for intellectual forces—forget about them. No one wants them. Of what benefit have been the many years I have studied them and prepared myself to apply them? That enormous organization of which I know nothing, but of which I form a part, has wished to cut me off and hurl me aside. And what can *I* do against such a desire?

However, enough. It is time to lie down and try to sleep. To-morrow I must get up very early.

* * * * *

I begged that no one should come to the station. But when I was already sitting in the waggon crammed full of men, I felt such a heart-pinching solitude and so homesick, that I would have given all the world to pass, if only a few minutes, with any one of my near relatives. Eventually the appointed hour arrived, but the train did not start. Something was delaying it. Half an hour went past, an hour, an hour and a half, and still we did not move. In this one and a half hours I could have gone home. . . . Perhaps, after all, someone will not be able to resist coming down. . . . No, they all imagine that the train has already gone. No one will think of it being late in starting. But still, perhaps . . . and I gaze anxiously in the direction whence they might come. Never has time dragged so.

The harsh notes of the bugle sounding the " assembly " made me shiver. Soldiers who had climbed out of the waggons and had crowded on to the platforms, hurriedly scrambled into their places. The train will be off in a minute, and I shall have seen no one. Then I catch sight of the Lvoffs. Brother and sister almost ran to the waggon, and I was madly glad to see them. I do not remember what I said to them, and do not remember what they said to me, except one sentence—" Kuzma is dead !"

* * * * *

This sentence ends the notes in my diary.

Under a lowering sky lies a broad snow-covered field surrounded by white hills, on which are trees, also white with frost, although there is a touch of thaw in the air. Above the rattle of musketry comes the frequent boom of guns. One of the hills is almost enveloped in smoke, through which, as it slowly rolls down on to the field below, can be seen a dark, moving mass. Looking more attentively, it is seen that this mass is composed of little black spots. Many of these spots are already motionless, but others are ever moving forward, although their goal, indicated only by the extra density of the smoke, is still far away, and although their numbers become less every second.

A battalion in reserve, lying in the snow with rifles in hand, is following the progress of this dark mass with its thousand eyes.

"They have started!—ours have started up!"

"But will they get there? Why do they keep us here? With our help they would quickly settle matters."

"Tired of life, are you?" said an elderly soldier surlily. "Lie still and thank God you are whole."

"Yes, old man, and I shall stay whole, don't make any mistake about that," replied a young soldier with a cheery face. "I have already been in four fights, and nothing happened. Only at first it is frightening, but then—— But the Barin—it is his first time; he will be probably asking God's pardon. Barin! Barin!"

"What is it?" replied a lanky, black-bearded man lying close by.

"You, Barin, cheer up!"

"I, my friend, am all right."

"You, Barin, will be near me in case ... I know, I have already been in it. Yes, our Barin is brave; he will not run away. But there was a volunteer before you who, as soon as we started, and directly the bullets began to fly, chucked away his knapsack and rifle, and bolted; but a bullet caught him up—hit him in the back. That sort of thing is forbidden because of the oath."

"Don't you be alarmed. I shall not run away," quietly replied the Barin. "You cannot get away from a bullet."

"No, the rascal," answered the young soldier. "Is it known where to get away from it? ... Holy! ... Surely ours have not stopped!"

COWARD

The black mass had stopped, and were being enveloped in the smoke from their rifles.

" Well, they have begun to fire. That means in a minute or two they will commence retiring. . . . No! they have gone ahead again. Save ! . . . Blessed Mother, again . . . and again. . . . How they are falling, and no one to pick them up !"

" A bullet ! a bullet !" exclaimed several around, as something whistled through the air. It was a chance bullet which had passed over the reserves. It was followed by another, then a third. The battalion began to stir.

" Stretcher-bearers !" someone cried.

The stray bullet had done its work. Four soldiers with a stretcher ran forward towards the wounded man. Suddenly little figures of men and horses appeared on one of the hills on the flank of the attack, and at the same moment a puff of smoke, white as snow, showed up.

" They are firing at us, the blackguards !" cried the cheery young soldier. There was the scream of a shell followed by a report. The youngster threw himself face down into the snow. When he raised his head he saw that the Barin was lying stretched out alongside him, his arms thrown out, with his head doubled unnaturally under his chest. Another stray bullet had struck him under the right eye, making a large black hole.

V

THE MEETING

A BROAD, trembling silvery band of moonlight stretched away for tens of versts. The remaining expanse of the sea was black, and the regular dull noise of the waves as they broke and rolled along the sandy shore reached the person standing on the cliff high above. Even more black than the sea itself were the gently rocking silhouettes of the vessels in the roadstead. One huge steamer ("Probably English," reflected Vassili Petrovich), within this bright strip of moonlight, was noisily blowing off steam in a series of small clouds, which dissolved as they lightly rose into the air. A moist, brine-laden breeze was coming from the sea. Vassili Petrovich, who had seen nothing of this kind previously, gazed rapturously at the sea, the moonlit strip, the steamers and sailing vessels, and, for the first time in his life, with a feeling of pleasure inhaled the sea air. He long gave himself up to the delights of this new sensation, turning his back on the town to which he had only this day come, and in which he was to spend many, many years. Behind him a heterogeneous crowd were promenading along the boulevard, whence could be heard scraps of Russian and other languages, the decorous, subdued conversation of local dignitaries mingling with the chatter of young girls, and the loud, merry voices of grown-up schoolboys, as they strolled past together in knots of twos and threes. A burst of laughter from one of these groups made Vassili

THE MEETING

Petrovich turn round. As it passed him, one of the youths was saying something to a young girl, whilst his comrades noisily interrupted his passionate and apparently apologetic speech.

"Don't believe him, Nina Petrovna! It is all lies! He is making it up!"

"But truly, Nina Petrovna, I am not in the least to blame."

"If you, Shevyreff, ever again dream of deceiving me . . ." said the girl stiffly, in a quiet young voice.

Vassili Petrovich lost the rest of the sentence as the speakers passed out of hearing. But a second later a further burst of laughter resounded in the darkness.

"This is the field of my future labours, in which, as the 'modest ploughman, I shall work,'" mused Vassili Petrovich, first because he had been appointed teacher in the local gymnasium, and secondly, because he was fond of figurative forms of thought, even when not expressed aloud.

"Yes, I must perforce toil in this modest field," he reflected, sitting down on a bench with his face to the sea. "Where are the dreams of a professorship, of being a publicist, of a great name? You haven't it in you, friend Vassili Petrovich, to carry out all these fine plans. We'll try work here."

And beautiful and pleasant thoughts passed through the brain of the new school-teacher. He thought of how he would discover the "spark divine" in the boys. How he would help those natures "striving to divest themselves of the chains of darkness." How, finally, his pupils in due course would become men of note. . . . In his imagination he even pictured himself, Vassili Petrovich, sitting, an old, grey-haired teacher, in his modest lodging, and being visited by his former scholars—one a professor of such and such a University, a man of renown in Russia and in Europe; another, an author, a well-known novelist; a third, a statesman also famous—

all of them treating him with respect. " It is the good seed sown by you, dear sir, when I was a boy, that has made me the man I am," the statesman would say to Vassili Petrovich, warmly pressing the hand of his old tutor.

However, Vassili Petrovich did not long occupy himself with such exalted reflections. His thoughts soon turned to matters directly concerning his present situation. He drew a new pocket-book from his pocket, and counting over his money, commenced to calculate as to how much would remain after payment of all necessary expenses. "What a pity I was so extravagant *en route!*" thought he. " Lodgings . . . we'll say twenty roubles a month, board, washing, tea, tobacco. . . . I shall save a thousand roubles in six months, anyhow. I am sure to be able to get lessons here at four, or even five, roubles each. . . ." A feeling of satisfaction took him, and he became possessed of a desire to feel in his pocket where two letters of recommendation to local " big-wigs " lay, and for the twentieth time to read their addresses. He pulled out the letters, carefully unfolded the paper in which they were wrapped, but was unable to read the addresses as the moonlight was not bright enough to admit of such satisfaction. A photograph was wrapped up with the letters. Vassili Petrovich turned it straight to the light of the moon, and endeavoured to look at the well-known features. " Oh, my darling Lise!" he murmured almost out loud, and sighed, not without a feeling of pleasure. Lisa was his fiancée, whom he had left behind in Petersburg, waiting until Vassili Petrovich should accumulate the thousand roubles which the young couple deemed necessary before setting up house.

Heaving a sigh, he hid the photograph and letters in the left side-pocket of his coat, and commenced to dream of his future married life. And these dreams were even more pleasurable than those about the statesman who was to come and thank him for the good seed sown in his heart.

THE MEETING

The sea fumed far away below him and the wind became fresher. The English steamer had disappeared from the strip of moonlight which was shining with a brilliancy melting into a thousand shimmering soft lights, and stretching far away over a seemingly endless expanse of water. Vassili Petrovich was loath to rise from his seat, to tear himself away from this picture and to return to the stifling atmosphere of the little room in the hotel at which he was stopping. However, it was now late, so he got up and went along the boulevard.

A gentleman in a light suit of greyish alpaca and a straw hat with a muslin pugaree (the summer costume of the local beaux), rose from a bench as Vassili Petrovich passed, and said :

" Can you give me a light ? "

" With pleasure," replied Vassili Petrovich.

The red glow of the flame lit up a familiar face.

" Nicolai, my good chap. Is it you ? "

" Vassili Petrovich ? "

" The same. . . . Ah, how glad I am ! I never thought of this, never dreamt of it !" said Vassili Petrovich, embracing his friend heartily. " What fate has brought you here ? "

" That's simply explained—my work. And you ? "

" I have been sent here as teacher in the gymnasium. I have only just arrived."

" Where are you staying ? If at an hotel, come along with me. I am glad to see you. You can scarcely have any acquaintances here ? Come with me, we will have some supper and talk over old times."

" Yes, let us," assented Vassili Petrovich. " I shall be delighted. I came here as if into a wilderness—and suddenly this happy meeting. ' Izvoschik !' " he called.

" Don't ; there is no need to call an izvoschik," said Vassili's friend, as he in turn called out " Sergei," and a smartly turned out koliaska drove up to the kerb. The friend jumped in, but Vassili Petrovich remained standing on the pavement, and looked with bewilderment at the carriage, the black horses, and the portly coachman.

"Kudriasheff, are the horses yours?"

"Mine, mine. What? You didn't expect it?"

"Wonderful.... Can it be you?"

"Well, who else if not me? But get in, and we will talk afterwards."

Vassili Petrovich got in, sat himself by the side of Kudriasheff, and the koliaska rolled over the cobbles. Vassili Petrovich, as he sat comfortably on the soft cushions, smiled. "What does it mean?" he thought. "Not long ago Kudriasheff was the poorest of students, and now—a koliaska!" Kudriasheff, stretching out his legs, placed them on the seat opposite, said nothing, but smoked his cigar. In five minutes' time the carriage stopped.

"Well, friend, we have arrived. I will show you my humble abode," said Kudriasheff, stepping down and helping Vassili Petrovich to get out of the carriage.

Before entering his " humble abode," the guest cast a glance at it. The moon was behind it, and did not light it up, so that he was only able to note that the " abode " was a one-storied building with some ten or twelve large windows. A portico with spiral columns picked out with gold hung over a heavy wooden door, in which was inserted a looking-glass. The handle was of bronze in the form of a bird's claw, which held an irregularly shaped piece of crystal. And a shining brass plate, bearing the owner's name, was affixed to the door.

"Your ' humble abode,' Kudriasheff! It is a palace," said Vassili Petrovich, as they entered the hall with its oak furniture and polished black fireplace. "Is it really your own?"

"No, my dear chap, I haven't got to that yet. I rent it. It is not expensive—one thousand five hundred roubles."

THE MEETING

"One thousand five hundred roubles!" gasped Vassili Petrovich.

"It is better to pay one thousand five hundred roubles than to spend capital which will give far higher interest if not converted into real estate. Yes, and it means a lot of money if you really build, not like this trash."

"Trash!" exclaimed Vassili Petrovich perplexedly.

"Yes, the house is nothing grand. But come along...."

Vassili Petrovich hurriedly took off his overcoat and followed his host. The general style in which the house was furnished gave him fresh food for amazement. A whole series of lofty rooms with parquet floors and expensive wall-papers with patterns of gold. The dining-room was furnished in oak with crude models of birds hanging on the wall, an enormous carved sideboard, and a large round dining-table, which was flooded with light thrown from a hanging bronze lamp ornamented with a dead white shade. In the lounge there was a grand piano, a quantity of furniture of all kinds—sofas, stools, chairs, etc. Expensive prints and villainous oleographs hung on the walls in gilded frames. The drawing-room had the customary silk upholstered furniture, and was crowded with numberless unnecessary things. It gave the impression that the owner had suddenly become wealthy—had won two hundred or three hundred thousand roubles,—and had hurriedly furnished his house on a lavish scale. All had been purchased at one time, and purchased not because it was wanted, but because the money was burning his pocket, and found an outlet in the purchase of a grand piano, on which, so far as Vassili Petrovich knew, Kudriasheff could only play with one finger; of the horrible old painting to which probably none paid the slightest attention— one of the tens of thousands which are attributed to some second-class Flemish master; of chessmen of Chinese work, so fine and ethereal that it was impossible to play with them, and on the heads of each of which were carved three balls, and of scores of other unnecessary articles.

The friends went into the study. Here it was more comfortable. A large writing-table, equipped with various bronze and china knick-knacks, and littered with papers, plans, and drawing implements, occupied the middle of the room. Huge coloured plans and geographical charts hung on the walls, and below them stood two low Turkish divans with silk cushions. Kudriasheff, taking Vassili Petrovich by the waist, led him straight to a divan, and sat him on the soft pillows.

"Well, I am very glad to meet an old comrade," said he.

"And I also. . . . Do you know what—to arrive here as if in a wilderness, and suddenly to meet . . . Do you know, Nicolai Constantinovich, meeting you has so stirred my mind, has raised so many recollections . . ."

"Of what?"

"How of what? Of our student days, of the time when we lived so well, if not in a material sense, at least morally speaking. . . . Do you remember . . ."

"Remember what? How you and I used to devour sausages made of dog? Enough, my friend; it bores me. Will you have a cigar? 'Regalia Imperiala,' or some such name—I forget what. I only know that they cost a poltinik each."

Vassili Petrovich took one of the proffered treasures, took a penknife out of his pocket, cut the end off, lit the cigar, and said:

"Nicolai Constantinovich, I feel absolutely in a dream. A few years—and you have got to such a position!"

"What position? It's worth nothing."

"But why? How much do you get?"

"What? Salary?"

"Yes, pay."

"As engineer and Provincial Secretary Kudriasheff (*2nd*)

THE MEETING

I receive a salary of one thousand six hundred roubles a year."

Vassili Petrovich's eyes dilated.

" But how ... Where does all this come from ?"

" Oh, my friend, what simplicity ! Where ? Out of water and earth, sea and dry land. But chiefly from here."

And he tapped his forehead with his finger.

" Do you see those drawings hanging on the walls ?"

" I see them," replied Vassili Petrovich, " and——"

" Do you know what they are ?"

" No, I don't," and Vassili Petrovich got up from the divan and went up to the wall. The blue, red, brown and black shades conveyed nothing to him, any more than the mysterious figures above the fine lines, drawn in red ink.

" Plans, of course they are plans ; but of what ?"

" Really, I don't know."

" These plans represent, my very dear Vassili Petrovich, a future mole. Do you know what a mole is ?"

" Well, of course. You must remember I am a teacher of the Russian language. A mole is—well, a dam. What ?"

" Precisely, a dam. A dam for the formation of an artificial harbour. On these drawings is the plan of the mole which we are now constructing. You saw the sea from above where you were standing ?"

" Certainly. A wonderful picture ! But I did not notice any kind of construction."

" It is difficult to notice it," said Kudriasheff, laughing. " Scarcely any of this mole, Vassili Petrovich, is in the sea. It is almost all here on dry land."

" Where ?"

" Where, here in this house, and at the houses of the other engineers—Knobloch, Puitsikovsky, etc. This is, of course, between ourselves. I am talking to you as an old friend. Why are you staring at me in that way ? It is a common occurrence."

"But really, this is awful! Surely you are not telling the truth? Are you really not above such unclean methods for obtaining this comfort? Has the past only resulted in bringing you to this . . . this? And you talk quite calmly of this . . ."

"Stop, stop, Vassili Petrovich! No strong words, if you please. You talk of 'dishonourable methods'? Tell me first what is meant by honourable and dishonourable. I myself do not know. Perhaps I have forgotten, but I didn't try to remember, and it seems to me you yourself do not remember, only pretend you do. But let us drop the subject. First of all, it is not polite. Respect freedom of judgment. You talk of—dishonour. Talk if you like, but don't swear at me. I do not swear at you because your opinions differ from mine. The whole matter, my dear friend, lies in the view, the point of view, and as there are many points of view, let us drop this matter and go to the dining-room, where we will have some 'vodka,' and talk on pleasanter subjects."

"But, Nicolai, Nicolai, it hurts me to look at you."

"Well, let it hurt as much as you like. Let it hurt. It will pass away. You will grow accustomed to it. You will look at it and will say, 'What a simpleton I am!' Yes, you will say it, remember my words! Come along, let us go and have a drink and forget about erring engineers. That's why a man has brains, in order to go astray. . . . Well, my dear tutor, how much are you going to get?"

"It is all the same to you."

"Well, for instance?"

"Well, I earn three thousand roubles with private lessons."

"There you are! For a paltry three thousand to drag out your whole life in giving lessons! And I sit here and look around. If I wish—I drink. If I don't wish, I don't. If the fancy came into my head to spit at the

THE MEETING

ceiling all day long, I could afford to do it. And money—so much money that it—' is dross for us.' "

When they went into the dining-room, they found everything ready for supper. The cold roast beef looked like a rosy mountain. There were pots of jam displaying a variety of English names and labels. A whole row of bottles raised their heads from the table. The friends drank a wineglass or so of vodka each, and consumed their supper. Kudriasheff ate slowly and with relish. He was absolutely absorbed in his occupation.

Vassili Petrovich ate and thought, thought and ate. He was greatly perplexed, and could not make up his mind what to do. Acting on his principles, he ought at once to leave his old friend's house and never look at it again. "All this is really stolen," he reflected, as he placed a piece of meat in his mouth, and sipped the wine poured out by his host; "and is it not disgraceful of me to be here eating and drinking it?" Many such thoughts passed through the brain of the poor teacher, but they remained thoughts, and behind them hid a certain secret voice which annexed each thought by "Well, and what then?" and Vassili Petrovich felt that he was not able to decide this question, and remained seated. "Well, I will watch," flashed through his brain in self-justification, followed by a sense of confusion mingled with shame. "Why should I observe? Am I a writer or what?"

"Ah, what meat!" commenced Kudriasheff. "Take note of it; you will not get anything like it throughout the town." And he related to Vassili Petrovich a long story of how he had dined at Knoblochs', and had been astonished by the beef there, and how he had found out where it could be got, and had eventually succeeded in getting it. "You have come just in the nick of time," he said, by way of conclusion of his story about the meat. "Have you ever eaten anything approaching it?"

"It is certainly excellent beef," replied Vassili Petrovich.

"Magnificent, my dear chap! I like everything to be as it ought to be. But why aren't you drinking? Wait a moment, I will pour you out some wine."

An equally long story of the wine followed, in which there figured an English ship's captain, a commercial house in London, and the same Knobloch and the Customs. As he talked about his wine, Kudriasheff drank it, and as he drank he became more excited. Bright spots appeared on his pallid cheeks, and his speech became more rapid and vehement.

"But why are you so silent?" asked he of Vassili Petrovich, who, as a matter of fact, had preserved a stubborn silence whilst listening to the panegyrics on meat, wine, cheese, and the other delicacies adorning the engineer's table.

"My dear fellow, I don't want to talk."

"Not want to? Bosh! I see you are still thinking about my confession. I am sorry, very sorry, I told you anything about it. We should have supped together with the greatest satisfaction but for this infernal dam. . . . Better not to think about it, Vassili Petrovich—put it aside . . . eh? Vassenka, have done with it! What is to be done, old chap? I have not realized your hopes. Life is not a school. Yes, and I don't know whether you will stick to your path long."

"I beg you not to make conjectures about me," said Vassili Petrovich.

"Offended? . . . Of course, you won't stick to it. What has your disinterestedness given you? Are you really contented now? Do you really never think every day as to whether your acts are in keeping with your ideals, and are you not convinced every day that they are not? Am I not right, eh? But drink, it is good wine."

He poured himself out a glassful, held it up to the light, sipped it, smacked his lips, and drank it.

THE MEETING

"Look here, my dear friend, do you think that I do not know what you are thinking of at the present moment? I know exactly. 'Why,' you are thinking, 'am I sitting here with this man? Is he necessary to me? Can I really not get on without his wine and cigars?' Listen—listen, let me finish. I do not for one moment imagine that you are sitting here only for my wine and cigars. Not at all. Even if you were in great need of them, you would not sponge on me. Sponging is a very burdensome thing. You are sitting here and talking with me simply because you cannot make up your mind as to whether or not I am really a criminal. Do I not disturb you, and that's all? Of course, it is very offensive to you, because you have certain convictions divided up under various headings in your head, and under them, I, your former comrade and friend, appear a scoundrel. At the same time you cannot feel any hostility towards me. Convictions are convictions, but I by myself am your comrade, and I may even say a good chap. You know yourself that I am incapable of offending anyone...."

"Wait a moment, Kudriasheff. Where have you got all this from? You yourself say it is not yours." Vassili Petrovich waved his hand. "The person from whom you have stolen is the offended party."

"It is easy to talk about the person from whom I have stolen. I think, and think, as to whom I have offended, but I cannot understand whom. You do not understand how this business is arranged. I will tell you, and then perhaps you will agree with me, that it is not so easy to find the offended party."

Kudriasheff rang, and the stolid figure of a man-servant appeared.

"Ivan Pavlich, bring me the drawing out of the study. It is hanging between the windows. You will see, Vassili Petrovich, what a gigantic business it is. I really have even begun to find poetry in it."

Ivan Pavlich carefully brought an enormous sheet

gummed on calico. Kudriasheff took it, pushed away the plates, bottles, and glasses near him, and spread out his drawing on the tablecloth, stained in places with red wine.

"Look here," he said. "This is a sectional drawing of our mole, and this is a longitudinal section. Do you see the part painted blue ? That is the sea. The depth here is so great that it is impossible to build up from the bottom, so we are first of all preparing a bed for the mole."

"A bed ?" asked Vassili Petrovich. "What a strange name !"

"A stone bed of enormous blocks of stone, each of which is not less than one cubic foot in size." Kudriasheff detached from his watch-chain a pair of miniature silver compasses, and took a little line by them on the drawing. "See, Vassili Petrovich, this is a sajene. If we measure the bed transversely, it will show a width of not less than fifty sajenes. Not what you would call a narrow bed, eh ? A mass of stone of this width is being raised from the bottom of the sea to within sixteen feet of the surface. If you picture to yourself the width of this bed and its enormous length, you will get some idea of the size of this mass of stone. Sometimes, do you know, for a whole day barge after barge will come to the mole and throw out its load, but when you measure, the increase is infinitesimal. The stones just seem to fall into a bottomless pit. . . . The bed is painted here on the plan a dirty grey colour. They are making progress with it, but from the shore other work is already commencing on it. Steam cranes are lowering on to this bed huge artificial stones, cubic-shaped blocks made of cobbles and cement, each of which is a cubic sajene in size, and weighs many hundreds of poods. The crane raises them, turns, and places them in rows. It is a strange sensation when you realize that with a slight pressure of the hand you can make this mass rise and lower at will. When such a mass

THE MEETING

obeys you, you are conscious of the might of man. . . . Do you see—here they are, these cubes." He pointed them out with the compasses. " They will be laid almost up to the surface of the water, and then the upper stone layer of hewn stone will be placed on them. So you see what sort of work it is. Second to no Egyptian Pyramid. These are the general features of the work, which has already lasted some years. How much longer, goodness only knows. The longer the better . . . at the same time, if it proceeds at its present rate it will last out our century."

" Well, and what else ?" asked Vassili Petrovich after a long silence.

" What else ? Well, we sit in our places and get as much as is necessary."

" But I still do not see from your story how you get what money you want."

" You innocent ! Listen ! By the way, we are, I think, of the same age. Only the experience which you lack has made me wiser—has made me older. This is how it is : You know that on every sea there are storms ? They do their work. Every year they wash away the beds, and we lay down a new one."

" But, still, I don't understand how . . ."

" We lay it down," calmly continued Kudriasheff, " on paper, here on the drawing, because it is only on the drawing that the storms wash it away."

Vassili Petrovich was completely bewildered.

" Because, waves cannot, in fact, wash away a bed only eight feet high. Our sea is not an ocean, and even in an ocean such moles as ours would stand. But with us in the two thousand sajenes depth, where the bed ends, it is almost a dead calm. Listen, Vassili Petrovich, how the thing is managed. In the spring, after the bad weather of the autumn and winter, we meet, and put the question, How much of the bed has been washed away this year ? We take the drawings and note. Well, then, we write,

'Washed away—let us say, by storms—so many cubic sajenes of work.' And they reply, 'Build and d——n you!' Well, we 'repair.'"

"But what do you repair?"

"Our pockets, of course," said Kudriasheff, laughing at his joke.

"No, no, this cannot be; it is impossible!" cried Vassili Petrovich, jumping up from his chair and running up and down the room. "Listen, Kudriasheff, you are ruining yourself . . . not to mention the immorality of it. . . . I simply want to say that they will catch you all in this, and you will be done for—will go to Siberia. Alas! what hopes! expectations! A capable, honourable young man—and suddenly . . ."

Vassili Petrovich launched out into heroics, and spoke long and fervently. But Kudriasheff quite calmly smoked a cigar and watched his excited friend.

"Yes, you are sure to go to Siberia," said Vassili Petrovich, as he concluded his harangue.

"It is a long way to Siberia, my friend. You are an extraordinary man; you don't understand in the least. Am I really the only one who . . . to put it more politely . . . 'acquires'? All around, even the air seems to pilfer. Not long ago a fresh hand appeared and began to write about honesty. What happened? We protected ourselves. . . . And always will protect ourselves. All for one, one for all. Do you imagine that man is his own enemy? Who will take upon himself to touch me when through me he himself may come to grief?"

"It means that everyone is guilty, as Kryloff said."

"Guilty, guilty! All take what they can from life and do not regard it platonically. . . . But about what did we begin to talk? Ah yes, of about whom I am insulting? Tell me whom? The lower class? Well, how? I don't take straight from the source, but I take what is ready and what has already been taken, and if I don't take it somebody worse than I will take it. At

THE MEETING

any rate, I don't live like a brute beast. I take some interest in intellectual matters. I subscribe to a whole bundle of papers and magazines. They cry out about science and civilization, but to what could it be applied if it were not for persons like us, people with means? And who would furnish science with the power to advance if not people with means? And means must be found somewhere, even in a so-called honest . . ."

"Oh, don't finish, don't say that last word, Nicolai Constantinovich."

"Word? What? Would it be better for your warped mind if I commenced to lie to justify myself? We rob, do you hear? Yes, if the truth were spoken, you are now robbing."

"Listen, Kudriasheff . . ."

"It is no use my listening," replied Kudriasheff with a laugh. "You, too, my friend are a robber, under a mask of virtue. What is your occupation—teaching? Will you really repay with your labour even the pittance which will be paid you? Will you turn out even one respectable man? Three-fourths of your pupils will become such as I am, and one-fourth like yourself—that is, a well-intentioned 'fainéant.' Are you not taking money for nothing? Answer me frankly. And are you so far apart from me? Yet you put on airs and preach honour!"

"Kudriasheff, believe me, that this conversation is extremely painful to me."

"And to me—not in the least."

"I did not expect to find what I have found in you."

"That's stupid. People change, and I have changed, but in what direction—you could not guess. You are not a prophet."

"It is not necessary to be a prophet to hope that an honourable youth will become an honourable citizen of the State."

"Bah! drop it! Don't use such words with me.

'An honourable citizen!' Out of what school-books have you dug up this archaism? It is time to finish with sentimentalism; you are not a boy. . . . Do you know what Vasia——" And here Kudriasheff took Vassili Petrovich by the arm. "Let us be friends and drop this infernal subject. Better to drink to our comradeship. Ivan Pavlich, bring another bottle of this."

Ivan Pavlich slowly appeared with a fresh bottle. Kudriasheff filled the glasses.

"Well, we will drink to prosperity . . . of what? Well, it's all the same for your and my prosperity."

"I drink," said Vassili Petrovich with feeling, "that you may come to your senses. That is my strongest wish."

"Be a good chap and don't talk about that. . . . If I come to my senses, it will be impossible to drink; then things will be in a bad way. Do you see what your logic amounts to? Let us drink just simply without any toasts. Let us drop this boring argument. It is all the same, we shall not come to any agreement. You will not put me on the true path, and I shall not convince you. It is not worth it. You will come round to my views."

"Never!" exclaimed Vassili Petrovich with warmth, banging his glass on the table.

"Well, we'll see. But why have I told you all about myself, and you have said nothing about yourself? What have you been doing, and what are your plans?"

"I have already told you I have been appointed teacher."

"Is this your first place?"

"Yes, before this I used to give private lessons."

"And do you intend to give them here?"

"If I can find any. Why?"

"We will find some, my dear chap; we will find some," and Kudriasheff slapped Vassili Petrovich on the shoulder. "We will hand over all the local youth to you. How much did you charge an hour in Petersburg?"

THE MEETING

"Very little. It was very difficult to get good lessons. About two roubles, not more."

"And for such pittance a human being wears himself out! Well, here, don't you dare to ask less than five roubles. It is hard work. I remember how I used to run after extra work during my first and second years. At the University there were times when I was glad to get fifty kopecks an hour. A most thankless and difficult work. I will introduce you to all our friends. There are some very nice families here, and young ladies. If you behave cleverly, I will get you engaged if you like. Eh, Vassili Petrovich?"

"No, thank you."

"What, engaged already? Really?"

Vassili Petrovich's face betrayed his confusion.

"Yes, I see it by your eyes. Well, old chap, I congratulate you. How soon? But Vasia! Ivan Pavlich!" shouted Kudriasheff.

Ivan Pavlich appeared at the door with a surly expression on his sleepy face.

"Bring some champagne!"

"There is none—all drunk," replied the man morosely.

"Don't bother, Kudriasheff. Why all this?"

"Silence, I am not asking you. Do you want to insult me, or what? Ivan Pavlich, don't come back without the champagne, do you hear? Be off!"

"But everything is closed, Nicolai Constantinovich."

"Don't argue with me. You have the money. Be off and get some."

The butler went off muttering something to himself.

"The sulky beast is still grumbling. And you, too, with your 'Don't bother.' If we are not to drink on such an occasion as this, what does champagne exist for? ... Well, who is she?"

"Who?"

"Who, why she, your fiancée. ... Pauper, heiress, nice?"

" It's all the same to you—you don't know her, so why tell you her name ? She has no money, and beauty— that is a matter of taste. In my opinion she is beautiful."

" Have you a photograph ?" asked Kudriasheff. " Bring it out. Do you carry it next to your heart ? Show it me ?"

And he stretched out his hand.

Vassili Petrovich's face, flushed from the wine, became still redder. Not knowing why, he unbuttoned his coat, took out his pocket-book and the precious photograph. Kudriasheff seized it and began to examine it.

" Not so bad, my dear chap. You know a good thing when you see it."

" Cannot you talk without using those expressions ?" said Vassili Petrovich curtly. " Give it me back. I will put it away."

" Wait a bit. Let me enjoy it. I wish you all luck and prosperity. Well, take it and put it back against your heart. Oh, you wonder, marvel !" exclaimed Kudriasheff, laughing.

" I don't understand what you have found laughable in this ?"

" Well, my dear chap, it is funny. I can picture to myself what you will be like in ten years' time : you in a dressing-gown, a wife, seven children, and no money with which to buy them shoes, breeches, hats, etc. Prosaic. Will you, then, carry this photograph about in your breast-pocket ? Ha, ha, ha !"

" It would be more to the point if you will inform me what poetry awaits you in the future ? Get money and spend it ? Eat, drink, and sleep ?"

" Not to eat, drink, and sleep, but to live. Live with a consciousness of one's freedom, and even a certain power."

" Power ? What power have you got ?"

" There is power in money, and I have money. I do what I like. . . . If I wish to buy you—I shall buy you."

THE MEETING

" Kudriasheff ! . . ."

" Don't get on the high horse about nothing. Surely old friends may joke with each other ? Of course, I shall not try to buy you. Live your own way as you like. All the same, I do what I wish. Oh, what a fool, an idiot, I am !" suddenly exclaimed Kudriasheff, hitting his forehead. " Here we are, and have been sitting for I don't know how long, and I haven't shown you *the* sight. You talk about eating, drinking, and sleeping. I will show you something in a minute which will make you take back your words. Come along. Bring a candle."

" Where ?" asked Vassili Petrovich.

" Follow me. You will see where."

Vassili Petrovich, as he rose from the table, felt that all was not as it should be. His legs were not altogether obedient, and he could not hold the candlestick without dropping candle-grease on the carpet. However, obtaining some sort of control over his recalcitrant limbs, he followed behind Kudriasheff. They passed through several rooms along a narrow passage, and appeared in a damp and dark compartment. Their footsteps resounded dully on the stone floor. The noise of falling water somewhere sounded in never-ceasing accord. Stalactites of dark blue glass hung from the ceiling. Artificial rocks rose here and there half covered by masses of tropical foliage and panes of glass glistened darkly in certain places.

" What is this ?" asked Vassili Petrovich.

" An aquarium to which I have devoted two years of time and much money. Wait a moment, and I will light it up."

Kudriasheff disappeared behind some foliage, and Vassili Petrovich went up to one of the panes of glass and commenced to examine what was behind it. The feeble light of the candle could not penetrate far into the water, but the fish, large and small, attracted by the bright light, collected in the part which was lighted up, and gazed stupidly at Vassili Petrovich with their round eyes, opening and shutting their mouths, and moving their gills and fins.

Farther off there loomed up the dark outlines of seaweed, amongst which some kind of reptile was moving, although Vassili Petrovich could not discern its precise form.

Suddenly a flood of blinding light compelled him momentarily to close his eyes, and when he again opened them, he did not recognize the aquarium. Kudriasheff had turned on electric light in two places. The light from the lamps penetrated the mass of blue water, swarming with fish and other live creatures, and filled with growth which showed up boldly against the undefined background in silhouettes of blood-red, brown, and dark green.

The rocks and tropical growth, made still darker by contrast, prettily framed the thick glass through which a view of the inside of the aquarium was opened up. In the aquarium all was a seething, hurrying mass, alarmed by the dazzling light. A whole shoal of small but big-headed chub rushed hither and thither, turning as if by word of command, sterlets wriggled about with their noses stuck to the glass, now rising to the surface, now sinking to the bottom of the water just as if they wished to break through the transparent but hard obstacle. A smooth black eel buried himself in the sand at the bottom of the aquarium, raising a whole cloud of mud. A ridiculous stumpy cuttle-fish detached himself from the rock on which he was resting, and swam jerkily backwards across the aquarium, dragging his long feelers behind him. Altogether it was so pretty and so new to Vassili Petrovich, that he was entranced.

" Well, Vassili Petrovich, what do you think of it ?" asked Kudriasheff, coming out to him.

" Marvellous ! Extraordinary ! How did you arrange all this ? What taste and effect !"

" Add also knowledge. I went to Berlin expressly to examine the aquarium there, and, without boasting, I will say that mine, although, of course, it is not so big, is not

in any way inferior in point of beauty and interest. . . .
This aquarium is my pride and consolation. However
bored, it is only necessary to come here, and I can sit
and gaze by the hour. I like all these fish, etc., because
they are frank, and not like our friend man. They go
for each other without the least shame. Look, look!
Do you see? A chase!"

A small fish was impetuously rushing now to the surface,
then to the bottom, and in every direction trying to escape
from some long marauder. In its mortal terror it kept
jumping out of the water into the air, or trying to conceal
itself in the recesses of the rocks, but keen teeth were
chasing it from all sides. The pirate was just on the point
of seizing his quarry, when suddenly another robber
darted in from the side, made a grab, and the little fish
disappeared in its jaws. The pursuer stopped perplexed,
and the robber hid itself in a dark corner.

"Snatched away," said Kudriasheff. "Idiot! got
nothing. Was it worth chasing simply for the booty to
be taken from under your very nose? . . . If only you
knew how they feed on these little fish: to-day a whole
shoal is put in, and by to-morrow it has disappeared, gone
—eaten up. They eat each other and never dream about
immorality; but we? I have only just got rid of this
fiddle-faddle, Vassili Petrovich. Don't you really in the
end agree that it is all fiddle-faddle?"

"What is?" inquired Vassili Petrovich, not taking his
eyes off the water.

"Why, these gnawings. What are they for? Your
conscience may prick you, but still . . . Well, I have got
rid of them now, and I try to imitate these creatures."

He pointed with his finger to the aquarium.

"Do as you like," said Vassili Petrovich with a sigh.
"Listen, Kudriasheff. Surely all this growth, all these
fish—it is all salt-water life."

"Yes, and the water is sea-water. I have laid down a
pipe on purpose."

THE MEETING

"What, from the sea ? But all this must cost an enormous lot ?"

"Yes. My aquarium costs about thirty thousand roubles."

"Thirty thousand !" exclaimed Vassili Petrovich in a horrified tone. "With a salary of one thousand six hundred roubles a year ?"

"Oh, drop this honour ! If you have looked at it we will go back. Ivan Pavlich by now should have brought the required . . . Only wait a moment whilst I switch off the light."

The aquarium again became plunged in gloom. The still burning candle appeared a dull, smoky little light to Vassili Petrovich.

When they reached the dining-room, Ivan Pavlich was waiting, and holding a bottle wrapped in a serviette in readiness.

VI

A NIGHT

I

A WATCH lying on the writing-table was hurriedly, and with wearying repetition, singing two notes. It was difficult even for a quick ear to distinguish between the two sounds, but to the owner of the watch, the wretched man sitting near this table, the ticking of the watch seemed a whole song.

"It is a joyless and disconsolate song," said he to himself. "It is the song of time itself, and it is being sung apparently for my benefit. It is for my edification that it is singing with such surprising monotony. Three, four, ten years ago the watch ticked as now, and in ten years' time will be ticking in just the same manner . . . exactly as now."

He threw a troubled glance at the watch, but immediately turned his eyes back to where he had been vacantly gazing.

"To the time of its ticking all life with its seeming variety is passing—its sorrows, joys, heart-breakings, and triumphs, hate and love. And only now, at night, when all and everything in this huge town and this huge house is asleep, and when there are no sounds other than the beating of my heart and the ticking of the watch—only now I perceive that all these sorrows, joys, and triumphs which go to make up life—all are unrealities, for some of which I have striven, and from others have fled without, in either case, knowing why. I did not know then that life holds only one reality—time. Time marching forward, passionless, pitiless, not halting where hapless man, living by minutes, would fain dwell, and not increasing its pace by one iota, even when reality is so grievous that it is desirable to make it a past dream ; time—conscious only of one refrain—that which I hear now with such painful clearness."

Thus thought this miserable man whilst the watch ticked on, maliciously repeating the eternal song of time, a song fraught with many memories for him.

" Truly it is strange ! I know that a certain scent, subject of conversation, or striking refrain will recall to memory a whole picture of the long, long past. I remember I was with a dying man, when an Italian organ-grinder stopped before the open window, and at the very moment the sick man was uttering his last disjointed words, and with bowed head was breathing in hoarse agony, there rang out an air from ' Martha,' and ever since, when I chance to hear this air—and I sometimes hear it : trivialities die hard—there immediately rises before my eyes a rumpled pillow, and on it a pale face. Whenever I see a funeral, the air which the little organ played immediately rings in my ears. Horrible ! . . . But all this is ' à propos ' of what ? I began to think. Ah ! I know—why should a watch, the sound of which, it would seem, should have long ago become familiar, remind me of so much ?—all my life !

" ' Do you remember, remember, remember ?' I remember ! Too well ! I even remember what it would be better not to remember. From these memories my face becomes distorted, my fist clenches and strikes the table a furious blow. . . . Ah, now ! that blow deadened the song of the watch, and for a moment I do not hear it ; but only for one moment, after which it again resounds insolently, evilly, and persistently.

" ' Do you remember, remember, remember ?' . . .

A NIGHT

Oh yes, I remember! There is no need for me to recall it. All my life! It is all in front of me. Is there anything in it of which to be proud?"

He shouted this aloud in a hoarse, choking voice. He imagined he saw before him all his life. He recalled a series of ugly and sombre pictures in which he was the principal figure. He recalled all that was worst in his life, turned it all over in his mind, but failed to find one clean or bright spot in it, and was convinced that none remained. "Not only none remained, but had never existed," he added in self-correction.

A weak, timid voice from some remote corner of his soul murmured: "Enough; did it really never exist?"

He did not hear this voice—or, at least, made pretence that he had not heard it, and continued to pull himself to pieces.

"I have thoroughly overhauled my memory, and it seems to me that I am right—there is nothing to stand on, no footing whence to make the first step forward. Forward!—whither? I do not know, only out of this vicious circle.

"There is no support in the past, because all is false, all is deception. I have lied, and deceived, and deluded even myself. Just as a swindler borrows money right and left, deceiving people with fictitious stories of his wealth—of wealth he has never received, but nevertheless declares to exist—so I all my life have lied to myself. Now the day of reckoning has arrived, and I am bankrupt—a fraudulent bankrupt."

He dwelt on these words with a perverted sense of enjoyment. He appeared to be almost proud of them. He did not perceive that in designating his whole life a fraud, and in besmearing himself, he was telling lies at that very moment—the worst possible description of lie—a self-lie, because he did not in reality place anything like so low an estimate on himself. Had anyone charged him with even a tenth part of what he had accused himself of during that long evening, his face would have flushed, but not with the flush of shame and recognition of the truth of such reproaches, but with the flush of anger. He would have known how to answer the offender who had touched the pride which he was himself now apparently trampling on so pitilessly.

Was he himself ?

He had arrived at such a state that he could not even say of himself, " I am myself." In his soul voices were speaking. They were speaking differently, and which of these voices was his own, his " ego," he himself could not tell. The first voice, full and clear, flayed him with welldefined, even eloquent, phrases. The second voice, vague but quarrelsome and persistent, sometimes drowned the first : " Why condemn yourself ?" it said. " Better deceive yourself to the end; deceive all. Make yourself out to others what you are not, and all will be well." There was yet a third voice—that voice which had said : " Enough ; did it really never exist ?" But this voice spoke timidly, and was scarcely audible. Moreover, he did not attempt to hear it.

" Deceive all. . . . Make yourself out what you are not. . . ."

" But, surely, have I not endeavoured to do this all my life ? Have I not deceived others ? Have I not played this farcical rôle ? And has it really turned out well ? It has resulted in my failure as an actor. Even now I am not what I am in reality. But do I really know what I actually am ? I am too much confused to know. But never mind, I have felt for some hours that I have broken down, and am uttering words which I do not myself believe, even now, when on the threshhold of death."

" Surely I am not really face to face with death ?

" Yes, yes, yes !" he shouted, viciously driving each word home with his fist against the table. " It is necessary once and for all to get out of this tangle. The knot is tied. It cannot be unloosed; it must be cut. Only why prolong matters and lacerate my soul already torn to tatters? Why, when once I have decided, do I sit like a statue from eight o'clock in the evening until now?"

And he hastily commenced to pull a revolver from out of a side-pocket of his shuba.

II

He had, indeed, sat in one place from eight in the evening until 3 a.m.

At seven o'clock of this last evening of his life he had left his flat, hired an izvoschik, and had driven, sitting huddled up in the sleigh, to the far end of the town, where an old friend of his lived, a doctor, who that evening, as he knew, was going with his wife to the theatre. He knew that he would not find his friends at home, and was not going for the sake of seeing them. He would be sure to gain admittance as an intimate friend, and that was all that was necessary.

"Yes, they are sure to let me in. I will say that I must write a note. If only Dunyasha won't think of standing by me in the room.... Hey, old man, get along faster!" he called out to the izvoschik.

The izvoschik — a little old man, his back bent with age, with a very thin neck enveloped in a coloured muffler, which stuck out above the wide collar of his coat, and with yellowish-tinged grey curls breaking out from under an enormous round cap, clicked his tongue—gave the reins a tug, again gave a click, and hurriedly murmured in a wheezy voice:

"We will get there, Your Excellency, never fear. Now, now!... Get on, you spoiled... Eh, but what a horse, may the Lord pardon!... Now, now!" He struck the horse with his whip, but the only response was a slight swish of its tail. "And I should be glad to please Your Excellency, but the master has given me such a horse—simply it is . . . The gentlemen are insulted, but what is to be done ? And the master says, ' Thou,' he says, ' Grandad, art an old man, and so here is an old beast for thee ; you will be a pair,' he says, ' and the young ones laugh. Glad to laugh. What is it to them ? They can scarcely understand. They do not understand."

"What do they not understand ?" inquired the passenger, occupied at this moment in thinking how not to let Dunyasha into the room.

"They do not understand, Your Excellency. They do not understand. How can they ? They are silly—young. I am the only old man in the yard. Is it permissible to insult an old man ? I have been eighty years in this world, and they are just showing their teeth. Twenty-three years I served as a soldier. . . . It is well known that they are stupid. . . . Well, you old rubbish, have you frozen stiff ?"

And he again hit the horse a whack with his whip, but as it paid not the slightest attention to the blow, he added : " What's to be done with it ? Also, I expect, twenty-one years old. Get on, you . . . Look, how it swishes its tail !"

On the illuminated face of a clock in one of the windows of a large building the hands pointed to half-past seven.

"They must have already started," thought the passenger of the doctor and his wife. " But perhaps not yet. . . . Grandad, don't hurry, please. Go slower. I am not in a hurry."

"That's known, sir," said the old man, pleased. " All the better slower. Now then, you old . . ."

They went along for a little time in silence, then the old man grew bold.

"Tell me, Your Excellency," he said, suddenly turning round towards his passenger, revealing a wrinkled face with red eyelids, and framed in a straggly grey beard, " why does this kind of thing happen to a man ? There was an izvoschik amongst us called Ivan, a young fellow, twenty-five or perhaps less years old. And who knows why, from what reason, he laid hands on himself."

" Who ? " quietly inquired the passenger in a hoarse voice.

" Why, Ivan Sidoroff. He lived amongst us izvoschiks. He was a bright young fellow and hard-working. Well, on Monday we had supper and laid down to sleep. But Ivan laid down without having any supper. His head, he said was breaking. We slept, but in the night he got up and went out. Only no one saw this. We went out in the morning to harness up, and there he was in the stable on a peg. He had taken the harness from off a peg, placed it alongside, and fastened a cord. . . . Ah me ! It was heart-breaking. And what was the reason this izvoschik hanged himself ? How could it have happened ? Wonderful ! "

" Why ? " asked the passenger, coughing, and with trembling hands wrapping himself up more closely in his shuba.

" There are no such thoughts with an izvoschik. Work is hard and difficult. In the early morning, when there is no light before dawn, harness up and away from the yard. Frost and cold. Only the traktir in which to get warm. Money to be earned so as to pay the two roubles and a half for hire of the horse, and money for the lodging to be found, and—sleep. It is difficult to think much then. But with you, sir, you know that everything crowds into the head with ' light ' food."

" With what kind of food ? "

" With bread lightly earned. Therefore the Barin will get up, put on his dressing-grown, drink his tea, and wander about his room with wicked thoughts around him. I have seen it. I know. In our regiment at T——, in the Caucasus, when I was serving, there was a young subaltern, Prince V—— They made me his servant . . ."

" Stop, stop ! . . ." suddenly called out the passenger. " Here, by the lamp. I will walk from here."

" As the Barin wishes. Walk if he wishes to walk. Thank you, Your Excellency."

The izvoschik turned and disappeared in the miatel which had arisen, and the passenger went on with dragging steps. In ten minutes' time he reached the house, and having arrived at the third story by way of the front staircase, he rang at a door covered with green baize, and ornamented with a highly polished brass name-plate. As he waited for the door to be opened, the few minutes seemed to drag as if they would never come to an end. A dull oblivion seized him ; everything disappeared ; the tormenting past, the chatter of the half-drunken izvoschik, so strangely apposite that it compelled him to walk, and even the intention which had brought him here—all had disappeared. Before his eyes was only a green-baize door edged with black tape studded with brass-headed nails. Naught else in the whole world.

" Ah, Alexei Petrovich !"

It was Dunyasha who, candle in hand, opened the door.

" And the Barin and Barinia have just gone out. Only this minute gone down the stairs. How is it you did not meet them ?"

" Gone ? Oh, what a pity !" He lied in such a strange voice that Dunyasha's face betrayed some bewilderment as she looked him straight in the eyes. " And I wanted to see them. Look here, Dunyasha; I am going into the Barin's study for a minute. . . . May I ?" he asked, even timidly. " I won't be a minute. Only just a note . . . it is a matter . . ."

He looked at her with an inquiring glance, not removing his shuba or galoshes, or moving from where he stood.

Dunyasha became confused.

"But what is the matter with you, Alexei Petrovich? Have I ever . . . it is not the first time," she said in an aggrieved tone. "Please come in."

"Yes, as a matter of fact, why all this? Why am I talking like this? However, she will come in after me. I must send her away. Where can I send her? She will guess, of course. She has even guessed already."

Dunyasha had guessed nothing, but was only extremely surprised at the strange appearance and behaviour of the visitor. She had been left alone in the flat and was glad, if only for five minutes, to be with a living being. Having placed the candle on a table, she stood by the door.

"Go away, go away, for goodness' sake!" Alexei Petrovich kept saying inwardly. He sat down at the table, took a sheet of paper, and began to think of what he should write, feeling Dunyasha's glance on him, which, it seemed to him, was reading his thoughts.

"Peter Nicolaivich," he wrote, stopping at each word, "I came to see you about a very important matter which . . ."

". . . Which, which," he muttered, "and she keeps standing and standing there. . . . Dunyasha, go and get me a glass of water," he suddenly said in a loud voice.

"Certainly, Alexei Petrovich." And she turned and went.

Then the visitor got up, and on tiptoe hurriedly went to the sofa, above which hung the revolver and sword the Doctor had used in the Russo-Turkish campaign, deftly unfastened the flap of the holster, pulled out the revolver, and slipped it into the side-pocket of his shuba; then he took some cartridges out of the pouch fastened on to the holster, and slipped them also into his pocket. Within three minutes Alexei Petrovich had drunk the glass of water which Dunyasha brought him, had sealed up the unwritten letter, and had started home.

"It must be finished, it must be finished," kept ringing

in his brain. But he did not finish it immediately following his arrival home. Going into his room and locking the door, he threw himself, without taking off his shuba, into an arm-chair, and, lost in thought, gazed vacantly, first at a photograph, then at a book, or at the pattern of the wall-paper, and listened to the ticking of his watch, which he had forgotten, and was lying on the table. He sat thus, without moving so much as a muscle, until far into the night, until that moment when we found him.

III

The revolver refused to come out of the narrow pocket; then, when it lay on the table, he discovered that all the cartridges except one had fallen through a small hole in the pocket into the lining of the shuba. Alexei Petrovich took off his shuba, and was about to take a knife to rip up the lining of the pocket and get out the cartridges, when he stopped, and a wry smile hovered at one corner of his parched lips.

"Why bother? One is enough. Oh yes, one of these little things is quite sufficient to make everything disappear once and for all. The whole world will disappear; there will be no regrets, no wounded self-esteem, no self-reproaches, no hateful people pretending to be kind and simple—people whom one sees through and despises, but before whom, nevertheless, one also dissembles, pretending to like them, and to be well-disposed towards them. There will be no deceit of self and others; there will be truth, the eternal truth of non-existence.

He heard his voice. He was no longer thinking but speaking aloud, and what he said was hateful to him.

"Again.... You are dying, killing yourself—and even cannot do that without apostrophizing. For whom, and before whom, are you posing? ... Before yourself! Ah, enough, enough, enough," he repeated in a tormented, despairing voice, and with trembling hands he tried to

A NIGHT

open the refractory breech of the revolver. At length the breech submitted and opened; the cartridge, smeared with fat, slipped into the chamber of the drum, and the hammer cocked apparently of its own accord. There was nothing to interfere with death! The revolver was a regulation officer's revolver; the door was locked, and no one could enter.

"Now then, Alexei Petrovich!" he said, firmly grasping the handle.

"But the letter?" suddenly flashed into his brain.

"Can I die without leaving behind me one line?"

"Why? For whom? All will disappear, there will be nothing. What concern is it of mine?"

"That may be, but all the same I shall write. May I not for once at least express myself absolutely freely, not embarrassed by anything? or, what is most important, by myself? This surely is a rare, very rare, the sole chance."

He laid down the revolver, took some writing-paper out of a box, and having tried several pens which would not write, but broke and spoilt the paper, he at length began, but not before he had spoilt several sheets: "Petersburg. 28 November, 187-." Afterwards his hand ran of its own accord along the paper, reeling off sentence after sentence, barely intelligible t o himse.

He wrote that he was dying calmly because regrets were useless. Life was one vast lie. People whom he loved—that is, if he had ever really loved anybody, and had not pretended to himself that he loved—were not able to make him live, because he had drawn all there was to be drawn out of them—no, no, not that—because there was nothing to draw out of them, but simply because they had lost all interest for him once he understood them. He wrote that he understood himself, and understood that in himself there was nothing but falsehood; that if he had done anything in his life, it was not from a wish to do good, but from vanity; that if he had done nothing wrong or dishonourable, it was not due to absence of evil qualities, but from cowardly fright of people. He wrote that, nevertheless, he did not think himself worse than those persons remaining to lie until the end of their days, and did not beg their pardon, but was dying with a contempt for people not less than his contempt for himself. A malicious, senseless phrase slipped in at the end of the letter : " Farewell, people ! Farewell, you bloodthirsty grimacing apes !"

It only remained to sign the letter. But when he had finished writing he felt hot ; the blood had surged to his head, and was beating against his perspiring temples. And forgetting about the revolver and the fact that by ridding himself of life he could avoid the heat, he got up, went to the window, and opened the fortochka. A steaming current of frosty air blew in on him. It had stopped snowing, and the sky was clear. On the opposite side of the street a dazzling white garden, wrapped in icicles, glistened in the moonlight. A few stars were gazing from out of a distant heaven, one of which was brighter than the remainder, and shone with a reddish tint.

" Arcturus," whispered Alexei Petrovich. " What years since I have seen Arcturus. Not since I was at school !"

He was unwilling to take his eyes off the star. Somebody shivering in a light overcoat, and stamping with his half-frozen feet on the pavement, passed hurriedly along the street. Then a carriage, the wheels of which rang on the frozen snow, and then an izvoschik went past, driving a fat man—and still Alexei Petrovich stood there as if carved.

" It must be done !" he said at last.

He went to the table. It was only a few paces from the window to the table, but it seemed to him as if he had been walking ages. He had already taken up the revolver, when through the opened window there came the distant but clear, vibrating sound of a bell.

A NIGHT

" A bell !" exclaimed Alexei Petrovich, astonished, and replacing the revolver once more on the table, he threw himself into the arm-chair.

IV

" A bell !" he repeated. Why a bell ? . . . Was it a service ? Prayers . . . church . . . suffocating heat. Wax candles. The decrepit priest, Father Michael, performing the service in a plaintive, cracked voice, and the deacon with his bass. A longing to sleep. Dawn just breaking through the window. His father standing next him with bowed head, making hurried little crosses. Behind them, in the crowd of moujiks and babas, constant prostrations. . . . How long ago it all was ! . . . So long ago that it was hard to believe it had ever happened, that he had himself once seen it, and had not read of it somewhere, or heard of it from somebody. No, no, it all happened, and it was better then. Yes, not only better but well. If only it was like that now, there would be no need to leave by aid of a revolver.

" Finish it !" something whispered to him. He glanced at the revolver, and stretched out his hand towards it, but immediately drew it back.

" Afraid ?" it whispered again.

" No, not afraid. There is nothing frightening in it. But the bell ! Why the bell ?"

He glanced at the watch.

" It must be early morning service. People will go to church. Many of them will feel easier for it. So they say, at all events. Besides, I remember I used to feel better for it. I was a boy then. Afterwards this passed off, perished, and I no longer felt easier for it. That's the truth . . . truth ! The truth has been found at last at this moment !"

And the moment seemed inevitable. He slowly turned his head and again looked at the revolver. It was a big

Government regulation pattern revolver, a Smith and Wesson. It had been "browned" once, but had now become lighter in colour, owing to its long rest in the doctor's holsters. It lay on the table with the butt towards Alexei Petrovich, who could see the worn wood of the handle with its ring for the cord, a part of the drum, with the cocked trigger and the muzzle of the barrel, which looked towards the wall.

"There lies death! It must be seized."

It was quiet in the street; no one was either driving or walking past. And from out of this stillness there again sounded the distant stroke of a bell. The waves of sound floated through the open window, and reached Alexei Petrovich. They spoke to him in a foreign tongue, but spoke something great, important, and solemn, stroke after stroke, and when the bell resounded for the last time, and the sound tremblingly died away into space, Alexei Petrovich experienced a real loss. The bell had delivered its message. It had recalled to a perplexed man that there is something besides his own narrow little world which had tormented him, and brought him to suicide. Recollections, fragmentary, disjointed, and all as if something entirely new for him, came flooding on him in an irresistible wave. This night he had already pondered over many things, had recalled much, and imagined that he had recalled all his life, that he had clearly seen himself. Now he felt that there was another side in him, that side of which the timid voice of his soul had spoken.

V

Do you remember yourself as a little child when you lived with your father in a far-away forgotten village? He was an unhappy man, your father, but he loved you more than all else in the world. Do you remember how you would sit together in the long winter evenings, he busy with accounts, you with your books, the tallow-

A NIGHT

dipped candle with its reddish flame burning more and more dimly, until, arming yourself with snuffers, you trimmed it? That was your duty, and you performed it with such importance that your father each time would raise his eyes from the big ledger, and with customary pathetic and caressing smile, look at you. Your eyes would meet.

" Look, papa, how much I have already read," you would say, and show the pages you had read, holding them together with your fingers.

" Read, read, my little friend," your father would say approvingly, and again bury himself in accounts.

He allowed you to read anything, because only good could remain in the mind of his adored little boy. And you read and read, understanding nothing of the arguments, but, nevertheless, taking it all in accordance with childish ideas.

Yes, red was red then, and not the reflection of red rays. Then everything was as it appeared. Then there were not ready-made receptacles for impressions, for ideas into which a man poured forth all that he felt, not troubling whether the receptacle was a fit one or sound. And if he loved someone, he knew without a doubt that he loved.

A pretty, laughing face rose before his eyes and vanished.

And she? You also loved her? I must acknowledge that, at all events, we played sufficiently with feeling. And it would seem that at least I spoke and thought sincerely at that time. . . . What torture it was! And when happiness came it did not seem at all like happiness, and if I had been able then actually to say to time, Stop! wait a little! here it is good—I should have still thought —Shall I order it to stop or not? And afterwards, very soon afterwards, it became necessary to drive time ahead. . . . But it is no use to think of that now. I must think of what was and not of what it appeared to be.

And there was very little to think of, only childhood.

And of that there remained in his memory only disjointed fragments which Alexei Petrovich began to collect with avidity.

He recalled the little house, the bedroom in which he slept opposite his father. He remembered the red canopy hanging above his father's bed. Every evening, as he fell asleep, he gazed at these curtains, and always found fresh figures in its fantastic patterns—flowers, birds, and faces of people. He remembered the early morning smell of the straw with which they warmed the house. The faithful Nicholas, the good man had already filled the passage with straw, which he had dragged in from outside, and was pushing whole bundles of it into the mouth of the stove. It used to burn brightly and clearly, and the smoke had a pleasing, but somewhat acrid smell. Alesha was ready to sit whole hours before the stove, but his father would call him to come and drink his morning tea, after which lessons would begin. He remembered how he could not understand decimals, and that his father would get rather hot, and try his utmost to explain them to him.

"I fancy he was not altogether clear about them himself," reflected Alexei Petrovich.

Then afterwards Biblical history. Alesha loved that more than all the other lessons. Wonderful, gigantic, and extravagant characters. Cain, the history of Joseph, the Pharaohs, the wars. How the ravens carried food to the prophet Elijah. And there was a picture of it. Elijah sitting on a stone with a large book on his knees, and two birds flying to him holding something round in their beaks.

"Papa, look, the ravens took bread to Elijah, but our Worka takes everything from us."

A tame raven with red beak and claws dyed with red paint, so Nicholas imagined, would jump sideways along the back of the sofa, and, stretching out his neck, try to drag a shiny bronze frame from the wall. In this frame

A NIGHT

there was a miniature water-coloured portrait of a young man with a very smooth forehead, dressed in a dark green uniform with epaulets, and a very high red collar, and a cross attached to a buttonhole. This was the same papa twenty-five years ago.

The raven and portrait flashed up and disappeared.

" And afterwards what ? Afterwards a star, a shed, manger. I remember that this word manger was quite a new one to me, although I had known of the manger in our stables and cow-house. But those stalls seemed something special."

They did not study the New Testament like the Old, not from a thick book with pictures. His father used to tell Alesha of Jesus Christ, and often read out to him whole chapters from the Gospels.

" ' But whosoever shall smite thee on thy right cheek, turn to him the other also.' Do you understand, Alesha ?" And the father began a long explanation to which Alesha did not listen, but suddenly interrupted his teacher by saying : " Papa, do you remember when Uncle Dmitri Ivanovich arrived ? That's exactly what happened. He struck Thomas in the face, and Thomas stood still, and then Uncle Dmitri Ivanovich struck him from the other side, and still Thomas did not move. I was sorry for him, and cried."

" Yes, then I cried," murmured Alexei Petrovich, rising from the arm-chair and commencing to pace the room. " Then I cried."

He became dreadfully sorry for these tears of a sixteen-year-old boy, sorry for that time when he could cry because a defenceless human being was struck in his presence.

VI

The frosty air was all this time entering the window. A cloud of steam was literally pouring into the already cold room. The big squat lamp, with its opaque shade, standing on the writing-table, burned brightly, but only lighted the surface of the table, and a portion of the ceiling on which it formed a trembling round spot of light. The rest of the room was in semi-darkness, through which could be discerned a bookcase, a large sofa, some other furniture, and a looking-glass on the wall, which reflected the lighted-up writing-table and the tall figure each time he strode past it in his restless movement from corner to corner of the room, eight paces there and eight paces back. Sometimes Alexei Petrovich stopped at the window. The cold current bathed his burning head, and his bared neck and chest. He shivered, but was not refreshed. He continued to recall those days in a series of fragmentary and disjointed reminiscences. He recalled numberless little trivial details, becoming confused in them, and unable to distinguish precisely what was important in them. He knew only one thing—*i.e.*, that up to twelve years of age, when his father sent him to school, he had lived an entirely different inner life, and he remembered that then it was better.

"What is drawing thee to that half-conscious life? What was there good in those childish years? A solitary child and a solitary grown-up man—a 'crushed' man, as you yourself called him after his death. You were right, he was a "crushed" man. Life had quickly and easily destroyed all the good in him, all the good which he had collected in his youth, but at least it had not introduced anything bad. And he lived his time, helpless, with a helpless love which he devoted almost entirely to you."

Alexei Petrovich thought of his father, and for the first time after many years felt that he loved him, in spite of all his smallness. He wished now, if only for one minute, to take himself back to his childhood, to the village, to the little house, and to caress this "crushed" man, caress him in regular childish fashion. He longed for that clean and simple love which only children know, and

A NIGHT

possibly the very clean, unspoiled natures of a few older people.

"And is it really impossible to return to this happiness? To this ability to recognize that what one says and thinks is true? How many years it is since I experienced it! One speaks warmly and *apparently* sincerely, but in one's soul there is all the time sitting a canker-worm, devouring it, and sucking it dry, and saying: 'My friend, are you not lying? Do you in reality think what you are now speaking?'"

Yet one more apparently senseless phrase took shape in the head of Alexei Petrovich. "Do you really think what you are thinking?" It was a senseless phrase, but he understood it.

Yes, then he really thought what he thought. He had loved his father, who knew that he loved him. "Oh, if there were but one genuine real feeling within me. Yet there exists such a world. The bell reminded me of it. When it sounded I remembered the church, the crowd, the enormous mass of humanity, the real life. That is where one must go—out of oneself—and that is where one must love, and love as children love. As children . . . just as it is said there. . . ."

He went to the table, drew out one of the drawers, and commenced to rummage in it. A little dark green book, bought by him once at some exhibition as a cheap curio, lay in a corner. He seized it joyously, quickly turning over the leaves with their two narrow columns of small print. Familiar words and sentences rose to mind. He began to read from the first page, and read it all without a pause, having forgotten even about the sentence in search of which he had got out the book. This sentence, which had so long been familiar and so long forgotten, astonished him, when he came upon it with the weight of the substance expressed in its words: "Except ye become as little children . . ."

It seemed to him that he understood all.

"Do I know what these words mean ' Become as a little child'? It means not to place oneself first in everything, to tear from one's heart this horrid little deformed god with its protuberant paunch, this repulsive ' ego ' which, like some canker-worm, sucks dry the soul, and ceaselessly demands of it fresh food. But out of where shall I tear it ? Thou hast already devoured all. All my time, all my forces, have been devoted to thy service. I have nourished thee, have revered thee. Although I hated thee I still worshipped thee, bringing to thee in sacrifice, and giving to thee all the good which I possessed, and for this I have bowed and bowed . . ."

He repeated this word as he continued to pace the room. But his gait was now unsteady. He staggered as if drunk, with his head lowered on his chest, which was heaving with sobs, not stopping to wipe his tear-moistened face. At last his legs refused to serve him any longer, and he sat down, pressing himself into a corner of the sofa. Supporting himself on his elbows, he dropped his fevered head into his hands and wept like a child. This loss of strength lasted for some time, but he was no longer in torture. The storm was abating, the tears were flowing, giving him relief, and he felt no shame in them. No matter who had entered the room at that moment, he would not have tried to restrain these tears which were carrying away hate with them. He felt now that all had not yet been swallowed up by the idol to which he had bowed for so many years. That there still remained love and even self-denial. That it was worth while living if only to pour forth this remnant; where, and on what, he did not know. At that moment it was not necessary to know where to take his guilty head. He recalled the grief and suffering which it had been his lot to witness in life—genuine living grief before which all his torments in solitude had no significance; and he understood that he ought to go to this grief, to take his share of it upon himself, and only then would there be peace in his soul.

A NIGHT

"It is terrible! I can no longer live on engrossed in my own fears and in myself. It is necessary, absolutely necessary, to bind myself with life in general, to suffer or to rejoice, to hate or to love, not for my own sake, not for my 'ego,' devouring all and giving nothing in return, but for the sake of truth, common to all, which is in the world, notwithstanding anything I may have said, which speaks in the soul in spite of all attempts to stifle it. Yes, yes," repeated Alexei Petrovich in awful excitement, "all this is written in the little green book, is said for ever and aye, and is truly said. It is necessary to 'reject' oneself, to kill one's 'ego,' to make for the road . . .''

"What use is it to you, madman?" whispered a voice. But another, once timid and unheeded voice, thundered in reply: "Silence! What benefit will it be to him if he tortures himself?"

Alexei Petrovich jumped to his feet and straightened himself to his full height. This argument rendered him enthusiastic. He had never yet experienced such enthusiasm from any life-success or from woman's love. This enthusiasm was born of his heart, burst from it, pouring out in a hot, wide wave, and flowed through all his limbs. In an instant his numbed, unhappy being flamed to life. Thousands of bells sounded in majestic triumph. A blinding sun flashed out, illumined the whole world, and disappeared. . . .

* * * * *

The lamp, which had burned throughout the long night, became dimmer and dimmer, and finally went out altogether. But it was no longer dark in the room. Day had broken. Its calm grey light little by little found its way into the room, faintly showing up the loaded weapon and the letter with its senseless ravings lying on the table, and revealing a peaceful, happy expression on the pallid face of a corpse stretched on the floor in the middle of the room.

VII

A TOAD AND A ROSE

ONCE upon a time in this world there lived a rose and a toad.

The bush on which the rose bloomed grew in a not very big crescent-shaped flower-bed in front of a country house in a village. The flower-bed was in a very neglected state. Grass and weeds grew thickly over its sunken surface, and along the paths, which no one had cleaned or sprinkled with sand for a long time. A wooden trellis, which had once been painted green, was now quite bare of any such decoration, had rotted, and was falling to pieces. Most of the long stakes of which the trellis-work was composed had been pulled up by the boys of the village for playing at soldiers, or by peasants coming to the house to defend themselves from a savage yard-dog.

But the flower-bed itself was none the worse for this desolation. Climbing hop tendrils entwined themselves amongst the débris of the trellis-work, mingling with the large white flowers of convolvuli. Broom hung from it in pale green clusters, dotted with lilac-tinted bunches of bloom. Prickly thistles grew so freely in the rich moist soil (the flower-bed was surrounded by a large shady garden), that they almost resembled trees. Yellow mullen raised blossom-covered shoots even higher. Nettles had taken possession of a whole corner of the bed. Of course they stung, but, from a distance, one could admire their dark

A TOAD AND A ROSE

foliage, especially when this foliage served as a background for the delicate, lovely pale blossom of a rose.

It burst into bloom on a beautiful May morning. When it had opened its petals, the early dew, before taking flight, had left on them a few transparent tear-drops, which made it look as if the rose was weeping. But all around was so beautiful, so clean and bright on this glorious morning when the rose first saw the blue sky and felt the caress of the morning zephyr, and the rays of a brilliant sun, giving a pinkish tint to its thin petals. All in the flower-bed was so peaceful and calm that had the rose really been able to cry, it would not have been from grief, but from the very joy of living. It could not talk; it could only diffuse around, with lowered head, a delicate fresh perfume, and this perfume was at once its words, tears, and prayers. But below it, amongst the roost of the rose-bush on the damp soil, as if glued to it by its flat belly, there sat a decidedly fat old toad, which used to hunt all night for worms and midges, and when morning came, would sit and rest from his labours, having first chosen the shadiest and dampest spot. He used to sit there, his toad's eyes, with their membranous lids, tightly closed, his scarcely perceptible breathing expanding his dirty-grey barbed and sticky sides, with one shapeless paw outstretched, too lazy to tuck it in. He was not rejoicing either in the brilliant morning sun or the beautiful weather. He had fed and meant to have a rest. But when the breeze chanced to die away for a minute, and the perfume of the rose was not borne to one side, the toad noticed it, and this caused him a vague uneasiness. However, for a long time he was too lazy to look and see whence this scent was coming.

It was a long time since anyone had come to the bed in which the rose was growing and the toad used to sit. In the autumn of the past year, on the very day that the toad, having discovered an excellent chink under one of the stones forming the basement of the house, had decided to take up his winter quarters therein, a small boy had come for the last time to this flower-bed in which he had sat every fine day throughout the summer. A lady, his grown-up sister, used to sit at the window reading or sewing, and from time to time used to look at her brother. He was a little fellow of seven, with large eyes and a large head on a thin little body. He was very fond of his flower-bed. It was his because only he used to go to this deserted part of the garden, and he would sit in the sunshine on a little old wooden seat standing on a dry, once-sanded path, which ran round the house itself, and along which servants used to go to shut the shutters, and he would commence to read the book he had brought with him.

" Vasia, shall I throw you your ball ? " his sister would call out. " Perhaps you would like to play with it ? "

" No, Masha, I am better like this with my book."

And he would sit for a long time and read. Then, when he was tired of reading about Robinson Crusoes, savage countries, and pirates, he would leave his book open on the seat and clamber into the thick of his flower-bed. He knew every bush, almost every stalk in it. He would squat on his heels before the thick stem of some shrub covered with rough, whitish leaves, three times as tall as himself, and look for hours at the world of ants hurrying up to their cows—green insects—and note how delicately the ants tapped the thin pipes sticking out along the backs of these insects, and collected the pure drops of sweet liquid which is at the end of these pipes. He would watch the dung beetle busily and zealously rolling its ball somewhere. He would mark own a spider which, having woven his clever rainbow-like web, was sitting on guard for flies, or a lizard basking in the sun, with its blunt little jaws open, and its back shining with little green scales. One evening he actually saw a hedgehog. He could scarcely restrain his delight, and almost shouted and clapped his hands,

A TOAD AND A ROSE

but, afraid of frightening the prickly little "beastie," he held his breath, and, with eyes dilated with joy, watched in ecstasies how, giving little grunts, it sniffed with its pig-shaped snout at the roots of the rose-bush, looking for worms, and how absurdly it went along with its fat little paws so ridiculously like a bear's.

"Vasia, dear, come along in now; it is getting damp!" his sister called out loudly.

And the hedgehog, frightened at the sound of a human voice, quickly pulled his prickly shuba over his head and hind paws, turning himself into a ball. The boy quietly touched its prickles, and the little animal still further contracted, breathing deeply and hurriedly, like a little steam-engine.

Afterwards the boy made friends with this hedgehog. He was such a delicate, quiet little fellow, that even the different animals seemed to understand and soon became accustomed to him. Imagine his joy when the hedgehog tasted some milk which the owner of the flower-bed brought out in a saucer.

This spring the child could not go out to his favourite nook. His sister, as before, was sitting near him, no longer, however, at the window, but by his bed. She was reading a book, not for herself, but aloud to him, because it was difficult for him to raise his head from the white pillows, and difficult to hold even the smallest book in his little wasted hands. Besides which, his eyes quickly tired from reading. Most likely he would never again go to his favourite flower-bed.

"Masha!" he suddenly murmured to his sister.

"What, dearie?"

"Is it nice in my garden now? Are the roses out?"

His sister bent down, kissed his white cheek, and furtively brushed away a tear.

"Very nice, darling, very nice. And the roses are out. On Monday we will go out together there. The Doctor will let you go."

The boy did not answer, and sighed heavily. His sister began to read aloud again to him.

"That is enough. I am tired. I would rather sleep."

His sister arranged his pillows and the white counterpane, and he with difficulty turned over on to his side and kept silent. The sun shone through the window, which looked on to the flower-bed, and threw brilliant rays on to the bed and the little emaciated form lying on it, lighting up the pillows and coverlet, and gilding the closely-cropped hair and wasted neck of the child.

The rose knew nothing of this. It had grown and become even more beautiful. The following day it would be in full blossom, and the third day begin to fade and shed its petals. This was the whole life of the rose. But even in this short life it was destined to experience no little trepidation and sorrow.

The toad had noticed it.

When he for the first time saw the flower with his evil and hideous eyes, something strange stirred his toad's heart. He could not tear himself away from the tender rose-petals, but all the time gazed and gazed at them. The rose attracted him immensely, and he felt a desire to be nearer such a fragrant and beautiful creation. But in order to express his tender feelings, he could think of nothing better to say than this :

"Wait a bit," he croaked. "I will gobble you up."

The rose shuddered. Why was she fastened to a stalk? Birds were free, twittering around her as they hopped and flew from branch to branch. Sometimes they went far away, where the rose did not know. The butterflies were also free ! How she envied them ! If only she were one ! How she would take wing and fly from those wicked eyes, persecuting her with their fixed gaze. The rose did not know that toads sometimes waylay butterflies too.

"I will gobble you up!" he repeated, all the time looking at the blossom. And the poor creation with

A TOAD AND A ROSE

horror saw how the disgusting, sticky, clammy paws fastened round the branches of the bush on which she was growing. However, it was difficult for the toad to climb. His smooth body could only crawl and jump easily in smooth places. After each effort to reach the rose, he would look up to where the blossom swung, and the rose froze with fright.

"Oh, please," she prayed, "if only I may die another death!"

But the toad still continued to clamber higher. However, when he reached where the older branches ended, and the young ones began, he had to suffer somewhat. The smooth dark green bark of the rose-tree was all covered with hard, sharp thorns. The toad kept pricking his paws and belly with them, and fell to the ground covered with blood. He looked at the flower with hatred.

"I have said I will gobble you up, and I will!" he repeated.

The evening came. It was necessary to think of supper, and the wounded toad, dragging himself along, seized incautious insects coming within his reach. Hatred did not prevent him from filling his inside as usual. Furthermore, his scratches were not very dangerous, and he decided, when he had had a rest, to try once again for the blossom which he hated but which so attracted him.

He rested for quite a long time. The morning came, midday passed, and the rose had almost forgotten about her enemy. She was now in full blossom, and was the most beautiful creation in the flower-bed. But there was no one to come to admire her. The little owner of the plot lay motionless in his bed. His sister never left him, and did not appear at the window. Only the birds and butterflies hovered round the rose, and the bees, buzzing, came and sometimes sat down inside the bloom, flying away quite covered with the yellow dust. A nightingale flew down, perched on the rose-bush, and sang his song. How different from the wheezing of the toad! The rose heard this song and was happy. It seemed to her that the nightingale was singing to her, and perhaps she was right. She did not see how her enemy was clambering up the branches. This time the toad was not sparing either his paws or belly. He was covered with blood, but bravely clambered up higher; and in the middle of the resonant tender trills of the nightingale, the rose suddenly heard the familiar wheeze:

"I said I would gobble you up—and I will gobble you up!"

His toad's eyes gazed at the rose from a neighbouring branch. The evil-looking thing had only one more move to make to seize the blossom. The rose understood that the end was at hand. . . .

* * * * *

The little master had long lain motionless on his bed. His sister, sitting in the depths of an arm-chair, thought he was asleep. On her lap lay an open book, but she was not reading it. Gradually her tired head drooped; the poor girl had not slept for several nights, had not left her sick brother, and now she was lightly dozing.

"Masha!" he suddenly whispered.

Her sister gave a slight jump. She had been dreaming that she was sitting at the window, that her little brother was playing as last year in his flower-bed, and had called her. Opening her eyes, and seeing him in bed, wasted and weak, she gave a deep sigh.

"What, dearest?"

"Masha, you told me that the roses are out. Can you get me . . . just one?"

"Of course I can, darling."

She went to the window, and looked at the rose-bush. There was one blossom, and it was a magnificent rose.

"There is a rose which seems to have come out purposely for you, and what a beauty! Shall I get it, and put it here in a glass for you on the table? Yes?"

"Yes, on the table. I want it."

A TOAD AND A ROSE

The girl took a pair of scissors, and went out into the garden. She had not been out of the house for a long time. The sun blinded her, and she felt dizzy from the fresh air. She got to the bush at the very instant the toad had meant to seize the flower.

"Oh, how disgusting!" she cried, and seizing the branch shook it violently. The toad fell flat on its belly to the ground. In fury it sprang at the girl, but could not jump higher than the edge of her dress, and was immediately sent flying by the toe of her slipper. He did not dare to try a second time, only from afar saw how the girl carefully cut off the rose and took it into her brother's room.

When the boy saw his sister with the rose in her hand, he smiled weakly for the first time for many a day, and with difficulty made a movement with his thin hand.

"Give it to me," he whispered; "I want to smell it."

His sister put the rose into his hand, and helped him to raise it to his face. He drew in the tender perfume, and, smiling happily, murmured:

"Ah, how good!"

Then his little face became serious and motionless, and he became silent for ever.

The rose, although she had been cut before she had begun to shed her petals, felt that it had not been for nothing. They placed her in a separate glass on the little coffin, on which were heaped whole wreaths and other flowers, but to tell the truth no one paid any attention to them. But the young girl, when she placed the rose on the table, raised it to her lips and kissed it. A tear fell from her cheek on to the flower, and this was the best incident in the whole life of the rose. When it began to fade they put the flower into an old thick book, and pressed it, and many years after gave it to me. That is why I know the whole history of it.

VIII

ATTALEA PRINCEPS

In a certain large town there was a botanical garden, and in this garden an enormous greenhouse of glass and iron. It was a very handsome building. Graceful spiral columns supported the whole structure, and on them rested ornamented arches interwoven by a whole web of iron frames, in which panes of glass were set. This greenhouse was especially beautiful when the setting sun was reflected redly against it. Then the whole building seemed alight. Crimson rays played and transfused just as in some gigantic, delicately-cut, precious stone.

Through the thick, but transparent, panes could be discerned the captive plants. Notwithstanding the size of the greenhouse its inmates felt cramped for space. Roots interlaced and robbed each other of moisture and sustenance. The branches of the trees interfered with the enormous leaves of palms, rotted and broke them, and pressing against the iron framework themselves rotted and snapped. The gardeners were constantly lopping off boughs and binding the palm-leaves with wires, so that they should not grow where they wished. But these efforts were of little avail. They needed space, their homeland and freedom. They were natives of hot climes, tender, luxurious creations. They remembered with longing the lands of their birth. However transparent the glass roof it was not the clear heavens. Occasionally in winter-time the panes became frosted, and then the

ATTALEA PRINCEPS

greenhouse became quite dark. The wind would howl and beat against the iron framework, causing it to vibrate. The roof would be covered with drift-snow. The plants standing within would listen to the beating of the wind, and recall another wind, warm and moisture-laden, which used to give them life and health. And then they would long to feel its breath once more so that it might sway their boughs and play with their leaves. But in the greenhouse the air was motionless, excepting when winter storms shattered some of the glass panes; then a cutting cold current, a veritable icicle, would burst in on them, leaving faded, shrivelled leaves in its wake.

But the broken panes were always promptly mended. The Director of the gardens was a most learned man, who allowed no disorder of any kind, notwithstanding that the greater part of his time was spent with a microscope in a special little glass sentry-box situated in the main greenhouse.

Amongst the plants there was one palm taller and more beautiful than all the others. The Director, sitting in his sentry-box, called it in Latin " Attalea Princeps." But this name was not its native name. Botanists had evolved this name. Botanists did not know its native name, which was not the name painted in black on the white board fastened to the trunk of the palm. Once a native from that hot country visited the gardens. When he saw this palm he laughed because it reminded him of home.

" Ah," said he, " I know this tree," and he called it by its home name.

" Excuse me," called out from his sentry-box the Director, who at that moment had carefully performed some operation with a razor on a little stalk, " you are mistaken. There is no such tree as you were pleased to mention. That palm is ' Attalea Princeps,' a native of Brazil."

" Oh yes," said the Brazilian, " I quite believe you.

I quite believe that botanists call it Attalea, but it has a proper native name."

"The proper name is that which is given by science," replied the botanist frigidly, and he locked the door of his little sentry-box so that he should not be disturbed by people incapable even of understanding that if a man of science says something they must keep silence and listen.

But the Brazilian long stood and gazed at the palm, and he became more and more sad. He recalled his native land, its sunny skies, its luxuriant forests with their wondrous denizens, its birds, its open prairies, and magic southern nights. And he recalled that he had never been really happy outside the land of his birth although he had toured the world. He touched the palm with his hand as if bidding it farewell, and left the garden. The next day he started off by steamer for "home."

But the palm remained. Life became even more burdensome to it now, although before this incident it had been very grievous. It towered five sajenes above the tops of all the other plants, and those other plants did not love it. They were jealous, and considered the palm proud. This growth caused the palm nothing but sorrow. Apart from the fact that the other plants were all together and it was alone, the palm best of all remembered its native skies, and mourned for them more than any of the others, because it was the nearest of all to that which supplanted those skies—a disgusting glass roof. Through it the palm occasionally saw something blue; it was the sky, strange and pale, yet for all that genuine blue sky. And when the plants talked amongst themselves Attalea always kept silent, fretted, and thought only of how good it would be to stand even under this pitiful heaven.

"Tell me, please, will they soon water us?" inquired a sago-palm which was very fond of moisture. "I really think I shall wither up to-day."

ATTALEA PRINCEPS

"Your words, my dear neighbour, astonish me," said a pot-bellied cactus. "Do you really mean that the enormous quantity of water which they pour over you every day is insufficient? Look at me! They give me very little, but all the same I am fresh and full of sap."

"We are not accustomed to be over-careful," replied the sago-palm. "We cannot grow in such dry and vile soil as do certain cacti. We are not accustomed to live in hand-to-mouth style; moreover, apart from all this, I may mention that you are requested not to make remarks." Having said this, the sago-palm took huff, and relapsed into silence.

"As far as I am concerned," broke in a cinnamon, "I am practically satisfied with my position. Of course it is dull, but at least I am sure that no one will strip me."

"But they used not to strip all of us," said a tree-fern. "Of course, to many even this prison would appear Paradise after the miserable existence which they led when free."

Thereupon the cinnamon, forgetting that they used to strip her, became offended, and started quarrelling. Some of the plants took her side and some took the part of the tree-fern, and a lively exchange of abuse commenced. They would undoubtedly have come to blows had they been able to move.

"Why are you quarrelling?" asked Attalea. "Does it really help you in any way? You only increase your unhappiness by being spiteful and losing your tempers. Far better to drop your quarrels and think. Listen to me! Grow taller and wider, throw out branches, press against the iron framework and glass panes, and then our greenhouse will break up into bits, and we shall gain freedom. If only one branch presses against the glass they will, of course, cut it off, but what will they do with a hundred strong and daring trunks? It is only necessary to be more friendly and to work together, and victory is ours!"

At first no one answered the palm. All kept silent, not knowing what to say. At last the sago-palm made up her mind.

"All ridiculous nonsense!" she declared.

"Ridiculous! Nonsense!" the trees chimed in, and everybody at one and the same time began to prove to Attalea that its proposal was awful nonsense.

"An impracticable dream!" they cried. "Bosh! Absurd! The framework is solid, and we shall never break it, and even if we did, what then? Men would come with knives and axes, lop off our boughs, mend the framework, and all would go on as before. All that would happen is that they would cut whole branches off us...."

"Well, as you like!" replied Attalea. "Now I know what to do. I shall leave you all alone. Live how you like, growl at each other, argue about sips of water, and stay for ever under a glass dome. I alone will find a way for myself. I want to see the sky and sun direct, not through this glass and grating . . . and I will."

And the palm proudly glanced with her green top at the forest of comrades displayed below. No one dared say anything, only the sago-palm quietly whispered to her neighbour: "Well, we shall see—we shall see how they will cut off her big head so that she does not get too conceited, Miss Proud!"

The others, although they kept silent, were angry with Attalea for her haughty words. Only one little herb was not angry with the palm, and not offended with what she had said. It was the most pitiful, contemptible herb of all the plants in the greenhouse, pale and poor, a creeper with fading, thickish leaves. There was nothing remarkable about it; and it was only used in the greenhouse to hide the bare soil. It had made itself the footstool of the big palm, and, listening to her, it seemed to the herb that Attalea was right. It did not know anything of Southern Nature, but it loved air and freedom. The greenhouse was a prison for it also. "If I, an insignificant faded herb, suffer so without my own grey sky, without my pale sun and cold rain, what must this beautiful and powerful palm suffer?" So thought the herb, and it tenderly entwined itself around the palm, caressing her the while. " Why am I not a great tree? I would listen to the advice. We would grow together, and together go out into freedom. Then the others would see that Attalea was right." But it was not a great tree, only a little faded herb. It could only entwine itself still more tenderly round the trunk of Attalea, and whisper words of love to her and wishes for success in her efforts.

" Of course, with us it is nothing like so warm; the sky is not so clear, the rain is not so luxurious as in your country, but for all that we, too, have a sky, a sun, a breeze. We have not such gorgeous plants as you and your companions are, with such gigantic leaves and beautiful blossoms, but we also have very nice trees— pines, firs, and birches. I am a little herb, and shall never attain freedom, but you are so great and strong! Your trunk is solid, and it will not be very long before you grow up to the glass roof. You will break it, and get out into God's world. Then you will let me know if it is all as beautiful there still as it used to be. I shall be content with this."

" Why, little herb, do you not wish to come out with me? My body is firm and strong; lean on it, climb up me. It will mean nothing to me to carry you."

" No; where could I go? Look at me! See how faded I am, and how weak! I cannot rise even to one of your branches. No, I am no mate for you. Grow and be happy! Only when you go out into freedom I beg you sometimes to remember your little friend."

Then the palm set to work to grow, and former visitors to the greenhouse were astonished when they came again at its gigantic growth. It grew taller and taller with every month. The Director of the botanical gardens attributed this rapidity of growth to the excellent care bestowed on it, and was proud of the skill with which he managed the greenhouse and did his business.

"Yes, look at Attalea Princeps," he would say; "such well-grown specimens are rarely met with even in Brazil. We have applied all our knowledge to ensure that the plants shall develop in the greenhouse just as freely as when wild; and it seems to me we have attained a certain measure of success."

And with a satisfied air he would strike the solid tree with his walking-stick, and the blows would resound loudly through the greenhouse. The leaves of the palm used to shake from these blows, and, oh! if only the palm could have groaned, what a howl of hate the Director would have heard.

"He imagines that I am growing for his delectation," thought Attalea; "well, let him."

And it grew, expending all its sap in order to extend itself, and thereby depriving its roots and leaves of moisture. Sometimes it seemed to the palm that the distance to the dome was not decreasing. Then it put forth all its strength, and the framework became closer and closer, and finally a young leaf touched the cold glass and iron.

"Look! look!" said the plants, "where she has got to! Does she really mean to do it?"

"How wonderfully she has grown!" said the tree-fern.

"What is there wonderful in her having grown up? There is nothing wonderful in that! Now, if she knew how to swell herself out like me," said a portly sicada, with a trunk like a round O. "And what's the good of stretching herself out? What will happen? Nothing will happen. It's all the same. The bars are solid and firm, and the glass thick."

Another month went by. Attalea continued to grow and raise herself. At last it was solidly against the framework. It could go no farther. Then the trunk began to bend. Its leafy top doubled up, and the cold

ATTALEA PRINCEPS

framework pierced into the tender young leaves, cut through them, and deformed them, but the palm was obstinate, and did not spare its leaves. Notwithstanding everything it continued to press against the bars, and the bars were already yielding although they were made out of strong iron.

The little herb followed the struggle with attention, and almost swooned from excitement.

"Tell me," it said, "surely it is painful for you? If the framework is so solid, would it not be better to give it up?" it inquired of the palm.

"Painful? What does it matter whether it is painful or not when I wish to gain my freedom? Did not you yourself encourage me?" replied the palm.

"Yes, yes, but I did not know it would be so difficult. I am sorry for you. You are suffering so."

"Silence, weak plant! Do not pity me. I shall free myself or die!"

And at that very moment there was a resounding crash. A thick iron bar had given way. Splinters of glass scattered around, and came ringing down. One splinter hit the Director's hat as he was leaving the greenhouse.

"What was that?" he exclaimed with a shudder, as he saw portions of glass flying through the air. He ran out of the greenhouse, and looked up at the roof. The green crown of the palm had straightened itself, and was proudly protruding above the glass dome.

"Only this," she thought, "and is it only for this that I have suffered so much and tortured myself so long? To attain which has been my greatest and highest aim!"

It was mid-autumn when Attalea straightened her top through the opening made. It was sleeting, a mixture of rain and snow. The wind was driving along low grey masses of clouds. It seemed to the palm that they would seize her. The trees were already bare, and resembled shapeless skeletons. Only the pines and firs retained their dark green tips. The trees looked at the palm sullenly. "You will be frozen," they seemed to say to her. "You do not know what frost is; you will not be able to stand it. Why have you come out of your hot-house?"

And Attalea understood that all was ended for her. She became numbed with the cold. Would it not be better to return under the roof? But she was no longer able to return. She would have to stand in the cold wind, feel its gusts and the biting touch of snowflakes. She would have to gaze at the drab sky, at beggarly Nature, at the unsavoury back-yard of the botanical garden, at the huge wearisome town looming through the fog, and wait until people below in the greenhouse decided what to do with her.

The Director gave instructions to saw the palm down. "We could build a special dome over it," he said, "but would it be for long? It would again grow up and smash everything. Besides which it would cost far too much. Saw it down."

They fastened ropes round the palm so that when it fell it should not destroy the walls of the greenhouse, and low down at its very roots they sawed it through. The little herb which had grown around the trunk did not wish to part from its friend, and also fell under the saw. When they dragged the palm out of the greenhouse, the torn stalks and leaves spoilt by the saw fell on to the stump that remained.

"Take out all this rubbish and throw it away," said the Director. "It has already turned yellow, and the saw has quite spoilt it. We will plant something new here."

One of the gardeners, by a clever stroke of a hook, pulled up the bunch of herb, placed it in a basket, carried it out, and threw it into the back-yard right on to the dead palm which was lying in the mud half buried by snow.

IX

"MAKE-BELIEVE"

(THAT WHICH WAS NOT)

One beautiful June day—and it was beautiful because there were twenty-eight degrees Réamur—one beautiful June day it was hot everywhere, but on a little plot in the garden, where there stood a mound of recently-mown hay, it was still hotter, because this spot was screened from any breeze by a thick, extremely thick, cherry orchard. Almost everything was sleeping. The men and women, having had their midday fill, were lying on their sides busily engaged in that profound meditation which generally follows the noonday meal. The birds were silent; even numbers of the insects were hiding from the heat, and as regards the domestic animals, " it goes without the saying." The cattle, large and small, were taking refuge under eaves. A dog which had dug a hole under a barn had betaken himself thither, and with half-closed eyes was stretched out, breathing spasmodically, and showing nearly half an arshin of crimson tongue. From time to time, no doubt from boredom caused by the stifling heat, he yawned to such an extent as to give little yelps. The pigs, mamma with thirteen children, had gone off to the river, and were lying embedded in greasy black ooze, showing only a row of sniffling, grunting snouts, long dirty backs, and huge flapping ears. Only the hens, fearless of the heat, were endeavouring to kill time by scratching up the dust opposite the kitchen door, in which there was not, as they well knew, even one single tiny grain, and things must have been going very badly with one of the cocks, because from time to time he assumed a ridiculous attitude, and at the top of his voice called out : " What a scandal ! "

We had come out of this plot where it was hottest of all, but a whole company of non-slumbering individuals were sitting there. That is to say, not all were sitting. The old bay horse, for instance, who, from fear for his sides of the whip wielded by the coachman, Anton, had been raking up the hay, being a horse, was quite unable to sit down. A caterpillar, the grub of some kind of butterfly, was resting on its belly rather than sitting ; however, it is not a matter of words. A small but very serious gathering had assembled under a cherry-tree—a snail, a beetle, a lizard, and the caterpillar already mentioned. A grasshopper also hopped up, and near by stood the old bay listening to the speeches with one bay ear lined inside with dark grey hairs turned towards them. There were also two flies sitting on the bay horse.

The gathering was politely, but quite excitedly, debating some question. As was proper, no one agreed with the other, as each highly prized the independence of his opinion and character.

" In my opinion," said the beetle, " a properly conducted animal should first and before all busy himself about his posterity. Life is labour for the future generation. He who wittingly carries out the obligations laid upon him by Nature stands upon sure ground. He knows his business, and whatever may happen will not be answerable for the future. Look at me ! Who works harder than I do ? Who for whole days rolls such a heavy ball—a ball made so ingeniously by me of manure for the great purpose of rendering it possible for future beetles like myself to be born ? I do not think anybody could say with so calm a conscience and so clean a heart as I can when new beetles appear, ' Yes, I have done all that I should or could have done in this world.' That is work."

" Go to, brother, with your work ! " said an ant, which, during the beetle's speech and notwithstanding the heat, had been dragging along a wonderful piece of dry stalk. It was resting for a moment, sitting on its four hind-legs, and with its two fore-legs was wiping the perspiration from its troubled face. " I, for one, work more than you do ! You work for yourself, or at all events for your species. We are not all so happily situated. You should try to drag beams along for the public, like I am doing. I myself do not know what compels me to work, exhausting my strength even in this awful heat.... No one will say thank you for it. We unhappy toiling ants, we all work, and in what way is our life beautiful ? Fate. . . .

" You, beetle, are too severe, and you, ant, are too pessimistic in your views of life," broke in the grasshopper. " No, beetle, I love to chirrup and jump, and no conscience, nothing, torments or worries me. Moreover, you have not in any way touched the question put by Madame Lizard. She inquired, ' What is the world ?' and you talk about your manure-composed balls. It is even impolite. The world in my opinion is a very nice place, because there is young grass in it for us, and sun, and breezes. . . . Yes, and how large it is ! You here amongst these trees can have no conception of its size. When I am in a field I sometimes jump as high as I can, and I assure you I attain an enormous height. And from it I observe that the world has no limit."

" True, true," affirmed the bay impressively, " but none of you, however, will ever see even one-hundredth part of what I have seen in my time. I regret you cannot understand what is meant by a verst. . . . A verst from here is a village, Luparevka, where I go every day with a barrel for water. But they never feed me there.

Then in the other direction there are Ephimovka and Kisliakovka. In Kisliakovka there is a church with bells. Then farther on there is Sviato-Troiska, and then Bogoiavlensk. In Bogoiavlensk they always give me hay, only it is of poor quality. But, Nicolaieff! that is a town for you—twenty-eight versts from here—there the hay is better, and they give you oats. However, I do not care about going there. Our master goes there sometimes, and orders the coachman to hurry up, and the coachman hits us in a most painful manner with the whip. . . . Then there is also Alexandrovka, Bielozerk, and Cherson, also a town . . . only how can you understand all this! That is the world; not all, we will admit, but nevertheless a considerable portion of it."

The bay stopped speaking, but his lower lip continued to quiver as if he was still whispering something. This was due to old age. He was seventeen years old, which age for a horse is what seventy-seven years of age would be to a man.

"I do not understand your sagacious, equine remarks, and will not bother to try and understand, but will accept them," said the snail. "As long as there is burdock for me it is sufficient. I have now been four days crawling on this plant, and I have not finished yet. And after this burdock is finished there is another, and in it I am sure a snail is sitting. And that's all. To jump is not necessary—that is all imagination and frivolity; sit and eat the leaf on which you are resting. If I had not been lazy in crawling I should long ago have gone away from you and your arguments. One's head aches from them, and nothing more."

"No; allow me to tell you why," interrupted the grasshopper. "It is so pleasing to chirrup a little, especially on such entrancing subjects as infinity, etc. Of course, there are practical natures which only trouble about how best to fill their insides, such as you or this beautiful caterpillar."

"Ah no, leave me in peace; I implore you, leave me in peace, and out of the question; do not bother about me," querulously cried the caterpillar. "I am doing this for the future life, only for the future life."

"What sort of a future life?" inquired the bay.

"Can it be you do not know that after death I become a butterfly with multi-coloured wings?"

The bay, lizard, and snail did not know this, but the insects had a kind of glimmering knowledge on the subject. And all kept silent for a short time, because no one knew how to say anything to the point respecting the future life.

"It is necessary to treat strong convictions with respect," chirruped the grasshopper at length. "Does no one wish to say anything more? Perhaps you ladies?" and he turned to the flies. The elder of them answered:

"We cannot say that things have gone badly with us. We have just come from a room where the 'gude wife' was potting jam, and we settled under a lid and had our fill. We are satisfied. It is true our mamma got entangled in the jam, but what is to be done? She had already lived a considerable time in the world, and we are satisfied."

"Gentlemen," said the lizard, "I am of the opinion that you are all entirely correct! But, on the other hand. . . ."

But the lizard did not state what was on the other hand, because she felt something firmly press her tail into the ground.

This was the coachman, Anton, who, having awakened, had come for the bay. He had unwittingly placed his huge foot on the assemblage and squashed it. Only the flies escaped, and flew away to buzz of their deceased mother departed in the jam. The lizard escaped, but with a reduced tail. Anton took the bay by the forelock, and led him out of the garden to harness him up to the barrel, and go for water, and said to him, "Get on, you old stump ! to which the bay only replied by whispering something to himself. The lizard remained without a tail. True it is that after a while it grew again, but it always remained somewhat blunted and blackish in colour, and whenever she was asked how she had damaged her tail, she used to reply :

"They tore it off because I dared to express my convictions."

And she was quite correct.

X

OFFICER AND SOLDIER-SERVANT

"UNDRESS!" said the doctor to Nikita, who was standing motionless, his eyes fixed on space. Nikita gave a start, and hurriedly commenced to unfasten his clothes.

"A bit faster, friend!" cried the doctor impatiently; "you see what a lot of you there are here."

He pointed to the crowd in the room.

"Turn round! . . . Lost your senses?" added by way of assistance the N.C.O. who was taking the measurements.

Nikita made even more haste, threw off his shirt and trousers, and stood in a state of nature. That there is nothing more beautiful than the human form has often been said by someone, somewhen, and somewhere, but if he who first made this pronouncement had lived in the seventies, and had seen the naked Nikita, he would certainly have retracted his words.

Before the Military Service Commission there stood a little man with a disproportionately large stomach, a legacy from generations of ancestors who had never tasted pure bread—and long withered arms furnished with huge black knotted fists. His long awkward body was supported by very short bandy legs, and the whole figure was crowned by a head . . . what a head it was! The facial bones had been developed at the expense of the skull. His forehead was low and narrow, and his eyes, without brows or lashes, were little more than slits. On an enormous flat face forlornly sat a little round nose which, although carried high, not only failed to give the face an expression of haughtiness, but, on the contrary, made it look still more woeful. The mouth, in contrast to the nose, was enormous, and presented the appearance of a shapeless chasm, unadorned, notwithstanding Nikita's twenty years, by one single hair. Nikita stood with his head lowered, his shoulders forward, his arms hanging like whipcords by his sides, and his feet slightly turned in.

"Ape!" said a rather stout, brisk-mannered Colonel, the military head of the Commission, leaning towards a spare young man with a handsome beard, a member of the Zemstvo Board, "a regular ape!"

"A splendid confirmation of Darwin's theory," murmured the Zemstvo official, to which the Colonel loudly assented, and turned to the doctor.

"Well, of course he is fit! He is sound," replied the latter.

"Only he will not go to the Guards, ha, ha, ha!" said the Colonel, laughing heartily, but not unkindly; then, turning to Nikita, he added in a quiet tone: "Present yourself here in a fortnight's time. The next man, Parfen Semenoff, undress!"

Nikita began slowly to dress himself; his arms and legs were all over the place, and refused to do as bid. He kept whispering something to himself, but precisely what it was he himself probably did not know. He understood only that they had declared him fit for service, and that within a fortnight they would drive him from home for some years. Only this was in his head, and only this thought pierced its way through the maze and stupor in which he was enveloped. Finally, having successfully reduced his arms to obedience, he put on his belt, and left the room in which the medical examination was taking place. A little doubled-up old man of some sixty years of age met him in the passage.

"Have they taken you?" he asked.

OFFICER AND SOLDIER-SERVANT

Nikita did not answer, and the old man knew that it was so, and did not ask any more questions. They went out into the street. It was a bright frosty day. A crowd of moujiks and babas were standing about waiting. Many were stamping their feet, and beating themselves with their arms to keep warm. The snow crunched under their bast shoes and boots, and steam was rising from their heads enveloped in shawls and from the little shaggy ponies which had brought their masters in from the surrounding villages.

The smoke from the chimneys in the little town was rising in straight tall columns.

"Have they taken yours, Ivan?" inquired an old man, a sturdy-looking moujik in a new tanned coat, a big sheepskin cap, and good boots.

"They have taken him, Ilia Savelich, taken him. It was God's will to do us this injury."

"What will you do now?"

"What is there to do? The will of God . . . there was one helper in the family, and now he's gone . . . and . . ."

Ivan made a gesture with his hand.

"You should have adopted him sooner," said Ilia Savelich, with an air of conviction, "then he would have been saved."

"Who knew of it? We knew nothing. He was instead of my son, and once again the only helper in the family. . . . I thought that for this reason the gentleman would have allowed it. 'No, no,' he said, 'impossible, because it is the law.' 'How can it be the law, Your Excellency,' I said, 'when his wife is in labour? Besides, Your Excellency,' I said, 'it is impossible for me, one . . .' 'No, we know nothing of this,' he said, 'and by the law as it stands he is an orphan, alone, and so he must serve. Who is to blame,' he said, 'that he has a wife and son? If he chose to marry when he was fifteen——'

"I wanted to explain to him, but he would not listen,

and got angry. ' Go, go away,' he said, ' there is plenty of work without you bothering me. . . .' What is to be done ? . . . God's will."

" Yours was a quiet young fellow ?"

" Yes, quiet and hard-working, and never have I heard a word in argument from him. Ilia, as I tell you . . . he has been better than a son to me. This is our grief. . . . God sent him, and God has taken him away. . . . Good-bye, Ilia Savelich ; and yours, will they look at him soon ?"

" That depends on the authorities . . . only they cannot call my son fit. He is a cripple."

" That's your happiness, Ilia Savelich."

" Eh, but what are you saying ! Are you not afraid to say that ? Eh, eh, ' happiness ' that a son was born lame."

" Well, Ilia Savelich, it has turned out for the better ; he will always be at home. Good-bye, and good health to you."

" Good-bye, friend . . . and what about that little loan ? Have you forgotten it ?"

" Impossible, Ilia Savelich . . . that is—cannot be done. It is only a trifle ; you can wait, and we are in such trouble. . . ."

" All right ! all right ! we will talk about it another time. Good-bye, Ivan Petrovich."

" Good-bye, Ilia Savelich, good health to you."

Nikita at this moment untied the horse from the post to which it was fastened, and he, with his adopted father, settled themselves in the sleigh, and started off. It was fifteen versts to their village. The little pony went along bravely, throwing up balls of snow with his hoofs, which broke up in their flight, falling in showers on Nikita. But Nikita lay silent near his father, wrapped up in his sheepskin, without saying a word. Twice the old man spoke to him, but received no reply. He seemed to have become petrified, and gazed fixedly at the snow, as if

OFFICER AND SOLDIER-SERVANT

seeking in it some point forgotten by him in the rooms of the Commission.

Having arrived, they went straight into the hut and gave the news. The family, which consisted, in addition to the men, of three women and three children of Ivan Petrovich's son who had died last year, commenced to wail.

Nikita's wife, Praskovia, collapsed. The women cried for a whole week. How this week passed for Nikita no one knows, because the whole time he maintained a rigid silence, his face preserving the same set expression of submissive despair.

Eventually it all came to an end. Ivan took the recruit to the town, and handed him over at the mustering-place. Two days later Nikita, one of a party of recruits, marched over the snowdrifts along the main road to the provincial capital where the regiment to which he had been drafted was quartered. He was clothed in a new short half-shuba, in trousers of thick black material, new valenkies, a cap, and mitts. In his wallet, besides two changes of linen and some pies, there lay a rouble note carefully wrapped up in a handkerchief. Nikita was indebted for all this to his adopted father, Ivan Petrovich, who had implored Ilia Savelich to make him a further advance so as to equip Nikita for service.

* * * * *

Nikita proved to be a very poor recruit. The instructor to whom he was handed over for his preliminary drills was in despair. Notwithstanding every conceivable explanation on his part to Nikita, amongst which cuffs and blows played a certain rôle, his pupil could not even entirely master the not difficult problem of forming fours. The figure of Nikita dressed up in uniform presented a sorry spectacle. In front of him projected his stomach, and in his efforts to draw it in he threw out his chest, leaning forward with his whole body at an angle which threatened to bring him down face forwards to the ground. Knock him about as they would, the authorities could not make out of Nikita even a most indifferent front-rank man. During company drill his Captain, having abused Nikita, would "tell off" the section N.C.O., who would pass it on to Nikita. The punishment awarded consisted of extra "fatigues." Soon, however, the N.C.O. guessed that this was no punishment, but a pleasure to Nikita. He was a wonderful worker, and the duties of carrying wood and water, attending the stores, but chiefly keeping the barrack quarters clean—*i.e.*, endless swabbing the floors with a damp mop—were to his liking. At any rate, whilst performing this work he was not obliged to think how not to get out of step, and not to go left when the command was "Right turn," and, besides, he felt quite safe from terrifying questions on that wonderful science known in soldier's language as "literature," such as : "What is a soldier ?" "What is a colour ?"

Nikita knew quite well what were colours. He was prepared with all possible zeal to carry out his obligations and duties as a soldier, and would probably have given his life in defence of the colours, but to define them verbatim as set forth in the book was beyond him.

"The colour is . . . which colour, colour . . ." he used to murmur, endeavouring as far as possible to straighten out his clumsy body, poking out his chin, and screwing up his eyes bare of all lashes.

"Fool !" would cry the consumptive N.C.O. giving the lesson. "Am I to teach you your alphabet ? How much longer am I to be tormented with you ? You idiot ! you clodhopper ! Tfy ! . . . How many times must I repeat it to you ? Now say it after me— the colour is a sacred banner. . . ."

Nikita could not repeat even these few words. The threatening aspect of the N.C.O. and his shouting had a stupefying effect on him. There was a ringing in his ears, stars were dancing before his eyes. He heard

OFFICER AND SOLDIER-SERVANT

nothing of the definition of a colour; his lips did not move. He stood silent.

"Go on; the D—— take you! The colour is a sacred banner."

"The colour . . ."

"Well? . . ."

". . . Banner . . ." continued Nikita in a trembling voice, with tears in his eyes.

"Is a sacred banner!" yelled the maddened N.C.O.

"Sacred which. . . ."

Then the N.C.O. would commence to rush from corner to corner, spitting and swearing, whilst Nikita remained perfectly still in the same place and in the same attitude, following his infuriated superior with his eyes. He was not upset by the abuse and epithets showered on him, but only grieved whole-heartedly at his inability to do his superior's bidding.

"Three days' extra duty!" the worn-out N.C.O. would gasp in a voice rendered faint and hoarse from shouting, and Nikita would thank God to be freed at least for a time from the hated "literature" and drill.

When it was noticed that the punishment awarded Nikita not only did not distress him, but even afforded him real pleasure, Nikita was placed under arrest. Finally, having exhausted all means for the reformation of the unfortunate man, the authorities washed their hands of him.

"Nothing can be done with Ivanoff," was the almost daily complaint of the Company Sergeant-Major, when making his morning report to the Company Commander.

"About Ivanoff? . . . Oh yes. Let me see, what is it he is doing?" the Captain would ask as he sat in his dressing-gown, smoking a cigarette between the intervals of sipping tea out of a glass in an electro-plated holder.

"Nothing, Your Excellency; he is not doing anything. As a man he is quiet, only he cannot understand anything."

"Try something," the Captain would say meditatively, blowing rings of tobacco smoke.

"We have tried, Your Excellency, but nothing comes of it."

"Well! What can I do with him? You will agree at least that I am but a mortal, and cannot work miracles. Eh? Well, idiot, do something with him . . . and get out!"

Eventually the Company Commander became bored with hearing daily complaints from the Sergeant-Major about Nikita.

"Stop talking about your Ivanoff!" he shouted. "Don't try to teach him; give him up. Do what you like with him, only don't bring him up before me."

The Company Sergeant-Major tried to arrange a transfer of Nikita Ivanoff to the "employed" men's Company, but there were already plenty of "employed" men. An attempt to make him an officer's servant was equally unsuccessful, as all the officers already had servants. Then Nikita was saddled with all the dirty work of the battalion, and all attempts to make him a soldier were abandoned. Thus he lived for a year until the arrival of a newly-appointed subaltern officer, Second Lieutenant Stebelkoff.

Nikita was told off as "permanent orderly" to him—in plain language, to be his soldier-servant.

* * * *

Alexander Michailovich Stebelkoff, Nikita's new master, was a very kind young fellow of average height, with a shaven chin and a magnificently pointed moustache, which he from time to time, not without a feeling of pride, used to stroke lightly with his left hand. He had just passed through the cadet school without having displayed during his time there any special taste for sciences, but had learnt his drill to perfection. He was thoroughly happy in his present position. The two years spent at the school on Government fare, under the strict supervision of the authorities, the entire absence of friends to whom

OFFICER AND SOLDIER-SERVANT

he could have gone on holidays in search of relaxation from the barrack life of the school, and not possessed of a kopeck of private money with which he could have amused himself, had all wearied him, and now, as an officer receiving forty roubles a month pay, commanding a half-company of soldiers, and a soldier-servant at his absolute disposal, he for the time at least wanted nothing more. " Good, very good," he thought, as he we. t to sleep, and again awaking he first of all remembered he was no longer a cadet, but an officer, that there was no longer need to jump out of bed on the instant and dress, under fear of the orderly-officer, but that he could roll over again, make himself snug, and smoke a cigarette.

" Nikita !" he would call, and Nikita, in a faded rose-coloured cotton shirt, black cloth trousers, and a pair of old big rubber galoshes (goodness knows how he had become possessed of them) on his bare feet, would appear at the door leading from the single room of Stebelkoff's flat into the passage.

" Cold to-day ?"

" I cannot tell you, Your Excellency," Nikita would reply timidly.

" Go and look ! and come and tell me !"

Off would go Nikita into the frost, and in the course of a minute reappear.

" Very cold, sir."

" Is there a wind ?"

" I cannot tell you, Your Excellency."

" Ass ! Why can't you tell ? Surely you were in the courtyard ?"

" In the yard there is none, sir."

" None. . . . Go out into the street."

Nikita would go out into the street, and return with the information that there was a " healthy " wind.

" No parade, sir, so Sidoroff says," he would venture to add.

" All right ; clear out !" and Alexander Michailovich

would then turn over in his bunk, pull the warm blanket over him, and, half dozing, would commence to think to the accompaniment of the crackling of brightly-burning wood in the stove which had been lit by Nikita. Cadet life appeared to him as an unpleasant dream, although it was not so long ago that the drum used to beat right at his ear, and he would have to jump out of bed shivering from the cold. . . . These recollections would awake others, also not particularly pleasing. Poverty, and the squalid surroundings and life of a small official, a habitually sullen mother, a tall lean woman, with a severe expression on her thin face which seemed a perpetual defiance to anyone bold enough to insult her. A crowd of brothers and sisters; the constant quarrels between them. His mother's railings against fate, an everlasting exchange of abuse between his parents whenever his father came home drunk. The school in which, in spite of all efforts, it was so difficult to learn. The teasing of his schoolmates, who for some unknown reason had bestowed on him the extremely insulting nickname of the "herring." His failure in the examination on Russian. The depressing, humiliating scene when he was turned out of the school in consequence, and arrived home in tears. His father was asleep on the chintz-covered sofa drunk. His mother was fussing about the kitchen at the stove preparing dinner. Seeing Sasha in tears with his books, she guessed what had happened, and after showering abuse on him had rushed off to his father, awakened him, and explained what had happened, and his father had thereupon beaten him.

Sasha was then fifteen years old. Two years later he took up military service as a volunteer, and at twenty years of age was already an independent man, a Second Lieutenant in an infantry regiment of the Line. . . .

"It is very nice," he would reflect, as he lay under the blanket. . . . "This evening at the Club there is to be a dance."

And Alexander Michailovich would picture to himself the hall of the Officers' Club brilliantly lighted up, the heat, and music, and young girls in long rows seated along the wall, only waiting for some young officer to invite them to take a few turns in a waltz. And Stebelkoff with a click of his heels (What a pity, dash it! he sighed, he could not wear spurs), and neatly bending before the Major's pretty daughter, with a graceful sweep of his hand would say " Permettez," and the Major's daughter, placing her little hand on his shoulder near his epaulette, they would glide away. . . .

" Yes, that's not being a ' herring '—how idiotic, and why a ' herring ' ? Those who attend the first course at the University are much more like herrings, going there and starving, but I . . . And why is it absolutely necessary to go to the University ? We will allow that a magistrate or doctor receives a bigger salary than my pay, but think how long it takes to get it ! . . . and all this time one must live at one's own expense. But with us, once you get into the school everything goes of itself. If one serves well it is possible to become a General. . . . Ah, then I would give it . . ." Alexander Michailovich did not say to whom or what he would give, for other reminiscences than of " herrings " at this instance flashed into his mind.

" Nikita," he called, " have we any tea ?"

" None at all, Your Excellency—all used."

" Go out and buy some ;" and then he would draw his new purse from under the pillow, and give Nikita the money, and whilst Nikita is out getting the tea Alexander Michailovich continues his reveries, but before Nikita returns has succeeded in going to sleep again.

" Sir ! Your Excellency !" whispers Nikita.

" What ? Eh ? Have you got the tea ? All right, I will get up in a moment. . . . Help me dress."

Alexander Michailovich, both at home and at the school, had always dressed himself (excepting, of course, during his babyhood), but having become possessed of a manservant, he in two weeks had absolutely forgotten how to put on or take off his clothes. Nikita pulls on his master's socks and boots, helps him with his trousers, throws around his master's shoulders the summer military cloak which does duty as a dressing-gown. And Alexander Michailovich, without washing, sits down to drink his morning tea.

They bring him the lithographed regimental orders, and Stebelkoff, reading it from beginning to end, notes with satisfaction that his turn for "guard" is still far off. "But what is this novelty?" he wonders as he reads:

"With a view to maintaining the standard of knowledge amongst officers of the regiment, Captain Ermolin and Lieutenant Petroff (2nd) are detailed from the commencement of next week to lecture, the former on tactics, the latter on fortification. Further special notice will be given as to the hours for these lectures, which will take place in the Officers' Club."

"Well! Goodness knows, I suppose I shall have to go and listen," thinks Alexander Michailovich. "They were boring enough at the school, and they will not say anything new, but will only read from the old handbooks."

Having read through the Orders and finished his tea, Alexander Michailovich orders Nikita to clear away the samovar, and settles himself down to roll cigarettes, continuing the while his never-ending cogitations about his past, present, and future, which last promises him, if not the embonpoint of a General, at least the substantial epaulettes of a Staff-Officer. And when all the cigarettes have been rolled he lies on his bed, and reads the back numbers of the *Niva*, looking at the already familiar pictures, and not missing a line of the text. Finally, from long lying and reading, his head begins to get dizzy.

"Nikita!" he shouts.

Nikita jumps up from the cloak stretched out on the

OFFICER AND SOLDIER-SERVANT 151

floor in the passage near the stove, which serves him as a bed, and rushes to the Barin.

" See what time it is ! . . . No, better bring me my watch."

Nikita gingerly takes up a silver watch, with its chain of new gold, from the table, and, having handed it to his master again, repairs into the passage to his cloak.

" Half-past one . . . about time to dine," thinks Stebelkoff, winding up the watch with a brass key which he had just purchased, and in the head of which was inserted a little photographic picture visible in magnified shape if held up to the light. Alexander Michailovich looks at the picture, screwing up his left eye, and smiles. " What extraordinarily amusing things they make nowadays, to be sure," he reflects, " and how clever. . . . However, I must be going. . . . Nikita !" he shouts.

Nikita appears.

" I want to wash."

Nikita brings an unpainted deal stool into the room, and places a wash-hand basin on it. Alexander Michailovich begins to wash. The icy cold water scarcely touches his hands before he yells out.

" How many times have I told you, you clown, to leave the water in the room over-night. This water is cold enough to freeze one's face. . . . Idiot !"

Nikita, fully conscious of the enormity of his crime, remains silent, and continues busily to pour water into the enraged gentleman's palms.

" Have you brushed my tunic ?"

" Yes, Your Excellency, I have brushed it," replies Nikita, as he gives the Barin a new tunic, with glistening gold shoulder-straps, decorated with a numeral and one star, which had been hanging on the back of a chair.

Before putting it on Alexander Michailovich attentively inspects the dark green cloth, and finds a piece of fluff on it.

" What's this ? Is this what you call cleaning ? Is

this the way you do your work? Clear out, you fool, and brush it again."

Nikita goes out into the passage, and begins to extract apparently from the brush, with the aid of the tunic, sounds known as "shooing." Stebelkoff, with the aid of a folding mirror in a yellow wooden frame and pommade hongroise, begins to bring his moustaches to the greatest possible perfection. Finally they are reduced to order, but the noise in the passage continues.

"Here, give me that tunic; you will go on cleaning it until the crack of doom. . . . I am already late through you, ass! . . ."

Then, carefully buttoning up his coat, fastening on his sword, and putting on his galoshes, Alexander Michailovich goes out into the street, stamping with his feet along the frozen boards of the path.

The rest of the day passes in dining, reading the *Russki Invalid*, and in conversation with his brother-officers about the Service, promotion, and pay. In the evening Alexander Michailovich goes to the Club, and flashes in the "whirl of a waltz" with the Major's daughter. He returns home late, tired, and a little excited from several drinks taken during the evening, but contented. . . . Life was varied only by drill, guards, camp in the summer, sometimes manœuvres, and occasionally by lectures on fortification and tactics which it was impossible to avoid. And so the years roll on, leaving no traces on Stebelkoff, save that the colour of his face changes and signs of baldness become manifest, whilst instead of one star on the shoulder-straps there appear two, three, and then four stars. . . .

What does Nikita do all this time? Nikita lies for the most part on his cloak near the stove, jumping up every few minutes in answer to the never-ending demands of the Barin. In the morning he has quite a lot to do. There is the stove to be lighted, the samovar prepared, water brought, boots and uniform to be cleaned, the

Barin to be dressed when he gets up, and the room to be swept and tidied. (It is true this last does not take up much time, as the whole furniture consists only of a bed, a table, three chairs, a cupboard, and a portmanteau.) Nevertheless all this is work for Nikita. When his master has gone out there commences a long, long day to be spent in the compulsory doing of nothing, broken only by a journey to the barracks for his dinner from the Company kitchen. Whilst living in barracks Nikita had learnt a little cobbling—how to patch and re-sole boots, and to piece heels. When he was transferred to Stebelkoff he thought of continuing his trade, and used to hide the bag containing his work behind the door in the passage as soon as there was a knock at the door. The Barin having noticed for several days that there was a strong smell of leather in the passage, sought out the cause, and gave Nikita a severe " head-washing," after which he ordered that it " must never occur again." Then there was nothing left for Nikita to do but to lie on his cloak and think. And he used to lie there thinking through whole evenings, dozing off and on until a knock at the door notified his master's return. Then Nikita would undress Alexander Michailovich, and soon afterwards the little flat would be buried in darkness—officer and servant both asleep.

The wind drones and howls, and the snow beats in whirling flakes against the window, representing to the sleeping Stebelkoff the noise of ball-room music. In his sleep he sees a brilliantly-lighted hall such as he had hitherto never seen, full of smartly-dressed strangers. However, he does not feel at all confused, but, on the contrary, the hero of the evening. There are people he knows in the hall, too. Their attitude towards him is not as it has been usually, but is one of enthusiasm. His Colonel, instead of giving him the usual two fingers, presses his hand warmly in his own fat fist. Major Khlobuschin, who had always looked somewhat askance at Stebelkoff's wooing of his daughter, himself now leads her to him, submissively bowing. What he had done or for what they are praising him he does not know, but that he had done something was evident. Glancing at his shoulders, he sees on them a General's epaulettes. The music resounds, the couples glide off, and he, too, floats away somewhere ever farther and farther, ever higher and higher. The brilliantly-lighted hall becomes a mere speck of distant light. Around him are a great number of persons in various uniforms. They are all asking his orders. He does not know about what they are asking, but gives his instructions. Orderlies gallop to and from him. The distant roar of cannon is heard. There is the clash of martial music as regiment after regiment marches past him. All are moving forward. The guns sound closer and closer, and Stebelkoff becomes terrified; "They are killing people," he thinks. And an awful yell resounds from every side. Terrible, monstrous, and ferocious beings, such as he had never seen anywhere, rush at him. They come ever closer; Stebelkoff's heart contracts with the indescribable fear experienced only in dreams, and he shouts "Nikita!"

The wind drones and howls, and the snow beats in whirling flakes against the window, and it seems to the sleeping Nikita a real wind and real bad weather. He dreams he is lying in his own hut alone. No one is near him—no wife, no father—not one of his belongings. He does not know how he got home, and is afraid he must have deserted. He is certain that they are after him, and feels that they are near, and wishes to run away and hide somewhere, but is unable to move a limb. Then he cries out, and the whole hut is filled with people, all his village acquaintances, but their faces are all extraordinary. "How do you do, Nikita?" they say to him. "All yours, my friend, have gone! God has taken them all. All have died. There they are; look there!" and Nikita sees his whole family in a crowd together—Ivan, his wife,

OFFICER AND SOLDIER-SERVANT

and Aunt Praskovia, and the children. And he understands that, although they are all standing together, they are all dead, and that all his village friends are dead. That is why they look so odd, and are laughing so strangely. They come towards him, and seize hold of him, but he breaks away from them, and runs over the snowdrifts, stumbling and falling. The dead are no longer pursuing him, but Lieutenant Stebelkoff, with soldiers. And he runs on and on, and the Lieutenant keeps crying out to him : " Nikita ! Nikita ! Nikita !"

" Nikita !" shouts out Stebelkoff in reality, and Nikita, awaking, jumps up, and gropes his way into the room in his bare feet.

" What's the matter with you ? D—— you ! Are you making a fool of me, or what ? How many times have I told you to place some matches near me ? You sleep like a lout ! I have been calling you for half an hour. Give me some matches."

The sleepy Nikita fumbles about the table and window until he finds the matches, then lights a candle stuck in a brass candlestick, which is turning green with verdigris, and, all the time blinking his eyes, gives it to his master. Alexander Michailovich smokes a cigarette, and within a quarter of an hour's time officer and soldier-servant are again wrapped in deep slumber.

XI

NADEJDA NICOLAIEVNA

I

I HAVE long wanted to commence my memoirs. A strange reason is compelling me to take up a pen. Some write their memoirs because there is much in them historically interesting, others because they wish by so doing to live the happy days of their youth once more, and yet others in order to sneer at and traduce persons long since dead, and to justify themselves before long-forgotten accusations. In my case it is not any one of these reasons. I am still young. I have not made history, nor have I seen how it is made. There is no reason for people to criticize me, and I have nothing concerning which I wish to justify myself. Once again to experience happiness? My happiness was so short-lived and its finale so terrible that to recall it does not afford me pleasure . . . no, far from it.

Why, then, does an unknown voice keep whispering of that happiness in my ear? Why, when I awake at night, do familiar scenes and forms pass before me in the darkness? And why, when one pale form appears, does his face blaze, his hands clench, and terror and fury arrest his breathing as on that day when I stood face to face with my mortal enemy?

I cannot rid myself of these recollections, and a strange thought has come into my head. Perhaps if I commit these recollections to paper I shall in this way settle accounts and finish with them. . . . Perhaps they will leave me, and allow me to die in peace. This is the strange reason which is compelling me to take up a pen. Perhaps somebody will read this diary, perhaps not; I care little. Therefore I do not apologize to any future readers either as regards style or the choice of subject upon which I am writing, a subject not in the least interesting to people accustomed to busy themselves in questions, if not of world-wide, at least of public interest. It is true, however, that I want one person to read these lines, but she will not condemn me. All that concerns me is precious to her. This person is my cousin.

Why to-day is she so long in coming? It is already three months since I came to myself after *that* day. The first face I saw was Sonia's. And from that time she has spent every evening with me. It has become a kind of duty with her. She sits by my bed or beside a big armchair when I am strong enough to sit up, talks with me, and reads aloud from the newspapers or from books. She is much distressed because I leave it to her, and am indifferent as to what she reads.

" Look here, Andrei, there is a new story in the *Viestnik Europa* called ' She thought it was otherwise.' "

" Very good, dear, we will have ' She thought it was otherwise.' "

" It is a story by Mrs. Hay."

And she commenced to read a long history of a Mr. Skripple and a Miss Gordon. After the first two pages she turned her big kind eyes on me, and said: " It is not a long one; the *Viestnik* always cuts the stories short."

" All right, I will listen."

And as she resumes her reading of the narrative concocted by Mrs. Hay, I look at her face bent over the book, and forget to listen to the edifying story. Sometimes in those places where, according to Mrs. Hay, I should laugh bitter tears choke me. Then she drops the book, and, looking at me in a searching, but timid, manner, places her hand on my forehead, and says :

"Andrei darling, again ! Now, my dear boy, that will do. Don't cry. It will all pass by and be forgotten . . ." just as a mother comforts a little child who has bumped and hurt his forehead. But my hurt will only pass away with my life, which, I feel, is little by little ebbing from my body ; nevertheless, I calm down.

Oh, my darling cousin ! How I appreciate your womanly caresses ! May God bless you, and allow the black pages in the beginning of your life—pages on which my name is written—to be replaced by a radiant narrative of happiness ! Only grant that this narrative will not resemble Mrs. Hay's tiresome story.

A ring ! At last ! She has come, and will bring an atmosphere of freshness into my dark and stifling room, will break its silence with her quiet tender talk, and will lighten it with her beauty.

II

I do not remember my mother, and my father died when I was fourteen years old. My guardian, a distant relation, packed me off to one of the Petersburg gymnasia, where, after four years, I completed my studies and was absolutely free. My guardian, a man immersed in his own numerous affairs, confined his solicitude for me to an allowance sufficient, in his opinion, to keep me from want. It was not a very handsome income, but it entirely freed me from care as to earning my crust of bread, and allowed me to choose my path of life.

The choice had long been made. For four years I had loved before all else in the world to play with paints and pencils, and at the end of my term at the gymnasium I already drew quite well, so I had no difficulty in entering the Academy of Arts.

Had I talent ? Now, when I shall never again stretch a canvas, I may without bias look upon myself as an artist. Yes, I had talent. And I say this not because of the criticisms of comrades and experts, not because I passed so quickly through the Academy, but because of the feeling which was in me, which made itself felt every time I commenced to work. No one who is not an artist can experience the painful but delicious excitement every time one approaches a new canvas for the first time. No one but an artist can experience the oblivion to all around when the soul is engrossed in. . . . Yes, I had talent, and I should have become no ordinary artist.

There they are, hanging on the walls — my canvases, studies, and exercises, and unfinished pictures. And there *she* is. . . . I must ask my cousin to take her away into another room. Or, no—I must have it hung exactly at the foot of my bed, so that she may all the time look at me with her sad glance, as if foreseeing execution. In a dark blue dress, with a dainty white cap, and a large tricoloured cockade on one side of it, and with her dark chestnut locks escaping from under its white frill in thick waves, she gazes at me as if alive. Oh, Charlotte, Charlotte ! Ought I to bless or curse the hour when the thought first entered my head to paint you ?

Bezsonow was always against it. When I first told him of my intention, he shrugged his shoulders, and smiled in a dissatisfied manner.

" You are mad people, you Russian painters," said he. " Have you so little of your own about which to paint ? Charlotte Corday ! What have you got to do with Charlotte ? Can you really transfer yourself to that time and those surroundings ?

Perhaps he was right. . . . Only, the figure of the French heroine so possessed me that I could not but take it for a picture. I decided to paint her full length, alone standing square before the spectators, with her eyes gazing ahead of her. She had already decided on her deed-crime, but it is only discernible as yet on her face. The hand which will deal the fatal blow at present hangs helplessly, and shows up delicately in its whiteness against the dark blue cloth of her dress. A lace cape, fastened crossways, tints the delicate neck, along which to-morrow a line of blood will pass. . . . I remember how her image shaped itself in my mind. . . . I read her history in a sentimental and perhaps untruthful book by Lamartine; from out of the false pathos of the garrulous Frenchman, delighting in his verbosity and style, the clean figure of the girl—a fanatic for the good cause—stood out in clear relief. I read over and over again all that I could get hold of about her, studied her portraits, and decided to paint a picture.

The first picture, like a first love, takes entire possession of one. I carried about mentally the figure which I had formed; I thought out the minutest details, and reached such a stage that, by closing my eyes, I could clearly see the Charlotte I had decided to put to canvas.

But, having begun the picture with a happy feeling of fear and tremulous excitement, I at once met an unexpected and almost unsurmountable obstacle. I had no model.

Or, rather, strictly speaking, there were models. I chose the one which seemed to me the most suitable from amongst those acting as models in St. Petersburg, and started zealously to work. But, alas! how unlike was this Anna Ivanovna to the creation of my fancy, as it appeared before my closed eyes! Anna posed splendidly. For a whole hour she would sit motionless, never stirring, and conscientiously earned her rouble, very pleased that she might sit draped.

" Ah! How nice it is to pose like this! " she said, with a sigh, and a slight flush on her face at her first sitting— " elsewhere——"

She had only been a model for two months, and could not as yet accustom herself to sitting in the nude. Russian girls, it would seem, never can quite accustom themselves.

I painted her hand, shoulders, and pose ; but when it came to her face, despair seized me. The small, plump, young face, with its slightly upturned nose, the kind grey eyes which gazed trustfully and somewhat dolefully from under very arched brows, shut out my vision. I could not transfer these nondescript features into that face. I wrestled with my Anna Ivanovna three or four days, then finally left her alone. There was no other model, and I decided to do what should never under any circumstances be done, to paint the face without a study— from " out of my head," as they say. I decided on this because I saw it as if living before me. But when work began, brushes went flying into the corner. Instead of a living face, a sort of sketch resulted, which possessed neither flesh nor blood.

I took the canvas from the easel and placed it in a corner, face to the wall. My failure surprised me greatly. I remember that I even tore my hair. It seemed to me that it was not worth living, to have thought out such a beautiful picture (and how beautiful it was in my imagination !), and not be able to paint it. I threw myself on my bed, and from grief and vexation tried to sleep. I remember that when I had already dropped asleep there was a ring at the door. The postman had brought me a letter from my cousin Sonia. She was rejoiced that I had thought out so big and difficult a task, and lamented that it was so difficult to find a model. " Would not I do when I leave the Institute ? Wait a little, Andrei," she wrote. " I will come to Petersburg, and you may paint ten Charlotte Cordays from me if you wish . . . if only there is a vestige of resemblance between me and that which you write now possesses your soul. . . ."

Sonia is not the least like Charlotte. She is incapable of inflicting a wound. She loves, rather, to heal them, and wondrously well she does it. And she would cure me . . . if it were possible.

III

In the evening I went round to Bezsonow.

I went into the room where he was sitting bent over his writing-table, which was littered with books, manuscripts, and cuttings from papers. His hand was travelling swiftly over the paper. He wrote very quickly, without making erasures, in a small, even, and florid hand. He gave me a rapid glance, and continued writing. A tenacious idea apparently possessed him, and he did not wish to stop his work until he had put it to paper. I sat down on a wide, low, and much-worn sofa (he slept on it), which stood in a dark corner of the room, and for some five minutes looked at him. His regular, cold profile was well known to me; I had often sketched it in my album, and had once painted a study from it. I have not got this study. He sent it to his mother. But this evening—perhaps because I was sitting out of the light, and a lamp with a green-coloured shade showed him up in brilliant relief, or perhaps because my nerves were unstrung—his face, for some reason, particularly attracted my attention. I looked at him and took in every detail of his head, and noted the smallest features which had hitherto escaped my notice. His head was indisputably the head of a strong man — perhaps not very talented, but strong.

The quadrangular-shaped skull, almost without a break passing into a wide and powerful nape; the abrupt and prominent forehead; the brows drooping in the centre and contracting the skin into a vertical fold; the strong jaw and thin lips—all appeared to me as something new to-day.

"Why are you looking at me like that?" he suddenly asked, having laid down his pen, and turning his face to me.

"How did you know?"

"I felt it. It is not fancy. I have several times experienced a similar feeling."

"I was looking at your face as a model. You have a very original-shaped head, Serge Vassilivich."

"Really!" said he, with a short smile. "Well! and let it be original."

"No; but, seriously, you are like someone . . . some famous . . ."

"Rogue or murderer?" he asked, not allowing me to finish. "I do not believe in Lavater. . . . Well—and you? By your face I see that things are not going well. Won't it work out?"

"No; things are not altogether right. I have given it up—chucked it," I replied in a despairing voice.

"Ah! as I thought. What is it? I suppose no model."

"No, no, no. You know, Serge Vassilivich, how I have searched. But it is all so unlike what I want that I am simply in despair—especially this Anna Ivanovna. She has absolutely worn me out. She has wiped out everything with her flat face. It even seems to me that the image itself is not as clear in my head as it used to be."

"Then, it was clear?"

"Oh yes, absolutely. If it had been possible to paint it with my eyes blindfolded, really, I think nothing better would have been wanted. With my eyes shut, I can see her now, there "—and I must have screwed up my eyes in a most ridiculous manner, because Bezsonow laughed loudly.

"Don't laugh. Seriously, I am in despair," I said.

He suddenly stopped laughing.

"If so, I'll stop. But, really and honestly, I am sorry for you, although I cannot help laughing. But didn't I tell you to have nothing to do with this subject?"

"And I have cast it aside."

"And how much labour, loss of nervous energy, how much vain lamenting now! I knew that it would not work out; and not because I foresaw that you would not find a model, but because the subject is unsuitable. One must have it in one's blood. One must be a descendant of those people who lived with Marat and Charlotte Corday, and those times. But what are you?—the mildest of well-educated Russians, lethargic and weak. One must be capable of doing such a deed oneself. But you! Could you, if necessary, throw away your brushes and—speaking figuratively—take up a dagger? For you this would be about as possible as a trip to the moon. . . ."

"I have often argued with you about this, Serge Vassilivich, and apparently you will never convince me, nor I you. An artist is an artist precisely because he can place himself in another's place. Was it necessary for Raphael to become the Blessed Virgin in order to paint the Madonna? It is absurd, Serge Vassilivich. However, I am beginning an argument, although I have said I don't wish to argue with you."

Bezsonow was going to say something, when he checked himself, and, with a gesture of the hand, said:

"Well, do as you like;" and, getting up from his chair at the table, began to pace from corner to corner of the room, making but little noise as he did so in his felt slippers.

"We will not quarrel about it. We will not irritate the sores of a secret heart, as somebody said somewhere."

"I do not think that anybody ever said that."

"Well, perhaps not; I usually misquote poetry. . . . What if we have the samovar in for consolation? It must be time."

He went to the door and shouted out, as if drilling a company of soldiers: "Tea!"

I disliked this manner of his with servants. For some time neither of us said a word. I sat buried in the cushions of the sofa, and he continued to pace from corner to corner. He was apparently thinking over something . . . and, finally stopping before me, he said, in a business-like tone :

"And if you had a model, would you try again ?"

"Oh, of course," I replied dismally ; "but where will you find her ?"

He again paced the room for a little while.

"Look here, Andrei Nicolaievich. . . . There is one person."

"If she is somebody important, she will not pose."

"No, she is not at all important—not at all. But . . . and I have a very big 'but' in connection with this matter."

"What kind of 'but,' Serge Vassilivich ? If you are not joking . . ."

"Yes, yes ; I am joking. It is impossible . . ."

"Serge Vassilivich . . ." I said, in an imploring tone.

"Listen to what I am going to say. You know that I have a high opinion of you," he began, standing still in front of me. "We are almost of an age. I am two years older, but I have lived and gone through as much as it will take you ten years and more, probably, to learn. I am not a nice man. I am bad and . . . immoral, depraved" (he rapped out each word). "There are many who are more so than I, but I consider myself more guilty. I hate myself for it and for not being able to be the clean-minded man I should like to be . . . like you, for instance."

"Of what sort of depravity and cleanness are you talking ?" I asked.

"I call things by their proper names. I often envy you your peace and clear conscience. I envy you for being what you are. . . . But it is all the same—impossible, impossible," he said to himself angrily. "We will not talk about it."

"If impossible, at least explain what or who I am," I replied.

"Nothing . . . no one. . . . But, yes, I will tell you.

Your cousin, Sophia Nicolaievna. She is not a very near cousin?"

"A second cousin," I replied.

"Yes, a second cousin. She is your fiancée," he said, in a positive tone.

"How do you know?" I exclaimed.

"I know. At first I guessed it, but now I know it. I found out from my mother. She wrote to me not long ago—and, besides, remember where she is. . . . Surely you know that in a provincial town everyone knows everything! Is it true that she is your fiancée?"

"Well, we will allow it is so."

"And from childhood? Your parents decided on it?"

"Yes, my parents arranged it. At first I regarded it as a joke, but now I see that it will take place. I did not want anyone to know this, and I am very sorry that you have found it out."

"I envy you for having a fiancée," he said quietly, his eyes taking on a far-away look, and he sighed deeply.

"I did not expect sentimentality from you, Serge Vassilivich."

"Yes, and I envy you because you have a fiancée," he repeated, not listening to me. "I envy you your cleanness, your expectations, your future happiness, your stock of as yet untouched love."

He took me by the arm, made me get up from the sofa, and led me up to a looking-glass.

"Look at me and at yourself," he said. "What are you? 'Hyperion before the goat-footed Satyr.' I am the goat-footed Satyr, and I am stronger than you. My bones are bigger and my health is naturally better. But compare us. Do you see this?"—he lightly touched his hair, commencing to get thin about his temples. "Yes, my dear fellow, all this ardour of the soul wasted in the wilderness. Yes, and what ardour it is! Simply . . . filth."

"Serge Vassilivich, let us get back to where we

started. Why do you refuse to introduce me to the model ?"

"Because she has taken part in this wasted ardour. I told you she is not an important person, and she most decidedly is not important—on the lowest rung of the human ladder. Below it is the abyss into which she perhaps will soon fall. The abyss is final ruin. Yes, and she has irrevocably perished."

"I am beginning to understand you, Serge Vassilivich."

"Ah ! Well, you see what kind of a ' but ' it is."

"You may keep that kind of a ' but ' for yourself. Why do you consider it your duty to act as my guardian and protector ?"

"I have said—because I like you, because you are clean—not only you, but both of you. You represent such a rarity, something fragrant and redolent of freshness. I envy you, and prize what I can see, even though I am but an outsider. And you wish me to spoil all this ! No, don't expect it."

"What, then, does all this amount to, Serge Vassilivich ? You cannot have much hope for the cleanness you have discovered in me if you fear such terrible consequences from a simple acquaintanceship with this woman."

"Listen ! I can give you this woman or not. I shall act as I think fit. I do not want to give her to you, and I shall not. *Dixi.*"

He sat down, whilst I excitedly walked about the room.

"And you think she is like ?"

"Very. But, no, not very"—he abruptly stopped—"not at all like. Enough about her."

I begged him, stormed, showed him the utter idiocy of the task he had taken upon himself of guarding my morals, but all in vain. He absolutely refused, and in conclusion said : " I have never said *dixi* twice."

"I congratulate you on the fact," I replied bitterly.

We talked only of trivialities over our tea, and then we parted.

IV

For a whole fortnight I did nothing. I went to the Academy merely to paint the programme picture, a terrible Biblical study—the turning of Lot's wife into a pillar of salt. Everything was ready—Lot and his family—but the pillar! I could not imagine it— whether to paint it as a sort of tombstone or a simple statue of Lot's wife made of rock-salt.

Life dragged along wearily. I received two letters from Sonia. I read her pretty prattle about life in the Institute—how she read secretly, evading the Argus-eyed class mistress—and I added her letters to the others, bound up by a pink ribbon. I had kept this ribbon for fifteen years, and up to the present had not been able to make up my mind to throw it away. Why throw it away? With whom did it interfere? But what would Bezsonow have said had he seen this evidence of my sentimentality? Would he again have gone into raptures over my "cleanness," or commenced to jeer?

However, it was no laughing matter which had vexed me. What was to be done? Give up the picture, or search again for a model?

An unexpected chance helped me. One day, as I was lying on my sofa, with a stupid translation of a French novel, and had lain there until my head ached and my brain reeled from stories of morgues, police detectives, and the resurrection of people who ought to have died twenty times over—the door opened, and in came Helfreich.

Imagine a pair of thin, rather bandy legs, a huge body crushed by two humps, a pair of skinny arms, high hunched-up shoulders, expressive of a sort of perpetual doubt, and a young, pale, slightly bloated, but kind-expressioned face on a head thrown well back. He was an artist. Amateurs know his pictures well. Painted for the most part on one subject. His heroes were cats. He has painted sleeping cats, cats with birds, cats arching their backs, even a tipsy cat, with merry eyes, behind a glass of wine. In cats he had reached the acme of perfection, but he never tried anything else. If in the picture there were certain accessories besides the cats—foliage, from out of which a pink-tipped nose with gold-coloured eyes and narrow pupils should appear, any drapery, a basket in which were a whole family of kittens with large transparent ears—then he used to turn to me. And on this occasion he arrived with something wrapped up in dark blue paper. Having given me his white, bony hand, he put the parcel on the table and commenced to unwrap it.

" Cats again ?" I asked.

" Again . . . You see, this one wants a little bit of carpet putting in . . . and in the other a corner of a sofa."

He unrolled the paper and showed me two not big paintings. The figures of the cats were quite finished, but were painted on a background of white canvas.

" Either a sofa, or something of that sort. . . . Invent it yourself. I am sick of it."

" Are you going to give up these cats soon, Simon Ivanovich ?"

" Yes, I ought to. They are hindering me very much. But what will you ? There is money in them ! For this rubbish, two hundred roubles."

And, spreading out his legs, he shrugged his already permanently hunched shoulders and threw out his hands, as if to express his astonishment that such rubbish found purchasers.

In two years he had obtained a reputation with his cats. Never before or since (with the exception of the late Huna) had there been such mastery in the depictment of cats of every possible age, colour, and condition. But, having devoted his attention exclusively to them, Helfreich had abandoned all else.

"Money, money . . ." he repeated musingly. "And why do I, a humpbacked devil, want so much money? And all the time I feel it is becoming harder and harder for me to take up regular work. I envy you, Andrei. For two years I have painted nothing but this trash. . . . Of course, I am very fond of cats, especially live cats. But I feel that it is sucking me drier and drier. And yet I have more talent than you, Andrei. What do you think?" he asked me in a good-natured tone.

"I don't *think*," I replied, smiling, "I *know* it."

"And what about your Charlotte?"

I waved my hand.

"Bad?" he asked. "Show me . . ." and, seeing that I made no move, he went himself and rummaged about in the heap of old canvases lying in the corner of the room. Then he placed the reflector on the lamp, put my unfinished picture on the easel, and lighted it up. He said nothing for a long time, and then exclaimed:

"I understand you. This might turn out all right. Only it is Anna Ivanovna. Do you know why I came here? Come along with me."

"Where?"

"Anywhere. For a walk. I am depressed, Andrei; afraid I shall again fall into sin."

"What nonsense!"

"No, it is not nonsense. I feel that something is already gnawing away at me here" (he pointed to the lower part of his chest). "I would fain forget and sleep"—he suddenly sang in a thin tenor—"and I have come here so as not to be alone. Once it begins, it will last a fortnight, and then afterwards I am ill. And, finally, it is very bad for me with such a body." And he turned himself round twice on his heels to show me both his humps.

"I tell you what," I suggested; "come and stay with me as my guest!"

"It would be very nice. I will think about it. And now come along."

NADEJDA NICOLAIEVNA

I dressed, and we went out.

We long sauntered along in the Petersburg slush. It was autumn. A strong wind was blowing from the sea, and the Neva had risen. We walked along the Palace Quay. The angry river was foaming and whipping the granite parapets of the Quay with its waves. From out of the blackness in which the opposite side had become hidden there came occasional spurts of flame, quickly followed by a loud roar. The guns in the Fortress were firing. The water was rising.

"I should like it to rise still higher. I have never seen a flood, and it would be interesting," said Helfreich.

We sat for a long time on the Quay, silently watching the stormy darkness.

"It will not rise any more," said Helfreich at length; "the wind seems to be dying down. I am sorry I have not seen a flood. . . . Let us go."

"Where?"

"Follow our noses . . . Come with me. I will take you to a place. Nature in a silly humour frightens me. Better to go and look at human folly."

"Where is it? Senichka?"

"I know. . . . Izvoschik!" he called out.

We got in and started off. On the Fontanka, opposite some gaudily painted wooden gates, decorated with carved work, Helfreich stopped the izvoschik. We passed through a dirty yard between the two-storied wings of an old building. Two powerful reflector lamps threw brilliant rays of light into our faces. They hung on either side of a flight of steps leading to the entrance, old, but also plentifully decorated with different coloured woodwork, carved in the so-called Russian taste. In front and behind us people were going in the same direction as ourselves—men in furs, women in long wraps of pretentiously costly material, silk-woven flowers on a plush ground, with boas round their necks, and white silk mufflers on their heads. All were making for the entrance, and, having gone up several steps of the staircase, were taking off their wraps, displaying for the most part pitiful attempts at luxurious toilettes, in which silk was half cotton, bronze took the place of gold, cut glass did substitute for brilliants and powder, carmine and *terre de sienne* took the place of freshness of face and brilliancy of eyes.

We took tickets at the booking-office, and passed into a whole suite of rooms furnished with little tables. The stifling atmosphere, reeking of strange fumes, seized me. Tobacco smoke mingled with the fumes of beer and cheap pomade. The crowd was a noisy one. Some were aimlessly wandering about, others were seated behind bottles at the little tables. There were men and women, and the expression on their faces was strange. They all pretended to be jovial, and were chatting away about something—what, goodness knows! We sat down at one of the tables, and Helfreich ordered some tea. I stirred mine with a spoon and listened, as, just alongside me, a short fat brunette with a gipsy type of face, slowly, and with a tone of dignity in her voice which betrayed a strong German accent and some pride, replied to a query from the young man with whom she was sitting as to whether she often came here.

" I come here once a week. I cannot come oftener, because I have to go to other places. The day before yesterday I was at the German Club; yesterday at the Orpheus; to-day here; to-morrow at the Bolshoi Theatre; the day after to-morrow at the Prikazchick; then to the operetta and the Château de Fleurs. . . . Yes, I go somewhere every day, and so the time passes, ' *die ganze Woche.*' . . ." And she proudly looked at her companion, who had already curled up at hearing so magnificent a programme of delights.

We got up, and began to stroll through the rooms. At the extreme end a wide door led into a hall for dancing. The windows had yellow silk blinds, the ceiling was a painted one; and there were rows of cane chairs along the walls; whilst in a corner of the hall there was a large white alcove, shell-shaped, in which the orchestra of fifteen men sat. The women, for the most part arm-in-arm, walked up and down the hall in pairs; the men sat on the chairs and watched them. The musicians were tuning their instruments. The face of the first violin seemed familiar to me.

"Is it you? Theodore Carlovich!" I asked, touching him on the shoulder.

Theodore Carlovich turned round towards me. My goodness! how flabby he had become! bloated and grey.

"Yes, it is I, Theodore Carlovich. And what do you want?"

"Don't you remember me at the Gymnasium? . . . You used to come with your violin for the dancing lessons. . . ."

"Ach! yes. And now I sit here on a stool in a corner of the hall. I remember you. . . . You waltzed very well."

"Have you been long here?"

"This is my third year."

"Do you remember how you came early, and in the empty room played Ernst's 'Elegy,' and I listened?"

The musician's bleary eyes glistened.

"You heard! you listened! I thought that no one heard. Yes, I could play once. Now I cannot. Here now, on all holidays. At the booths in the day-time, and night-time here. . . ." He remained silent for a bit. "I have four boys and one girl," he murmured quietly. "One of the boys finishes at the Anne Schule this year, and is going to the University. I cannot play Ernst's 'Elegy.'"

The leader waved his bâton several times, and the small but loud orchestra broke into a deafening polka. The leader, having marked the time three or four times, joined with his squeaky violin in the general noise. Couples began to revolve whilst the orchestra thundered,

"Come on, Senia," I said; "this is boring. Let's go home and have some tea, and talk of something nice."

"'Of something nice?'" he inquired, with a smile. "All right; let's go."

We began to push our way through towards the exit, when suddenly Helfreich stopped.

"Look!" said he. "Bezsonow!"

I looked, and saw Bezsonow. He was sitting at a marble-topped table, on which stood bottles of wine, glasses, and something else. Bending over, his eyes sparkling, he was whispering something in an animated manner to a woman dressed in black silk sitting at the same table, but whose face I could not see. I could only note her well-made figure, delicate hands and neck, and her black hair smoothly done up on the top of her head.

"Thank Fate!" said Helfreich to me. "Do you know who she is? Rejoice! That is your Charlotte Corday."

"She? Here!"

V

Bezsonow, holding a glass of wine in his hand, raising a pair of excited and very red eyes, saw me, and his face clearly expressed his dissatisfaction.

He got up from his place and came to us.

"You here? What has brought you here?"

"We came to look at you," I replied, smiling; "and I am not sorry, because, because——"

He caught my glance as it ran over his friend, and he abruptly interrupted me.

"Do not hope for this.... Helfreich has told you this.... But nothing will come of it. I will not allow it. I shall take her away...." And, briskly going up to her, he said loudly:

"Nadejda Nicolaievna, let us go.

She turned her head, and I saw for the first time her astonished face.

Yes, I saw her for the first time in this haunt. She

NADEJDA NICOLAIEVNA

was sitting here with this man who sometimes descended from his life of egoism and arrogant self-conceit to this debauchery. She was sitting behind an empty bottle. Her eyes were a little bloodshot, her pale face was worn, her dress was untidy and loud. Around us pressed a crowd of holiday-makers—merchants despairing of the possibility of living without drinking, unfortunate shopmen spending their lives behind counters and getting away from their wretched thoughts only in these haunts of fallen women, and girls whose lips had only just touched the horrible cup, a few young milliners' hands, and shop-girls. . . . I saw that *she* was falling into that abyss of which Bezsonow had spoken to me, if, indeed, she had not already fallen.

"Come along, come along, Nadejda Nicolaievna! Let us go," exclaimed Bezsonow impatiently.

She rose, and looking at him with surprise, asked:

"Why? Where?"

"I don't want to stop here. . . ."

"Well, then, you can go. . . . This, I think, is your friend and Helfreich."

"Did you hear what I said? Listen, Nadia . . ." said Bezsonow roughly.

She knitted her brows and threw a look of hate at him.

"Who gave you the right to talk to me like this? Senichka, old boy, how are you?"

Simon took her hand and gave it a hearty squeeze.

"Look here, Bezsonow," said he; "stop fooling. Go home if you want, or stay here; but Nadejda Nicolaievna will stay here with us. We have some business with her, and it is very important business. Nadejda Nicolaievna, allow me to introduce my friend, and his friend also," pointing to the frowning Bezsonow, "and an artist."

"How she loves pictures, Andrei!" suddenly said he to me in raptures. "Last year I took her to the Exhibition, and we saw your studies. Do you remember?"

"Remember?" she answered.

"Nadejda Nicolaievna!" said Bezsonow once again.

"Leave me alone. . . . Go where you like. I am going to stay here with Senia and this Mr. . . . Lopatin. I want to have a rest . . . from you . . ." she suddenly exclaimed, seeing that Bezsonow was going to say something more. "I am sick of you. Leave me alone. Clear out ! . . ."

He turned abruptly, and went off without saying a word to any of us.

"That's better. . . . Now he has gone . . ." said Nadejda Nicolaievna, giving a deep sigh.

"Why do you sigh, Nadejda Nicolaievna ?" asked Senichka.

"Why ? Because what is allowable for all these cripples "—with a movement of her head she indicated the crowd which surged around us—" is not allowable for him. . . . Well, never mind ; it is sickening and boring. No, not boring ; it's worse. There is no word for it. Senichka, treat me with something to drink."

Simon looked at me plaintively.

"You see, Nadejda Nicolaievna, I should be glad to, but I cannot ; he . . ."

"What about him ? He can drink with us."

"He will not stay."

"Well, then, you."

"He will not let me."

"That's bad. . . . Who can stop you ?"

"I have given my word that I will obey him."

Nadejda Nicolaievna looked at me closely.

"That's it, is it ?" she said. "Well, do as you like. If you don't want to, you needn't. I will drink by myself. . . ."

"Nadejda Nicolaievna," I began, "forgive me that at our first meeting . . ."

I felt the crimson rush to my cheeks. She smiled and looked at me.

"Well, what ?"

"That at our first meeting I ask you . . . not to do this,

NADEJDA NICOLAIEVNA

not to behave like this. . . . I wanted to ask you yet another favour."

Her face took a mournful expression.

"Not to behave like this?" said she. "I am afraid that I cannot behave in any other way. I have lost the habit. Well, all right; so as to please you I will try. And the favour?"

With a lot of stuttering and mixing up of my words I confusedly explained to her the matter. She listened attentively, fixing her grey eyes straight on me. Either the strained attention with which she listened to my words or something else gave her glance a stern and almost cruel expression.

"All right," she said at length. "I understand what you want. I will make my face like that."

"That will not be necessary, Nadejda Nicolaievna; only your face. . . ."

"All right, all right. When shall I come?"

"To-morrow at eleven o'clock, if possible."

"So early? Well, that means I must get to bed now. Senichka, will you see me home?"

"Nadejda Nicolaievna," said I, "we have not arranged about one thing: it cannot be done for nothing."

"What! you will pay me?" she said; and I felt that there was a ring of wounded pride in her voice.

"Yes, pay; otherwise it is off," said I decisively.

She threw a scornful, even insolent, glance at me; but almost immediately her face took on a thoughtful expression. We both kept silent. I felt awkward, whilst a faint flush showed on her cheeks, and her eyes glinted.

"All right," she said; "pay. Give me what other models get. How much shall I get altogether for Charlotte, Senichka?"

"Sixty roubles, I should think," he replied.

"And how long will it take to paint her?"

"A month."

"Good, very good!" she exclaimed vivaciously. "I will try to earn your money. Thank you!"

She put out her thin hand and firmly pressed mine.

"He is spending the night with you?" she asked turning to me.

"Yes, yes, with me."

"I will let him go directly he has seen me home."

In half an hour's time I was home, and five minutes later Helfreich returned. We undressed, laid down, and put out the candles. I had already begun to doze.

"Are you asleep, Lopatin?" suddenly sounded Senichka's voice through the darkness.

"No; why?"

"Because I would straight away give my left hand if only this woman was a good and pure one," said he in an agitated voice.

"Why not the right hand?" I asked sleepily.

"Duffer! How would I be able to paint then?" he asked me seriously.

VI

When I awoke the next day the grey morning was already looking in through the window.

Having glanced at the dimly lighted, pale, kind-looking face of Helfreich asleep on the couch, and having recalled the evening before, and that I had a model for my picture, I turned over on my side and again lapsed into a light early morning slumber.

"Lopatin!" resounded a voice. I heard it in my sleep. It accorded with my dream, and I did not awake, but somebody touched me on the shoulder.

"Lopatin! wake up!" said the voice.

I jumped to my feet and saw Bezsonow.

"Is that you, Serge Vassilivich?"

"Yes; you did not expect me so early?" said he quietly. "Speak softer; I do not want to wake up the hunchback."

"What do you want?"

"Dress, wash, and I will tell you. We will go into the other room. Let him sleep."

I collected my clothes under my arm, and, picking up my boots, went to dress in the studio. Bezsonow was very pale.

"You apparently did not sleep last night?" I asked.

"No, I slept; but I got up very early and worked. Tell them to give us tea, and we will talk. By the way, show me your picture."

"Not worth while now, Serge Vassilivich. But wait a bit; I shall soon finish it in its corrected and proper form. Perhaps it is displeasing that I have gone contrary to your wishes, but you would not believe how glad I am that I shall finish it, and that this has happened. Anyone better than Nadejda Nicolaievna I could not wish for."

"I shall not allow you to paint her," said he dully.

"Serge Vassilivich, you have apparently come here to quarrel with me."

"I will not allow her to be with you every day, to spend whole hours with you.... I will not allow her."

"Have you such power? How can you forbid her? How can you forbid me?" I asked, feeling my temper rising.

"Power ... power.... A few words will be sufficient. I will remind her what she is. I will tell her what sort of person you are; I will tell her of your cousin, Sophy Michailovna...."

"I will not allow you to make mention of my cousin.... If you have any right to this woman—even if it is true what you have told me of her; even if she has fallen; if tens of others have the same right as you to her—you may have a right to her, but you have no right to my cousin. I forbid you to mention anything about my cousin to her! Do you hear me?"

I felt that there was a threatening ring in my voice. He was beginning to exasperate me.

" Oho ! you are showing your claws ! I did not know you had any. Very well ; you are right. I have no rights whatever to Sophy Michailovna. I will not dare to take her name in vain. But this other . . . this . . ."

In his excitement he several times paced from corner to corner of the room. I saw that he was seriously upset. I did not know what was to be done with him. In our last conversation he had in words and tone expressed such undisguised contempt for this woman, and now . . . surely ? . . .

" Sergé Vassilivich," I said, " you love her !"

He stopped short, looked at me in a strange manner, and abruptly said :

" No."

" Well, then, what's the matter with you ? Why have you raised this storm ? I cannot believe that you are consumed with the rescuing of my soul from the claws of this imaginary devil ?"

" That's my business," said he. " But, remember, by hook or by crook I shall stop you. . . . I shall not allow it. Do you hear ?" he cried out hotly.

I felt the blood rush to my head. In the corner where I was standing at this moment there was a heap of odds and ends—canvases, brushes, a broken easel, and there was also a stick with a sharp iron tip, on to which a large umbrella was screwed for summer work. By chance I had taken this lance into my hand, and when Bezsonow said, " I will not allow," I drove the sharp end with all my might into the floor. The piece of iron went a vershok into the wood.

I did not say a word, but Bezsonow looked at me with puzzled and, it seemed to me, even frightened eyes.

" Good-bye," said he ; " I am going. You are over-irritated."

I had already succeeded in cooling down.

"Wait a moment," said I; "stop."
"No, I cannot. Au revoir."

He went. With an effort I pulled the lance out of the floor, and I remember I felt with my finger the slightly warm, bright piece of iron. For the first time it entered my head that this was an awful weapon, with which it would be easy to kill a man outright.

Helfreich went off to the Academy, and I waited calmly for my model. I put on an entirely new canvas, and made all the necessary preparations.

I cannot say that I thought then only of my picture. I recalled the evening before, with its strange setting, such as I had never previously seen, and the unexpected and, for me, happy meeting with this strange woman—this fallen woman, who at once attracted all my sympathy—and the strange behaviour of Bezsonow. . . . What does he want from me ? Is he really not in love with her ? If not, why this contemptuous attitude towards her ? Could he not surely save her ?

I thought of all this as my hand travelled over the canvas with the charcoal. Again and again I made sketches of the pose in which I wanted to place Nadejda Nicolaievna, only to wipe them out one after another.

Punctually at eleven o'clock the bell rang. A minute later she appeared for the first time on the threshold of my room. Oh, how well I remember her pale face when, in agitation and shamefacedly (yes, shame had replaced her yesterday's expression), she stood silently at the door ! She literally did not dare to come into this room where she afterwards found happiness, the sole bright ray in her life, and . . . destruction—but not that destruction of which Bezsonow spoke. . . . I cannot write about this. I will wait a little and get calm.

VII

Sonia does not know I am writing these bitter pages. She sits every day, as of old, near my bed or arm-chair. My other friend also often comes—my poor old hunchback. He has grown very thin, and has wasted away, and for the most part keeps silent. Sonia says he is working stubbornly. God grant him happiness and success!

She came, as she promised, punctually at eleven o'clock. She entered timidly, bashfully answered my greeting, and, without saying another word, sat down in an armchair standing in a corner of the studio.

"You are very punctual, Nadejda Nicolaievna," I said, squeezing some paints on to a palette.

She glanced at me, but did not reply.

"I do not know how to thank you for agreeing to sit," I continued, feeling myself turning red from confusion. I wanted to say something quite different to her. I had been so long unable to find a model that I had quite given up the picture.

"Are there really none at the Academy?" she asked.

"Yes, there are, only not suitable. Look at this face."

I took the picture of Anna Ivanovna from amongst the bundle of rubbish lying on the table, and handed it to her. She looked at it, and smiled faintly.

"Yes; she is not what you want," said she. "That is not Charlotte Corday."

"You know the history of Charlotte Corday?" I asked.

She glanced at me with a strange expression of surprise, mixed with some bitterness of feeling.

"Why should I not know?" she asked. "I have been to school. I have forgotten much now, leading this kind of life; but, for all that, I remember some things, and such things as the story of Charlotte Corday it is impossible to forget."

NADEJDA NICOLAIEVNA

" Where were you at school, Nadejda Nicolaievna ? "

" Why do you want to know ? If possible, let us begin."

Her tone suddenly changed. She spoke these words jerkily and gloomily, as she had spoken the night before to Bezsonow.

I said nothing. Having got out of a cupboard the dark-blue dress long ago made by me, the cap, and all the accessories of the costume of Charlotte Corday, I begged her to go into the next room and change. I had scarcely got everything ready when she came back.

Before me stood my picture !

" Ah, my goodness, gracious me ! " I exclaimed, with enthusiasm. " How grand it is ! Tell me, Nadejda Nicolaievna, have we not seen each other before ? Otherwise it is impossible to explain it. I pictured this subject to myself just exactly as you look now. I think I have seen you somewhere. Your face must unconsciously have impressed itself on my memory. . . . Tell me, where have I seen you ? "

" Where could you have seen me ? " she asked in return. " I do not know ; I never met you before last night. Begin, please. Put me as you want me ; paint."

I begged her to stand, arranged the folds of the dress, lightly touched her hands, giving to them that helpless position which I always pictured to myself, and went to the easel.

She stood before me. . . . She stands before me now, there on the canvas. . . . She is looking at me as if alive. She has the same sorrowful and thoughtful expression, the same tokens of death on the pale face as on that morning.

I wiped off all the charcoal from the canvas, and rapidly sketched in Nadejda Nicolaievna. Then I began to paint. Never before or since have I worked so quickly and successfully. The time flew by unnoticed, and only after an hour, when glancing at my model's face, I noticed that she was on the point of falling from fatigue.

"Forgive, forgive me . . ." I said, leading her down from the dais on which she was standing, and sitting her in a chair. "I have quite worn you out."

"Never mind," she replied, pale, but smiling. "If one earns one's living, one must suffer a little. I am glad that you were so engrossed. May I look?" said she, nodding her head towards the picture, the face of which she could not see.

"Of course, of course!"

"Oh, what a daub!" she cried. "I have never before seen the beginning of an artist's work. But how interesting! . . . And, do you know, even in this mess I see what it will be. . . . You have thought out a good picture, Andrei Nicolaievich. I will try to do all to make it a success . . . so far as it depends on me."

"What can you do?"

"I told you yesterday. . . . I will put on the expression. It will make the work easier. . . ."

She quickly went to her place, raised her head, dropped her white hands, and on her face was reflected all that I had dreamt of for my picture. Determination and longing, pride and fear, love and hate . . . all were there.

"Like that?" she asked. "If like that, then I will stand as long as you like."

"I do not want anything better, Nadejda Nicolaievna; but, surely, it will be difficult for you to keep up that expression for long. Thank you. We will see. It is still far from that. . . . May I ask you to have lunch with me?"

She refused for a long time, but at last consented.

My faithful old nurse, Agatha Alexeievna, brought in the lunch, and we for the first time sat at table together. How often did this happen afterwards! . . . Nadejda Nicolaievna ate little and kept silent. She was evidently embarrassed. I poured her out a glass of wine; she drank it off almost at a gulp. The crimson played on her pallid cheeks.

"Tell me," she suddenly asked, "have you known Bezsonow long?"

I did not expect this question. Recalling all that had passed between me and Bezsonow about her, I felt confused.

"Why do you blush? But never mind; only answer my question."

"A long time, since childhood."

"Is he a good man?"

"Yes, in my opinion he is a good man. He is honourable, and works hard. He is very talented. He behaves very well to his mother."

"He has a mother? Where is she?"

"In ——. She has a little house there. He sends her money, and sometimes goes there himself. I have never seen a mother more in love with her son."

"Why does he not bring her here?"

"Apparently she does not want to come. . . . But I do not know. . . . She has her house there, and is accustomed to the place."

"That is not true," said Nadejda Nicolaievna musingly. "He will not bring his mother here because he thinks she will be in the way. I do not know, but only think so. . . . She embarrasses him. She is a provincial, the widow of some small chinovnik. She would *shock* him."

She pronounced the "shock" bitterly and deliberately.

"I do not like the man, Andrei Nicolaievich," she said.

"Why? He is, all the same, a good fellow."

"I do not like him. . . . I am afraid of him. . . . Well, never mind; let us get to work."

She went to her place. The short autumn day was drawing to a close.

I worked up to twilight, giving Nadejda Nicolaievna a rest now and then, and only when the paints began to become mingled in their colours, and the model standing before me on the dais had already become merged in the darkness, did I lay down my brushes. . . . Nadejda Nicolaievna changed her dress and went.

VIII

The same day in the evening I moved Simon Ivanovich to my room. He lived in the Sadovaia Street, in a huge house filled from top to bottom with people, and occupying almost an entire block between three streets. The most aristocratic part of the house faced the Sadovaia, and was taken up with furnished rooms in the possession of a retired Captain Grum-Skjebitski, who rented out his quite large, but somewhat dirty, rooms to budding artists, the wealthier class of students and musicians. These formed the preponderating element of those lodging with the stern Captain, who was severely solicitous for the good name of what he called his "hotel."

I went up the iron staircase and entered the passage. From the first door came fleeting passages by a violin; a little farther on a 'cello was booming away; at the end of the corridor a piano was thundering. I knocked at Helfreich's door.

"Come in!" he called in a high voice.

He was sitting on the floor, and was packing his household goods into a huge case. A trunk, already corded, lay near it. Simon Ivanovich was stowing away things into the case without any attempt at system. At the bottom he had placed a pillow, on it a lamp, which had been taken to pieces and wrapped in paper; then followed a small leather cushion, boots, a bundle of studies, a box of paints, books, and all sorts of odds and ends. Alongside the case sat a huge ginger-coloured cat, which gazed into its master's eyes. This cat, according to Helfreich, was always on duty for him.

"I am ready, Andrei," said Helfreich. "I am very

glad you have come to fetch me. Tell me, was there a sitting to-day? Did she come?"

"Yes, yes; she came, Senia..." I replied, with triumph in my heart. "Do you remember in the night you said something about giving your left hand?"

"Well?" said he, sitting on the case and smiling.

"I understand you a little now, Senia...."

"Ah! Look here, Andrei, Andrei! help her out of it! I cannot. I am a stupid, humpbacked devil. You yourself well know that I cannot even drag through life, bearing only my own burden, without outside help—without you, for instance—and how could I support another? I am myself in want of rescue from darkness, of someone to take me, make me work, keep my money, paint baskets, couches, and all the setting for my cats. Ah, Andrei, Andrei! What should I do without you?"

And in an unexpected burst of tenderness Senichka suddenly jumped up from the case, ran towards me, seized my hands, and pressed his head to my chest. His soft silky hair touched my lips. Then he just as quickly left me, ran to the corner of the room (I have a strong suspicion that the dear chap brushed away a tear), and sat himself down in an arm-chair standing in the corner in the shadow.

"Well, you see, I am not fit for that. But you ... you—it is different. Take her out of it, Andrei."

I said nothing.

"There was yet another who could have done so," continued Simon Ivanovich, "but he was unwilling."

"Bezsonow?" I inquired.

"Yes, Bezsonow."

"Has he known her long, Senichka?"

"A long time—longer than I have. He is a man whose brain is nothing but compartments and drawers. He will open one, take out a ticket, read what is on it, and act in accordance. That is the way in which he saw this case. He sees a fallen woman, and immediately he refers to his brain (the compartments are alphabetically arranged), opens the drawer, and reads: 'They never return.'"

Simon Ivanovich said no more, but, resting his chin in his hand, thoughtfully looked straight ahead into space.

"Tell me how they got to know each other. What are the extraordinary relations between them?"

"Afterwards, Andrei; I will not begin now. And perhaps she will tell you herself. Not ' perhaps,' but for certain she will. You are that sort of man . . .." said Simon smilingly. Come along; I must settle with the Captain."

"Have you any money?"

"Yes, yes. The cats save me."

He went into the passage, called out something to a servant, and a minute later the Captain himself appeared. He was a sturdy, thick-set old man, very fresh-looking, with a smooth, clean-shaven face. Coming into the room, he bowed affectedly, and gave his hand to Helfreich; he made the same silent deep bow to me.

"What does the gentleman require?" he inquired courteously.

"I am leaving you, Captain."

"That is your business," he replied, elevating his shoulders. "I have been very pleased with you, sir. I am glad when well-behaved and well-educated people patronize my hotel. . . . The gentleman's friend is also an artist?" he inquired, turning towards me with a second and very exaggerated bow. "Allow me to recommend myself: Captain Grum-Skjebitski, an old soldier."

I put out my hand and gave him my name.

"Mr. Lopatin!" exclaimed the Captain, his face assuming an expression of respectful astonishment. "It is a famous name. I have heard it from all students at the Academy. Very happy to make your acquaintance.

I wish you the fame of Semiradsky and Mateik. . . .
Where are you going to ?" the Captain inquired of
Helfreich.

" To him . . ." replied Helfreich, smiling confusedly.

" Although you are taking an excellent lodger from
me, I do not regret it. Friendship has that right . . ."
said the Captain, again bowing. " In a minute I will
bring my book. . . ."

He went out, holding his head well up, with a somewhat
military gait.

" Where did he serve ? " I asked Senia.

" I don't know ; I only know he is not a Russian
Captain. I found that out from his passport. He is
simply dvorianin Kesari Grum-Skjebitski. He tells everyone in confidence that he was in the Polish Rebellion.
There is an old musket hanging on the wall of his room."

The Captain brought his book and accounts. Having
referred to them for two or three minutes, he informed
Helfreich of the amount owing for his board and lodging
up to the end of the month. Simon Ivanovich settled,
and we parted on very friendly terms. When they had
taken out all his belongings, Simon Ivanovich took the
ginger-coloured cat under his arm. It had for some time
been rubbing itself against his leg, holding its tail high
and stiff like a stick, every now and then giving a short
mew (probably the desolate look of the room alarmed
it), and off we started.

IX

Another three or four sittings passed by. Nadejda
Nicolaievna used to come to me at ten or eleven o'clock,
and remain until it was dark. Time and again I begged
her to stay and have dinner with us, but as soon as the
sitting was ended she invariably hurried off into the next
room, changed the dark blue dress for her black dress,
and left.

Her face changed greatly during these few days. A melancholy and wistful expression became noticeable about her mouth and in the depths of her grey eyes. She seldom spoke to me, and only brightened up a little when Helfreich, who continued—in spite of my efforts to make him take up something seriously—to paint one cat after another, sat in the studio at his easel. Besides his ginger model, some five or six cats of various ages, sex, and colour appeared from somewhere in our flat, which Agatha Alexeievna invariably fed, although she waged a never-ending war with them, consisting principally in taking several of them up under her arm and throwing them out on to the back-stairs. But the cats used to mew piteously at the door, and the soft heart of our faithful domestic could not withstand such appeals; the door would open, and the models again take possession of our flat.

How dearly I remember those long quiet sittings! The picture was nearing completion, and an indefinable feeling of depression was gradually stealing into my heart. I felt that when Nadejda Nicolaievna ceased to be necessary for me as a model we should part. I recalled my conversation with Helfreich on the day he came to live with me. Often when I looked at her pale, melancholy face, his words, "Ah, Andrei, Andrei, take her out of it," would ring in my ears.

Take her out of it! I knew almost nothing about her. I did not even know where she lived. She had left her old address, to which Helfreich escorted her the evening after our first meeting, and was living in another lodging, but where neither Senia nor I could discover. Neither of us knew her surname.

I remember once I asked her it at a sitting, when Helfreich was absent. He had gone that morning to the Academy (I made him go, if only rarely, to the study class), and we spent the whole day alone. Nadejda Nicolaievna was a little brighter than usual, and a little more talkative. Encouraged by this, I dared to say :

"Nadejda Nicolaievna, even now I do not know your surname."

She took no apparent notice of my question. An almost imperceptible shadow crossed her face, and for a second her lips compressed, as if something had taken her by surprise; then she went on talking. She spoke of Helfreich, and I saw that she was thinking of what to say in order to direct my attention and evade my question. Finally she stopped.

"Nadejda Nicolaievna," I said, "tell me why you do not trust me. Have I ever shown even . . ."

"Stop!" she replied sadly. "I not trust you! Nonsense. . . . Why should I not trust you? What harm can you do me?"

"Why do you . . ."

"Because it is not necessary. Paint, paint; it will soon be dark," she said, trying to speak more brightly. "Simon Ivanovich will soon be here, and what will you be able to show him? You have done almost nothing to-day. We spend the whole time in talking."

"It will be all right. . . . I am tired. . . . If you like, get down and rest a little."

She came down and sat on a stool which stood in the corner. I sat at the other end of the room. I had a wild longing to talk with her and question her, but I felt it was becoming more difficult with every sitting. I noted how she sat, bending forward and holding her knees with her hands, and her lowered eyes fixed on some spot on the floor. One of Senia's cats was rubbing against her dress, and looking up in a friendly way into her face, purring quietly and kindly. She seemed to have become frozen in this pose. . . . What was happening in that proud and unhappy soul?

Proud! Yes, it was no idle word which my pen has torn from me. At that time I already felt that her ruin had come from her refusal to bend. Perhaps, had she made some concession, she would have lived like the rest, would have been an interesting girl " with inscrutable eyes "; then she would have married and have become engulfed in the sea of a colourless existence side by side with her husband, occupied in some unusually important business in some service. She would have become a lady of fashion, have had her *jour fixe*, have educated her children (son at the Gymnasium and daughter at the Institute) ; she would have dabbled in " good works," and, going along the path ordained by the Almighty, would have given her husband an opportunity of making public on the next day in the *Novoe Vremia* his " deep affliction." But she had gone off the track. What had compelled her to leave the mapped-out life of a " decent woman " ? I did not know, and tormentingly endeavoured to read the reason in her face. But it remained immobile. Her eyes were all the time fixed on one spot.

" I have had a rest, Andrei Nicolaievich," she said, suddenly raising her head.

I got up, looked at her, then at the canvas, and answered :

" I cannot work any more to-day, Nadejda Nicolaievna."

She glanced at me, seemed about to say something, but refrained, and without a word went out of the room to dress. I remember I threw myself into an arm-chair and covered my face with my hands. An unintelligible longing feeling filled me ; a vague expectancy of something unknown and terrible ; a passionate longing to do something for which I could not account, and a tenderness towards this unfortunate being, together with a timorous feeling which possessed me in her presence—all this fused into one suffocating impression, and I do not remember how long I sat buried in almost complete oblivion.

When I came to myself she was standing before me, eady dressed in her own clothes.

"Au revoir."

I rose and gave her my hand.

"Wait a little.... I want to say something to you."

"What is it?" she asked anxiously.

"A great, great deal, Nadejda Nicolaievna.... Sit down, for goodness' sake, for a little, if only for once not as a model."

"Not as a model? What else can I be to you? God grant that if not a model, I may not be for you what I have been... what I am," she added hurriedly. "Good-bye. Will you soon finish the picture, Andrei Nicolaievich?" she asked at the door.

"I don't know.... I think I shall have to ask you to come to me for another two or three weeks."

She remained silent, as if unable to make up her mind to say what she wanted to say.

"Do you want something, Nadejda Nicolaievna?"

"Do any of your friends want a ..." she stammered.

"A model...?" I interrupted. "I will try to arrange it. I will do all I can, Nadejda Nicolaievna."

"Thank you. Good-bye."

I had barely stretched out my hand, when the bell rang. She turned pale, and sat down on a chair. Bezsonow came in.

X

He entered with a free and jaunty air. He seemed at first to have grown thinner the few days we had not seen each other, but after a few minutes I changed my opinion. He greeted me merrily, bowed to Nadejda Nicolaievna, who remained seated in her chair, and spoke with great animation.

"I have come to have a look. Your work interests me very much. I want to find out if you really can do anything now when you have a model better than which you cannot want."

He shot a glance at Nadejda Nicolaievna. She remained seated as before. I expected and wanted her to go, but she remained as if transfixed to her chair, and did not take her eyes off Bezsonow.

"That's true," I replied. "I do not want a better model. I am very grateful to Nadejda Nicolaievna for sitting to me."

Saying this, I moved the easel from the wall and placed it as it ought to be.

"May I look?" said he.

He devoured the picture with his eyes. I saw that it astonished him, and my author's pride was pleasantly tickled.

Nadejda Nicolaievna suddenly rose.

"Au revoir!" she said dully.

Bezsonow turned round impetuously, and made several steps towards her.

"Where are you off to, Nadejda Nicolaievna? I have not seen you for so long, and when I meet you almost by chance you apparently run away from me. Stop a little longer, if only five minutes more. We will go together and I will escort you home. I have not been able to find you. At your old lodging they told me you had left the town. I knew that wasn't true. I tried at the Inquiry Bureau, but they had not your address. I meant to ask again to-morrow, hoping that by this time they had your address, but now, of course, it is not necessary. You will tell us where you live, and I will see you home."

He spoke quickly and with a tenderness in his tone quite new and strange to me. How different this tone from that in which he had spoken to Nadejda Nicolaievna the evening I and Helfreich had chanced upon them.

"It is not necessary, Serge Vassilivich, thank you," replied Nadejda Nicolaievna. "I can get home by myself. I do not want any escort, and . . . with you," she added quietly, "I have nothing to talk about."

He made a movement of the hand as if he wished to

say something, but only a strange sort of noise came from his lips. I saw that he was restraining himself. . . . He made several paces, and then, turning towards her, said quietly :

" Go ! . . . If you do not need me, so much the better for both of us . . . perhaps for all three. . . ."

She went, giving my hand a slight squeeze, and we were left alone. Soon Helfreich arrived. I asked Bezsonow to stay and dine with us. He did not answer at first, occupied with some thought, then suddenly remembered himself and said :

" Dine ? Thank you. . . . I have not been here for a long time. I wanted to have a talk with you to-day."

And he did. At the beginning of dinner, he, for the most part, was silent or gave disjointed replies to Senichka, who talked without ceasing about his cats, which he must certainly give up, and about the necessity of taking up serious work ; but afterwards, perhaps under the influence of two glasses of wine, Helfreich's spirits infected him, and I must say that I never saw him so animated and eloquent as he was at that dinner and on that evening. Towards the end he entirely monopolized the conversation, and read us whole lectures on Foreign and Home politics. Two years of " leader " writing on every conceivable kind of question had made him capable of talking with absolute freedom on all those matters about which Helfreich and I, engaged in our studies, knew little.

" Simon Ivanovich," said I, when Bezsonow left, " I am sure Bezsonow knows Nadejda Nicolaievna's surname."

" How do you know ?" inquired Helfreich.

I told him of what had happened before he came in.

" Why did you not ask him ? But I understand, I know myself. . . ."

Why, indeed, had I not asked Bezsonow ? Even now I cannot answer that question. Then I knew nothing of the relations between him and Nadejda Nicolaievna ;

but even then an uncomfortable premonition filled me of something unusual and mysterious which was to take place between these two persons. I wanted to stop Bezsonow in his impassioned speech about opportunism ; I wanted to interrupt his dissertation as to whether capitalism was spreading in Russia or not, but every time the word died away on my tongue.

I told Helfreich this. I told him that I did not myself know what it was which prevented me from talking of her. There was something between them. I did not know what. . . .

Senichka said nothing as he paced the room ; then, going up to the dark window and gazing into the black space, replied :

" But I know. He despised her, and now he is beginning to love her. Because, you see. . . . Oh ! what a hard, egotistical and jealous heart this man has, Andrei !" he exclaimed, turning towards me and waving his arms. " Beware, Andrei ! . . ."

Jealous heart ? Jealous. . . . Of what can it be jealous ?

XI

From the Diary of Bezsonow.—Yesterday Lopatin and Helfreich met with me Nadia. Against my wish they became acquainted. This morning I went to Lopatin, and tried to stop their coming together, but could do nothing. They will see each other, will sit together for several hours every day, and I know how it will end.

I am trying hard to answer the question why I am taking such an interest in all this ? Is it not all the same to me ? Granted that I have known Lopatin many years, and sincerely sympathize with this talented youth. I do not wish him ill, but an intimacy with a fallen woman, who has passed through fire and water, is—a catastrophe, especially for such a pure nature as his. I have known this woman, comparatively speaking, for a long time. I knew her when she was already what she is. I must confess to myself that there was a time when I had a feeling for her, and when I was attracted by her not altogether ordinary appearance and, as I thought, her uncommon personality. I thought of her more than I should have done. But I quickly conquered myself. Knowing already for a long time that it is easier " for a camel to go through the eye of a needle " than for a woman who has tasted of this poison to return to a normal and honourable life, and watching the woman myself, I convinced myself that there were no guarantees in her that could make her an exception to the general rule, and with sorrow at heart I decided to leave her to her fate. Nevertheless, I continued to see her. I shall never forgive myself for the mistake I made that evening when Lopatin came to complain of his failure. I made a blunder when I told him that I knew of somebody who would make a good model. I do not understand why Helfreich never mentioned this to him. He has known her as long, if not longer, than I have.

My indiscretion and garrulity to-day have ruined the whole affair. I should have been milder. I even drew this soft-hearted man out of himself. He seized a kind of lance and drove it into the floor with such force that the window-panes rattled and I, seeing that he was irritated to the last degree, had to leave.

I have not seen Lopatin for several days. Yesterday I met Helfreich in the street and cautiously led the conversation on to his friend.

She goes there every day; the picture is progressing rapidly. How does she behave? Modestly, with dignity. Never says a word. Dresses in black, and poorly. Takes money for her sittings. Well, and Lopatin is very pleased at having found such a model. At first he was very lively, but now he is inclined to be thoughtful.

" I do not know, Bezsonow, why you are so interested

in all this," said the hunchback to me in conclusion. "You have never done anything for this woman, and there was a time when you could have easily saved her. . . . Now, of course, it is too late . . . that is too late for you. . . ."

Too late for you ! . . . Too late for you ! . . . What did he mean to say by this ? Was it not that, if too late for me, it is not too late for his friend ? Fools !

Nonsense ! And this Helfreich, who considers himself his friend, who knows better than I Lopatin's relations with his cousin-fiancée—and yet cannot he understand what troubles they are preparing ? They will not save this woman. Lopatin will break a loving girl's heart and his own.

I feel that I must, that I am in duty bound to do something. I will go to Lopatin to-morrow, and try to prove to him how far he has gone. And to-day I will go to her.

I have been, but did not find her in. She has gone no one knows where. They told me she had sold all her clothes. I tried to find her, but, notwithstanding the Inquiry Bureau and the efforts of the dvorniks, I could not find a trace of her. To-morrow I will go and see Lopatin.

I must abandon my former tactics. I have made a mistake with Lopatin. I thought from his softness of manner that I could adopt an authoritative tone with him. I must say that our former relations to a certain degree justified this opinion. I must, without touching him, work on this woman. There was a time she seemed to be a little interested in me. I think that if I make a certain amount of effort I shall separate them. Perhaps I shall reawaken in her the old feeling, and she will come to me !

Courting Nadejda Nicolaievna ! The idea is a wild one, even to myself, but I will not stop before it. I feel that I have no right to permit the fall of Lopatin and the ruin of his whole life.

This woman is laughing at me. I appealed to her with all the tenderness of which I am capable. I even, perhaps, spoke with her in a manner humiliating to myself, but she went off only saying insulting, contemptuous words.

She has changed marvellously. Her pale face has taken on a certain impression of dignity not at all in keeping with her " calling." She is modest and at the same time apparently proud. Of what is she proud? Looking intently at Lopatin's face, I thought I should read there the story of his relations towards her, but I can see nothing in particular. He is somewhat agitated, but apparently only about his picture. It will be a magnificent bit of work. She stands on the canvas as if alive.

I hid my rage, and, not showing that I felt insulted, remained with Lopatin and Helfreich. We talked, and they listened attentively to my opinions on various matters in which I am at present engaged.

But what is to be done? Let the matter go as it is? Once I gave Lopatin my word not to drag his cousin, Sophy Michailovna, into this business. Of course I must keep my promise. But may I not write to my mother? She sees Sophy Michailovna, although not often, and can tell her. I shall not be breaking my word, and at the same time. . . .

No, and such a matter as this cannot be left to run its own course. I have no right to do so. I will compel this woman, no matter what the cost, to give up her prey. . . . It is only necessary to find out where she lives. Then I will talk with her . . . and now I will leave all this and go on with my work. In the empty and colourless grinding mill we call life there is only one real absolute happiness—the satisfaction of the worker when buried in his labours. He forgets all the trivialities of life, and then, having completed his task, can say to himself with pride: " Yes, to-day I have done something beneficial and of use."

XII

Diary of Lopatin.—Six days have passed since the meeting between Bezsonow and Nadejda Nicolaievna, and she has not been. She merely wrote a few lines in which she begged me to excuse her, and mentioned something about some business.

I showed the note to Helfreich, and we both decided that she is ill. We must find her at all costs. If we knew her name, we could find her address at an Inquiry Bureau, but neither I nor he knew it. It was useless to ask Bezsonow. I was in despair, but Simon Ivanovich promised me to hunt her out " even if she were at the bottom of the sea." Getting up early the next morning, he dressed with as much care and determination as if he was starting on some dangerous expedition, and disappeared for the whole day.

Left alone, I tried to work, but the work wouldn't go. I took a book from a shelf, and began to read. The words and ideas passed through my brain without conveying any impression. I made every effort to devote my whole attention, and yet could not get beyond a few pages.

I shut the book—a clever and good book which a few days ago I had read, although with some difficulty, nevertheless with attraction and pleasure such as good reading always affords—and went out to stroll through the town.

A half-conscious, vague hope of meeting, if not Nadejda Nicolaievna herself, at least someone who could give me a hint about her, was present the whole time, and all the time I looked closely at the passers-by, and several times crossed over to the other side of the street when I saw a woman at all reminding me of her in appearance. But I met no one except Captain Grum-Skjebitski about four o'clock (it was the end of December, and already dark), who was walking along the Nevsky Prospect with a stately air of importance. It was very warm for the time of the year. The Captain was walking along in quite a smart fur, unbuttoned and opened about the neck. A flowered-silk tie with a bright tie-pin showed out from the fur. The Captain's tall hat shone as if polished, and in his hand, encased in a fashionable yellow glove with broad black stripes, he carried a big ivory-headed cane.

Seeing me, he smiled pleasantly in a patronizing way, and, making a gracious movement of the hand, came up to me.

" Glad to see you, Monsieur Lopatin," said he. " A very agreeable meeting."

He pressed my hand, and, in reply to my question as to his health, continued :

" Quite well, I thank you. Are you merely out for a stroll or hurrying somewhere ? If the former is the correct case, will you not walk a little with me ? I would willingly turn and go with you, but habit, Monsieur Lopatin ! I go for a walk daily, and take the Nevsky twice up and down. It is a law of mine."

I wanted to return home, and so turned and went with the Captain. He carried on a dignified conversation.

" This is the second pleasant rencontre to-day," said he. " I came across Mr. Bezsonow also on the Nevsky, and learnt that he is also a friend of yours."

" Wonderful, Captain ! So you know Bezsonow, too ?"

" Ask me whom I do not know !" replied the Captain, shrugging his shoulders. " When Mr. Bezsonow was a student he resided at my hotel. We were excellent friends, upon my word of honour. Who has not lived with me, Monsieur Lopatin ? Many now well-known engineers, jurists, and authors know the Captain—yes, very many famous people remember me."

And with this the Captain politely bowed to someone

who passed by rapidly with a preoccupied clever face. A look of perplexity was followed by a smile and a friendly nod of the head.

"He does not forget old friends, although he is now of high rank. That gentleman, Monsieur Lopatin, is the famous engineer, Petritseff. Also lived as student with me."

"And Bezsonow?" I inquired.

"Bezsonow is a very nice gentleman. Has a certain weakness for *les beaux yeux* of the fair sex . . ." added the Captain, stooping towards my ear.

I felt my heart beat faster. It struck me that the Captain must know something also of Nadejda Nicolaievna.

The Captain again bowed to some acquaintance, and continued:

"Yes, if he had not been such a very nice young gentleman, we should have quarrelled, Monsieur Lopatin; but I remember my own youth; besides, an old soldier even now is not indifferent to *les beaux yeux*."

He gave me a sidelong glance and winked, whilst his shrivelled-up little eyes became somewhat oily.

"Captain," I began, "I—I am very glad that you know Bezsonow. . . . I, you understand, did not know this."

"He only lived with me for a very short time."

"Was he acquainted . . ."

I suddenly became ashamed of myself. Something held my tongue, ready to utter the name of Nadejda Nicolaievna. I looked at the Captain. His eyes, which had suddenly changed their expression, were fixed intently on me. At this moment he resembled a vulture.

"But you probably do not know. Forgive me," I finished confusedly.

He looked at me, assumed a most unconcerned air, and flourished his stick.

"Yes, an old soldier has something to remember . . ." he continued, as if I had asked him nothing. "I am in my sixtieth," he added, mournfully shaking his head. " I must confess that I envy you, Monsieur Lopatin, but only your youth."

" Where did you serve, Captain ? " I inquired, remembering Helfreich's words.

The Captain once more became quite changed. His face became preternaturally serious. He glanced to the right and left, looked behind him, and, bending down so close that his moustache even brushed against my ear, whispered :

" Between ourselves, as gentlemen ! You see before you, Monsieur Lopatin, a warrior of Miekoff and Opatoff." And he stepped back a pace and looked at me in a manner which seemed to demand astonishment on my part. I made an effort to assume an expression suitable to the occasion.

" This is the secret which I confide only to my most intimate friends . . ." added the Captain, as again he bent down and again jumped back from me, regarding me with a triumphant look.

There was nothing left but to thank him for his confidence, and part as we had reached the " Police " bridge.

I was angry with myself. I had almost mentioned Nadejda Nicolaievna's name to this man, whom I did not trust in the least.

When I arrived home, Alexeievna informed me that " our cat man " had not yet returned. She served dinner and stood at the door, her face expressing keenest sympathy at my lack of appetite.

" What has happened, Andrei Nicolaievich, that she does not come ? " she asked.

" She must be ill, Alexeievna."

She shook her head, and, sighing deeply, went off to the kitchen to bring me my tea. It was long since I had dined without Helfreich, and I was very lonely.

XIII

After dinner they brought me a letter from Sonia.

I have never hid anything from her. When I die—which will be soon; even now death is not creeping stealthily towards me, but is advancing with a firm tread, the sound of which I hear clearly on sleepless nights when I am feeling worse, when I am racked with pain, and the past comes up before me—when I die and she reads this diary, she will know that I have never, never lied to her. I have written to her all I have thought and felt, and only that which I have not myself suspected as being in my soul, or have not acknowledged even to myself, but perhaps vaguely felt, has not found a place in my long letters to her.

But she understood me. Although but nineteen, her sensitive, loving soul understood what I did not dare to confess to myself, what I have never once said to myself in actual words.

"You love her, Andrei. God grant you happiness...."

I could not read further. A gigantic wave surged over me, overwhelmed me, and almost deprived me of consciousness. I leant back in the chair, and, holding the letter in my hand long, sat there motionless and with closed eyes, conscious only of this wave which was roaring and surging in my soul.

It was true. I loved her. I had not experienced this feeling up till now. I had described my attachment to my cousin as love. I was prepared in the course of a few years to become her husband, and perhaps should have been happy with her; I should not have believed it had anyone told me that I could love another woman. It seemed to me that my fate had been settled. "Here is thy wife," had said the Lord to me, "and thou shalt have none other." And in this I concurred, undisturbed for the future, and assured in my choice. To love another woman seemed to me an unnecessary and unworthy caprice.

And then came this strange, unhappy being, with her broken life and all her suffering in her eyes. Pity first possessed me; indignation against the man who had expressed his contempt for her made me still more inclined to take her part, and then . . . Then, I do not know how it happened . . . but Sonia was right. I loved her with the distraction and passion of the first love of a man who has reached twenty-five years of age without knowing love. I longed to snatch her from the horrors which were tormenting her, to take her in my arms somewhere far, far away, to fondle and press her to my heart, so that she might forget, so as to bring a smile on her suffering face. . . . And Sonia had said all this in one line of her letter. . . .

"Do not think of me. I do not want to say, forget me entirely, but only that you should not think of my suffering. I will not commence to complain of a broken heart—and do you know why? Because it is not at all broken. I have been accustomed to look upon you as a brother and future husband. The first was real; the second, I think, people thought of and arranged for us. I love you above all others in this world. I need not have written this, because you yourself know it, but when I read your last three letters and told myself the truth about you and Nadejda Nicolaievna—believe me, dear, I experienced not one atom of grief. I understood that I am a sister for you, and not a wife; I understood this from my own joy at your happiness—joy mingled with fear for you. I do not hide this fear, but God grant that you may save her, and be happy, and make her happy.

"From what you have written me of Nadejda Nicolaievna, I think she is worthy of your love. . . ."

I read these lines, and a new joyous feeling gradually took possession of me. I did not share Sonia's fears. What and why should I fear? How or when this happened I do not know, but I believe in Nadejda Nicolaievna. All her past life, of which I did not know, her fall—the only thing I knew of in her life—appeared to me as some accident, unreal, some mistake of Fate, for which Nadejda Nicolaievna was not herself to blame. Something had rushed at her, surrounded her, knocked her off her feet, and thrown her in the mud, and I would lift her out of this mire, would clasp her to my heart, and there calm this life so full of suffering.

A sudden furious ring made me jump, I do not know why, and not waiting for Alexeievna, shuffling along in her slippers to open the door, I rushed to it and pushed back the bolt. The door flew open, and Simon Ivanovich seized me with both hands, danced about, and cried out in a radiant, squeaky voice:

"Andrei, I have brought her, have brought her, brought her! . . ."

Behind him stood a dark figure. I rushed to her, seized her trembling hands, and commenced to kiss them madly, not listening to what she was saying in an agitated voice as she strove to restrain her sobbing.

XIV

We three long sat together on that, for me, memorable evening. We talked, joked, laughed; Nadejda Nicolaievna was calm, and even merry. I did not ask Helfreich where and how he found her, and he himself did not say a word about it. Between us nothing was said which hinted at what I had thought and felt before her arrival. I cannot say it was modesty or indecision on my part which kept me silent. It was simply I felt it unnecessary and superfluous. I feared to alarm her wounded soul. I had never been so talkative and merry. Helfreich displayed a kind of noisy enthusiasm, appeared radiant, chattered without ceasing, and sometimes compelled Nadejda Nicolaievna to laugh at his sallies. Alexeievna laid the cloth and brought in the samovar. When she had done so she stood in the doorway, and, resting one cheek on her hand, she looked at us all for a few minutes, and at Nadejda Nicolaievna, as she made the tea and did the hostess.

" Do you want anything, Alexeievna ?" I asked.

" Nothing, my dear ; I only want to look at you . . . and you are offended !" she said. " An old woman may not even stand for a minute. I was looking to see how the young lady would act as mistress. She does it very well."

Nadejda Nicolaievna bowed her head.

" See how well. Formerly only men came to you, who poured out the tea and did everything. Excuse me for saying so, Andrei Nicolaievich, but even I, to tell you the truth, missed there being no woman about."

She turned, and with short steps went along the passage. Our gaiety came to an end. Nadejda Nicolaievna got up and commenced to pace the room. My picture stood in the corner. These last several days I had not gone near it, and the colours had dried. Nadejda Nicolaievna looked at the picture for some time, and then, turning to me, said with a smile :

" Well, now we shall soon finish it. I will not give you any more of these breaks. It will be ready long before the Exhibition opens."

" How like you it is !" broke in Senichka.

She suddenly stopped still, as if some sudden thought prevented her speaking, and, with a frown on her face, went away from the picture.

" Nadejda Nicolaievna, what is the matter ? Frowning again ?" I said.

" Nothing in particular, Andrei Nicolaievich. . . . I really am very like this picture. It has come into my mind that many will recognize me—too many. . . . I can see how it will be. . . ."

She sighed, and the tears welled in her eyes.

" I am thinking of how many stories, questions, you will have to hear," she continued. " Who is she ? Where did he find her ? And even people who know will ask who I am, where did I come from. . . ."

" Nadejda Nicolaievna. . . ."

" You have not been ashamed of me, Andrei Nicolaievich, you and dear old Senichka ; you have treated me as a human being. . . . The first time for three years. And I could not believe it. Do you know why I left you ? I thought (forgive me for thinking it)—I thought that you were like the rest.

" The picture was coming to an end ; you had been polite and delicate with me, and I have got unaccustomed to such treatment, and did not trust myself. I did not wish to get a blow, because the blow would have been very painful, very painful to me. . . ."

She sat down in a big arm-chair, and pressed her handkerchief to her eyes. . . .

" Forgive me," she continued. " I did not trust you, and waited with terror for the moment when you would look upon me in the way to which I have become too accustomed during these last three years, because during these three years no one has looked at me in any other way. . . ."

She stopped ; her face twitched spasmodically, and her lips trembled. She gazed into the far corner of the room as if she saw something there.

" There was one, only one, who looked at me not like all those . . . and not like you. . . . But I . . ."

I and Helfreich listened to her with bated breath.

" But I killed him. . . ." she said in a scarcely audible tone, and a terrible access of despair seized her. A wail burst from her tortured breast, and a heart-rending, child-like sobbing resounded through the room.

XV

From the Diary of Bezsonow.—I am waiting to see what will happen. I was there the other day, and saw them together. All the strength of will I possess was insufficient to enable me to continue wearing my mask of indifference and politeness. I felt that had I stayed here another quarter of an hour I should have thrown it off and revealed my true self. It is impossible to recognize this woman. I have known her for three years, and have become accustomed to see her as she has been these three years. Now I see the change which has taken place in her, and I do not understand her, and do not know whether this change is genuine, or whether it is only a rôle being played by one accustomed to deceive herself and other contemptible beings.

I do not in the least understand their relations. I do not even know whether she has become his mistress. For some reason I do not think so, and if I am right she is more clever than I thought. What is her object ? To become his wife ?

I have read over these lines, and I see that all I have written is incorrect, except that she has altered. I myself three years ago saw something unusual in her, rarely met amongst women in her position. I myself almost took on the rôle of rescuer which Lopatin is now magnanimously playing. But I was more experienced then than she is now. I knew that nothing would come of it, and gave it up without even trying to do anything. Her character, besides the ordinary obstacles in this respect, possessed one peculiarity—her fearful stubbornness and impudence. I saw that she would wash her hands of everything, and oppose my first attempt, and I did not make this attempt.

Has Lopatin made it ? I do not know. I only see that it is impossible to recognize this woman. I know for certain that she has abandoned her former mode of life. She has gone to some little room into which she does not allow either Helfreich or her rescuer to enter. She sits for him, and, in addition, does sewing. She lives very poorly. She is like the drunkard who has signed the pledge. Will she keep it? Will this sentimental artist, who has not seen life and knows nothing of it, help her to keep it?

Yesterday I wrote mother a long letter. She is sure to do all, as I imagine she will—women love to meddle in such affairs—and will tell everything to Sophy Michailovna. Perhaps that will save him.

Save him! Why should I worry about his salvation? It is the first time in my life that I have concerned myself so deeply in other people's affairs. Is it not all the same to me what Lopatin does with this woman, whether he drags her out of the mire or sinks into it with her, and, in fruitless attempts, undoes his own life and casts aside his talents?

I am not accustomed to indulge in reflections or to dig into my soul; for the first time in my life I have been looking deeply into it and analyzing my feelings in detail. I do not understand what is taking place within me now, and what is compelling me to rouse myself. I thought (and now think) that it was only a disinterested desire to avert a great calamity from a man whom I like. . . . But upon analyzing my thoughts I see it is not altogether that. Why, in working to save him, do I think more of her? Why is it *her* face, once brazen and impudent, but now downcast and tender, which rises before me every minute? Why does *she* and not he fill my soul with a strange feeling which I cannot define, but in which unkind feelings predominate? Perhaps it is true that it is not so much that I wish to do *him* good as to do her . . .

What? Harm? No, I do not wish to do her harm, and yet I would like to tear her from him, to deprive her of his protection, in which lies, perhaps, her sole hope.

. . . Oh, surely it is not that I would like to stand in Lopatin's place!

I must see her to-day. This business won't let me work or live in peace. My work is being neglected, and these last two weeks I have not done as much as formerly I used to do in two days. I must put an end to it somehow, come to an understanding, and explain all to myself . . . and afterwards what?

Give her up? Never! All my pride rebels at the mere thought. I found her. I could have saved her, and would not. Now I would.

XVI

Diary of Lopatin.—Helfreich ran for the doctor who lived on the same landing as ourselves. I brought water, and she quickly got over her hysterics. Nadejda Nicolaievna sat in a corner of the sofa to which I and Helfreich had carried her, and only now and then quietly sobbing. I was afraid of upsetting her, and went into the next room.

Unable to find the doctor, Simon Ivanovich came back, and found her already quiet.

She decided to go home, and he declared his intention of escorting her. She pressed my hand, looking straight into my eyes with her own full of tears, and I noted a kind of timid expression of gratitude on her face.

A week, another, a month passed. Our sittings continued. To tell the truth, I tried to draw them out. I do not know if she understood that I was doing it intentionally. I only know that she constantly hurried me on. She became much calmer, and occasionally, but rarely, was quite bright.

She told me her whole history. For a long time I wondered whether I would write it here or not. And I have decided to say nothing of it. Who knows into what hands this diary may fall? If I could know for certain that only Sonia and Helfreich would read it, I should not talk of Nadejda Nicolaievna's past. They both know it well. I, as of old, have hid nothing from my cousin, and in my letters have written her the whole of Nadejda Nicolaievna's long and bitter story. Helfreich heard it all from her herself. Consequently her history in my diary is not necessary for him. As for others . . . I do not want others to judge her. She told me her whole life. I was her judge, and forgave her all which, in the opinion of men, required forgiveness. I listened to her painful confession and narrative of her misfortunes, the most dreadful misfortunes, such as only a woman can experience, and it was not accusation which stirred in my soul, but the shame and humiliating feeling of a man who feels himself guilty of the evil about which they are speaking to him. The last episode in her history filled me with horror and pity. Her words the evening that Helfreich found her were no empty ones. She really had killed a man unintentionally. He had wished to save her, but could not. His weak hands were not strong enough to restrain her from the brink of the abyss, and, unable to restrain her, he had hurled himself instead into the pit. He shot himself. Dry-eyed and with a kind of set determination, she related to me the whole of this awful history, and I long thought over it. Can her crushed heart come once more to life? Can such terrible wounds heal?

They did apparently heal. She became gradually calmer and calmer, and a smile was no longer a rarity. She used to come to me every day, and stayed to dinner. After dinner we three used to sit together for hours, and whatever the subject of conversation between Helfreich and myself, Nadejda Nicolaievna only occasionally put in a word.

I well remember one of these talks. Helfreich, without giving up his cats, had begun seriously to paint studies. Once he confessed that he was working so hard only because he had thought out a picture which he intended to paint, " perhaps in five, perhaps in ten years' time."

NADEJDA NICOLAIEVNA 213

"Why so far ahead, Senichka?" I asked, with an involuntary smile at the important way in which he had announced his intention.

"Because it is a serious subject — a matter of life, Andrei. Do you think that only tall people with straight backs and chests can think out serious subjects? Oh, you conceited hop-poles! Believe me," continued he, with an air of assumed importance, "that between these humps of mine great ideas can reside, and in this long box (he struck himself on the head) great ideas are born."

"This great idea—is it a secret?" inquired Nadejda Nicolaievna.

He looked at us both, and after a moment's pause said:

"No, it is not a secret. I will tell you. I have had this idea for a long time. Listen. Once upon a time Vladimir (Krasnoe Solnishko) became angry at the bold words of Ilia Murometz. He ordered him to be seized, taken away, and locked up in a deep vault, which was to be covered up with earth. They led the old Cossack away to death. But, as always happens, the Princess Evprakseiushka at that moment became "wise." She found out a way to Ilia, and used to send him bread each day, and water, and wax candles by the light of which to read the Gospel. And she sent him the Gospels."

Senichka stopped and thought, and was silent for so long that at length I said:

"Well, Simon Ivanovich?"

"Well, that's all. Of course, the Prince soon wanted the old Cossack. The Tatars came, and there was no one to save Kieff. Then Vladimir was sorry, bitterly regretted. Then Evprakseiushka sent people straightway to the deep vaults, and led out Ilia by the hand. Ilia did not bear malice, sat on a steed, and so on, routed the Tatars—and that's all."

"But where's the picture, Simon Ivanovich?"

Simon looked at me with an expression of exaggerated astonishment, and threw up his arms.

"Artist! Oh, artist! Oh, Lopatin, Andrei Lopatin! There are thirty, three hundred, three thousand pictures, if you want them, but I shall choose one only, and shall paint it. I shall die, but I shall paint it first! Cannot you see him sitting in the vault? Can you not see it as if real? Listen! the cave, vault, generally a burrow of some kind like the Kieff caves. The narrow approaches and the small niche in the wall. The dust and mildew, frightening and fantastic in the light of the wax candle. And Ilia sits on the steps, before him a desk, and on the desk there lies an old sacred book with thick, warped, yellowing leaves of parchment, inscribed with letters of black and red. The old Cossack is sitting in a shirt only, and is reading attentively, turning over the rebellious leaves of the book with his big, uncouth peasant's hands, accustomed to the campaign and lance, to the sword and to the cudgel. These hands have laboured much, and, from the hard work which they have performed all his life, they are tremulous, and with difficulty turn over the leaves of the sacred book. . . . Eh, my friend," suddenly said Helfreich in the middle of all this, "only one calamity: there were no such things as spectacles at that time. If there had been, Evprakseiushka would undoubtedly have sent him spectacles—huge round ones with silver rims. Perhaps he was long-sighted from life on the steppe? What do you think?"

We both laughed. Helfreich looked at us, surprised, and then, as if understanding why we laughed, himself smiled. But the solemn spirit of his narrative again took hold of him, and he continued.

"I will not begin to tell you what his eyes were like; that will be hardest of all to paint. But I can see it all— his eyes and lips. And so he sits and reads. He has opened the book at the description of the Sermon on the Mount, and he reads how, having received a blow, it is necessary to turn the other cheek. He reads this, and does not understand. Ilia has worked without ceasing all his life. He has destroyed a mighty number of Pechenegs and Tatars and brigands. He has conquered many knights of old. He has passed a century in valorous deeds and in artifices, so that evil should not befall Christianized Russ, and he believed in Christ, and prayed to Him, and believed that he was fulfilling Christ's teaching. He did not know what was written in the book. And now he sits and ponders. ' " Whosoever shall smite thee on thy right cheek, turn to him the other also." How can this be ? O Lord ! is it good if they shall strike me, insult a woman, or touch a child, or if the pagans shall come and commence to rob and kill Thy servants, O Lord ? Not to touch them ! To let them kill and plunder ? No, Lord, I cannot obey Thee. I will get astride a steed, lance in hand, and will go out to fight in Thy name, because I do not understand Thy wisdom. Thou hast put a voice into my soul, and I listen to it, and not to Thee ! . . .' And his hand trembles, and the yellow page with its red and black lettering trembles in it. The candle burns dimly ; above it a thin black streak rising from the wick vanishes into the darkness, and only Ilia and his book—only these two are lighted by this light. . . ."

Simon Ivanovich stopped and pondered, having thrown himself back into his chair with his eyes raised to the ceiling.

"Yes," I said, after a long silence, " it is a good picture, Senichka. Only it is easier to narrate than to paint in oils on a canvas. How will you express all this ?"

"I will, without a doubt ; I will do this—all this," Senichka cried with warmth. "Yes, I will paint it. I will put this note of interrogation. Ilia and the Gospel ! What is there common between them ? For this book there is no greater sin than murder, and Ilia has killed all his life, and journeys on his war-steed all hung around with weapons of slaughter—not murder, but execution, because he executes. And when this arsenal is insufficient, or he has not got it with him, he puts sand in his cap, and uses that as a weapon. And he is a saint. I saw him in Kieff. . . . He lies amongst them all, and justly so."

"That is all right, Senichka, but I cannot help saying the paints will not express all this."

"Why not ? Bosh ! And even if they do not, what harm ? They will ask the question. . . . But wait, wait a minute," broke in Senichka excitedly, seeing I wanted to say something. "You will say that the question is already put ? Quite true ! But that is little. It is necessary to put it every day, every hour, every second. People must not be allowed peace. And if I think that I shall succeed in making even ten people think of this question, I must paint this picture. I have long thought of it, but all these have prevented me."

And he leant forward, and, bending down, picked up the ginger cat, which was sitting on the carpet near him, and had seemingly listened attentively to his speech, and placed it on his knee.

"Would you not surely do the same ?" continued Senichka. "Your picture, surely, is it not the same question ? Do you really know if this woman did right ? You will make people think—that's the whole point. And, apart from the æsthetic feeling which every picture arouses, and which of itself is not worth much—is not this the idea which animates our work ?"

"Simon Ivanovich, my dear fellow," said Nadejda Nicolaievna suddenly, " I never saw you like this before. I always knew that you had a most kind heart, but . . ."

"But you thought that I was a fool of a hunchback ? Do you remember you called me that once ?"

He looked at her, and, perhaps seeing the shadow on her face, added :

"Forgive me for recalling that. Those years must be wiped out of memory. All will go well. It is true, Andrei, is it not ? All will go well ?

I nodded my head. I was very happy then: I saw that Nadejda Nicolaievna was little by little becoming calmer, and—who knows?—perhaps her life for the last three years will become for her nothing more than a distant recollection, not of years lived through, but only a vague and distressing dream, after which, having opened her eyes and seeing that the night is quiet and that all is as usual in the room, she rejoices that it was only a dream.

XVII

The winter passed. The sun rose higher and higher in the heavens, and with ever-increasing strength warmed the streets and roofs of St. Petersburg. Everywhere water was pouring down all the spouts; bits of ice with the noise of thunder came jumping out of them on to the pavements, or into the buckets put to catch them; droshkies appeared rattling along the roads, now bare of snow in places, with a familiar but strangely new sound to the ear.

I have finished my picture. A few more sittings, and it will be possible to take it to the Academy before the Court of Exhibition experts. Helfreich has congratulated me already on my success. Nadejda Nicolaievna is delighted. Looking at the picture and at her face, I often see an up to this time unfamiliar expression on it of quiet satisfaction. Sometimes she has been even gay, and has joked—for the most part with Senichka, who is engrossed in the reading of numerous books which he says he must read for his picture, in looking at albums, at all sorts of antiquities, and in studying the Gospels. His cats have gone. Only the faithful ginger cat has stayed on, and even he lives in peace, almost undisturbed by his master, and uncalled upon to act as a model. Since our conversation about Ilia Murometz, Simon Ivanovich has only painted one cat picture, and, having sold it for a hundred and fifty roubles, considers himself assured of money for a long time—the more so that he, to my great astonishment, is not the least embarrassed with his long stay in my flat, where living costs him nothing.

We three spent almost all our spare time together. Helfreich managed to get Nadejda Nicolaievna an enormous manuscript containing a scheme by some important person —a scheme by which Russia must be loaded with benefits in a very short time—and she has copied it out in a dainty large hand. As this benefiting of Russia demanded a large amount of thinking, the scheme has been amended and supplemented without end, and, it seems, has not even now been completed. Somebody is probably copying it now after Nadejda Nicolaievna!

At any rate, she had a little money. What she earned by copying, and the money she received from me for her sittings, sufficed her. She lived in the same little room to which she had changed when she hid from us. It was a narrow, low room, with one window looking out on to a blank wall. A bedstead, chest of drawers, two chairs, and a card-table, which did duty as a writing and dining table, made up its furniture. When we used to go and see her, Senichka would go to the kitchen and beg a stool for himself from the landlady. But we seldom visited her. The room, which nothing could induce Nadejda Nicolaievna to leave, was uninviting and gloomy, and we seldom went there. For the most part, we forgathered in my rooms, which were spacious and light.

I never once spoke to her of what was passing in my mind. I was calm and happy in the present. I understood that any incautious reference to her, perhaps still open, spiritual wounds would reflect painfully on her. I might lose her for ever if I insisted now in carrying out my secret idea, wish, and hope. Perhaps I could not have behaved so quietly and restrained myself so long had not this hope been so strong. I firmly believed that after another six months, a year, or even two (I was not afraid of time), when she had become calm and restored

NADEJDA NICOLAIEVNA

to health, she would see around her a firm support on which she could lean and would become mine for life. I even did not hope, I actually knew she would be my wife.

I do not know if she used to see Bezsonow. . . . He came occasionally to me, upsetting our tranquillity and introducing an awkwardness into our conversation. Apparently he was calm, and looked upon Nadejda Nicolaievna with indifference. She did not talk to him, although she answered his questions and listened to his long dissertations on the most varied subjects. He was very well read and spoke well. Somehow it seemed to me that he was so talkative and instructive in order to hide from us something concealed behind the flow of speech which would not give him peace. Subsequently I knew that this was so, and that under his outward calm he was hiding the mortal ulcer which was killing him, just as that French priest of reputed invulnerability used to wear a red cloak in battles, so that the blood which used to pour from his wounds should not be seen. But when I found this out it was already too late.

For some reason he again went to live with the Captain. I went there once. His new room, like his old one, was all littered with books, newspapers, and papers, but it seemed to me that they all lay in great disorder and covered with dust, as if it was long since anyone had put a finger to work. I felt an intruder, and decided not to go any more to him. I asked him, by the way, whether he knew anything of the Captain, and was it true that he was a " hero of Miekoff and Opatoff."

" He is inventing," said Bezsonow. " He is really half a Pole. He became Orthodox long ago. I think he simply wishes to impress young fellows when he discloses this sham secret."

I came away from Bezsonow. Soon afterwards two incidents opened my eyes to his behaviour.

First, Sonia wrote me a letter describing the plot between Bezsonow and his mother. The old lady used sometimes to go to the Institute on visiting days, remembering the interest which Sonia's mother had taken in her and her son. According to my cousin, on this occasion she arrived in an agitated and mysterious state, and, after a few preliminary remarks, disclosed the reason of her visit. Serge Vassilivich had written to her all details of what was happening. He could not find words with which to paint the position of affairs as black as he wished. He had *not asked* his mother to inform Sonia of the contents of the letter, but the old woman herself, out of a feeling of gratitude, had decided to come and tell her everything in order to warn her so that she might act whilst it was yet possible to save me. The old lady was very surprised when she found out my cousin knew all. She was much upset. She, as an old woman, was ashamed to talk of such things to a young girl still at an Institute, but what was to be done ? The unhappy Andrusha must be saved at all costs. If she were Sonia, she would leave the Institute at once and go to St. Petersburg in order to open my eyes.

" Serge Vassilivich," wrote Sonia, " is playing some strange part in all this story. I do not believe he wrote all this to his mother without knowing that she would infallibly tell me all; and, I will go further, he hoped she would tell me.

" I will come to St. Petersburg, but only after the examinations. If you are agreeable, we will pass the summer somewhere together in a dacha, and I will do a little work, so that it will not be too hard for me when I begin my studies."

This letter upset me, but when I received a second long anonymous epistle, it was more than I could stand.

In high-flown, florid sentences, the anonymous author warned me against the doleful fate of all young people who give themselves up blindly to their passions, not discriminating between the qualities and deficiencies of the being with whom they are intending to enter into alliance—" the fetters of which are light and unnoticeable at the commencement, but which subsequently become converted into a heavy chain resembling that which unfortunate galley-slaves drag." This was the style in which the unknown author of the latter expressed himself. " Believe the kindly meant word of an older and more experienced man, Mr. Lopatin." Then followed a whole indictment against " Nadejda," whose soul was characterized as " booty for the stove " (an expression from which I conclusively recognized the hand of the Captain). She was accused of a long life of vice which she could have left had she chosen, " because she has relatives, albeit very distant ones, who—I am convinced of this—would have rescued her from her fallen social position ; but her natural bent is vicious ; she preferred to wallow in the mire from which you, in vain hope to save her, and into which, without doubt, you will yourself fall, and lose your life and wonderful talent." She was accused of the murder of a man, " also very correct, not distinguished by talents such as you possess, but a first-rate man, receiving fifty roubles a month salary, and having a prospective increase of salary which would have been sufficient for both to live on, because what could such a creature as this contemptible being rely on ? However, her nature was such that she preferred to reject the marriage offers of this young man, Mr. Nikitin, so as to be free to continue her vile life."

The letter was a very long one, and before I came to its end I had thrown it into the stove. That Bezsonow had had a share in this appeared to me undoubted. Why otherwise should the Captain bother about my soul's salvation ? All the blood rushed to my head, and my first impulse was to rush to Bezsonow. I do not know what I should have done to him. I did not bother about the Captain. This renegade hiding his treason had been talked over, bought over with drink perhaps, or frightened into it by some means. I seized my hat, and was already at the door, when I recovered myself. It would be better to calm down, and then decide upon what to do.

I decided in this sense, and, whilst waiting for Nadejda Nicolaievna, tried to paint in some of the accessories of the picture, thinking by this means to calm myself down for work, but my brush jumped about the canvas, and my eyes did not see the paints. I dressed so as to go out and get a breath of fresh air. As I opened the door, I found Nadejda Nicolaievna standing in front of me, pale, breathless, with a terrified expression in her wide-opened eyes.

XVIII

From Bezsonow's Diary.—Heartsick and longing ! This sickness of heart is persecuting me, no matter where I am or what I may do in order to forget, to appease it by some means or other. My eyes have at last opened. A month has gone by, and in this month all has been settled. What has become of my boasted philosophic tranquillity ? Where are my sleepless nights passed in work ? I, the same I who prided myself on possessing character in our characterless time, have been crushed and destroyed by the storm which has rushed on me. . . . What storm ? Is it really a storm ? I despise myself. I despise myself for my former pride, which did not prevent me from giving way to an empty passion. I despise myself for having allowed this devil in the shape of a woman to take possession of my soul. Yes, if I believed in the supernatural, I could in no other way explain what has happened.

I have read over these lines. . . . What humiliating, pitiful wails ! Oh, where art thou, my pride ? Where is that strength of will which made it possible for me to break myself, and live, not as life willed, but as I wished to live ? I have lowered myself to petty intrigue. I wrote to my mother, and she, without doubt, told all I wanted told to his cousin, and nothing has come of it ;

NADEJDA NICOLAIEVNA

impatiently, I made an old fool write an illiterate letter to Lopatin—and I know nothing will come of this. He will throw the letter into the fire, or, still worse, will show it to her, his mistress, and they will read it together, make fun of the illiterate effusions of the Captain's soul, and will jeer at me because they will understand that no one but I could have urged the Captain to commit this idiotic act.

His mistress ? Is she ? The word was torn from me, but I do not know whether it is true. And if untrue ? Is there still any hope for me ? What makes me think that he has fallen in love with her, excepting vague suspicion roused by mad jealousy ?

Three years ago everything was possible and easy. I lied in this very diary when I wrote that I gave her up because I saw it was impossible to save her. Or, if I did not lie, I deceived myself. It would have been easy to save her. It only meant bending down to pick her up, but I would not stoop. I understand this only now, when my heart is aching with love for her. Love ! No, it is not love ; it is more : it is a raging passion, a fire which is consuming me. How shall I extinguish it ?

I will go to her. I will collect all my forces and speak calmly. Let her choose between him and me. I will only speak the truth. I will tell her that it is impossible to rely on this impressionable fellow, who to-day is thinking of her, and to-morrow will be engrossed with something else and will forget her. I will go ! One way or the other this must come to an end. I am too worn out, and cannot. . . .

The same day.

I have been to her. I am going to him directly.

These are the last lines which will be written in this diary. Nothing can hold me back. I have no control over myself. . . .

XIX

Lopatin's Notes.—Why drag it out any longer ? Is it not better to end my reminiscences in these lines ?

No, I will write them to the end. It is all the same ; if I throw down my pen and this diary, that awful day will be lived by me a thousand times. For the thousandth time I am experiencing the horror and torment of conscience and the agony of loss ; for the thousandth time the scene of which I am going to write now will pass before my eyes in all its details, and each detail will lie on my heart with fresh, awful emphasis. I will go on to the very end.

I led Nadejda Nicolaievna into the room. She could scarcely stand, and was trembling as if in a fever. She gazed at me all the time with the same frightened glance, and for the first minute could not utter a word. I sat her down and gave her some water.

" Andrei Nicolaievich, beware ! Lock the door ! . . . Let no one come in. He will be here in a minute."

" Who ? Bezsonow ?"

" Lock the doors !" she gasped.

Rage possessed me. It was not sufficient to write anonymous letters ; he had resorted to violence.

" What has he done to you ? Where have you seen him ? Calm yourself. Drink some more water, and tell me. Where did you see him ?"

" He has been to see me."

" For the first time ?"

" No, not for the first time. He has been twice before. I did not want to tell you, so as not to upset you. I begged him to stop coming to me. I told him it distressed me to see him. He said nothing, and went, and for three weeks did not come near me. To-day he came early, and waited until I had dressed. . . ."

She stopped. It was difficult for her to continue.

" Well, and further ?"

" I have never seen him before like he was. He began

by speaking quietly. He spoke of you. He said nothing bad about you, only that you were impressionable and fickle, and that I could not rely on you. He said straight out that you would throw me aside because you would tire of me. . . ."

She stopped and began to cry. Oh, never was I possessed with such love and pity for her. I took her cold hands and kissed them. I was madly happy. Words flowed without restraint from my lips. I told her I would love her for life, that she must be my wife, and that she would see and know that Bezsonow was wrong. I spoke a thousand senseless words—words of delirious happiness for the most part, having no outward sense— but she understood them. I saw her dear face, radiant with happiness, resting close to my heart. It was an entirely new, somewhat strange face—not the face with a secret suffering writ on its features that I had been accustomed to see.

She laughed and cried, and kissed my hands, and pressed towards me. And at that moment the world held only us two. She spoke of her good fortune, and how she had loved me from the very first meeting, and had run away from me frightened at this love. She declared she was not worthy of me, that it terrified her that I should link my fate with hers, and she again embraced me, and again shed tears of joy and happiness. Finally she sobered down.

" But Bezsonow," she said suddenly.

" Let Bezsonow come," I replied. " What has Bezsonow got to do with us ?"

" Wait ; I will finish what I began to tell you of him. Yes, he spoke of you, then of himself. He said he was a far more hopeful support than you. He reminded me that three years ago I loved him and would have gone with him, and when I told him he was deceiving himself his whole pride blazed out, and he so lost control of himself that he rushed at me. . . . Wait, wait," said

Nadejda Nicolaievna, seizing me by the hand as I jumped to my feet ; " he did not touch me. . . . I am sorry for him, Andrei Nicolaievich . . . he threw himself at my feet, this proud man. If only you had seen him !"

" What did you say to him ?"

" What was there to say ? I was silent. I could only tell him that I did not love him, and when he asked me if it was because I loved you, I told him the truth. . . . Then something strange came over him, which I could not understand. He rushed at me, clasped me to himself, and whispered " Good-bye, good-bye," and went to the door. I have never seen such an awful face. I fell into a chair. At the door he turned, and, smiling strangely, said, ' But I shall see you with him,' and his face was so awful. . . ."

Suddenly she stopped speaking and turned deadly pale, fixing her eyes on the door of the studio. I turned round. In the doorway stood Bezsonow.

" You did not expect me ?" he said stammeringly. " I did not disturb you, and came in by the back entrance."

I jumped to my feet and faced him. We stood for some time like this, measuring each other with our eyes. He was indeed a terrifying spectacle. He was white, his bloodshot eyes, full of raging hate, were fixed on me. He said nothing, but his thin lips trembled, and seemed to be whispering something. Suddenly a wave of pity for him swept over me.

" Serge Vassilivich, why did you come ? If you want to talk to me, come along and calm yourself."

" I am quite calm, Lopatin. . . . I am ill, but calm. I have already decided, and I have nothing to excite me."

" Why have you come ?"

" To say a few words to you. You imagine you will be happy with her ?" With a wave of his hand, he pointed to Nadejda Nicolaievna. " You will not be happy ! I will not allow it."

" Leave this place," said I, making tremendous efforts

to speak quietly. " Go away—go and rest. You yourself say you are unwell."

" That's my business. Listen to what I am going to tell you. I have made a mistake. . . . I am to blame. I love her. Give her to me."

" He has gone out of his mind," flashed through my mind.

" I cannot live without her," he continued in a dull, hoarse voice. " I will not leave you until you say ' Yes.' "

" Serge Vassilivich !"

" And you will say ' Yes,' or . . ."

I took him by the shoulders and turned him towards the door. He went quietly, but when we reached the door, instead of taking hold of the handle, he turned the key in the lock, then, with a sudden violent movement, threw me off and stood in a threatening pose. Nadejda Nicolaievna gave a shriek.

I saw him transfer the key from his right hand into his left, and put his right hand into his pocket. When he drew it out, something glistened in it which I had not time to name. But its sight terrified me. Not knowing what I was doing, I seized the lance standing in the corner, and when he pointed the revolver at Nadejda Nicolaievna, I rushed at him with a wild yell. Everything reverberated with a terrific report. . . .

Then the slaughter began.

I do not know how long I lay unconscious. When I came to I remembered nothing, only that I was lying on the floor, that I could see the ceiling through a strange dove-coloured mist, that I felt there was something in my chest preventing me from moving or speaking—all this did not astonish me. It seemed to me that it was all a necessary part of some matter which had to be done, but what I could not in any way remember.

The picture ! Yes. Charlotte Corday and Ilia Murometz. . . . He is sitting and reading, and she is turning the leaves for him and laughing wildly. . . . What nonsense ! . . . It is not that ; that is not the question about which Helfreich is speaking.

I make a movement, and feel great pain. Of course, that is as it should be—otherwise is impossible.

Absolute quiet. A fly is buzzing in the air, and then bumps itself against the window-pane. The double windows have not yet been taken out, but through them comes the rattle of the droshkies passing along the street. The faint smoke clears away before my eyes—a strange bluish smoke—and I see clearly on the ceiling a coarsely modelled rosette round the hook for a candelabra. I think that this is a very strange ornament. I have never noticed it before. And somebody is touching my arm. I turn my head and see somebody's hand—a little soft white hand lying on the floor. I cannot get at it, and I am dreadfully sorry, because this is Nadia's hand, whom I love more than anybody or anything else in the world. . . .

And suddenly a bright gleam of consciousness illuminates me, and in a flash I remember all that has happened. . . . He has killed her.

Impossible ! Impossible ! She is alive. She is only wounded. " Help ! help !" I cry, but no sound is heard. Only a kind of gurgling in my chest which chokes me, and a rosy froth collects on my lips. He has killed me also.

Collecting my strength, I raised myself and looked at her face. Her eyes were closed and she was motionless. I felt how the very hair on my head moved. I wanted to become unconscious. I fell on her breast, and commenced to smother with kisses the face which but half an hour ago had been full of life and happiness, and had so confidingly snuggled to my heart. Now it was still and severe. The blood had already ceased to trickle from a little wound over one eye. She was dead.

When they burst open the door and Simon Ivanovich rushed towards me, I felt that I was at my last gasp. They lifted me up and placed me on the sofa. I saw how they took hold of her and carried her out. I wanted to cry out, to beg, implore them not to do it, but to leave her alongside me. But I could not cry out. I only noiselessly whispered whilst the doctor examined my chest, through which a bullet had passed.

They took him out. He lay with a severe and terrible face covered in blood, which had poured like a wave from a mortal wound on his head.

I am finishing now. What is there to add?

Sonia arrived almost immediately, summoned by a telegram from Simon Ivanovich. They have been treating me for a long time, and persistently continue to treat me. Sonia and Helfreich are convinced that I shall live. They want to take me abroad, and rely on this journey as on a mountain of stone.

But I feel I have only a few days more. My wound has closed, but my chest is being racked by another disease. I know I have consumption. And, thirdly, a still more terrible disease is helping it. I cannot for one minute forget Nadejda Nicolaievna and Bezsonow. The appalling details of that last day stand eternally before my mental gaze, and a voice without ceasing whispers into my ear that I have killed a man.

They did not try me. The case was quashed. It was recognized that I killed in self-defence.

But for the human conscience there are no written laws, no doctrine of irresponsibility, and I am suffering punishment for my crime. I shall not suffer it long. Soon the All-Merciful will forgive me, and we three will meet where our passions and sufferings will seem insignificant in the light of everlasting love.

XII

THE SCARLET BLOSSOM

I

" IN the name of His Imperial Majesty the Lord Emperor Peter the First, I order a revision of this Asylum !"

These words were uttered in a loud, strident, resounding voice. The clerk who had registered the patient in a large dilapidated book lying on an ink-bespattered table could not restrain a smile. But the two young men who had escorted the patient did not smile. They could scarcely keep on their feet after forty-eight hours without sleep, passed alone with the lunatic whom they had just brought along by train. At the station immediately preceding their destination the attack had increased in its intensity, and they had succeeded in obtaining a strait-jacket from somewhere, which, with the assistance of the train-conductors and a gendarme, they had placed on the patient, and had brought him to the town, and finally to the Asylum in this dress.

He was dreadful to look at. Over his body and above his grey suit, which had been torn into rags during his paroxysms, was stretched a jacket of coarse canvas opened in front ; its sleeves, which were fastened behind, forced his arms crosswise against his chest. His blood-shot eyes (he had not slept for ten days) blazed with a fixed and intense glare. His lower lip was twitching with a nervous tremor, whilst his tangled, curly hair fell mane-like over his forehead. With rapid, agitated steps, he

THE SCARLET BLOSSOM

paced from corner to corner of the office, gazing inquisitively at the old shelves laden with documents, and the chairs covered with a kind of oilcloth. Occasionally he glanced at his recent fellow-travellers.

"Take him to the ward. To the right."

"I know—I know; I was here with you last year. We went over the Asylum. I know all about it, and it will be difficult to deceive me," said the patient.

He turned towards the door. The keeper opened it before him, and, with the same rapid gait, holding his head well up, he left the office, and, almost running, went to the right, to the ward for mental patients. Those who were escorting him could scarcely keep up with him.

"Ring! I cannot. You have tied my arms." The porter opened the door, and they entered the Asylum.

It was a large stone building, an old Government structure. Two large halls—one the dining-hall, the other a general room for quiet patients; a wide corridor with a glass door leading into a flower-garden, and some twenty separate rooms where the patients lived occupied the lower story. Here, also, were two dark rooms—one lined with mattresses, the other with boards—in which violent patients were placed; and an enormous, gloomy, vaulted room, which was the bath-room.

The upper story was occupied by women, whence there came a confused din, interspersed with yells and howling. The Asylum had been built for eighty patients, but as it was the only one available for some distance around there were nearly three hundred accommodated within its walls. Each small cubicle held four or five beds. In winter-time, when the patients were not allowed into the garden and all the iron-barred windows were tightly closed, the building became unendurably stifling.

They led the new patient into the room in which were the baths. Even on a sane person this room was calculated to produce a feeling of depression, and on a distorted, excited imagination the impression would be so much the greater. It was a large vaulted room with a greasy stone floor, and lighted by one window in a corner. The walls and arches were painted a dark red. Two stone baths, like two oval-shaped holes, and full of water, were let into, and on a level with, the floor, which had become almost black from the accumulated dirt of ages. A huge copper stove with a cylindrical boiler for heating the water, and a whole system of copper tubes and taps, filled the corner opposite the window. Everything bore an unusually gloomy and, for a disordered mind, fantastic character, which impression was further heightened by the forbidding physiognomy of the stout, taciturn warder in charge of the baths.

When they led the patient into this terrifying room in order to give him a bath, and, in accordance with the curative method of the principal medical officer of the Asylum, to place a large blister on the nape of his neck, he became terrified. Fantastic ideas, each one more monstrous than the other, came crowding into his head. What was this? An inquisition? A place for secret executions where his enemies had decided to put an end to him? Perhaps even Hell itself? Eventually he became possessed of the idea that this was to be some kind of trial. They undressed him, in spite of his frantic resistance. With a strength rendered twofold by his affliction, he easily wrenched himself free from several warders, hurling them to the ground; but eventually four of them threw him down, and, having seized him by his arms and legs, lowered him into the warm water. It seemed to him to be boiling, and into his disordered brain flashed disjointed fragmentary thoughts about trial by boiling water and red-hot iron. Choking with the water, convulsively struggling with his arms and legs, by which the warders were firmly holding him, he screamed out disjointed sentences, surpassing in reality any possible description. Supplications alternated with curses. As long as he possessed the strength to do so, he continued to cry out in this fashion; then, becoming quiet, and with scalding tears, and having no connection with anything he had previously said, he murmured: " Holy and greatest of all martyrs—St. George !—into thy hands I surrender my body. But my spirit !—no, never !"

The warders continued to hold him, although he had become quiet. The warm bath and the bag of ice placed on his head were having their effect. But when they took him, almost unconscious, out of the water and laid him on a bench in order to apply a blister, the balance of his strength and the fantastic ideas again returned.

" Why ? Why ?" he shouted. " I never wished anyone harm ! Why kill me ? O-O-O-O Lord ! Oh, you have already tormented me. I implore you ! Spare me !"

The burning hot application to the back of his neck made him struggle desperately. The attendants, unable to cope with him, did not know what to do. " You can do nothing," said the soldier who had performed the operation ; " we must rub."

These simple words sent the patient into convulsions of fear: " Rub ! Rub what ? Rub whom ? Me !" he reflected, and in mortal terror he closed his eyes. The soldier, taking the two ends of a coarse towel and pressing heavily, quickly drew it across the nape of the patient's neck, tearing from it both the blister and the outer layer of skin, and leaving an open red sore. The painfulness of this operation, almost unendurable even for a quiet and sane person, seemed to the patient the end of all things. He made a desperate effort with his whole body, wrenched himself free of the warders, and his naked body slid along the stone slabs. He thought they had cut off his head. He wished to cry out, but could not. They carried him to his cubicle in a state of unconsciousness, which passed into a profound, deathlike sleep.

II

It was night when he awoke. All was quiet. The heavy breathing of patients sleeping in the large room near was audible. A patient, placed for the night in the dark room, was talking to himself in a strange and monotonous voice. Above, in the women's ward, a hoarse contralto was singing some wild song. The patient listened to these sounds. He felt a terrible weakness and lassitude in all his limbs. His neck was dreadfully painful.

"Where am I? What has happened to me?" came into his head. Then suddenly, with extraordinary vividness, his life during the last month came before him, and he understood that he was unwell, and in what way he was unwell. He recalled a series of absurd thoughts, words, and actions which made him shudder throughout his whole being. "But that is ended; thank God, it is ended!" he whispered to himself, and again fell asleep.

An opened window, but guarded with iron bars, looked out on a little corner between the big buildings and a stone wall. Into this corner no one ever went, and it was overgrown with some wild shrub and a lilac in gaudily full blossom at this time of the year. Behind these bushes directly opposite the window a high wall loomed, from behind which, in turn, glanced lofty tops of trees, and through their leafy branches pierced the moonlight, which was bathing all around, including the big garden from which these trees arose. On the right was the white building of the Asylum, with its iron-barred windows, through which the lights were visible. On the left, white and brilliant in the moonlight, was the blank wall of the mortuary. The moon's rays, shining past the iron bars of the window into the room, fell on to the floor, and lighted up a part of the bed, bringing into relief the worn pallid face of its occupant lying with closed eyes. There was no trace of insanity in its features now.

THE SCARLET BLOSSOM

It was the deep, heavy sleep of an exhausted being, dreamless, motionless, and almost breathless. For a few seconds he awoke, fully conscious, and apparently sane, only to rise in the morning from his bed again bereft of reason.

III

"How do you feel?" asked the doctor of him the following morning.

The patient, having only just awakened, was still lying in bed.

"Splendid!" he replied, jumping out of bed, putting on his slippers, and wrapping himself up in his dressing-gown—"first-rate! Except for one thing. Look!" He pointed to the nape of his neck. "I cannot turn my head without pain. But it is nothing. All is good if you understand it, and I understand."

"You know where you are?"

"Of course, doctor! I am in an Asylum. But once you understand, it is absolutely all the same—absolutely."

The doctor looked him fixedly in the eyes. His handsome, attractive face, with its well-tended golden beard and the calm blue eyes which looked through gold-rimmed spectacles, was immovable and inscrutable. He was observing his patient.

"Why are you looking at me so fixedly? You will not read what is in my mind," continued the sick man, "and I can clearly read what is in yours. Why do you do evil? Why have you collected this crowd of unfortunates here, and why do you keep them here? To me it is all the same. I understand everything, and am calm, but they! What is the purpose of all this torture? To one who has recognized that in his mind there exists a mighty idea—to him it is a matter of indifference where he lives or does not live, and what he feels. It is a matter of indifference even whether he lives or dies. Is not that so?"

"Perhaps," replied the doctor, seating himself on a chair in a corner of the room so as to watch the patient, who shuffled rapidly from corner to corner in a pair of huge, horse-hide slippers, waving the folds of his dressing-gown, made of some cotton material on which was printed wide stripes and large flowers. The " dresser " and head warder, who had accompanied the doctor, remained standing to attention at the door.

"And I have this idea!" exclaimed the patient; "and when I discovered it I felt reborn. My senses have become more acute, my brain works as it never did formerly. What was once attained by a long process of conjecture and reasoning I now know intuitively. I am an illustration of the great idea that space and time—are fictions. I live in all centuries. I live outside of space, everywhere or nowhere, as you wish. And therefore it is all the same to me whether you detain me here or release me, whether I am free or bound. I have noticed that there are several such here. But for the remainder their position is appalling. Why do you not release them? To whom is it necessary?"

"You say," interrupted the doctor, "that you live apart from time and space. But you cannot, however, deny that we are with you in this room, and that now"—here the doctor pulled out his watch—" it is half-past ten on May 6, 18—. What are your views on this?"

"None. To me it is all the same where and when I live. If to *me* it is all the same, does it not mean that *I* am everywhere and always?"

The doctor laughed.

"Rare logic," he said, rising. "Au revoir. Would you care for a cigar?"

"Thank you." The patient stopped, took the cigar, and nervously bit off its end. "This will assist me to think," he said. "This world is a microcosm. At one end alkali, at the other—acid. Such is the equilibrium

THE SCARLET BLOSSOM

of the world in which opposing principles neutralize each other. Good-bye, doctor!"

The doctor went farther. The greater part of the patients awaited him standing to attention. No chief enjoys such respect from his subordinates as does the mental doctor from those placed under his care.

Our patient, left alone, continued to stride from corner to corner of his cubicle. They brought him a large mug of tea, which he emptied in two gulps without sitting down; and a large slice of white bread, which disappeared as if by magic. Then he left his room, and for several hours without cessation paced in his rapid and agitated manner from end to end of the whole building. It was a rainy day, and the patients were not allowed into the garden. When the " dresser " went to look for the new patient, the others pointed to him at the end of the corridor. He was standing there with his face pressed close to the pane of the glass door leading into the garden, and was staring fixedly at a flower-bed. An unusually bright scarlet blossom of the poppy variety had attracted his attention.

" Please come and be weighed," said the " dresser," touching him on the shoulder, and nearly falling down from fright when the patient turned round, such wild malice and hatred were burning in his imbecile eyes. But, seeing the " dresser," his expression immediately changed, and he followed obediently behind the official without saying a word, apparently engrossed in profound thought. They entered the doctor's room, and the patient of his own accord stood on the platform of the weighing-machine. The " dresser " entered his weight as 109 pounds. The following day he weighed only 107 pounds, and the day after 106 pounds.

" If he continues like this, he will not live," said the doctor, and gave instructions that he was to be given the best dietary.

But, in spite of this, and notwithstanding his enormous

appetite, the patient continued to lose weight, and grew thinner and thinner. He scarcely ever slept, and spent the whole and almost every day in uninterrupted movement.

IV

He understood that he was in a madhouse. He knew even that he was ill. Sometimes, as during the first night, he would awake in the quietness after a whole day of violent exercise, feeling exhaustion in every limb and a dreadful heaviness in his head, but fully conscious. Perhaps it was the absence of impressions in the stillness of the night and half-light. Perhaps it was the feeble working of the brain of a but just awakened being that caused him during such moments to understand fully his position, and made him apparently sane. But when morning arrived with the light and awakening of life in the Asylum, delusions again engulfed him as in a wave. The diseased brain could not grapple with them, and he once more became insane. His condition was a strange mixture of correct reasoning and nonsense. He understood that all around him were lunatics, but at the same time he saw in each of them somebody mysterious, a person hiding or hidden whom he had known previously, or of whom he had read or heard. The Asylum was inhabited by persons of all ages and nationalities, dead and living. Here there were the famed and strong of the world, and soldiers killed in the last war, but now resurrected. He saw himself in some magic enchanted circle, having collected to himself all the forces of the earth, and in proud delirium he deemed himself the centre of this circle. All his comrades in the Asylum were gathered there to perform a duty which, in a confused manner, appeared to him as a gigantic enterprise directed towards the extinction of evil on earth. He did not know in what the task would consist, but felt himself possessed of sufficient strength to execute it. He could

THE SCARLET BLOSSOM

read the thoughts of others. He saw in things their whole history. The large elms in the Asylum garden revealed whole legends of the past to him. The building, which really was of old construction, he considered a structure of Peter the Great, and was convinced that that Tsar had lived in it at the time of the Poltava battle. He read this in the walls, the plaster which had fallen, in the pieces of brick and Dutch tiles found by him in the garden. The whole history of the house and garden was written in them. He peopled the little building which did duty as a mortuary with tens and hundreds of persons long since dead, and fixedly gazed into the little window of its cellar, which looked into the garden, seeing in the uneven reflection of light on the old rainbow-tinted and dirty glass familiar features encountered by him at some period in life or seen in portraits.

In the meanwhile there came a period of bright fine weather. The patients spent the whole day out of doors in the garden. Their part of the garden, small and thickly overgrown with trees, was, wherever possible, planted with flowers. The Superintendent insisted that all who were capable of so doing should work in the garden. Every day they swept and sprinkled the paths with sand, weeded and watered the flower-beds, vegetables, and fruit which they themselves had planted. In a corner of the garden was an overgrown cherry orchard. Alongside it stretched an avenue of elms, in the centre of which, on a small artificial mound, there was laid out the prettiest flower-bed in the garden. Bright-coloured flowers grew along the edges of the upper space, whilst the centre was adorned by a large full and rare yellow dahlia with red spots. It formed the centre of the whole garden, rising above it, and it was noticeable that many of the patients invested it with some secret significance. To the new patient it also appeared to be something out of the common, some palladium of the garden and building. All around the paths had also been planted by the patients. Here there was every possible flower met with in the gardens of " Little " Russia : high-growing roses, bright petunias, groups of tall tobacco-plants with small rose-coloured bloom, mint, nasturtiums, pinks, and poppies. Here, too, not far from a flight of steps, grew three small clusters of a particular kind of poppy. It was much smaller than the ordinary variety, and differed in its extraordinarily brilliant blood-red blossom.

It was this blossom which had astonished the patient when, on the first day after his admission into the Asylum, he had seen it through the glass door. Going out for the first time into the garden, he first of all, without leaving the steps which led from the corridor, looked at the brilliant blossoms. There were only two of them. By chance they had grown apart from the other flowers and in an unweeded spot, so that they were surrounded by a thick growth of weeds and grass.

The patients filed, one by one, out of the glass door, at which stood a warder, who gave to each as he passed a thick white cotton cap having a red cross in front. These caps had been intended for hospital use during the war, and had been bought at an auction. But the patients, of course, attributed a special hidden meaning to the cross. The new-comer took off his cap, and looked first at the cross, then at the poppy-blossoms. The latter were the brighter.

" It wins," said he ; " but we will see ;" and he went down the steps. Having hastily glanced around, and having failed to notice the warder standing behind him, the patient stepped on to the flower-bed and stretched out his hand towards the flower, but could not decide to pluck it. He experienced a warm and stinging sensation at first in his outstretched hand, and then throughout his whole body, as if some powerful shock from a force unknown to him was emanating from the red petals and was penetrating through him. He moved closer, and put out his hand towards the actual blossom, but it seemed

THE SCARLET BLOSSOM 241

to him that it was defending itself and giving out a poisonous deadly exhalation. His head was reeling, but nevertheless he made one last desperate effort, and had already seized the stalk, when a heavy hand was laid suddenly on his shoulder. It was the old warder.

" It is forbidden to pluck the flowers," said he, " and you must not go on to the flower-beds. If each of you is going to pick the flower which attracts you, the whole garden will be spoilt," continued he with conviction, still holding the culprit by the shoulder.

The patient looked him in the face, without saying a word freed himself, and, in a state of excitement, passed on along the path. " Oh, unhappy ones !" he thought ; " you do not see. You are so blind that you defend it ! But at all costs I will put an end to it. If not to-day, then to-morrow we will measure forces. And if I perish, is it not all the same ?"

He walked about in the garden until the evening, making acquaintances and carrying on strange conversations first with one and then with another of his companions, and at the end of the day was still more convinced that " all was ready," as he said to himself. " Soon, soon the iron bars will fall asunder ; all these prisoners will issue hence, and will flash to all ends of the earth. The whole world will tremble, will divest itself of its ancient covering, and will appear in new and wondrous beauty." He had almost forgotten the blossoms, but, on leaving the garden and mounting the flight of steps, he again saw them in the thick grass which had already become covered with dew, whereupon, keeping back from the rest of the patients, he awaited a favourable opportunity. No one saw him as he jumped across the flower-bed, grasped the flower, and hurriedly hid it against his chest under his shirt. When the fresh dew-covered leaves touched his body he became deathly pale, and, in an agony of fear, opened his eyes widely. A cold perspiration broke out on his forehead.

Inside the Asylum they had lit the lamps, and the majority of the patients, whilst waiting supper, were lying on their beds. A few restless ones were pacing the corridor and halls. Amongst these was the patient with the flower. He walked with his hands crossed on his chest. It seemed as if he wished to crush the plant hidden on it. When meeting the other patients, he passed them at a distance, fearing to come into contact with any part of their clothes. "Do not come near! Do not come near me!" he cried out. But in the Asylum little attention was paid to such exclamations, and for two hours he paced thus in a kind of ecstasy, ever faster and faster, and with ever-increasing strides.

"I will tire thee out, I will stifle thee," he muttered maliciously. Sometimes he ground his teeth.

Supper was served in the dining-hall. Wooden painted and gilded bowls were placed at intervals on the large tables bare of cloths. These bowls contained a liquid wheaten gruel. The patients sat on benches, and each was given a portion of black bread. They ate with wooden spoons, eight to every one bowl. Those who were ordered better food were served separately. Our patient quickly gulped down his portion, which had been brought to his room by a warder; then, still unsatisfied, he went into the common dining-room.

"Allow me to eat here?" he said to the Superintendent.

"But surely you have had your supper," replied he, pouring out an extra portion into a bowl.

"I am very hungry, and it is most necessary for me to recruit my strength. All my support is in food. You know that I do not sleep at all."

"Eat and get well, my friend," said the Superintendent, giving orders to a warder to give the patient a spoon and some bread.

He sat down near one of the bowls, and ate a further enormous amount of gruel.

"That is enough now," said the Superintendent at last,

THE SCARLET BLOSSOM

when all had finished their supper; but our patient still continued to sit in front of the bowl, scraping the gruel out of it with one hand, and holding the other tightly to his chest. "You will overeat yourself."

"Ah! if only you knew how much I am in need of strength! Good-bye, sir," said the patient, at last rising from the table and warmly pressing the Superintendent's hand. "Good-bye."

"But where are you going?" inquired the Superintendent, with a smile.

"I? Nowhere. I am staying here. But perhaps we shall not see each other to-morrow. I thank you for all your kindness." And he again warmly clasped the Superintendent's hand, whilst his voice trembled and tears came welling into his eyes.

"Calm yourself, my good friend — calm yourself," replied the Superintendent. "What is the use of such dismal thoughts? Go and lie down and sleep well. You want more sleep. If you sleep well, you will soon recover."

The patient sobbed. The Superintendent turned round to order the warder to clear away the remains of the supper more quickly, and in half an hour afterwards all in the Asylum were already asleep, with the exception of one patient, who lay on his bed in the corner of the room fully dressed. He was trembling as if in a fever, and spasmodically held his chest, impregnated, as it seemed to him, with a strange and deadly poison.

V

He did not sleep all night. He had plucked the flower because he saw in this action a deed he was in duty bound to perform. At the very first glance through the glass door the blood-red petals had attracted his attention, and it seemed to him that from this moment it was perfectly clear what in particular he was called upon to perform on earth. In this brilliant red flower was collected all the evil existent on earth. He knew that opium is made from poppies, and perhaps this knowledge, taking some fantastic, distorted form, had induced him to create this terrible and monstrous phantom. In his eyes the flower was the personification of all evil. It flourished on all innocent bloodshed (which was why it was so red), on all tears, and all human venom. It was a mysterious, awful being, the antithesis of God—Ahriman —who had taken a modest and innocent form. It was necessary to pluck and kill it. But more than this was necessary ; it was necessary not to allow it to emit all its evil into the world. Therefore he had hid it in his chest. He hoped that by the morning it would have lost all its strength, that its evil would have passed into his body, his soul, and there be conquered or conquer—when, if the latter, he would himself perish, die, but die as an honourable knight and the first to wrestle at once with all the evil in this world. " They have not seen it. I saw it. Could I let it live ? Better death !"

And he lay wearing himself out in a struggle, phantom and unreal, but nevertheless exhausting. In the morning the " dresser " found him scarcely alive. But this notwithstanding, in a short time excitability once more gained the upper hand. He jumped up from his bed, and resumed his former race through the passages of the Asylum, conversing with the other patients and himself more loudly and disjointedly than at any previous time.

They would not let him into the garden. The doctor, seeing that his weight was daily decreasing, and that he never slept, but continued incessantly to walk and walk, ordered that a strong dose of morphia be injected hypodermically. He did not resist. Luckily, on this occasion his disordered brain in some manner accepted the operation. He quickly fell asleep, the feverish activity ceased, and the great motive which was its constant companion ceased to ring in his ears. He forgot all, and ceased to think of anything, even of the second blossom which it was necessary to pick.

However, he plucked it after an interval of three days before the very eyes of the old warder, who was unable to prevent him doing so. The warder gave chase, but with a loud triumphant yell the patient rushed into the Asylum and, hurling himself into his room, hid the plant on his chest.

" Why do you pick the flowers ?" asked the warder, who had followed after him. But the patient, who was already lying on his bed in his usual position with his arms crossed, commenced to rave so incoherently that the warder went away. And once more the phantom struggle commenced. The patient felt that from the flower an evil was exuding in long, gliding, snakelike streams. It was wrapping around him, pressing and crushing his limbs, and was impregnating the whole of his body with its awful substance. He wept and prayed in the intervals between the curses he showered on his enemy. By the evening the flower had quite faded. The sick man stamped on the blackened blossom, collected the pieces from the floor, and carried them to the bath-room. Throwing the shapeless bruised piece of erstwhile green into the red-hot stove, he long watched how his enemy hissed, diminished, and finally became converted into a tender snow-white ball of ash. He blew, and it all disappeared.

The following day the patient became worse. But although dreadfully pale, with hollow cheeks and burning eyes which had sunken far into their sockets, he continued his frenzied walking, raving almost without cessation, tottering and stumbling from weakness.

" I do not wish to have resort to force," said the senior doctor to his assistant, " but if this goes on much longer he will die in two or three days' time. We must stop this walking. To-day he weighs only ninety-three pounds. Yesterday morphia had no effect." Then, after a short silence, he gave instructions that the patient should be bound, expressing at the same time doubts as to his ultimate recovery. And they bound him. He lay clothed in a strait-jacket on his bed, tightly fastened by wide strips of calico to the iron framework of the bed. But the frenzied activity increased rather than diminished. For many hours he strove persistently to free himself. Eventually by a strenuous effort he succeeded in bursting one of his pinions, freed his legs, and having slipped from under the rest of his fetters, began, with his arms still bound, to pace his room, giving vent to wild, unintelligible utterances.

The warder, coming into the room, called loudly for help, and with two of his brother-warders threw themselves on the patient, whereupon a long struggle commenced, tiring for them and torturing for the patient, who was in this way using up the remnants of his almost exhausted forces. Finally, they laid him on his bed and bound him tighter than before.

"You do not understand what you are doing!" he panted. "You will perish. I saw a third scarcely opened blossom. Now it must be ready. Let me finish my work! It must be killed—killed—killed! Then all will be finished and all saved. I would send you, but only *I* can do this. You would perish merely from contact with it."

"Be quiet—stop talking!" said the old warder left to watch near his bed.

VI

The patient suddenly stopped talking. He had decided on stratagem. He decided to deceive his warder. They kept him bound all day, and left him so during the night. Having given him his supper, the old attendant placed a mat near the bed and laid down. In a few moments he was sound asleep, and the patient began his task.

Contorting his body so as to get at the ironwork of the bedstead, and feeling for the edge of the iron frame with his wrist hidden in the long sleeves of the strait-jacket, he commenced quickly and vigorously to rub the sleeve on it. After a short time the thick canvas gave way, and he had freed his wrists and the first finger of one of his hands. Then matters progressed more speedily. With an ingenuity born of insanity he untied the knot behind his back which secured the sleeves, unlaced the jacket, and then for a long time listened intently to the snoring of the warder. Satisfied that the old man was sleeping soundly, the patient took off the jacket and slid from the bed. He was free! He tried the door. It was locked from the inside, and the key was probably in the warder's pocket. Afraid of awaking him, he did not dare to search his pockets, and so decided to get out of his room through the window.

It was a still, warm, dark night. The window was open. The stars were shining. He gazed at them, recognizing familiar constellations, and rejoicing that they, as it seemed to him, understood and were in sympathy with him. His mad resolution increased. It was necessary to get rid of the iron bar which formed the grating of the window in order to be able to clamber through the narrow opening into the corner of the garden, overgrown just here with bushes, and to scale over the high stone wall. Then would come the last struggle, and afterwards—mayhap death!

He tried ineffectually to bend the thick iron bar with his bare hands. Then he made a cord by twisting up the strong canvas sleeves of the strait-jacket, and fastened it to the forged spike on the end of the bar. Upon this he hung with the whole weight of his body. After frantic efforts, almost exhausting his remaining stock of strength, the spike gave way, and the narrow passage was open. He squeezed through it, bruising and lacerating his shoulders, elbows, and bared knees, and pushed his way through the bushes, but came to a stop before the wall. All was quiet. The light of the small lamps used in the rooms showed feebly through the windows of the building. No one was to be seen inside it. Nobody saw him. The old warder watching by his bed was probably still sound asleep. The twinkling rays of the stars seemed to penetrate into his very heart, giving him renewed spirit.

"I am coming to you," he whispered, glancing upwards.

Having fallen at the first attempt to scale the wall, with torn nails and bleeding hands and knees he began to search for a suitable place. A few bricks had become detached from the wall where it met the wall of the Mortuary, and making use of the hollows thus formed, the patient climbed on to the wall, seized hold of the branches of an elm growing on the other side, and quietly let himself down the tree on to the ground.

He rushed to the well-known spot near the flight of steps. The blossom with its closed petals showed up clearly and darkly in the dewy grass.

"The last!" whispered the patient—"the last! To-day is victory or death! But it is all the same to me. Wait," said he, gazing up to the starry sky, "I will soon be with you."

He rooted up the plant, tore it to pieces, and holding it crushed in his clenched hand, he returned to his room the same way he had left it. The old warder still slept. The patient, barely reaching the bed, fell on to it senseless.

In the morning they found him dead. His face was calm and serene. The tired features, with the thin lips and deeply sunken closed eyes, wore an expression of proud happiness. When they had laid him on a stretcher they attempted to open his clenched hand and remove the scarlet blossom. But it was too late, and he carried his trophy to the grave.

XIII

THE BEARS

In the Steppe the town of Bielsk nestles on the River Rokhla at a point where it makes several sharp curves linked up by branch streams, the whole forming a network which, if looked at on a clear summer day from the lofty right bank of the channel through which the river runs here, resembles a gigantic bow of blue ribbon. At this point the bank rises some three hundred and fifty feet sheer above the level of the river as if it had been cut by a huge knife. So steep is it that to clamber from the water's edge to the top, where the limitless Steppe commences, is possible only by taking hold of the bushes of spindlewood, birch, and hazel thickly covering the face of the slope. From this summit a clear view of forty versts opens out on every side. On the right to the south and on the left to the north stretch the gradients of the right bank of the Rokhla, descending abruptly into valleys such as the one from above which we are gazing. Some of the ridges show up white with their chalk tops and naked sides destitute of soil. Others are covered for the most part with short and withered grass. In front to the east stretches the illimitable undulating Steppe, yellow with haystacks, over which some useless weed is growing thickly, or verdant with growing crops, here showing the dark purple-black of newly upturned fallow, there the silvery grey of feather-grass. Viewed from where we are standing, the Steppe appears level, and only the accustomed eye can trace on it the scarcely discernible lines of ridges, of invisible ravines and gullies. Here and there an old half-sunken tumulus meets the view, its sides scarified by the plough, and no longer possessed of its stone slab, now perhaps adorning the courtyard of the Kharkoff University, or perhaps taken away by some peasant, and now forming part of the wall of his cattle-yard.

Below, the winding river runs from north to south, alternately receding from its high bank into the Steppe or flowing immediately under its ledge, fringed at intervals with clusters of pine-trees and about the town by gardens and grazing-plots. At some distance from the bank to the side of the Steppe a strip of quicksand runs almost the entire length of the river, barely supporting the red and black shoots of small shrubs growing on it, and its thick carpet of fragrant lilac-coloured charbrets. Amongst these sands, two versts from the town, lies the cemetery, resembling from a distance a little oasis with the small wooden bell-tower of the cemetery chapel rising from its centre. The town itself presents no outstanding features, and is much like all district towns, apart from the astonishing cleanliness of its streets, due not so much to a solicitous municipal administration as to the sandy soil on which the town is built, which absorbs any moisture an incensed heaven may pour forth, and thereby places the town swine in great difficulties, compelling them to seek suitable accommodation for themselves at least two versts' distance from the town in the dirty banks of the river.

In September of 1857 the town of Bielsk was in a state of unwonted excitement. The usual routine of life was disturbed. Everywhere, whether in the Club, streets, or on the benches outside the gateway entrances of courtyards, indoors and outdoors, animated conversation was being carried on. It might have been supposed that the Zemstvo elections, which were taking place at this time,

THE BEARS

were the cause of disturbance; but there had been previous Zemstvo elections, and with all their scandals they had never produced any special impression on the native of Bielsk. On these occasions, if meeting in the street, the citizens would merely exchange brief remarks with each other.

"Have you been?" one would ask, indicating by a glance the building in which the Zemstvo offices were housed.

"Yes," would reply the other, with a gesture of his hand; and, accustomed to this mode of expression of thoughts, the interrogator would understand and simply add:

"Who?"

"Ivan Petrovich."

"Whom?"

"Ivan Parfenovich."

Then they would both smile and part.

But now it was quite different. The town was in an uproar just as at fair-time. Crowds of urchins kept running backwards and forwards in the direction of the town common grazing-ground. Respectable, sober individuals in loose summer suits of alpaca silk were also wending their way thither, and the damsels of the town, with parasols and various coloured hoop-petticoats (they wore them in those days), occupying so much of the wide street that young Rogacheff, the merchant, driving a dapple grey, was obliged to draw in almost against the walls of the houses. The ladies were accompanied by the local cavaliers in grey overcoats with black velvet collars, carrying walking-canes and wearing straw hats or caps with cockades. Among these beaux were, of course, the brothers Isotoff, the leaders of all public gaieties, who knew how during a quadrille to call out "Grand Rond!" and "Au rebours!"—that is, when they were not running through the town imparting the latest news to their lady acquaintances.

"They have arrived from the Valuinsk District, and occupy half the ground of the Common right up to the river," said Leonid, the elder brother.

"I regarded the view from the summit of the eminence," added Constantine, the younger brother, who delighted in expressing himself in the most flowery language—"an entrancing picture!"

"Eminence" was the name he gave to the hill from which a view of the town and its vicinity could be obtained.

"Ah, what a good idea! Listen! I have a splendid idea. Let us order the lineika, and drive out to the eminence. It will be like a picnic, and we will watch from there."

This proposal by the first lady of Bielsk, the wife of the brother of the Treasurer (almost the whole town called her husband, Paul Ivanovich, the brother of the Treasurer), who had arrived eight years ago from Petersburg, and was therefore the authority on fashions and good tone, met with general approval. The fat old bay horse was harnessed into the lineika, which is only met with in provincial capitals, and consists of long boards with two long seats so placed that the occupants, usually twelve in all, sit in two rows of six or seven a side and back to back. The party, which consisted of some dozen persons, seated themselves in the lineika, and started off through the town, overtaking mobs of boys, strings of damsels, and crowds of every description of public, all making their way to the Common. The lineika, having negotiated the sandy streets of the town, crossed the bridge and made for the steep right bank of the river. The bay, with dogged pace, wrinkling the sleek folds of his glossy haunches, clambered up the long slope, and in half an hour the picnickers were seated on the edge of the three hundred feet high ridge, with its overgrowth of bushes, gazing at the view with which we are already acquainted. Below, under their feet, immediately under this wall, the

THE BEARS

river was quietly flowing along its course, and behind it opened out the common on which the general attention was concentrated.

In the variety of colouring it resembled a huge patchwork carpet. The dull white of tents, numberless vehicles, and a motley crowd were all visible. Dark figures of men in kaftans and dirty grey shirts intermingled with the bright yellow and scarlet dresses of the women. A dense crowd surrounded the gipsy encampment which had been formed. It was a magnificent day, not too hot, and absolutely still. Above the roar of a multitudinous crowd could be heard the ring of sledge-hammers on iron, the neighing of horses, and the roar of scores of tame bears—the mainstay of the gipsies who had brought them hither out of the neighbouring Districts.

Olga Pavlona gazed at this kaleidoscope through binoculars, and went into raptures.

"How interesting it all is! What a big one! Look, Leonid, what a huge bear there on the right! And the young gipsy alongside it—a perfect Adonis!"

She handed the glasses to the young man, who through them saw the figure of a well-built and exceedingly dirty youth who was standing near and petting a beast which kept shuffling about and changing from one leg on to another.

"Allow me to look," said a stout, clean-shaven man in a duck suit and straw hat. For some time he looked attentively through the glasses, and then, turning to Olga Pavlona, said with a deep sigh: "Ye-es, Olga Pavlona, an Adonis. But this Adonis will turn out a first-class horse-thief."

Olga Pavlona uttered an exclamation of impatience.

"Why," said she, "do you always try to turn everything poetical into prose? Why a horse-thief? I will not believe it! He looks so good!"

"That may be, but how is he going to support his beautiful body without that bear? To-morrow they are slaughtering all these bears, and one-half of all the gipsies in this encampment will be without a living."

"They can work as blacksmiths and shoeing-smiths, tell fortunes . . ."

"Tell fortunes! Ilia, the horse-doctor, came to me yesterday. You go and talk with him. 'Thomas Thomasovich,' he said, 'those greys of yours are very good, only beware of our brother.' 'What!' I said; 'surely you will not steal them?' He smiled, the blackguard! Tell fortunes! Those are the sort of fortunes he is telling!"

Out of the lineika they took a large basket, from which appeared eatables and drinks, and the company began to seat themselves in groups, chatting merrily the while, and scarcely paying any attention to the picture displayed at their feet. The sun had set, and the gigantic shadow of the height quickly spread to the Common, town, and Steppe. Outlines softened, and, as happens in the South, day was quickly replaced by night. Lights began to flicker in the town, and fires were lighted in the camp, which showed up redly through the mist rising from the slumbering river below, the distant bends of which glistened in the cold moonlight. And above the river, on the height itself, Constantine and Leonid kept up a ceaseless flow of ridiculous stories, at which Olga Pavlona occasionally smiled with condescension, and the younger ladies of the party giggled or even laughed aloud. Candles protected by glass shades were lighted, and the coachman with the maid prepared the samovar in the bushes near by—a process apparently necessitating occasional, but at the same time very cautious, squeaks on the part of the maid. Portly Thomas Thomasovich alone remained silent, and finally interrupted Leonid at the most interesting point of one of his anecdotes.

"When, then, have they finally decided to have this slaughter of bears?" said he.

"Wednesday morning," said the brothers Isotoff simultaneously.

THE BEARS

The unhappy gipsies had journeyed hither from four Districts of the Government with all their household effects, horses, bears, etc. More than a hundred of these awkward beasts, ranging from tiny cubs to huge " old men " whose coats had become grey or whitish from age, had collected on the town common. The gipsies awaited the fatal day with terror. Those who had been the first to arrive had already been encamped here more than a fortnight. The Authorities were waiting until all should arrive, so that the business of killing the bears might be carried out in one day and finished with once and for all. The gipsies had been given five years' grace from the publication of the Order prohibiting performing bears, and now this period had expired. They were now to appear at specified places and themselves destroy their supporters.

They had completed their last round through the villages with the familiar goat and big drum—the invariable companions of the bears. For the last time, having espied them afar off coming down from the Steppe into the steep gully and bank of the river, the usual site of Little Russian villages, a crowd of boys and girls had run a verst to meet them, returning triumphantly with them, a confused rabble, back to the village, where the fun of the fair had already commenced. And what fun it was ! What festivities took place ! They would halt by the inn or some bigger house, or if it was an estate before the proprietor's house, and begin their performances, cures, trade, barter, fortune-telling, horse-shoeing, and repairs of waggons, continuing right throughout the long summer day until the evening, when the gipsies would leave the village for the cattle-grazing ground, and, setting up their tents or simply stretching the canvas over the shafts of the waggons, would light their fires and prepare supper, whilst far into the night an inquisitive crowd would stand around the encampment.

"Come along now; it is time to go home," my father would say to me, a little boy, but no less unwilling to leave, would wait in response to my entreaties for "just a little longer—a little longer." Together we would sit in the cart, the old horse Vasia, with his head turned towards the fires and ears pricked towards the bears, standing quietly, save for an occasional snort. The fires of the camp cast dancing red lights and vague trembling shadows. A light mist was rising from the ravine to the side of us, whilst behind the camp stretched the Steppe. The dark wings of a windmill stood out as if painted against the sky, and behind it was limitless mysterious space enfolded in a silvery twilight. Amidst the din of the encampment could be heard those subdued sounds so characteristic of the Steppe at night. First from some distant pond would come the solemn reverberating chorus of frogs, then the regular but hurried chirrup of the grasshopper and the cry of the quail. Again, faint, indistinguishable harmonious sounds would be wafted to our ears—mayhap the sound of some distant bell borne on the breeze, or the voice of Nature, whose tongue we do not understand.

But in the encampment all is becoming quiet. Gradually fires are extinguished. The bears under the carts to which they are tethered growl deeply from time to time, as with a jingling of their chains they restlessly change their position. Their owners, too, are settling down to sleep. One of them in an uncultivated tenor is singing a strange song in his native language, unlike the songs of Moscow restaurant gipsies and operatic singers—a song characteristic, wild, mournful, strange to the ear. No one knows when it was composed, what Steppe, forest or mountain gave it birth. It has remained a living testimony of a land forgotten even by those who sing it now under the burning stars of a foreign sky and in alien Steppes.

"Come along," says my father. Vasia bravely starts,

THE BEARS

and the droshky wends its way along the winding road below into the valley. A thin dust rises half-heartedly from under the wheels, and then, as if also overcome with sleep, falls back on to the dewy grass.

" Papa, does anyone know gipsy ?"

" The gipsies themselves, of course, do, but I have never met others who could speak to them."

" I should like to learn it. I should like to know what he was singing about. Papa, are they heathens ? Perhaps he was singing about his gods, how they lived and fought."

We arrive home, and as I lie under the coverlet my imagination still works and forms strange fancies in the little head already on the pillow.

Now, bears no longer wander through the villages, and even the gipsies themselves seldom wander. The greater number of them live where they have been told to live, and only occasionally pay tribute to their century-old instincts, select some common, stretch their smoky canvas, and live whole families together, busy with the shoeing of horses, horse-curing, and dealing. I have even seen how tents have given place to hastily erected wooden shelters. This was in the provincial capital not far from the hospital and the fair-ground, on a piece of land as yet unbuilt on and running alongside the main road. On this plot the gipsies had built quite a little town. Only the swarthy faces, quick-glancing eyes, curly hair, and dirty clothes of the men, with the equally dirty, gaudy rags of the women and the naked bronzed children, reminded me of the former picture of a wandering gipsy encampment. The clang of iron was coming from these shelters, and I looked into one of them. An old man was making horseshoes. I looked at his work, and saw that this man was no longer a gipsy blacksmith, but an ordinary workman who had taken some order, and was working as quickly as possible to finish it so as to take up a new job. He was forging shoe after shoe, throwing them one after another into a heap in a corner of the shanty. He was working with a gloomy concentrated air, and at a great rate. This was in the daytime. Going past late that night, I went up to the shelter, and saw the old man still at the same work. It was a factory. And it was strange to see a gipsy encampment almost in the heart of the town situated between the Zemstvo hospital, the bazaar, and some kind of enclosed square where soldiers were being drilled, and from which came the sound of sharp orders given by the instructors. It was alongside a road from which the wind was raising clouds of dust, smothering with it the boarded shelters and the fires with their pots, in which the womenkind, their heads adorned with gaudy handkerchiefs, were boiling some sort of gruel.

They had gone through the villages giving their shows for the last time. For the last time the bears had displayed their histrionic talents, had danced, wrestled, showed how little boys steal the peas, imitated the mincing step of the young girl and the waddling gait of the old woman. For the last time they had received their reward in the form of a tumbler of vodka, which the bear, standing on its hind-legs, would seize with both front paws, place against his shaggy muzzle, and, throwing his head back, pour the contents down his throat, after which he would lick his jaws and express his satisfaction in a quiet rumble and strange deep sighs. For the last time old men and women were coming to the gipsies to be cured of their ailments by the true and tried process of lying on the ground under a bear, which would place his belly on the patient, spread himself out on all fours, and remain in this position until the gipsies considered the séance had lasted long enough. For the last time they had entered huts, when, if the bear voluntarily entered, he was led into the front portion of the dwelling,

THE BEARS

and all sat there and rejoiced at his graciousness as a good omen, but if, in spite of all entreaties and caresses he refused to cross the threshold, the occupants would be sorrowful, and their neighbours would shake their heads.

The greater part of the gipsies had come from the Western Districts, so that they were obliged to descend into Bielsk by a long hill nearly two versts long, and, seeing from a distance the site of their coming misfortune —this little town with its thatched and iron roofs and two or three bell-towers—the women commenced to wail, the children to cry, and the bears from sympathy, or perhaps—who knows ?—understanding from their masters the bitter fate in store for them, to roar in such a way that carts which met them turned aside from the road so that the bullocks and horses should not be frightened, whilst the dogs with yelps of alarm crawled under the carts, taking refuge behind the grease and tar-pots which the peasants of these parts fasten under the body of their carts.

Several of the old men amongst the gipsies had collected at the entrance gates of the house in which the ispravnik of Bielsk resided. They had decked themselves out so as to present a respectable appearance before the Authorities. All wore black or dark blue under-tunics, and belts brocaded with silver and black enamel-work, silk shirts having a narrow piping of gold lace round the collar, plush trousers, high boots which in some cases were embroidered and slashed with a pattern, and the majority wore astrachan caps. This dress was worn only on the most solemn occasions.

" Is he asleep ?" inquired a tall, upright gipsy, tanned from age, of a gorodovoi who came out of the courtyard —one of the eleven gorodovois entrusted with the preservation of law and order in the town of Bielsk.

" He is getting up—is dressing. He will send for you soon," replied the gorodovoi.

The old men, who up till now had been sitting or standing motionless, began to move and to speak in low tones amongst themselves. The senior of them drew something out of the pocket of his baggy trousers; the remainder all collected around him and looked at the object which he held in his hands.

"Nothing will come of it," he said at last. "What, indeed, can he do? It is not his doing. It is the Minister at Petersburg who has given the order. They are killing the bears everywhere."

"We will try, Ivan. Perhaps he can do something," said another of the old men.

"Of course we can try," replied Ivan dismally. "Only he will take our money and will not help in any way."

The ispravnik sent for them. They went in a crowd into the entrance-hall, and when he came out to them— a whiskered man in an unbuttoned police uniform, which exposed a red silk shirt—the old men fell at his feet. They implored his assistance, offered him money, and many of them wept.

"Your Worship," said Ivan, "will himself judge what is to happen to us. What will become of us? We had bears; we lived quietly, insulted no one. Amongst us are young men who engage in evil work, but are there not horse-thieves amongst the Russians? No one was insulted by our beasts, Your Worship; they amused all. Now what is going to happen to us, Your Worship? We must go into the world, and if not thieves, must be vagabonds. Our fathers, our grandfathers, Your Worship, led bears around. We do not know how to plough the land; we are all blacksmiths. It has been hard work travelling the wide world over as blacksmiths in search of work, and now work will not come of itself to us. Our young men will become horse-thieves—nothing else to do, Your Worship. Before God I speak frankly, concealing nothing. A great evil has been done us and good people by taking away our bears from us. Perhaps you will

THE BEARS

help us. God will reward you for it. Kind sir, help us!"

The old man fell on his knees and prostrated himself at the feet of the ispravnik. The others followed suit. The Major stood with a gloomy expression on his face, smoothing his long moustaches with one hand and the other thrust into the pocket of his dark blue overalls.

The old man pulled out a bulging pocket-book and offered it to him.

"I will not take it," said the ispravnik surlily. "I can do nothing."

"But if you will take it, Your Worship," said the crowd, "perhaps something—if you would write."

"I will not take it," repeated the ispravnik more loudly than before. "On no account. It is useless. It is the law. You were given five years' grace. What can be done?" And he made a motion with his hands. The old men remained silent. The ispravnik continued: "I know what a misfortune this is for all of you—and to us. Now we shall have to look out for our horses, but what can I do? You, old man, put away your money. I will not take it. If I have to give you trouble through your children over horses do not be angry with me, but to take money for nothing is not one of my customs. Put it away—put it away, old man; your money will be useful to you."

"Your Worship," said Ivan, still holding the pocket-book in his hands, "be so good as to give the order for the slaughter. Please to-morrow "—the old man's voice trembled—" please to-morrow finish it. We are tired, worn out. Two weeks ago I came here with mine. We have lived quite——"

"There is still one lot to come in, old man," broke in the ispravnik. "We must wait. It must be done all at one time, and finished. The whole town has gone off its head over you all."

"They have arrived already, Your Worship. As we

came to Your Excellency they were coming down the hill. Do us this kindness, sir. Do not torment us!"

"Well, if they have arrived, then to-morrow at ten o'clock I will come to you. Have you guns?"

"We have guns, but not all of us."

"All right, I will tell the Colonel to lend you some rifles. God be with you! I am sorry, very sorry for you all!"

The old men turned towards the door, but the ispravnik called them back.

"Wait a moment," he said. "I will tell you something. Go to the chemist's shop next to the church. Go and say I sent you. The chemist will buy all the bears'-fat from you; he will make it into pomade. Perhaps he will buy the skins, too. He will give you a good price. He will not lose by it."

The gipsies thanked him, and in a crowd trooped off to the chemist's shop. Their hearts were torn; almost without bargaining they sold the mortal remains of their old friends. Thomas Thomasovich bought all the fat at fourteen kopecks a pood, and promised to speak about the skins later on. The young merchant, Rogacheff, who happened to be there, bought all the bear-hams at five kopecks a pound, hoping to make a good deal out of the transaction.

In the evening of that day the brothers Isotoff rushed breathless to the house of the brother of the Treasurer.

"Olga Pavlona! Olga Pavlona! they have settled it for to-morrow! All have arrived! The Colonel has already given out the rifles!" they shouted, vying against each other in their haste to tell the news. "Thomas Thomasovich has bought all the fat at fourteen kopecks a pood, and Rogacheff the hams, and——"

"Stop, stop, Leonid!" interrupted Olga Pavlona. "Why has Thomas Thomasovich bought the fat?"

"For ointment, pomade. It is a splendid thing for making the hair grow." And forthwith Constantine

THE BEARS

related an interesting anecdote of how a certain bald gentleman, through rubbing his head with bears'-fat, even grew hair on his hands.

"And he was forced to shave them every two days," added Leonid; and then the two brothers burst out laughing.

Olga Pavlona smiled and pondered over the news. She had long worn a chignon, and this information about bears'-grease interested her very much. When that same evening Thomas Thomasovich came round to play cards with her husband and the Treasurer, she cleverly succeeded in making him promise to send her some bears' ointment.

"Of course—of course, Olga Pavlona," he had said, "and it shall be scented. Which do you prefer—patchouli or ylang-ylang?"

The day broke cloudy and cold—a genuine September day—with an occasional slight drizzle, but this notwithstanding, numbers of both sexes and of all ages went to the Common to see the interesting spectacle. The town was almost deserted. All the vehicles the town boasted of — one carriage, several phaetons, droshkies, and lineikas—were engaged in taking out the curious. They left them at the encampment, and returned for fresh loads. By ten o'clock all were already out there.

The gipsies had lost all hopes. There was not much noise in the camp. The women were hiding in the tents with the little ones, so as not to see the massacre, and only occasionally a despairing wail was wrung from one or another of them. The men were feverishly making the last preparations. They had dragged the waggons to the edge of the camping-ground, and had tied the bears to them.

The ispravnik, with Thomas Thomasovich, passed along the rows of condemned. The bears themselves were not altogether calm. The unusual surroundings, the strange preparations, the enormous crowd, the large number of bears collected together—all this had excited them, and they tugged or gnawed at their chains, uttering occasional low growls. Old Ivan stood near his enormous bear crooked with age. His son, an elderly gipsy whose black hair was already streaked with silvery grey, and his grandson—that same Adonis whom Olga Pavlona had noticed—with ghastly faces and burning eyes were hastily tying up the bear.

The ispravnik came up level with the trio.

"Well, old man," said he, "tell them to commence."

A wave of excited expectation passed over the crowd of onlookers, conversation redoubled, but soon after all became quiet, and amidst a profound silence was heard a low but authoritative voice. Old Ivan was speaking.

"Allow me, sir, to speak." Then, turning to his fellow-gipsies, he continued : "Comrades, I beg you to let me be the first to finish. I am older than any of you. Next year I shall have seen ninety years. I have led bears from my infancy, and in the whole camp there is no bear older than mine."

He lowered his grey curly head on to his chest, shaking it sorrowfully from side to side, and wiped his eyes with his fist. Then he drew himself up, raised his head, and continued in a louder, firmer voice than before :

"Therefore I want to be the first. I thought I should not live to see such grief. I thought—that my bear, my loved one, would not live, but apparently Fate has willed otherwise. With my own hand I must kill him, my provider and benefactor. Loose him ; let him be free. He will not go away ; he, as with us old men, will not flee from death. Loose him, Vasia ! I do not wish to kill him bound, as they kill cattle. Do not be afraid," said he, turning to the crowd, which showed signs of alarm ; "he will not move."

The youth freed the huge beast, and led him a short distance away from the waggon. The bear sat on his

THE BEARS

haunches, letting his front paws hang loosely, and swayed from side to side, breathing heavily and hoarsely. He was very old, his teeth were yellow, his coat had grown a reddish colour and was falling out. He gazed in a friendly but melancholy manner at his old master with his one small eye. All around was an absolute silence, broken only by the noise of the ramrods against the barrels of the rifles as the wads were pressed home.

"Give me the gun," said the old man firmly.

His son gave him the rifle. He took it, and, pressing the muzzle against the old animal's breast, again began to address the bear:

"I am going to kill thee in a minute, Potap. God grant that my old hand may not tremble, and that the bullet may find its way into thy very heart. I do not want to torture thee. Thou dost not deserve such, my old bear, my good, my kind old mate. I caught thee a little cub. One of thy eyes had gone, thy nose was rotting from the ring, thou wert suffering from consumption. I tended thee as a son, and pitied thee, and thou grew up a big and powerful bear. There is not such another in all the camps which have collected here. And thou grew up and did not forget my kindness. Never have I had such a friend amongst men such as thou hast been. Thou hast been kind and quiet and clever, and hast learnt all. Never have I seen a beast kinder, more clever than thou. What would I have been without thee? My whole family have lived by thy labour. Thou hast bought me two troikas. It was thou who built me a hut for the winter. Thou hast done yet more for me. Thou saved my son from being a soldier. Ours is a large family, but all, from the oldest to the youngest, thou hast supported up till now. And I have loved thee greatly, and have not beaten thee too much, and if I have in any way offended against thee, forgive me. At thy feet I bow."

He threw himself at the bear's feet. The beast quietly

and plaintively growled. The old man lay on the ground, his whole body quivering convulsed with sobs.

"Shoot, daddy," said his son. "Do not tear our hearts!"

Ivan rose. The tears no longer flowed. He threw back the grey mane which had fallen over his brow, and continued in a steady, resounding voice:

"And now I must kill thee. They have ordered me, an old man, to shoot thee with my own hands. Thou must no longer live on this earth. Why? May God in Heaven judge us!"

He cocked the trigger, and with a firm, steady hand aimed at the beast's heart under the left paw. And the beast understood. A pitiful, heart-rending sound broke from the bear. He stood up on his hind-legs, and raised his fore-paws as if to hide his face with them from the terrifying gun. A wail went up from the gipsies; in the crowd many were openly crying. With a sob the old man threw aside the rifle, and fell senseless to the ground. His son rushed forward to pick him up, and the grandson seized the gun.

"It must be," he cried in a wild, hysterical voice, with blazing eyes. "Enough! Shoot, comrades; let us end it!" And, running up to the beast, he placed the muzzle of the rifle against the bear's ear and fired. The bear fell to the ground a lifeless mass. Only his paws moved convulsively, and his jaw dropped as if yawning. Throughout the encampment rang out shots and the despairing cries of the women and children. A light breeze carried the smoke towards the river.

"One has got loose—broken loose!" resounded through the crowd, and, like a flock of frightened sheep, all rushed helter-skelter. The ispravnik, fat Thomas Thomasovich, urchins, Leonid and Constantine, young ladies—all fled, panic-stricken, running into the tents, against the carts and waggons, screeching and falling over each other.

THE BEARS

Olga Pavlona almost fainted, but fear gave her strength, and, picking up her petticoats, she fled along the Common, regardless of the disordered state of her costume caused by such hasty flight. The horses, harnessed up in anticipation of the return of their owners to town, commenced to get out of control, and bolted in various directions. But the danger was by no means great. A still quite young brown bear, maddened by fright, with a broken chain hanging from his neck, was running away with astonishing rapidity. Everyone and everything made way in front of him, and, like the wind, he fled straight into the town. Some of the gipsies, rifles in hand, were running after him. The few pedestrians who chanced to be in the streets pressed themselves against the walls if too late to take refuge in gateways. Shutters were bolted, everything living hid, even the dogs disappeared.

Past the church went the bear, and up the main street, sometimes rushing to one or other side as if seeking a place in which to hide, but everywhere was bolted. As he flashed past the shops he was met with fiendish cries from the shopmen and boys who wished to frighten him. He fled past the bank, the school, and barracks, to the other end of the town, rushed along the road leading to the bank of the river, and stopped. His pursuers were out-distanced. But soon after a crowd, no longer composed of gipsies only, appeared from the street. The ispravnik and the Colonel were in a droshky with rifles in their hands. The gipsies and a squad of soldiers were following behind them at the double. Alongside the droshky ran Leonid and Constantine.

" There he is ! there he is !"cried out the ispravnik. " The deuce take him !"

A volley of shots followed. One of the bullets grazed the bear, and in mortal fright he fled faster than ever. A verst from the town, up the Rokhla, whither the bear was running, is a large water-mill, surrounded on all sides by a small but thick wood. The animal made for this wood, but, becoming confused in the branches of the river and the dams, lost his way. A wide expanse of water separated him from the dense overgrowth, where he could perhaps find, if not safety, at least respite. But he decided not to swim. On this side there was a species of bush which grows thickly, and is only found in Southern Russia. Its long, supple, branchless stalks grow so closely together that it is impossible for anyone to make his way through it, but at its roots there are corners and bare patches into which dogs can crawl, and as they often do this to escape from the heat when the weather is warm, and widen the paths leading to them by the pressure of their flanks on the bushes, a whole labyrinth of passages is formed. It was into this undergrowth the bear rushed. The mill men, who were watching from the upper story of the mill, saw this, and when the breathless, exhausted chase arrived, the ispravnik ordered the bear's hiding-place to be surrounded.

The unfortunate animal forced its way into the very depth of the bushes. The wound made by the bullet was very painful. He rolled himself into a ball, buried his muzzle in his paws, and lay motionless, deafened by the noise, mad with fright, and deprived of the possibility of defending himself. The soldiers fired into the bushes, hoping by chance to touch him and make him roar, but to hit, firing at random, is difficult. They killed him late that evening, having smoked him out of his shelter by setting fire to the bushes. Everyone who had a rifle thought it his bounden duty to plant a bullet into the dying beast, so that when they skinned it the skin was useless.

Not long ago I chanced to be in Bielsk. The town has scarcely changed. Only the bank has smashed, and the school is now larger and of a higher grade. They have changed the ispravnik, who was given promotion as pristaff in a provincial capital for zealous service. The brothers Isotoff, as of old, shout "Grand rond!" and "Au rebours!" and run about the town relating the last piece of gossip. The chemist, Thomas Thomasovich, has grown even fatter, and notwithstanding that he made a good thing out of the purchase of the bears'-fat at fourteen kopecks per pound by selling it at eighty kopecks, which brought him in all no small sum, even now speaks with disapproval of the slaughter of the bears.

"I said then to Olga Pavlona that through it her Adonis would become a horse-thief . . . and what happened? Less than a week afterwards he stole my pair of greys, the blackguard!"

"And do you know it was he who stole them?"

"Who else could it have been? Last year they tried him for horse-stealing and robbery. He was sent to penal servitude."

"Ah, how sorry I was for him!" said Olga Pavlona sorrowfully.

The poor lady has grown decidedly older these last years, and notwithstanding the fact, according to Thomas Thomasovich, who told me in confidence, that she has smeared her head with four pounds of bears'-grease, her hair has not only *not* become thicker, but even grown thinner. But her chignon hides it so well that it is absolutely unnoticeable.

XIV

THE FROG WHO TRAVELLED

ONCE upon a time there lived in this world a frog. She used to sit in a swamp and catch mosquitoes and midges, and in the spring used to croak loudly in company with her friends. And but for an event which occurred she would have lived happily her whole life through—provided, of course, a stork had not eaten her.

One day she was sitting on a crooked branch which stuck out of the water, and was revelling in a warm, slight drizzling rain.

" Ah me, what beautiful damp weather to-day !" she thought. " What a delight it is to live !"

The drizzle damped her striped polished back, and the raindrops trickled down under her belly behind her paws, which was extraordinarily pleasant—so pleasant that she almost gave a croak. But luckily she remembered that it was already autumn, and that frogs don't croak in the autumn—the spring is the time for that—and had she croaked she might have lost her " frogly " dignity. So she kept quiet and continued to take her ease.

Suddenly a thin, intermittent, whistling noise resounded in the air.

There is a species of duck which, when it flies, makes a singing, or rather a whistling, sound with its wings as they cleave the air. " Phew, phew, phew, phew !" sounds through the air when a covey of such ducks fly high above us, although the birds themselves are invisible, so

THE FROG WHO TRAVELLED

high do they fly. On this occasion the ducks, having described an enormous semicircle, swooped down and settled in the very same swamp in which the frog lived.

"Quack, quack!" said one of them. "We have still a long way to fly; we must have something to eat."

And the frog instantly hid herself, and, although she knew that the ducks would not eat her—a big and fat frog—she all the same dived under the log in case of accidents. However, having thought it over, she decided to stick her head with its protruding eyes out of the water. She was very curious to know to where the ducks were flying.

"Quack, quack!" said another duck. "It is already quite cold. Let us get away as quickly as possible to the South."

And all the ducks began to quack loudly in token of their approval.

"Mesdames ducks," said the frog, plucking up her courage, "what is the 'South' to which you are flying? Please excuse me for disturbing you."

The ducks crowded round the frog. At first they evinced a decided inclination to eat her, but each on reflection came to the conclusion that she was too big to be swallowed. And then they all began to quack and flap their wings.

"It is very nice in the South! It is warm there now! And what lovely warm swamps there are there! What worms! It is nice in the South!"

They quacked to such a degree that they nearly deafened the frog. She could scarcely prevail on them to be quiet, and begged one of them, who seemed to her the fattest and most intelligent of them all, to explain to her what was the "South." And when the duck told her all about the South, the frog went into ecstasies, but, nevertheless, at the end of the description, because she was a cautious frog, she asked him:

"And are there midges and mosquitoes there?"

"Oh, I should just say so—clouds of them!" replied the duck.

"Croak!" said the frog, and immediately turned round to see if there was any friend near who could have heard her and scolded her for croaking in the autumn. She really could not restrain herself from giving at least one little croak. "Take me with you!"

"You astonish me!" exclaimed the duck. "How can we take you? You have no wings!"

"When do you fly?" asked the frog.

"Soon, soon!" cried out all the ducks. "Quack, quack, quack! Here it is cold! To the South! to the South!"

"Allow me to think only five minutes," said the frog. "I will come back directly. I am sure to think of something good."

And she flopped from the branch, on to which she had again clambered, into the water, dived into the mud, and absolutely buried herself in it, so that no extraneous matter should distract her thoughts. Five minutes passed, and the ducks had all collected to fly, when suddenly from out of the water near the branch on which the frog had sat her mouth appeared, and it wore an expression of delight such as only a frog's mouth can assume.

"I have thought it out; I have found a way!" she said. "Let two of you, one at each end, take a twig in your beaks, and I will hang on to it in the middle. You will fly and I will travel. Only, whatever happens, you must not quack nor I croak—and then all will be superb."

Now, although, goodness knows, it is by no means a joke to carry a frog three thousand versts, keeping silent all the time, still the ingenuity of her plan sent the ducks into such a delirium of delight that they unanimously resolved to take the frog with them. They agreed to relieve each other every two hours, and as there were as many and many ducks as could be, and only one frog,

THE FROG WHO TRAVELLED 273

no duck's turn to carry the frog would come very often. They found a good strong twig, two ducks took it in their beaks, the frog caught hold in the middle with her mouth, and the whole covey rose into the air. The terrific height to which they flew up took the frog's breath away. Besides which, the ducks did not fly evenly, and kept giving the twig jerks. The poor frog swung in the air like a paper " tumbling tommy," and hung on by her jaw with all her might, so as not to be thrown off and flop to the ground. However, she soon became accustomed to her surroundings, and even began to look around her. Beneath her fields, meadows, rivers, and mountains passed by in rapid succession, but it was very difficult for her to take stock of them, because, hanging as she was from the twig, she could only see backwards and towards the sky; nevertheless, she managed to see something, and was very pleased and proud with herself.

" What a splendid idea it was of mine!" she thought to herself.

And as the rest of the ducks flew along behind the first pair which carried her they cried out to her and praised her.

" Our frog has an astonishingly clever head," they said. " It would be difficult to find anything like it even amongst us ducks."

The frog could scarcely restrain herself from thanking them, but, remembering that if she opened her mouth she would fall from a terrific height, she closed her jaw still tighter, and decided to resist the temptation. She swung in this manner for a whole day. The ducks who were carrying her relieved each other on the wing, cleverly catching hold of the twig. This was most terrifying. Several times the frog almost croaked from fright, but it was necessary to have plenty of presence of mind, which she possessed. In the evening the whole company halted in a swamp. At dawn the ducks with the frog continued their journey, but this time their passenger, in order to see the better what was happening, fastened on with her back and head to the front. The ducks flew over mown fields, woods turning yellow, and over villages full of corn-stacks. They could hear the people talking, and the noise of the machines with which they were threshing the rye. The villagers looked at the ducks, and, noticing something strange in their midst, pointed to it. And the frog longed to fly lower down, so as to show herself and to hear what they were saying about her. At the next halt she said:

"Is it possible for us to fly not quite so high? It makes my head swim, and I am afraid of falling if I should suddenly feel bad."

The kind ducks promised her to fly lower, and the following day they travelled so low that they could hear what was said.

"Look, look!" cried the children in one of the villages; "the ducks are carrying a frog!"

The frog heard this, and her heart jumped.

"Look, look!" "grown-ups" cried in another village. "That's an extraordinary thing!"

"Do they know that it was I who thought of this, and not the ducks?" the frog wondered to herself.

"Look, look!" they cried in a third village. "What a wonder! And who thought of such a clever dodge?"

Thereupon the frog could stand it no longer, and, throwing caution to the winds, cried out at the top of her voice:

"It was I—I!"

And with this cry she went tumbling over and over to the ground. The ducks quacked loudly, and one of them tried to catch hold of their unfortunate fellow-traveller as she was falling, but missed her. The frog, frantically waving all four paws, quickly fell to the ground, but as the ducks were flying very fast, she did not fall just at the spot above which she had cried out, and where there was a hard road, but much farther on, which was ex-

THE FROG WHO TRAVELLED

tremely lucky for her, because she flopped into a muddy pond on the edge of the village.

She quickly appeared from out of the water, and with all her might began to cry out :

" It was I—it was I who thought of it !"

But there was no one near her. The local frogs, frightened by the unexpected splash, had all disappeared under water. When they began to reappear they gazed at the new arrival with astonishment.

And she related to them a wonderful story of how she had thought all her life about the matter, and had at last invented a new, unusual method of travelling by ducks. How she had her own special ducks which carried her where she wanted to go. How she had been in the beautiful South, where it was so nice, where there are such lovely warm swamps, and such quantities of midges, and every other kind of edible insects.

" I have come here to see how you live," she said. " I shall stay with you until the spring, until my ducks which I have let go, return."

But the ducks never returned. They thought that the frog had been smashed to pieces by her fall, and were very sorry for her.

XV

A VERY SHORT ROMANCE

Frost and cold. January is approaching, and is making its coming known to every unfortunate being—dvorniks and gorodovois—unable to hide their noses in some warm place. It is also letting me know. Not because I have been unable to find a warm corner, but through a whim of mine.

As a matter of fact, why am I stumping along this deserted quay? The lamps are shining brightly, although the wind keeps forcing its way inside them and making the gas-jets dance. Their bright light makes the dark mass of the sumptuous Palace, and especially its windows, look all the more gloomy. The wind is moaning and howling across the icy waste of the Neva. Through the gusts of wind comes the sound of the chimes of the Fortress Cathedral, and every stroke of the mournful bells keeps time with the tap of my wooden leg on the ice-covered granite slabs of the pavement and with the beating of my aching heart against the walls of its narrow cell.

I must present myself to the reader. I am a young man with a wooden leg. Perhaps you will say I am imitating Dickens. You remember Silas Wegg, the literary gent with the wooden leg (in " Our Mutual Friend ") ? No, I am not copying him. I really am a young man with a wooden leg. Only I have become so recently.

" Ding-dong, ding-dong !" The chimes again ring out

their doleful chant, and then one o'clock strikes. Only one o'clock! Still seven hours before daylight, then this black winter night, with its cold, wet snow, will give place to a grey day. Shall I go home? I do not know. It is absolutely all the same to me. I have no need of sleep.

In the spring, also, I loved to spend whole nights walking up and down this quay. Ah, what nights those are! What can surpass them? They are not the scented nights of the South, with their strange black heaven and big stars with their pursuing gaze. Here all is light and bright. The sky with its varied hues is coldly beautiful, and throughout the night remains gilded north and east with the rays of a scarce-setting sun. The air is fresh and keen. The limpid Neva rolls onwards proudly, its dancing wavelets contentedly lapping against the stonework of the quay. I am standing on this quay, and on my arm a young girl is leaning. And this girl——

Ah, good people! why have I begun to tell you of my wounds? But such is the stupidity of the poor human heart. When it is stricken it dreams of seeking relief from each it meets, and does not find it. This is, however, quite intelligible. Who is in want of an old undarned stocking? Everyone endeavours to throw it away—the farther the better.

My heart was in no need of mending when in the spring of this year I met Masha—the best of all Mashas in this world. I met her on this same quay, which was not, however, as cold as it is now. And I had a real leg instead of this disgusting wooden stump—a real well-made leg, like the one that I have left me. Taking me all round, I was a well-made fellow, and, of course, did not walk, as now, like some bandy-legged fool. Not a nice word to use, but at present I cannot pick my words. And so I met her. It happened quite simply. I was walking along; she was walking along. (I am not a Lothario, or rather *was* not, because now I have a wooden stump.)

I do not know what impelled me to do so, but I spoke. First of all I, of course, told her I was not one of those sort of blackguards, etc., then I declared my intentions were honourable, and so on. My face (on which there is now a deep furrow above the bridge of my nose (a very gloomy-looking furrow) calmed her fears, and we walked together as far as her home. Sue was returning from her old grandmother, to whom she used to read. The poor old lady was blind.

Now the grandmother is dead. This year many have died, and not only old grandmothers. I could have died very easily, I assure you. But I have not. Oh, how much trouble can a man stand ? You do not know, and neither do I.

Very well, Masha ordered me to be a hero, and therefore I had to join the army.

The times of the Crusades have passed, and knights are extinct ; but if she whom you love were to say to you, " I am this ring," and throw it into a fire, even were it the greatest possible conflagration, would you not throw yourself into the flames to get that ring ? Oh, what a quaint fellow ! " Of course not," you reply—" of course not. I should go to the best jeweller and buy her another ring ten times more valuable." And she would say : " This is not the same ring, but is it an expensive ring ? I will never believe you." However, I am not of the same opinion as you, gentle reader. Perhaps the woman who would appeal to you would act in that way. You, no doubt, are the proud possessor of many shares and stocks, and can gratify any wish. You perhaps even subscribe to a foreign journal for your amusement. Perhaps you remember as a child having watched a moth which had flown into a flame ? That also amused you in those days. The moth lay on its back quivering and fluttering its little striped wings. This interested you ; then, when it no longer amused you, you squashed it with

A VERY SHORT ROMANCE

your finger, and the unhappy little thing ceased to suffer. Ah, kind reader, if only you would squash me with your finger, so that I might cease to suffer!

She was a strange girl. When war was declared she went about dreamily, and without speaking, for several days, and nothing I did would amuse her. "Listen," she said to me at length, "you are an honourable man?"

"I may admit that," I replied.

"Honourable people prove their words by deeds. You were for the war; you must fight." She puckered her brows and warmly pressed her little hand into mine.

I looked at Masha, and said seriously: "Yes."

"When you return I will be your wife," she said to me on the station platform. "Come back!" Tears dimmed my sight, and I almost sobbed aloud. But I kept my self-control, and found strength to answer Masha:

"Remember, Masha, honourable people——"

"Prove their words by deeds," said she, finishing the sentence. I clasped her to my heart for the last time, and jumped into the railway-carriage.

I went to fight for Masha's sake, but I did my duty by my country honourably. I marched bravely through Roumania amidst rain and dust, heat and cold. Self-sacrificingly I gnawed the ration biscuit. When we first met the Turks I did not fail, but won the "Cross" and promotion as N.C.O. In the second action something happened, and I fell to the ground. Groans, mist; a doctor in white apron with blood-covered hands; hospital nurses; my leg, with its birth-mark, taken off below the knee. All this happened as in a dream. Then the ambulance-train, with its comfortable cots and dainty lady in charge, brought me to St. Petersburg.

When you leave a town in the usual and proper way with two legs, and return to it with one leg and a stump instead of the other—believe me, it costs something.

They placed me in a hospital. This was in July. I begged them to find out the address of Mary Ivanovna

G——, and the good-natured attendant brought it me. I wrote, then again, and a third time—but no answer. My kind reader, I have told you all this, and, of course, you do not believe me. What an unlikely story! you say. A certain knight and a certain crafty traitress—the old, old story. My intelligent reader, believe me there are many such knights besides myself.

Eventually they fitted me with a wooden leg, and I was able now to find out for myself the cause of Masha's silence. I drove to her house, and then stumped up the long staircase. How I had flown up it eight months ago! At last the door. I ring with a sinking at my heart. I hear footsteps, and the old servant opens the door to me. Without listening to her joyous exclamations I rush (if it is possible to rush when your legs are of different kinds) into the drawing-room. Masha!

She is not alone, but is sitting with a very nice young fellow, a distant relative, who was at the University with me, and was expecting to obtain a good appointment eventually. Both congratulated me very tenderly (probably owing to my wooden leg), but both were somewhat confused. Within a quarter of an hour I understood all.

I did not wish to stand in the way of their happiness. The intelligent reader smiles sceptically. Surely you do not want me to believe all this? Who would gratuitously surrender the girl he loves to any good-for-nothing fellow?

First, he is not a good-for-nothing fellow; and, second, —well, I would tell you that second only you would not understand, because you do not believe that virtue and justice exist nowadays. You would prefer the unhappiness of three persons to the misery of one. You do not believe me, intelligent reader? Then don't!

The wedding took place two days ago, and I was best man. I performed my duties at the ceremony with dignity, and gave to another what I most prize in this

A VERY SHORT ROMANCE

world. Masha from time to time glanced timidly at me, and her husband regarded me with a perplexed air of bewilderment. The wedding was a merry one. Champagne flowed, her German relatives cried " Hoch !" and called me " der Russische Held." Masha and her husband were Lutherans.

" Aha !" exclaims the intelligent reader ; " see how you have betrayed yourself, sir hero ! Why must you make use of the Lutheran religion ? Simply because there are no orthodox marriages in December ! That is the whole reason and explanation, and the whole narrative is pure invention."

Think what you like, dear reader. It is a matter of absolute indifference to me. But were you to come with me on these December nights along the Palace Quay, and listen to the storm and chimes, and the tap of my wooden leg on the pavement ; if you could feel what effect these winter nights have on me ; if you could believe——

" Ding-dong, ding-dong !" The chimes are sounding four o'clock. It is time to go home, and throw myself on to my lonely bed and sleep.

" Au revoir," reader !

XVI

FROM THE REMINISCENCES OF PRIVATE IVANOFF

I

On the 4th of May, 1877, I arrived at Kishineff, and half an hour later had learnt that the 56th Division of Infantry was passing through the town. As I had come with the view of enlisting in some regiment and going to the war, I found myself, on the 7th of May, at 4 a.m., standing in the street amongst the grey ranks which had been formed up before the quarters of the Colonel of the 222nd (Starobielsky) Regiment. I was in a grey overcoat with red shoulder-straps and dark blue facings and a kepi, around which was a dark blue band. On my back was a knapsack, at my waist were cartridge-pouches, and I was holding a heavy Krinkoff rifle.

The band struck up as they brought out the colours from the Colonel's quarters. Words of command rang out and the regiment presented arms. Then followed a fearful row. The Colonel gave a command which was taken up by the battalion, company, and, finally, section commanders, and as the result of all this shouting a confused and, to me, absolutely incomprehensible movement of grey overcoats took place, which ended in the regiment drawing itself out into a long column and marching off with measured tread to the sound of the regimental band as it thundered out a quick step. I too stepped out, trying to keep my dressing and to keep in step with my neighbour. My knapsack pulled me backwards, the heavy ammunition pouches pulled me forward; my rifle kept jumping off my shoulder, and the grey collar of my overcoat rubbed my neck. But in spite of all these little discomforts, the music, the rhythmic, ponderous movement of the column bristling with bayonets, the freshness of early morning, and the sight of the sunburnt and stern faces, all combined to inspire a feeling of calm determination.

Notwithstanding the earliness of the hour, people flocked to the courtyard gates of the houses, and half-dressed figures gazed at us from windows. We marched through the long straight street past the bazaar, where the Moldavians were already commencing to arrive in their ox-carts. The street wound up the hill and stopped at the town cemetery. The morning became overcast, and a cold drizzle commenced. The trees of the cemetery were discernible through the mist, and glimpses of tombstones could be caught above its gates and walls. As we skirted the cemetery, leaving it to our right, it seemed to me that it gazed perplexedly at us through the mist, asking: " Why are you going thousands and thousands of versts to die on foreign fields when it is possible to die here—to die peacefully, and lie beneath my wooden crosses and stone slabs? Stop here!"

But we did not stop. An unknown, mysterious force was drawing us—the strongest force in human life. Each of us, taken separately, would have gone home, but the whole mass went forward in obedience to discipline, and not from any recognition of the justice of the cause, nor from any feeling of hatred towards an unknown enemy; not from any fear of punishment, but moved solely by that hidden and unconscious something which will, for many a long day yet, lead humanity to sanguinary slaughter—the most potent cause of every description of human ill and suffering.

A wide and deep valley which stretched away beyond sight into the mist opened out behind the cemetery.

The rain became heavier. Somewhere far, far away, the clouds had made way for a ray of sunshine which caused the slanting and perpendicular strips of rain to glisten like silver. Through the mist which rolled along the green slopes of the valley could be distinguished long columns of troops ahead of us. Now and then there was the gleam of bayonets. And the guns, as they came into the sunlight, shone like some bright star, only to vanish in the course of a few moments. Sometimes the clouds came together; it became darker and the rain more frequent. An hour after our start I felt a little stream of cold water begin to trickle down my back.

The first stage was not a long one, the distance from Kishineff to the village of G—— being in all only eighteen versts. However, not being accustomed to carry a weight of 20 to 35 pounds, I was at first unable even to eat when we at length reached the cottage told off to us. I leant against the wall, resting on my knapsack, and stood like this for some ten minutes fully equipped with my rifle in my hand. One of the soldiers going to the kitchen for his dinner took pity on me and took my canteen with him. But on his return he found me sound asleep. I slept until four o'clock in the morning, when I was awakened by the insufferably harsh sounds of a bugle sounding the "assembly," and five minutes later I was again plodding along the muddy, sticky road under a fine drizzling rain. Before me jogged a grey back, on which was strapped a brown calfskin knapsack and an iron canteen, which rattled incessantly. The grey back had a rifle on one shoulder. On either side and behind me were similar grey figures. For the first few days I could not distinguish them one from the other. The 222nd Infantry Regiment of the Line which I had joined consisted for the most part of peasants from the Governments of Vyatka and Kostroma. They all had broad faces, now blue with cold, prominent cheek-bones, and small grey eyes. Most of them were fair, with light-coloured hair and beards. Although I knew the names of several, I could not pick out their owners. A fortnight later I was unable to understand how I could ever have mixed up my two comrades, the one marching alongside me, and the other the possessor of the grey back which was constantly before my eyes. At first I had called them Feodoroff and Jitkoff indifferently, continually making mistakes, although they did not in the least resemble each other. Feodoroff, a corporal, was a young man of twenty-two, of average height, and splendidly built. His face, with its beautifully chiselled nose and lips, was as regular in its features as if it had been the work of some sculptor. His chin was covered with a fair curly beard, and there was a merry twinkle in his blue eyes. When the command was "Singers to the front!" he used to be the leader of our company. He was the possessor of a tenor voice, and would sing falsetto when high notes were necessary. He was a native of the Vladimir Government, but had lived since childhood in St. Petersburg. Contrary to the general rule, Petersburg "education" had not spoilt him, but had merely polished him, and had taught him to read the papers and to speak "wise words."

"Of course, Vladimir Mikhailovich," he used to say to me, "I can judge better than 'Uncle' Jitkoff, because 'Peter'* has set its mark on me. There is a civilization in 'Peter,' but nothing but ignorance and savagery in the provinces. However, as he is not a young man, but, so to speak, has seen things and undergone various vicissitudes of fate, I cannot shout at him. He is forty, and I am only in my twenty-third year. But I am a corporal."

"Uncle" Jitkoff was a gnarled-looking peasant of extraordinary strength and a perpetually morose visage. His face was swarthy. He had prominent cheek-bones and little eyes, which looked out from under his eyebrows.

* The people's name for St. Petersburg.

He never smiled, and rarely spoke. He was a carpenter by trade, and was on "indefinite leave" when the mobilization order was issued. He had only a few months more to serve in the reserve when the war broke out and compelled him to take part in the campaign, leaving a wife and five small children behind him at home. In spite of an unprepossessing exterior and perpetual moroseness, there was something attractive in him—something kind and strong. Now, as I have said, it seems quite unintelligible to me how I could ever have mixed up these two neighbours, but for the first two days they seemed alike to me. Each was grey; each was tired and benumbed with the cold.

The rain was unceasing during the whole first half of May, and we were marching without tents. The seemingly never-ending sticky road rose over hills and dipped into gullies almost every verst. It was heavy marching. Clumps of mud stuck to our feet, a leaden grey sky hung low and threateningly over us, and rained a continual fine drizzle on us, and there was no end to it. There was no hope of drying and warming ourselves when we reached the night's camp. The Roumanians would not let us into their cottages, and, indeed, there was no room anywhere for such a mass of men. We used to march through the town or village and camp anywhere on the common.

"Halt! . . . Pile arms!"

And there was nothing for it, when we had eaten our hot broth, but to lie down actually in the mud. Water below, water above. It seemed as if one's whole body was permeated with water.

Shivering, we wrapped ourselves up in our great-coats, and, gradually getting warm with a moist warmth, slept soundly until again awakened by the universally detested "assembly." Then again the grey column, the grey sky, muddy road, and dismal dripping hills and valleys. It was hard on us.

"They have opened all the windows of heaven," said, with a sigh, our squad leader, a N.C.O. named Karpoff, a veteran who had served through the Khiva campaign. "We are soaked and soaked without end."

"We shall get dry, Vasil Karpich! Look, there is the sun peeping out; it will dry us all. The march will be a long one. We shall have time to get dry and wet again before we reach the end of it. Mikhailich!" said my neighbour, turning to me, "is it far to the Danube?"

"Another three weeks yet."

"Three weeks! But we shall get there in two weeks...."

"We are going straight into the clutches of the devil," muttered "Uncle" Jitkoff.

"What are you growling about, you old blackguard? You are only making mischief. Where the devil are we going to? Why do you say things like that?"

"Well, are we going on a holiday?" snarled Jitkoff.

"No, not on a holiday, but as our duty calls us, to carry out our oath.... What did you say when you were sworn in? Not sparing your life. You old fool! Take care what you are saying!"

"But what did I say, Vasil Karpich? Am I not going? If to die, then to die.... It's all the same...."

"Well, don't let's hear any more of it."

Jitkoff relapsed into silence. His face became still more morose. For the matter of that, it was no time for talking. The going was too heavy. The feet kept slipping, and men kept constantly falling into the sticky mud. Deep swearing resounded through the battalion. Only Feodoroff did not hang his head, but kept unwearyingly relating to me story after story of Petersburg and the country.

However, there is an end to all things. One day, when I woke up in the morning in our bivouac near a village where a halt had been arranged, I saw a blue sky, huts with white plastered walls, and vineyards bathed in the bright morning sun, and heard gay, animated voices. All had already risen, had dried their clothes, and had recovered from the arduous ten days' march in the rain without tents. During the halt they were brought up. The soldiers immediately stretched them out, and, having pitched them properly, driven in the tent-pegs, and tightened the canvas, were almost all lying in their shade.

"They did not help us when it was raining. They will guard us from the sun."

"Yes, so the 'Barin's' face shan't get burnt," joked Feodoroff, slyly winking towards me.

II

We had only two officers in our company—the company commander, Captain Zaikin, and a subaltern officer, a lieutenant of the reserve named Stebelkoff. The company commander was a man of middle age, rather stout, and of jovial disposition. Stebelkoff was a youth only just out of the Academy. They lived on good terms with each other. The Captain took care of the Lieutenant, messed him, and during the rain even sheltered him under his own waterproof cloak. When they issued out the tents our officers camped together, and as the officers' tents were spacious, the Captain decided to take me in with him.

Tired out by a sleepless night, our company had been told off to help the transport, and had spent the whole night in dragging it out of gullies, and had even pulled the carts and waggons out of swollen streams by singing.

I was sleeping soundly after dinner, when the Captain's servant awoke me by cautiously touching my shoulder.

"Sir, Mr. Ivanoff, Mr. Ivanoff——" he whispered, as if he did not want to awake me, but rather was trying all he could not to disturb my sleep.

"What's the matter?"

"The Captain wants you." Then, seeing me putting

on my belt and bayonet, added : " He said I was to bring you just as you were."

A whole crowd had assembled in Zaikin's tent. Besides its usual occupants there were two more officers—the regimental Adjutant and the commander of the rifle company, named Ventzel. In 1877 a battalion did not consist, as now, of four companies, but of five. On service the rifle company brought up the rear, so that the rear files of our company were in touch with their front files. I often marched almost amongst the riflemen, and I had already several times heard from them the most uncomplimentary remarks about Staff-Captain Ventzel. All four officers were seated around a box which took the place of a table, and on which stood a samovar, plates and dishes, etc., and a bottle, and were drinking tea.

" Mr. Ivanoff ! Come in, please," cried out the Captain. " Nikita ! Bring a cup, mug, or glass, or whatever you have. Ventzel, move up a bit, and let Ivanoff sit down."

Ventzel stood up and bowed very courteously. He was a short, raw-boned, pale, and nervous-looking young man. What restless eyes ! and what thin lips ! were the thoughts which came into my head when I first saw him. The Adjutant, without rising, stretched out his hand. " Lukin," he said briefly, introducing himself.

I felt awkward. The officers were silent. Ventzel was sipping tea in which was some rum. The Adjutant was pulling at a short pipe, and Stebelkoff, the Lieutenant, having nodded to me, went on reading a battered volume, a translation of some novel which went through the march from Russia to the Danube with him in a portmanteau and subsequently returned home in a still more battered state. My host poured out some tea into a large earthenware mug and added an enormous go of rum.

" How are you, Mr. Student ? Don't be angry with me. I am a plain man. Yes, and all of us here, you know, are just common folk. But you are an educated man, so you must excuse us. Isn't that so?"

And he seized my hand with his huge fist as a bird of prey seizes its booty, and waved it several times in the air, looking at me with a kind expression in his prominent round little eyes.

"Are you a student?" inquired Ventzel.

"Yes, sir, I was."

He smiled and raised his restless eyes on me. I recalled the soldiers' stories I had heard about him, and doubted their truth.

"Why 'sir'? Here in this tent we are all alike. Here you are simply an intelligent man amongst others like yourself," he said quietly.

"An intelligent man! Yes, that's true," exclaimed Zaikin. "A student! I like students, although they are such insubordinate beggars. I should have been a student myself if it had not been for fate."

"What was your particular fate, Ivan Platonich?" inquired the Adjutant.

"Why, I simply could not work up for exams. Mathematics were not so bad, but as for the rest . . . it was hopeless. Literature, composition. I never learnt to write properly when I was a cadet. Honestly!"

"Do you know, Mr. Student," said the Adjutant between two gigantic puffs of smoke, "how Ivan Platonich makes four spelling mistakes in one simple word?"

"Come, come, don't tell lies, old chap," said Zaikin with a wave of his hand.

"It's quite true; I am not lying," said the Adjutant, laughing heartily as he spelt the word *à la* Zaikin.

"Laugh away! But the Adjutant himself is no better," said Zaikin, giving a specimen in his turn.

The Adjutant roared with laughter. Stebelkoff, who happened to have his mouth full of tea, spluttered it over his novel and put out one of the two candles which lighted the tent. I too could not help laughing. Ivan Platonich, thoroughly pleased with his witticism, went off into peals of deep laughter. Only Ventzel did not laugh.

"It was literature, then, Ivan Platonich?" he inquired quietly as before.

"Literature. . . . Yes, and other things. It reminds me of a man who only knew of the equator in geography and the meaning of the word 'era' in history. But, no, I am speaking rot. That wasn't the reason. It was simply that I had money and would never do any work. I, Ivanoff . . . I beg your pardon, what's your name?"

"Vladimir Mikhailich."

"Vladimir Mikhailich? Thank you. . . . Well, I was a light-headed fellow from the very first, and what tricks I used to play! You know the song about the boy who had money.

"I entered this famous, although a purely line regiment, as a junker. They sent me to school. I only just passed, and now I have been twenty years slaving in the service. Now we are dodging after the Turk. Drink up, gentlemen—drink properly! Is it worth while spoiling good tea? Let us drink, gentlemen, to 'Food for powder.'"

"Chair à canon," said Ventzel.

"Well, all right, in French, if you like. Our Captain, Vladimir Mikhailich, is a clever man. He knows several languages, and can repeat a lot of German poetry by heart. Look here, young man, I sent for you to propose you should transfer yourself into my tent. Where you are now there are six of you, and it is stifling and crowded with soldiers. Besides, they are not over clean. In any case, you will be better off with us."

"Thank you, but please allow me to refuse your offer."

"Why? Bosh! Nikita! Go and fetch his knapsack! Which tent are you in?"

"The second on the right. But please allow me to

stay there. I have to be more with the men, and it is better I should be altogether with them."

The Captain looked at me attentively, as if desirous of reading my thoughts. Having pondered a little, he said:

"What is it? You want to make friends with the men?"

"Yes, if it is possible."

"That's right. Don't change. I respect you for it."

And he grabbed my hand and once more waved it in the air.

Soon afterwards I took farewell of the officers and left the tent. It had grown dark. The men were putting on their great-coats in preparation for evening prayers. The companies were drawn up in their lines, so that each battalion formed a closed square, within which were the tents and piled arms. Owing to the halt, the whole of our division had got together. The drums were beating tattoo, and from afar could be heard the words of the command preparatory to prayers:

"Remove caps!"

And twelve thousand men bared their heads. "Our Father which art in Heaven," began our company. The chant was taken up around us. Sixty choirs of two hundred men each, and each choir singing independently. There were discordant notes to be heard, but, nevertheless, the hymn produced a stirring and solemn effect. Gradually the choirs came to an end. Finally, the last company of the battalion at the far end of the camp sang, "But deliver us from evil." The drums gave a short roll, and the order:

"Put on head-dress!" was given.

The soldiers laid themselves down to sleep. In our tent, where, as in the other tents, six men occupied a space of two square sajenes, my place was near the walls of the tent, and for a long time I lay gazing at the stars, at the camp-fires of other troops far from us, and listening to the low, confused murmur of a large camp. In the

REMINISCENCES OF PRIVATE IVANOFF

neighbouring tent someone was telling a fairy-tale, everlastingly interspersed with " And after that . . ." " and after that this prince went to his spouse and began to scold her about everything. And after that she . . . Lutikoff, are you asleep ? Well, sleep, then, and God be with you," murmured the narrator of the tale, and lapsed into silence.

The sound of conversation was audible from the officers' tent also, and the movements of the officers sitting there were revealed in distorted form against the canvas by the light of the candles. From time to time could be heard the noisy laugh of the Adjutant. An armed sentry was pacing his beat in our lines. Opposite, and not far from us, was the artillery camp, with yet another sentry with drawn sword. The stamping of the horses picketed in their lines, and their deep bretahing as they quietly chewed their oats, could be plainly heard, a sound which recalled nights passed at post-stages in now far-away homeland on just such quiet starlight nights as this one.

The Great Bear constellation was shining low down on the horizon, much lower down than with us in Russia. Gazing at the North Star, I pondered as to the exact direction in which St. Petersburg lay, where I had left my mother, friends, and all dear to me. Above my head familiar star groups were shining. The Milky Way shone in a bright, majestically calm, band of light. Towards the South burned the great stars of some constellations unknown to me, one with a red, and the other with a greenish fire. I wondered whether I should see any other strange stars when we were across the Danube and Balkans, and into Constantinople.

As I did not feel sleepy, I got up and commenced to stroll along the damp grass between our lines and the artillery. A dark figure came up with me, and, guessing by the clinking of a sword that it was an officer, I turned to my front. It proved to be Ventzel.

"Not asleep, Vladimir Mikhailich?" he inquired in a soft, quiet voice.

"No, sir."

"My name is Peter Nicolaievitch . . . and I also cannot sleep. . . . I sat and sat with your Captain. But it was boring. They sat down to cards, and were all drinking too much. . . . Ah, what a night!"

He walked alongside me, and, reaching the end of our lines, we turned and continued to pace backwards and forwards in this manner several times, neither of us saying anything. Ventzel was the first to break the silence.

"Tell me, you have started on this campaign voluntarily?"

"Yes."

"What induced you to do so?"

"How can I explain?" I replied, not wishing to go into details. "Chiefly, of course, a desire to experience and see things personally."

"And probably to study the people in the person of its representative—the soldier?" inquired Ventzel. It was dark, and I could not see the expression on his face, but I detected the irony in his tone.

"How could one study here? How can one study when one only thinks of how to get to the night's camp and sleep?"

"No; without joking, tell me why you would not transfer yourself to your Captain's tent? Surely you do not value the opinion of a moujik?"

"Certainly I value the opinion of anyone whose opinion I have no reason not to respect."

"I have no reason to disbelieve you. Besides, it is the fashion nowadays. Even literature presents the moujik as a masterpiece of creation."

"But who is speaking of masterpieces of creation, Peter Nicolaievitch? If only they would recognize him as a man."

"Enough of such sentimentality, please ! Who does not recognize him as a man ? A man ? Well, granted he is a man, but what sort is another question. . . . Well, let's talk of something else."

We did, in fact, talk a great deal. Ventzel had evidently read a great deal, and, as Zaikin had said, " knew languages."

The Captain's remark that he could recite poetry also proved to be true. We talked about French writers, and Ventzel, having censured the " Realist " school, went back to the thirties and forties, and even recited with feeling Alfred de Musset's " A December Night." His rendering of it was good, simple, and expressive, and with a good accent. Having recited it, he was silent, and then added :

"Yes, it is good, but all the French authors put together are not worth ten lines of Schiller, Goethe, or Shakespeare."

Until he got his company, he had charge of the regimental library, and had followed Russian literature closely.

Talking of it, he expressed himself strongly against what he termed its " boorish tendency." The conversation then reverted to the old subject. Ventzel argued heatedly :

"When I was almost a boy, I entered the regiment, and I did not then think what I am telling you now. I tried to act by mere force of word. I endeavoured to obtain some moral influence over the men. But after a year they had exhausted me. All that remained from the so-called good books coming into contact with actuality proved to be sentimental bosh, and now I am convinced that the only way of making oneself understood is—that !"

He made some sort of gesture with his hand. But it was so dark that I did not understand it.

"What, Peter Nicolaievitch ?"

"A clenched fist!" he interjected.

"But good-night; it is time to sleep."

I saluted and went back to my own tent, sorry and disgusted.

They were apparently all asleep, but a minute later, when I had laid down, Feodoroff, who was sleeping alongside me, asked quietly:

"Mikhailich, are you asleep?"

"No, why?"

"Were you walking with Venztel?"

"Yes."

"How was he? Quiet?"

"All right—quiet and even kind."

"Well, well. What it means to be a brother Barin! He isn't like that with us."

"What do you mean? Is he really very bad-tempered?"

"I should just think so—awful. He makes their teeth rattle in the second rifle company, the beast!"

And Feodoroff forthwith fell asleep, so that in reply to my next question I heard only his even and calm breathing. I wrapped myself up more tightly in my big cloak. My thoughts became at first confused, and then disappeared in sound sleep.

III

The rain was followed by heat. About this time we left the little village where our feet used to stick in the slippery mud, and came on to the main road leading from Yass to Bukarest. Our first march along this road from Tekuch to Berlada will always be remembered by those who made it. It was thirty-five degrees (Réaumur) in the shade, and the distance was forty-eight versts. It was perfectly still. A fine dust, full of lime, which was being raised by thousands of feet, hung over the road. It got into our noses and mouths, and powdered our hair so thickly that it was impossible to distinguish its colour.

REMINISCENCES OF PRIVATE IVANOFF 297

Settling all over our perspiring faces, it became mud, and turned us into niggers. For some reason we marched in our tunics instead of in our shirt-sleeves. The black cloth drew the sun, which literally baked our heads through our black shakos. The almost red-hot stones of the metalled road could be felt through the soles of our boots. The men kept on " falling out." To add to our misfortunes, there were few wells along the route, and there was for the most part so little water in them that the head of our column (it was a whole division) exhausted the supply, and after frightful crushing and pushing at the wells, we found only a sticky liquid more resembling mud than water. When there was not even this, the men used to fall, utterly done up. On this day in ou battalion alone about ninety men fell out along the road. Three died from sunstroke.

Compared with my comrades, this trial affected me but lightly. Possibly because the majority of my battalion hailed from the North, whereas I had been accustomed from childhood to the heat of the Steppe. Perhaps, also, there was another cause. I had occasion to note that the common soldier, speaking generally, takes physical suffering more to heart than is the case with those drawn from the so-called privileged classes. (I am referring only to those who went to the war as volunteers.) To the ordinary soldier physical misfortunes were a source of genuine grief, capable of producing depression and, in general, mental torture. Those who were going to the war as volunteers of course suffered, physically speaking, no less, but rather more, than the soldier drawn from the lower class—owing to a more tender upbringing, comparative bodily weakness, etc., but inwardly were calmer. Their spiritual world could not be disturbed by bleeding feet, insufferable heat, and deadly tiredness. Never have I experienced such complete spiritual calm, such peace within myself, and such contentment with life as when I was undergoing these hardships, and went forward under a rain of bullets to kill people. All this may seem wild and strange, but I am only writing the truth.

However that may be, when others fell by the roadside I still kept up.

In Tekuch I supplied myself with an enormous calabash water-bottle, holding at least four flaskfuls. It often cost me dear to fill it. Half of the water I used to keep for myself, and the other half I shared out to my comrades. A man would force himself to plod along, but in the end the heat would claim him. His legs would begin to bend under him, his body reel as if drunk. Through the thick layer of grime and dust could be seen the apoplectic hue of his face as his trembling hands gripped his rifle. A gulp of water would revive him for a few minutes, but eventually the man would fall senseless into the road thick with lime-dust. Hoarse voices would cry out "Orderly!" It was the orderly's duty to drag the fallen man to one side, and assist him although he was himself almost in the same condition. The ditches along the road were sown with prostrate men. . . . Feodoroff and Jitkoff were marching alongside me, and, though obviously suffering, were endeavouring to hold out. The heat was affecting each reversely, according to his temperament. Talkative Feodoroff kept silent, merely giving an occasional deep sigh, and a piteous look was in his beautiful but now dust-inflamed eyes. "Uncle" Jitkoff, on the other hand, kept up a continuous flow of abuse and argument.

"Look at him, tumbling down—he will stick me with his bayonet, d——n him! . . ." he would cry angrily, avoiding some fallen soldier, the point of whose bayonet had nearly caught him in the eye. "Lord! why are you sending this on us? If it wasn't for that brute I should fall myself."

"Who is the brute, 'Uncle'?" I asked.

"Niemtseff, the Staff-Captain. He is orderly officer

to-day, and is in the rear. Better to go ahead or else he will beat me black and blue."

I already knew that the men had changed the name Ventzel into Niemtseff. The two names were not unlike in Russian. I stepped out of the ranks. It was a little easier marching along the side of the road. There was less dust and not so much jostling. Many were doing this. On this unfortunate day nobody cared about keeping the ranks. Gradually I dropped behind my company, and found myself at the tail of the column.

Ventzel, worn out and breathless but excited, caught me up.

"How are you getting on?" he inquired, in a hoarse voice. "Let us go along the side of the road. I am absolutely worn out."

"Do you want some water?"

He greedily took several gulps from my water-bottle.

"Thank you, I feel better now. What a day!"

For a little time we marched side by side in silence.

"By the way," he said, "you have not transferred yourself to Ivan Platonich?"

"No."

"More fool you. Excuse my outspokenness. Au revoir. I am wanted at the tail of the column. For some reason many of these tender creations are falling down."

Having gone a few paces farther, I turned my head and saw Ventzel bend over a fallen soldier, and drag him by the shoulder.

"Get up, you blackguard! Get up!"

I literally did not recognize my educated conversationalist. He was pouring out an endless flow of the coarsest abuse. The soldier was almost senseless, and his lips were murmuring something as he gazed up with a hopeless expression at the infuriated officer.

"Get up! Get up immediately, Aha! you won't? Then take that, and that, and that!"

Ventzel had seized his sword, and was dealing blow after blow with its iron scabbard over the wretched man's shoulders, all blistered and aching from the weight of his knapsack and rifle. I could stand it no longer, and went up to Ventzel.

"Peter Nicolaievitch!"

"Get up! . . ." His arm with the sword was once more raised for a blow, when I succeeded in seizing it firmly.

"For God's sake, Peter Nicolaievitch, leave him alone!"

He turned a frenzied face towards me. He was a terrifying sight with his eyes half out of his head, and a distorted mouth, which was convulsively twitching. With a sharp movement he wrenched his arm from my hold. I thought that he would roar at me for my boldness (to seize an officer by the arm was certainly most daring), but he restrained himself.

"Listen, Ivanoff; never do this. If, in my place, there was some other brute, such as Schuroff or Timothieff, you would have paid dearly for your pleasantry. You must remember that you are a private, and that for such action you could be without further words—shot."

"It is all the same to me. I could not see and not interfere."

"It does honour to your tender feelings. But apply them elsewhere. Can one act otherwise with these? . . ." (His face assumed an expression of contempt—nay, more, hatred.) "Perhaps ten of these scores who have given way and fallen down like a lot of old women are really absolutely played out. I am doing this not from cruelty. I have none in my nature. But one must maintain discipline. If it was possible to reason with them, I would talk, but words have no effect on them. They understand and feel only physical pain."

I did not hear him out, but started to overtake my company, which was already far away. I caught up

Feodoroff and Jitkoff as our battalion debouched from the road into a field and was halted.

"What were you talking about, Mikhailich, with Staff-Captain Ventzel?" asked Feodoroff, when, thoroughly exhausted, I threw myself down near him, after having with difficulty piled my arm.

"Talking," muttered Jitkoff.

"Can you call it talking? He seized him by the arm."

"Take care, Ivanoff, sir. Be careful of Niemtseff. Don't be misled because he likes to talk with you. It will cost you dear."

IV

Late that evening we reached Fokshan, passed through the unlighted, silent, and dusty little town, and came out somewhere into a field. It was as dark as pitch; the battalions were camped anyhow, and worn-out men slept as if dead. Scarcely anyone cared to eat the "dinner" which had been prepared. The soldier's food is always dinner, whether it is early morning, daytime, or night. All night long stragglers were coming in. At dawn we were again on the march, but consoled ourselves with the act that at the end of it there was to be a day's halt.

Once again the moving ranks, once again the knapsack presses benumbed shoulders, once again the pain of sore and bleeding feet. But the first ten versts were performed in a kind of stupor. The short sleep we had had was not able to destroy the fatigue of yesterday, and the men practically slept as they marched. I slept so soundly that when we had our first halt I could not believe we had already covered ten versts, and could not recall any one part of the road we had traversed. Only when, as a prelude to a halt, the columns begin to close in and re-form does one awake and think with joy of an hour's rest and the possibility of throwing off one's pack, of boiling water in one's canteen, and lying free whilst sipping hot tea. As soon as arms are piled and knapsacks removed the majority commence collecting firewood—almost always the dry stalks of last year's maize-crops. Two bayonets are stuck into the ground, a ramrod is laid on them, and two or three canteens hung on it. The dry, brittle stalks burn brightly and merrily. The flames lick the blackened canteens, and within ten minutes the water is boiling hard. The men used to throw the tea straight into the kettle, allowing it to boil for a short time, which resulted in a strong, almost black, tea, drunk for the most part without sugar, as the commissariat, while issuing plenty of tea (the men even smoked it when out of tobacco), gave us very little sugar. The tea was drunk in enormous quantities. A canteen which held about seven glasses was the usual one man's portion.

Perhaps it seems strange that I go into such details. But a soldier's life, when campaigning, is so hard, and entails so much deprivation, and the future holds out so little hope, that even tea or some such similar small luxury gives enormous pleasure. It was necessary to see, to realize with what serious, contented faces sunburnt, rough, and stern soldiers, young and old—true it is that there were scarcely any over forty years of age amongst us—like children, laid little sticks and stalks under the canteens, looked after the fire, and advised each other.

"You, Lutikoff, push them to the edge. That's it. . . . They have begun to burn. Now the water will boil soon."

Tea, and sometimes in cold and rainy weather a glass of vodka, or a pipe of tobacco, comprised the sum-total of a soldier's pleasures, excluding, of course, all-healing sleep, when it was possible to forget bodily misfortunes and thoughts of a dark and terrifying future. Tobacco played no small rôle amongst these joys of life, exciting and supporting exhausted nerves. A tightly filled pipe would go round ten men, and, being returned to its owner, he would take the last pull, knock out the ash, and, with

REMINISCENCES OF PRIVATE IVANOFF

an air of importance, secrete the pipe in the upper part of his jack-boot. I remember my grief at the loss of my pipe by one of my friends to whom I had lent it for a smoke, and how he, too, was grieved and ashamed about it, just as if he had lost a whole fortune entrusted to him.

At the chief halt (about midday) we used to rest for an hour and a half to two hours. After drinking our tea everyone would sleep. Quiet would reign in the bivouac. Only the sentry on the colours would pace to and fro, and some one or other of the officers would keep awake.

We would lie on the ground with our knapsacks under our heads, neither asleep nor awake. The scorching sun would burn our faces and necks. Flies would keep buzzing everlastingly around us, making real sleep impossible. Dreams mingled with reality. It was so short a time ago that life had been so different that in half-conscious slumber one expected to wake and find oneself at home; that this Steppe would disappear; this bare soil, with thorny bushes in place of grass; this pitiless sun and hot wind; these thousands of strangely attired men in dust-stained shirts; these piles of arms. It was all like some hideous nightmare.

Then the powerful voice of our little bearded battalion Major, Chernoglazoff, would give the command, "Ri-ise," in a long-drawn-out and severe tone of voice, and the prostrate crowd of white shirts would move, stretch itself, rise, and commence to strap on its equipment, and form ranks—"Unpile arms!"

We take our rifles. Even now I well remember my rifle, No. 18,635, with its stock rather darker than the others, and a long scratch along the dark varnish. Yet another command, and the battalion, forming column, turns on to the road. At the extreme front of the column the Major's horse was led, a prancing bay stallion called Vavara. The Major only rode on extreme occasions, always marching at the head of the battalion with Vavara, a true infantryman. He wished to show the soldiers that the " authorities " also endeavoured to do their duty, and the soldiers loved him for it. He was always cool and collected, never joked nor smiled. He was the first to rise in the morning and the last to lie down at night. His manner toward the men was firm and restrained, and he never allowed himself to rage or shout without reason. It was said that but for him goodness knows what Ventzel might have done.

To-day is hot, but not like yesterday. We are no longer marching along the metalled road, but parallel with the railway, along a narrow by-road, so that most of us are marching over grass. There is no dust. Clouds are racing overhead. At intervals there are big raindrops. We gaze upwards at the clouds and stretch out our hands to see if it is really raining. Even yesterday's stragglers have taken heart. It is no distance now, only some ten versts, and then a rest—the longed-for rest—not merely for one short night, but all night, the next day, and even that night too. The men, having cheered up, want to sing, and Feodoroff breaks out into the well-known song about Poltava. Having sung how suddenly a mischief-making bullet found its way into the Imperial head-dress, he switched off into an idiotic and somewhat obscene, but extremely popular, song amongst men, about a certain Liza who went into the woods and found a bee-hive there, and all that happened from this find. Then followed the historic song about Peter the Great and the Senate, and, finally, a song of some fifty verses, an effort by the local talent of our battalion.

" Feodoroff," I asked one day, " why do you sing all that bosh about Liza ? "

I mentioned several other songs, idiotic and cynical to a degree.

" Orders, Vladimir Mikhailich. But why ? Do you really call it singing ? It is really a kind of screeching, just to work the chest and to make marching more lively."

The singers tire themselves out, and the band begins to play. It is much easier to step out to the measured, loud, and, for the most part, lively marches. All, even the most tired, pull themselves together, march strictly in step, and keep their dressing. It is difficult to recognize the battalion. I remember how once we marched more than six versts in an hour without feeling tired, thanks to the band. But when the exhausted bandsmen ceased playing, the influence of the music went, and I felt as if I should drop straightaway, and so I should have done had not there been an opportune halt.

About five versts from our halt we came upon an obstacle. We were marching through the valley of some little river. On the one side there were mountains and on the other a narrow and somewhat high railway embankment. The recent rains had flooded the valley and converted our road into a kind of lake about thirty sajenes wide. The bed of the railway rose above it like a dam, and we had to cross over by it. A ganger on the line let the first battalion over, which thus successfully avoided the lake, but then declared that a train was due in five minutes' time, and we must wait. We halted and had just piled arms, when the well-known carriage of the Brigadier-General appeared at the turn of the road.

He was a great man. I have never heard such a voice as he possessed, either on the operatic stage or amongst cathedral choirs. The echoes of his bass resounded in the air like a trumpet, his big well-fed figure, with its red, big head, enormous dark-coloured whiskers waving in the breeze, and heavy black eyebrows surmounting tiny little eyes, which shone like needles, was a most inspiring sight as he sat on his horse giving commands to the brigade. On one occasion on the manœuvre-ground at Moscow during some evolutions, his appearance and general demeanour were so martial and inspiring that an old man in the crowd in a fit of enthusiasm shouted out :

" Bravo ! That's the sort we want !"

Since which occasion the General has always been known as "Bravo."

He had ambitions. He carried several small volumes on military history throughout the campaign. His favourite topic of conversation with his officers was criticism of the Napoleonic campaigns. I, of course, only knew of this from hearsay, as we seldom saw our General. Generally he caught us up midway in the day's march in his carriage, drawn by a troika. Having arrived at the quarters for the night, he would occupy a lodging and stay there until late the next morning and again catch us up during the day, when the men would always remark on the particular degree of purple in the face and the hoarseness accompanying his deafening salute to us:

"Health to you, Starobieltzi!"

"We wish Your Excellency health," the men would reply, adding to themselves: "Old Bravo is off for another booze."

And the General would go ahead, sometimes without any incident, and sometimes bestowing *en route* a thunderous "head-washing" on some poor company commander.

Noticing that the battalion had halted, the General rushed at us and jumped out of his carriage as quickly as his corpulency would admit. The Major went up to him.

"What's this? Why have you halted? Who gave you leave?"

"Your Excellency, the road is under water, and a train is expected shortly over the rails."

"Road under water? Train? Bosh! You are making old women of the men, teaching them to be mollycoddles. Don't halt without orders! Consider yourself, sir, under arrest . . ."

"Your Excellency . . ."

"Don't answer me!"

The General raised his eyes threateningly and turned his attention on another victim.

"Why, what's this? Why is the commander of the second rifle company not in his place? Staff-Captain Ventzel, come here, please!"

Ventzel went forward, and the General poured a torrent of rage on him. I heard how Ventzel tried to reply, raising his voice, but the General shouted him down, and it was only possible to guess that Ventzel had said something disrespectful.

"You dare to reply? To be impertinent?" thundered the General. "Hold your tongue! Take his sword from him. Go to the money-chest, under arrest! An example to the men.... Afraid of water! My men, after me! Remember Suvoroff!"

The General went rapidly past the battalion with the cramped gait of one who has been sitting for a long time in a carriage.

"Follow me! Children! Remember Suvoroff!" he repeated, and waded in his patent-leather jack-boots into the water. The Major, with a malicious expression on his face, glanced back and went forward with the General. The battalion moved after them. At first the water was knee-high, then it reached the waist, then higher and higher. The tall General moved freely, but the little Major was already striking out with his arms. The men, just like a flock of sheep when crossing a stream, jostled each other and staggered from side to side as they pulled their feet out of the soft clayey bottom in which they kept sticking. The company commanders and the battalion Adjutant, who were riding, and could have, in consequence, crossed over very comfortably, seeing the example set by the General, followed it, dismounted, and, leading their horses, waded into the muddy water, which had been churned up by hundreds of soldiers' feet. Our company, composed of the tallest men in the battalion, crossed with comparative comfort, but the eighth company, which was marching abreast of us, and was composed of undersized men, were almost up to their ears in the water. Some of them even began to choke and clutch at us. A little gipsy soldier, with blanched face and terrified, wide-opened eyes, seized " Uncle " Jitkoff by the neck with both hands, having thrown away his rifle. Luckily for the gipsy, somebody seized it from going to the bottom.

Ten sajenes farther on the water became shallower, and everyone, being now out of danger, commenced to scramble out as quickly as possible, pushing and swearing at each other. Many of us laughed, but it was no laughing matter for the soldiers of the eighth company. Many of their faces were blue not only from cold. Behind us pressed the riflemen.

" Now then, whipper-snappers, scramble out ! They have sunk !" they cried.

" Very easy to have drowned," replied the eighth company. " It was all right for him ; he only wetted his whiskers. What a hero ! People could be drowned here."

" You should have sat in my canteen. I would have taken you over dry."

" I didn't think of that," replied the little soldier good-humouredly at the gibe.

The cause of all this bustle having already succeeded in freeing his feet from the sticky bottom, and having got out of the water, was standing in a majestic pose on the bank, looking at the struggling mass of humanity in the water. He was wet to the skin, and had in reality soaked himself and his long whiskers. The water was trickling from his clothes. His polished leather top-boots were bulging with water, but he continued to shout encouragement to the men.

" Forward, my children ! Remember Suvoroff !"

The soaking officers with gloomy faces were crowding around him. Amongst them was Ventzel, with distorted face, and minus his sword. Meanwhile the General's coachman, having reached the bank, and having pushed off into the water, sat on the box with a huge whip, and got over successfully, a little to one side of the spot where he had crossed, and where the water scarcely reached the axles of the carriage-wheel.

"That is where, Your Excellency, we should have crossed over," said the Major quietly. "Will you order the men to dry themselves?"

"Certainly, certainly, Sergei Nicolaich," replied the General calmly. The cold water had quenched his ardour. He got into his carriage, sat down; then again stood up and cried out at the top of his extraordinarily powerful voice:

"Thank you, Starobieltzi! You are good fellows."

"Pleased to try, Your Excellency!" replied the men in salute somewhat confusedly. And the dripping General drove off ahead.

The sun was still high. There were only five more versts to go, so the Major made a prolonged halt. We undressed, lit fires, dried our clothes, boots, knapsacks, and pouches, and two hours afterwards started off again, even laughing at the recollection of our bath.

"And so old Bravo has sent Ventzel off under arrest!" said Feodoroff.

"A good job. Let him march a day or two with the money-chest," came the reply from someone in the riflemen company behind us.

"What's that to do with you?"

"With me! Not only with me, but for the whole company it will be easier. At least we shall have a rest for a couple of days. We can't stick him—that's what it is to do with me!"

"Patience brings everything about."

"Patience is all right, but it doesn't always bring everything," said Jitkoff in his usual surly tone. "If only the Turk will kill him!"

"And you, 'Uncle' Jitkoff, don't despair. You have

to think about our no longer being wet, that we are marching dry, and old Bravo is riding wet," said Feodoroff, amidst general laughter.

V

We continued to march parallel with the railway. Trains filled with men, horses, and supplies were continually passing us. The men looked enviously at the goods waggons being whirled past us, through the open doors of which were to be seen horses' muzzles.

"Eh? But what luck for the horses! Meanwhile we have to walk."

"A horse is stupid, and gets thin," argued Vasili Karpich. "But you are a man, and can look after yourself properly."

Once, when we were halted, a Cossack galloped up to the Major with an important piece of news. We were ordered to fall in without knapsacks or arms, just in our white shirts. None of us knew what this meant. The officers examined us. Ventzel, as usual, was shouting and swearing, tugging at badly-put-on belts, and with kicks ordering men to adjust their shirts. Then they marched us to the bed of the railway, and after a good deal of manœuvring, the regiment was stretched in two ranks along the route. The line of white shirts extended more than a verst.

"Children," shouted the Major, "His Majesty the Emperor is passing by!"

And we commenced to await the Emperor. Our division was an outlying one, stationed far from Petersburg and Moscow. Barely one-tenth of the men composing it had ever seen their Tsar, and all waited the Imperial train impatiently. Half an hour passed by, and no train. The men were allowed to sit down, and began to talk.

"Will the train stop?" asked someone.

"Don't reckon on that! Stopping for every regiment! He will look at us out of the window, and that's good enough for us."

"And we shall not distinguish which is he. There are a number of Generals with him."

"I shall know. The year before last I saw him at K—— as close as that;" and the soldier stretched out his hand to show how close he had been to the Emperor.

Finally, after two hours' expectancy, smoke appeared in the distance. The regiment rose and took up its proper dressing. First passed the train with the servants and kitchen. The cooks and their assistants in white caps looked at us out of the windows, and for some reason laughed. About 200 sajenes behind came the Imperial train. The engine-driver, seeing the regiment drawn up, slackened speed, and the carriages slowly rumbled past before eyes greedily searching the windows. But all had the blinds drawn. A Cossack and an officer, standing on the platform of the last carriage, were the sole persons on the train whom we saw. We stood gazing after the faster and faster receding train for another three minutes, and then returned to our bivouac. The men were disappointed, and expressed their disappointment.

"When shall we ever see him now?"

But we were soon to see him. They told us that the Emperor would review us before the town of Ploeshti.

We marched past before him, as on the march, in the same dirty white shirts and trousers, in the same browned and ·dusty boots, with the same ugly strapped-on knapsacks, ration-bags, and bottles on string. The soldier had nothing of the young dandy or dashing hero in appearance. Each much more closely resembled a simple common moujik. Only the rifle and ammunition-pouches showed that this moujik was off to the war. We were drawn up in columns of fours, as we could not have marched through the narrow streets of the town in any other formation. I marched by the side, and tried above all not to get out of step and to keep my dressing, and reflected that if the Emperor and his suite chanced to be standing on my side, I should pass close to him, right under his eyes. Chancing to glance at Jitkoff marching abreast of me, at his face, as always, severe and sombre, but now flushed, I became infected with the general excitement, and my heart beat quicker, and I suddenly felt that it all depended on us as to how the Emperor regarded us. I felt much the same sort of sensation the first time I came under fire.

The men marched faster and faster, the pace became longer and the gait freer and more firm. There was no need for me to adapt myself to the general pace. All tiredness had vanished just as if we had all grown wings which were bearing us forward to that point whence already we could hear the crash of bands and deafening hurrahs. I don't remember the streets through which we passed, nor the people in them, or whether they looked at us. I remember only the excitement which possessed me, and the consciousness of the compelling, tremendous strength of the mass of which I was a member. One felt that nothing was impossible for this mass, that the torrent of which I was a struggling component part could know no obstacle, but could smash, extirpate, destroy all in its path, and each one thought that He, past whom this torrent was streaming, could, with one word, by one wave of the hand, alter its courses, turn it back, or again hurl it at terrifying obstacles. Each one wished to find in the word of this one man, and in the movement of his hand, the unknown something which was sending us to death. "Thou art sending us"—each one thought—" and we are giving thee our lives. Look at us and rest assured. We are ready to die."

And He knew we were ready to die for him. He saw the terrifying rows of determined men which were passing him almost at the double, the men of his own poor country, poorly clad, simple soldiers, they were all going to death calm and free of responsibility.

He was sitting on a grey horse which stood motionless with ears pricked alert at the music and the mad, enthusiastic shouts. A brilliant suite was round him. But I do not remember any of the brilliant crowd of horsemen excepting that one man on a grey horse in simple uniform and white cap. I remember his pale worn face—worn with the consciousness of the weighty decision taken. I remember how tears like big raindrops were running down his cheeks, falling on the dark cloth of his uniform in bright glistening splashes. I remember the trembling lips murmuring something which was doubtless a welcome to the thousands of young lives about to perish and for whom he was weeping. All this appeared and disappeared, lighted up with the rapidity of lightning, as I, breathless, not from running, but from mad, delirious enthusiasm, doubled past him with rifle raised high in one hand, and with the other waving my cap above my head, yelling a deafening hurrah, which, however, I could not even hear in the general roar.

All this flashed up and disappeared. The dusty streets bathed in a scorching heat, the exhausting excitement, the soldiers worn out by excitement and from having doubled for a distance of nearly one verst under a baking sun. The shouts of the officers calling on the men to keep formation and in step—that is all I saw and heard five minutes later.

After we had marched a further two versts through the stifling town and reached the common on which we were to bivouac, I threw myself to the ground, utterly worn out, body and soul.

VI

Difficult marches, dust, heat, fatigue, bleeding feet, brief halts by day, deathlike slumber by night, the hated bugle waking us at scarce dawn, and all the time fields—

fields. Not like those in our own country, but covered with high, green, loudly-rustling, long, silky leaves of maize or wheat, already in places turning yellow.

The same faces, the same regimental life, the same topics of conversation and tales of home, of the halt in the provincial town, and criticisms of the officers.

Of the future we seldom and unwillingly spoke. We only knew vaguely that we were going to war, notwithstanding the fact that we had halted not far from Kishineff for a whole six months, although quite ready to march. It would have been possible during that time to have explained why we were preparing for war, but I suppose it was not considered necessary. I remember a soldier one day asked me:

"Vladimir Mikhailich, shall we soon arrive in Bokhara?"

I thought at first that I had not heard correctly, but when he repeated the question I replied that Bokhara was beyond two seas, four thousand versts away, and we were never likely to get there.

"No, Mikhailich, don't talk like that. One of the regimental clerks has told me. He says that we shall cross the Danube, and then we shall be in Bokhara."

"Not Bokhara—Bulgaria!" I exclaimed.

"Well, Bokhara or Bulgaria, whichever you call it, isn't it all the same?"

And he said no more, evidently dissatisfied.

We only knew that we were going to kill the Turk because he had shed much blood. And we wanted to kill him, not so much for the blood he had shed of persons not known to us, but because he had upset so many people that, through it, we were forced to experience a hard campaign ("for which we are going a thousand versts to him, the unclean beast!"). Those on furlough and reservists were obliged to leave home and family, and all go together somewhere under shell and bullet. The Turk was pictured as a rioter and ringleader, whom it was necessary to pacify and subdue.

REMINISCENCES OF PRIVATE IVANOFF

We occupied ourselves much more with our family, battalion, and company affairs than in the war. In our company all was quiet and peaceful. But matters went from bad to worse with the rifle company. Ventzel did not grow more sensible. Secret indignation grew, and after one incident, which, even now, five years afterwards, I cannot remember without becoming worked up, it developed into regular hatred.

We had just passed through a town, and had come out on to a field where the first regiment, marching ahead of us, had already pitched its tents. The camp was a good one. On one side was a river, on the other an old clean oak grove, probably a resort of the local inhabitants. It was a nice warm evening. The sun was setting. We halted and piled arms. I and Jitkoff began to pitch our shelter. We had fixed up the supports. I was holding one edge of the sheet, and Jitkoff was hammering in a peg with a stick.

"Tighter, hold it tighter, Mikhailich." (He had for some days past commenced to address me in this intimate way.) "There, that's right."

But at this moment from behind us there came some strange measured smacking sounds. I turned round.

The riflemen were standing in line. Ventzel, shouting out something hoarsely, was hitting one of the soldiers in the face. The man, with a face pale as death, holding his rifle at the order and not daring to avoid the blows, was trembling all over. Ventzel's thin, small body swayed with the force of the blows he was dealing with both hands, first the right and then the left. Everyone around was silent—only the smack was heard and the hoarse muttering of the infuriated commander. Everything went dark, and began to swim before me. I made a movement. Jitkoff understood it, and tugged with all his strength at the tent sheet.

"Hang on to it, d——n you, you awkward——" he shouted, showering the most abusive epithets on me.

"Have your hands withered or what ? Where are you looking ? Have you never seen it before ?"

The blows continued to resound. Blood was trickling from the man's upper lip and chin. At last he fell, Ventzel turned round, and glaring full at the whole company, shouted :

"If anyone else dares to smoke, I will treat the blackguard worse. Lift him up, wash his ugly face, and put him in the tent. Let him lie there. Pile arms !" he commanded.

His hands were trembling, red, swollen, and covered with blood. He took out a handkerchief, wiped his hands, and left the men, who had piled their arms and were dangerously silent. Several of them, muttering amongst themselves, collected around the bruised victim, and raised him. Ventzel was walking with a nervous, worn-out gait. He was pale and his eyes glistened. The twitching of his muscles told how hard his teeth were set. He went past us, and, meeting my searching look, he smiled with his thin lips, only in an unnatural, derisive manner, and, muttering something, went on.

"Bloodsucker !" said Jitkoff, with hatred in his voice. "And you too, sir. . . . What did you want to go there for ? Do you want to be shot ? Wait a little, and they will get even with him."

"Will they complain ?" I asked. "If so, to whom ?"

"No, there will be no complaint. We also will do something."

And he muttered something almost to himself. I dared not understand him. Feodoroff, who had already been amongst the riflemen and asked what it was all about, came back to us.

"He bullies the men without any reason," he said. "This little soldier, Matushkin, was smoking on the march. When they halted he ordered his rifle, keeping the cigarette between his fingers. Evidently, and unluckily for him, he forgot all about it. But Ventzel

REMINISCENCES OF PRIVATE IVANOFF

noticed it. Brute, beast!" he added sorrowfully, laying himself down in the tent, which was now ready. "The cigarette was out. It's quite clear the poor beggar had forgotten."

In the course of a few days we marched into Alexandria, where an enormous number of troops had collected. Whilst still coming down the high mountain, we saw an enormous expanse dotted with white tents and the black figures of men, long horse lines and glistening rows of guns with their green carriages and limbers. Whole crowds of officers and men were wandering through the streets of the town. Lugubrious, mournful Hungarian music, mingling with the clatter of dishes and loud conversation, came from the open windows of crowded and dirty hotels. The little shops were crammed with Russian purchasers. Our soldiers, Roumanians, foreigners, and Jews shouted loudly at each other, without making themselves understood. Quarrels as to the rate of exchange on the paper rouble could be heard at every step.

"Where is the Post-Office?" with exaggerated courtesy and touching the peak of his kepi with his hand, inquires of a smartly-dressed Roumanian an officer equipped with a "Soldier's Translator," a little book with which the troops had been supplied. The Roumanian explains. The officer turns over the pages of the book, looking for a translation of the unintelligible words, and understands nothing, but still thanks him politely. "Tfy, you comrades! What a people! Our priests and our churches, and yet you can't understand a word!"

"Will you take a silver rouble for this?" a soldier shouts at the top of his voice, holding up a shirt in his hands to a Roumanian trading at an open stall. "How much for the shirt? Five francs? Four francs?"

He draws out the money, shows it, and the business ends in mutual satisfaction.

"Make way, make way, chums, the General's coming."

A tall, young-looking General, in a smart jacket and high boots, with a cossack whip hanging by its lash over his shoulder, came rapidly along the street. Several paces behind him was an orderly, a little Asiatic in a coloured robe and turban, with an enormous sword and a revolver at his belt. The General, holding his head well up, and with good-natured indifference looking at the men as they saluted and made way for him, passed into an hotel. Here I, Ivan Platonich, and Stebelkoff were ensconced in a corner swallowing down some local dish composed of red pepper and meat. The dilapidated room, laid out with little tables, was full of people. The clatter of dishes, the popping of corks, and the hum of sober and drunken voices, were all hidden by the orchestra, which was seated in a kind of alcove decorated with red stuff curtains. There were five musicians. Two violins were scraping away furiously. A 'cello was booming on two or three notes, whilst a double-bass roared. But all these instruments merely formed an accompaniment for a fifth. A swarthy, curly-haired Hungarian, almost a boy, sat in front of all. From inside the wide velvet collar of his coat there projected a strange-looking instrument, a wooden flute of the precise pattern that Pan and the Fauns are always depicted as playing. It consisted of a row of uneven wooden pipes, so fastened together that their open ends rested against the lips of the artist. The Hungarian, turning his head first to one side then to another, blew into these pipes, producing powerful, melodious sounds, not unlike those of a flute or clarionet. He executed the most tricky and difficult passages by shaking and turning his head. His black greasy locks danced on his head and fell over his forehead. His red face was covered with perspiration, and the veins stood out on his neck. It was evidently a difficult job. . . . Against the discordant accompaniment of the stringed instruments, the sound of the pan-pipes stood out sharply, clearly, and wildly beautiful.

The General took his place at a table around which were some officers known to him, bowed to all who had risen at his entry, and loudly said, "Be seated, gentlemen," which applied to the rank and file present. We finished our dinner in silence. Ivan Platonich ordered a bottle of red Roumanian wine, and after the second bottle, when his face had taken on a jovial expression and his cheeks and nose had become brightly tinted, he turned to me:

"You, young man, tell me.... Do you remember when we had the big halt?"

"I do, Ivan Platonich."

"Did you speak with Ventzel then?"

"I did."

"Did you seize him by the arm?" inquired the Captain, in a preternaturally solemn tone. And when I replied I had done so he gave a prolonged deep sigh and began to blink in an agitated manner.

"You did wrong... you acted stupidly. Look here, I don't want to reprimand you. You did very well... that is, it was contrary to all discipline.... Oh, damn it! what am I saying? You will excuse me...."

He remained silent, gazing at the floor and breathing heavily. I also was silent. Ivan Platonich gulped down half a glass and then smacked me on the knee.

"Give me a promise that you will not do such a thing again. I quite understand.... It is difficult for a newcomer. But what good can you do by it? He is such a mad dog, this Ventzel. Well, look here...."

Ivan Platonich evidently could not find the right word, and after a long pause again had recourse to his glass.

"That is... you see... he is a good chap really. It is a kind of... deuce knows what—a kind of madness of his. You yourself saw how I, too, knocked one of the men about a little not long ago. But if the idiot won't understand his mistakes.... You know he is such a wooden... But I, Vladimir Mikhailich, act like a father to them. I swear I have no malice against them, even though I do flare up sometimes. But as for Ventzel, it has got into his system. Hey, you!"—he shouted to one of the Roumanian waiters—" another bottle. . . . And some day he will be court-martialled or even worse. The men will get revengeful, and the first time under fire. . . . It will be a pity, because all the same he is a good man, as you know. And even a warm-hearted fellow."

"What!" Stebelkoff exclaimed. "What warm-hearted man would act like he does?"

"You should have seen, Ivan Platonich, what your warm-hearted man did the other day."

And I told the Captain how Ventzel had knocked about one of the men for smoking in the ranks.

"There you are, there you are. . . ."

Ivan Platonich turned red, puffed, stopped short, and again commenced to talk. "But for all that he is not a beast. Whose men are best fed? Ventzel's. Which are the best-trained men? Ventzel's. In which company are there practically no fines? Who never sends his men up for court-martial, unless a man does something very bad? Always Ventzel. If it were not for this unhappy weakness of his the men would carry him shoulder high."

"Have you spoken about it to him, Ivan Platonich?"

"I have spoken and argued a dozen times. What can you do with him? 'Either they are soldiers or militia,' he says. Those are the silly kind of speeches he makes. 'War,' says he, 'is so cruel that even if I am cruel with the men it is but a drop in the ocean. . . .' 'They,' he says, 'are in such a low state of development. . . .' In a word, the deuce knows what he doesn't say. All the same he is an excellent chap. He doesn't drink or play cards. He is a conscientious soldier, helps his old father and a sister, and is a splendid companion. Moreover, he is the best-read man in the regiment. And mark my word, he will either be court-martialled, or they"—he nodded his head towards the window—"will deal with him. It's a bad job. And that's how the matter stands, my most worthy trooper."

Ivan Platonich gave me a kindly pat on my shoulder-strap and then dived his hand into his pocket, brought out a tobacco-pouch, and commenced to roll a gigantic cigarette, which he stuck into an enormous amber mouth-piece on which was the inscription " Caucasus " in oxidized silver. Sticking the holder into his mouth, he silently pushed the pouch towards me. We were all three smoking, and the Captain recommenced:

" Sometimes it is impossible not to hit them. They are really like children. Do you know Balunoff ? "

Stebelkoff suddenly burst out laughing.

" Well, what's the matter, Stebelkoff ? " grunted Ivan Platonich. " Balunoff is an old soldier who has often been punished. He has served twenty years, and yet they will not let him go on account of his various offences. Well, this rascal once . . . You weren't with us then. When we were leaving a village near Kishineff an order was given to inspect all the extra pairs of boots. I drew the men up in line, and walking behind them to see if any of the boot-tops were sticking out of the knapsacks, saw that Balunoff had none. 'Where are your boots ? ' ' I have put them inside my knapsack for safety, sir.' 'That's a lie.' 'Not at all, sir. They are in my knapsack so as not to get wet,' the blackguard replied.

" ' Take off your knapsack and open it. I noticed he didn't open it, but dragged the tops of the boots from under the cover.

" ' Open it.' ' I can take them out without opening it, sir.' "

" However, I made him open the knapsack, and what do you think ? He dragged a live sucking-pig by the ears out of it. Its snout was tied up with string so that it shouldn't squeak. With his right hand at the salute he stood and grinned, and with his left hand held the pig.

He had stolen it, the rascal, from the Moldavians. Well, of course I hit him, but not hard."

Stebelkoff roared with laughter, and, scarcely able to speak, said: "Yes ... and do you know, Ivanoff, what he hit him with? ... With the pig!"

"Yes, but couldn't you have avoided that, Ivan Platonich?"

"Oh you! Upon my word, it makes me tired to listen to you. I couldn't court-martial him for it, could I?"

VII

On the night of the 14th to 15th of June Feodoroff woke me.

"Mikhailich, do you hear?"

"What is it?"

"Firing. They are crossing the Danube."

I began to listen. A strong wind was blowing, driving before it lowering black clouds which hid the moon. It blew against the canvas of our tents, making them flap, whistled through the guy-ropes, and made a faint sighing sound through the piles of arms. Through these sounds could be heard occasional deep reports.

"Many are being killed now," whispered Feodoroff with a sigh. "Will they order us forward or not? What do you think? It sounds like thunder."

"Perhaps it is only a thunderstorm?"

"No, it is so regular. Listen, do you hear them one after another?"

The booming was certainly very regular in its intervals. I crawled out of the tent and gazed in the direction of the sounds. No flashes of flame were visible. Sometimes a light appeared to be visible to the straining eyes in the direction whence the reports were coming, but it was only fancy.

At last it has come, I thought.

And I tried to picture to myself what was happening in the darkness there. I imagined a wide black river with precipitous banks, utterly unlike the real Danube as I afterwards saw it. Hundreds of boats are crossing. These measured, frequent shots are at them. Will many of them escape? A cold shiver ran down my back. " Would I like to be there?" I asked myself involuntarily.

I gazed at the sleeping camp. All was quiet. In the intervals between the distant thunder of guns and the noise of the wind could be heard the heavy breathing of the men. And I had a sudden passionate longing that all this should not take place, that the march should continue, that all these soundly sleeping men and with them myself should not be obliged to go where the firing was taking place.

Sometimes the cannonade became heavier. Sometimes I heard confusedly a less loud deep noise. They are firing volleys, I thought, not knowing that we were still twenty versts from the Danube and that a painfully strained imagination was creating these sounds. But though imaginary, they roused, nevertheless, quickened fancy, causing it to picture fearful scenes. In imagination I heard the cries and groans, I saw thousands of human beings falling, and heard the desperate hoarse hurrahs. I pictured the bayonet charge, the carnage. And if beaten off, it will all be for nothing!

Grey dawn commenced in the dark east. The wind began to die away. The clouds parted, disclosing stars waning in the paling heavens. It grew lighter. Somebody in the camp awoke and, hearing the sounds of battle, aroused the others. They spoke little and quietly. The unknown had approached closely to us. No one knew what the morrow would bring. No one cared to think or speak of it.

I slept until daylight and awoke rather late. The cannon continued to rumble deeply, and, although no news had come from the Danube, there were rumours amongst us, each one more improbable than the other. Some said that we had already crossed and were pursuing the Turks, others said the attempt to cross had failed and whole regiments had been destroyed.

"Some had been drowned, others had been shot," said someone.

"And you are lying," interrupted Vassili Karpich.

"Why am I lying, if it is true?"

"True! Who told you?"

"What?"

"The truth? Where did you hear it?"

"We all know. The firing goes on and nothing more."

"All say it. A Cossack has been to the General, and..."

"Cossack! Did you see him? What is he like, this Cossack?"

"An ordinary Cossack... just as he ought to look."

"As he ought to! What a tongue you have got—just like an old woman. Better to keep your mouth shut. No one has been, so no one could know."

I went to Ivan Platonich. The officers were sitting fully equipped and ready, with their revolvers fastened to their waist-belts. Ivan Platonich, as usual, was red, puffing, and breathing heavily, and was wiping his neck with a dirty handkerchief. Stebelkoff was excited, bright, and for some reason had pomaded his usually drooping moustaches so that they stuck out in pointed ends.

"Look at our Lieutenant! He has got himself up for action," said Ivan Platonich, winking at him. "Ah, my dear chap, I am sorry for you. We shall have no such moustaches in our mess! They will do for you, Stebelkoff," said the Captain jokingly. "Well, you are not afraid?"

"I shall try not to be," said Stebelkoff in a brave voice.

"Well, and you, you warrior, is it terrifying?"

"I don't know, Ivan Platonich.... Has nothing been heard from there?"

"Nothing. The Lord only knows what is happening

there." Ivan Platonich sighed deeply. "We move off in an hour's time," he added after a short pause.

The fly of the tent opened, and the Adjutant Lukin poked his head in. He looked very serious and pale.

"You here, Ivanoff ? Orders have been given to swear you in. . . . Not now, but when we move off. Ivan Platonich, a fifth packet of cartridges to the men."

He refused to come in and sit down, saying that he had much to do, and went off somewhere. I also left.

About twelve o'clock dinners were served. The men ate little. After dinner we were ordered to remove our sight-protectors (leather covers) from our rifles and extra ammunition was issued. The men began to prepare for action. They commenced to examine their knapsacks and throw away anything superfluous. Torn shirts and drawers, various kinds of rags, old boots, brushes, greasy handbooks—all were thrown away. Some of the men appeared to have brought a quantity of useless things in their knapsacks as far as the Danube. I saw a "schelkun" —a small piece of wood used in time of peace before parades and reviews for polishing kit-straps—lying on the ground, heavy stone pomade jars, all sorts of small boxes and bits of boards, and even a whole boot-tree.

"Go on ; throw away. It will be easier marching. *We* shall not want them to-morrow."

"Five hundred versts I have carried you . . . and what for ?" argued Lutikoff, examining some rag. "I can't take you with me."

It became the fashion that day to throw away things and to clean out knapsacks. When we left the camp it showed up in the dark background of the Steppe as a quadrangular space dotted with multi-coloured rags and other articles.

Before marching, when the regiment was already standing waiting the word of command, several officers and our young regimental chaplain collected in front. I was called out of the ranks with four "volunteers" from other regiments. All had enlisted for the campaign. Having handed over our rifles to neighbours, we went forward and stood near the colours. My unknown comrades were in a state of agitation, and I, too, felt my heart beating faster than usual.

"Take hold of the colours," said the battalion commandant. The colour-bearer lowered the colour and others of the colour-party removed the case. An old faded green silk fabric unfolded to the wind. We stood around it, and, grasping the pole with one hand and holding the other aloft, we repeated the words of the chaplain, as he read out the ancient military oath of Peter's time. They recalled to me what Vassili Karpich had said on our first march. Where does it come in? thought I, and after a long list of the occasions and places on and in which His Imperial Majesty had served, I heard these words: "Do not spare your life." We five all repeated them in one voice, and, glancing at the rows of gloomy men ready for action, I felt that they were no empty words.

We returned to our places. The regiment stirred, and dissolving into a long column, set off with forced step for the Danube. The firing which we had heard had now ceased.

* * * * *

As through a dream I remember that march. The dust raised by the horses of Cossack regiments as they overtook us, the broad steppes sloping down to the Danube, the opposite bank showing up blue, fifteen versts away. The fatigue, heat, and the jostling and fighting at the wells under Zimnitza. The dirty little town filled with troops, some Generals who waved their caps at us from a balcony and shouted "Hurrah!" to which we replied.

"They have crossed! They are over!" buzzed voices around us.

"Two hundred killed, five hundred wounded."

VIII

It was already dark when, having come down from the bank, we crossed a tributary of the Danube by a small bridge, and marched over a low sandy island still wet from the water which had but just receded from it. I remember the sharp clank of the bayonets of the soldiers as the men collided with each other in the darkness, the deep rumble of the artillery which had overtaken us, the black expanse of the wide river, the lights on the other bank, where we had to cross to-morrow, and where, I reflected, to-morrow would be a fresh battle. . . . Better not to think, better to sleep, I decided, and laid down on the watery sand.

The sun was already high when I opened my eyes. Troops, transport, and parks were swarming over the sandy shore. At the very edge of the water they had already dug out gun-pits and trenches for the riflemen. Across the Danube, on its steep cliff could be discerned gardens and vineyards in which our troops swarmed. Behind these the land rose higher and higher, abruptly restricting the horizon. To the right, three versts from us, and showing white on the hills, were the houses and minarets of Sistovo. A steamer with a barge in tow was transferring battalion after battalion to the other side. On our side a little torpedo-boat was noisily blowing off steam.

"A successful crossing, Vladimir Mikhailich," said Feodoroff to me gaily.

"The same to you. Only we have not crossed yet."

"We shall directly. Look; the steamer will soon take us over. They say a Turkish ironclad is not far away. This little samovar is ready for it." He pointed to the torpedo-boat.

"Great God ! but what a number have been killed," he continued, changing his tone. "They are already bringing and bringing them over from that side. . . ."

And he related to me the well-known details of the Battle of Sistovo.

"Now it is our turn. We chall cross over to that side. . . . The Turks will attack us. . . . Well, anyhow, we have had a respite. We at least are alive, but those there . . ." He nodded his head to a group of men and officers standing not far from us, who were crowded round some object not visible to us at which they were all gazing.

"What is it?"

"They have brought over our killed. Go and look, Mikhailich. How terrible!"

I went up to the group. All were silent, and with heads bared were gazing at the bodies lying side by side on the sand. Ivan Platonich, Stebelkoff, and Ventzel were also there. Ivan Platonich was frowning angrily, clearing his throat and breathing heavily. Stebelkoff, with frank horror, was stretching out his thin neck. Ventzel was standing wrapped in thought.

There were two of them lying on the sand. One was a full-grown, handsome Guardsman of the Finland Regiment, from the Composite Guards half-company—the same half-company which had lost half its strength during the attack. He had been wounded in the stomach, and must have suffered long agonies before he died. Suffering had left a faint impression of something spiritual, had left a shadow of refinement and something painfully tender on his face. His eyes were closed, and his arms were crossed on his chest. Had he himself adopted this position before death, or had his comrade tended him? His appearance did not excite terror or revulsion, but only infinite pity for the life so full of energy which had perished.

Ivan Platonich bent over the body and taking up the man's cap lying near the head, read on the peak, "Ivan Jurenko, 3rd Company." "The poor chap was a Little Russian," he said quietly. It recalled to me my birthplace, the warm wind of the Steppe, the village nestling in the ravine, the gullies, the overgrown willows, the little white mud hut with its red shutters. . . . Who is waiting you there?

The other was a linesman of the Volhynia Regiment. Death had taken him suddenly. He was running madly to the attack, breathless from shouting. The bullet had struck the bridge of his nose and had penetrated into his head, leaving a black gaping wound. He lay with wide-opened eyes, now dimmed, with gaping mouth, and face already discoloured, but still distorted with rage.

"They have paid their accounts," said Ivan Platonich; "they are in peace and want nothing more."

He turned away. The soldiers hurriedly parted to let him through. I and Stebelkoff followed him. Ventzel caught us up.

"Well, Ivanoff," he said, "did you see?"

"I have seen, Peter Nicolaievitch," I replied.

"And what did you think as you looked at them?" he inquired moodily.

A sudden rage rose within me against this man and a mad desire to say something hard to him.

"Much. And most of all I thought that they were no longer 'food for powder,' that they no longer needed welding and discipline, and that nobody would now bully them for the sake of this welding. I thought that they are no longer soldiers, no longer subordinates," I said in a trembling voice—"they are men!"

Ventzel's eyes flashed. A sound came from his throat and broke off. No doubt he wished to answer me, but once more restrained himself. He walked by my side with lowered head, and after taking a few paces, not looking at me, said:

"Yes, Ivanoff, you are right. . . . They are men. . . . Dead men."

IX

They took us across the Danube. For some days we halted near Sistovo awaiting the Turks. Then the troops started off into the heart of the country. We, too, started off. For a long time they sent us first here, then there. We were near Tirnova and not far from Plevna. Three weeks passed by, and still we had not been in action. At length we were told off to form part of a special division whose duties were to hold the advance of a large Turkish army. Forty thousand were stretched over seventy versts of country. There were about one hundred thousand Turks in front of us, and only the cautious movements of our commander—who would not risk his men but contented himself by opposing the advance of the enemy—and the dilatoriness of the Turkish Pacha enabled us to carry out our task—not to allow the Turks to break through and cut off our main army from the Danube.

We were few and our line was enormous; consequently we were seldom able to have a rest. We marched round numbers of villages, appearing first in one place, then in another, in order to meet the anticipated attack. We penetrated into such remote parts of Bulgaria that the transport with food did not find us, and we were obliged to starve, making our two days' ration of biscuit last over five and more days. The hungry men used to thresh unripe wheat with sticks on outstretched sheets of our tents, and made a disgusting soup from it and sour wild apples, without salt (because we could not get any), and got sick from it. Battalions faded away, although not in action.

In the middle of June our brigade, with several squadrons of cavalry and two batteries of artillery, arrived at a ruined and half-burned Turkish village which had been abandoned by its inhabitants. Our camp was situated on a high, precipitous mountain. The village was below, in the depth of the valley along which a little river wound its course. Steep, high cliffs rose on the other side of the valley. It was, as we imagined, the Turkish side, but no Turks were, as a matter of fact, near us. We camped several days on our mountain, almost without bread, only obtaining with great difficulty any water, as it was necessary to descend far below for it to a spring which came out at the bottom of the cliff. We were absolutely detached from the army, and did not know in the least what was going on in the world. Fifteen versts in front of us were Cossack patrols. Two or three sotnias of them were distributed over a distance of twenty versts. There were no Turks there either.

Notwithstanding the fact that we could not find the enemy, our little column took every precautionary measure. Day and night a strong chain of advanced posts surrounded the camp. Owing to the nature of the ground its line was a long one, and every day several companies were told off for this inactive but very tiring work. Inaction, almost constant starvation, and ignorance of the state of affairs acted prejudicially on the men.

The regimental hospitals became overflowing. Each day men, weakened and tortured by fever and dysentery, were sent to the divisional hospital. The companies were only one-half or two-thirds of their proper strength. All were gloomy, and everyone longed to come to grips. Anyhow, it would have been a change.

At length it came. A Cossack orderly came galloping in from the commander of a Cossack squadron with the information that the Turks had begun to advance and that he had been compelled to call in his men and fall back five versts. Afterwards it appeared that the Turks went back without thinking of continuing the attack, and we could have quietly remained on the spot, the more so as nobody had ordered us to advance. But the General commanding us then, who had but recently arrived from St. Petersburg, felt, as did all of us in the column, that it was insufferable to the men to sit with folded arms or stand for whole days on guard against an invisible and, as all were convinced, non-existent enemy, to eat horrible food, and await their turn to fall sick. All were eager for the fray; and the General ordered an attack.

We left half the column in camp. The situation was so little known that there was a possibility of being attacked from both sides. Fourteen companies, the Hussars, and four guns moved out after midday. Never had we marched so fast and light-heartedly, with the exception of the day on which we marched past the Emperor.

We marched along the valley, passing, one after another, deserted Turkish and Bulgarian villages. In the narrow thoroughfares bordered by hedges higher than a man nothing was to be met—neither human beings, cattle, nor dogs. Only clucking hens flew away on our approach, on to the hedges and roofs, and geese, with a cry, raised themselves ponderously in the air and endeavoured to fly away. In the gardens could be seen plum-trees of every description, the branches of which were literally obscured by ripe fruit. In the last village, five versts from the spot we imagined the Turks to be in, we halted for half an hour. During this spell the half-starved men shook down quantities of plums, ate them, and crammed their ration bags with them. A few would catch and kill the hens and geese, pluck them, and bring them along in their knapsacks. I remembered how the same soldiers before the crossing at Sistovo, in anticipation of a fight, had thrown everything out of their knapsacks, and I mentioned it to Jitkoff, who was at the moment busily engaged in plucking an enormous goose.

" Well, Mikhailich, although we have not been in action we have become accustomed to wait. It seems as if you will only march and not take any part in the fighting. And even if you do you need not necessarily be killed."

" Are you frightened?" I asked him involuntarily.

" But perhaps nothing will happen," he answered

slowly, frowning, and assiduously plucking out the last remnants of white down.

"But if it does?"

"If it does, frightened or not frightened, its all the same, one has to go. They don't ask us. Go, and God help you. Lend me your knife. It is such a good one."

I gave him my big hunting-knife. He cut the goose in two, and held out one half to me.

"Take it in case. And about being frightened or not frightened, don't think of it, sir. It is better not to think of it. All rests with God. You cannot get away from what He designs."

"If a bullet or shell comes at you, where can you go?" added Feodoroff, who was lying near us. "I think this, Vladimir Mikhailich, that it is even more dangerous to run away, because a bullet must travel like that"—he showed with his finger—"and the heaviest fire comes from the rear."

"Yes," said I, "especially with the Turks. They say they fire high."

"Well, clever one," said Jitkoff to Feodoroff, "go on talking. There they will show you a trajectory. Yes, certainly," he added, thinking, "it is better to be in front."

"It depends on our officers," said Feodoroff, "and our officer will go ahead and not be afraid."

"Yes, he will go ahead all right. He isn't afraid. And Niemtseff also."

"'Uncle' Jitkoff," inquired Feodoroff, "what do you say? Will he live through the day or not?"

Jitkoff lowered his eyes.

"What are you talking about?" he asked.

"Well I never! Have you seen him? Every nerve is on the go."

Jitkoff became still more surly.

"You are talking rot," he growled.

"Well. What did they say before we crossed the Danube?" said Feodoroff.

"*Before* we crossed the Danube! ... The men were angry then, and didn't know what they were saying. It's a fact that they couldn't stand him."

"What do you think? That they are blackguards?" said Jitkoff, turning and looking Feodoroff straight in the face. "Have they no thought of God in them? They do not know where they are going! Perhaps some will to-day have to answer to the Lord God, and can they think of such a thing at such a moment? *Before* the crossing of the Danube! Yes, I too then said the same thing to the gentleman" (he nodded his head at me). "I said exactly the same thing because ... it was sickening to look at. It's not worth while remembering what happened before we crossed the Danube."

He felt in his boot-top for his tobacco-pouch, and, continuing to mutter, filled his pipe and commenced to smoke. Then, replacing the pouch, he settled himself more comfortably, seized his knees with his hands, and became buried in some moody reflections.

Half an hour later we left the village and began to clamber up from the valley into the mountains. The Turks were behind the ridges, over which we were to cross. When we reached the summit there opened out before us a wide, hilly and gradually descending expanse, covered here with fields of wheat and maize, there with overgrown bushes and medlar-trees. In two places glistened the minarets of villages hidden behind the green hills. We were to take the one on the right. Behind it, on the edge of the horizon, could be seen a whitish streak. It was the main road which had been previously held by our Cossacks. Soon all this became lost to sight. We entered into a dense undergrowth intersected at intervals by small fields.

I don't remember much about the commencement of the battle. When we came out into the open on the summit of a hill the Turks could plainly be seen. As our companies emerged from amongst the bushes they formed up and opened out. A single cannon-shot thundered out. They had fired a shell. The men started, and all eyes were attracted by a white puff of smoke which was already dispersing and slowly rolling down the hill. At the same instant the screeching sound of a shell as it flew, apparently directly, over our heads made everyone duck. The shell, passing over us, struck the ground near the companies in rear of us. I remember the dull thud of its burst was followed by a pitiful cry from someone. A splinter had torn off the company sergeant-major's foot. I heard of this later. At the time I could not understand the cry; my ears heard it—that was all. Then everything merged into that confused indescribable feeling which takes possession of anyone coming under fire for the first time. They say that there is no one who is not afraid in action. Any modest and truthful man, to the question, "Were you frightened?" replies, "Yes." But it is not the physical fear which takes hold of a man at night, in some obscure alley, when encountering a footpad. It is the full, clear recognition of the inevitability and proximity of death. And, fantastic and strange as these words may appear, this recognition does not make men stop, does not force them to think of flight, but compels them to go ahead. Bloodthirsty instincts are not awakened; there is no desire to go ahead in order to kill somebody. But there is an irresistible force which drives one forward at all costs. Thoughts as to what must be done during action cannot be expressed in words. It is necessary to kill, or rather—one's duty to die.

Whilst we were crossing the valley the Turks succeeded in firing several shots. As we slowly climbed up to the village we were separated from the Turks only by the last piece of thick undergrowth. As we entered the bushes everything became quiet.

It was difficult going. The dense, often prickly, bushes grew thickly, and it was necessary either to go round them or to push one's way through them. The sharpshooters in front of us were already extended, and from time to time called gently to each other so as not to lose touch. Up to the present the whole company was together. A profound silence reigned in the wood.

Then there came the first rifle-shot, not very loud and resembling the thud of a woodman's axe. The Turks were beginning to fire at random. Bullets whistled high above in the air in varying tones; they flew noisily through the bushes, cutting off branches, but were not touching us. This noise like wood-chopping became more and more frequent, and finally melted into an uniform tapping. The squealing and snarling of single bullets could no longer be heard. The very air itself seemed to be yelping. We hurriedly advanced. I and all around me were whole. This much astonished me.

Suddenly we emerged from the bushes. A deep gully along which ran a little stream intersected the road. The men halted a few minutes and drank.

From here the companies extended on either side so as to outflank the Turks. Our company was left in reserve in the gully. The skirmishers were to go direct through the bushes and rush the village. The Turkish fire was as frequent as formerly, unceasing, but much louder.

Having climbed up to the other side of the gully, Ventzel formed up his company. He said something to the men which I did not hear.

"We will try, we will try!" resounded the voices of the men.

I looked at him from below. He was pale, and it seemed to me, sorrowful, but calm. Seeing Ivan Platonich and Stebelkoff, he waved to them with his handkerchief, and then looked towards us as if in search of something. I guessed that he wished to bid me farewell, and I stood up so that he should notice me. Ventzel smiled, nodded his head several times at me, and ordered his men to go up into the fire. The men extended right and left,

REMINISCENCES OF PRIVATE IVANOFF

forming a long line, and were at once lost to sight in the bushes, with the exception of one man, who suddenly bounded forward, threw up his hands, and fell heavily to the ground. Two of ours jumped out of the gully and brought in his body.

There was a torturing half-hour of suspense.

The fight developed. Rifle-fire became more frequent and became one menacing howl. Guns boomed on our right flank. Blood-bespattered men, some walking, some crawling, commenced to appear from out of the bushes. At first only a few, but their numbers increased every moment. Our company assisted them down into the gully, gave them water, and dressed their wounds waiting the arrival of the stretcher-bearers. A rifleman with a shattered wrist, crying out terribly and rolling his eyes, his face pallid from loss of blood and pain, arrived by himself and sat down by the stream. They tied up his arm and placed him on his great coat. The bleeding stopped. He was in a highly feverish state. His lips trembled, and he was sobbing nervously and convulsively.

" Mates, mates ! . . . dear comrades ! . . ."

" Are many killed ?"

" Yes, they are falling."

" Is the company commander all right ?"

" Yes, as yet. But for him we would have been beaten back. We will take it. With him they will take it," said the wounded man in a weak voice. " Three times he led, and they beat us back. He led for the fourth time. They (the Turks) are sitting in a gully. They have heaps of ammunition, and go on firing and firing. . . . But no !" the wounded man screamed suddenly, rising and waving his injured hand. " You are joking, it cannot be. . . . They must . . ."

Then, rolling his delirious eyes and shouting out the most awful curses, he fell forward senseless.

Lukin appeared on the bank of the gully.

"Ivan Platonich!" he shouted out in an unnatural voice, "Bring them on!"

* * * * *

Smoke, reports, groans, and a mad "hurrah." A smell of blood and powder.... Strange men with pale faces enveloped in smoke.... A savage, monstrous, inhuman struggle. Thank God that such moments are remembered only as in a dream, mistily.

* * * * *

When we reached them Ventzel had led the remnant of his company for the fifth time at the Turks, who were raining lead on him. This time the riflemen gained the village. The few Turks still defending it succeeeded in getting away. (The second rifle company lost in the two hours' fighting fifty-two men out of a little over one hundred.) Our company, having taken but little part in the action, lost only a few.

We did not remain on the position we had won, although the Turks had been defeated all along the line. When our General saw battalion after battalion take the road out of the village, when he saw masses of cavalry move off and long lines of guns, he was horrified. It was evident the Turks did not know our strength, concealed by the bushes. Had they known that only fourteen companies in all had driven them out of the deep roads, gullies, and hedges surrounding the village, they would have returned and annihilated us. They were three times as many as ourselves.

By the evening we were back again at our old camp. Ivan Platonich called me in to have some tea.

"Have you seen Ventzel?" he asked.

"Not yet."

"Go to him. He is in his tent. Tell him we want him. He is killing himself. 'Fifty-two! fifty-two!' is all you can hear. Go to him."

A thin piece of candle was feebly illuminating Ventzel's tent. He was crouching in one of the corners with his bowed head resting on some boxes, and sobbing bitterly.

XVII

THE ACTION AT AISLAR

I

We halted two weeks at Kovachitsa. Camp-life is wearisome and monotonous when there is nothing to do, especially in such an out-of-the-way spot; at the same time it would not be just to call Kovachitsa by such a name. The staff of our corps had its quarters in the place and there was a postal section—in a word, the means of finding out what was going on in the world surrounding us, but chiefly at the two theatres of war and in our dear, far-away Homeland. However, it must be said in all justice that we were not spoiled by the freshness and wealth of the news, and it often appeared to us to be mutilated and exaggerated. Sombre rumours of the early failures at Plevna were so exaggerated that only papers two or three weeks old dispersed the gloom reigning amongst the officers. It seemed that the direct road from Plevna was not as close to us as the route via Petersburg and Moscow; however, " the shortest cut is the longest way round," as the saying goes.

Our brigade began to get bored. It is true that once a portion of the Niejinsky Regiment went out reconnoitring, or, more correctly speaking, to punish the armed inhabitants of Lom, who had risen. Having taught them a lesson, the regiment returned with the loss of one killed. Another soldier escaped by a miracle, as will be seen from the following narrative of his:

THE ACTION AT AISLAR

"We had begun to turn back, and the Bashi-Bazouks commenced to fire from afar. I lagged behind a little, and turned to fire. I had only just started to overtake them when it hit me in the back. But it was a bad shot—it buried itself in my great-coat. It went through seven folds and stuck in the eighth."

"It" was, of course, a bullet. When the soldier opened out his great-coat there were actually seven holes in it.

"And I had only time to cross myself when—look!—my ration-bag had two holes in the very bottom of it, and biscuit crumbs began to dribble out."

It had a bite of them and went.

"Our Russian biscuits are not tasty," said somebody jokingly.

Meanwhile, whilst we were halted in Kovachitsa, and, to use the popular expression, "were going sour," there were constant skirmishes ahead of us at the front, near Papkio.

On the 9th of August our regimental doctor ordered a "medical inspection" to assemble in the lines of the third battalion (which was camped apart from us). Our company was the first of all to muster, and after they had formed us up, we were marched to the appointed parade-ground. It was not a large piece of ground, but was free of tents and guns. Here we halted. There was no doctor, and we were obliged to wait for him. Having nothing to do I began to gaze at the camp. A camp in time of war presents a strange appearance. The little tents of the soldiers shone brightly white bathed in sunshine. The piles of arms and different coloured figures of soldiers lent a variety to this white background. Lilac-coloured shirts predominated; then came red, yellow, crimson, and green. The black tunics were only worn if on some duty. Everyone preferred the most immoderate *déshabille*. Some were bare-footed, others with bared chest and back. Boots were not worn because of the heat, besides which a thousand versts' march had taught the men the necessity of taking care of them.

THE ACTION AT AISLAR

We waited quite a time. Someone went to inform the doctor that the men were on parade. But it became evident to us that we were not to undergo a " medical inspection." The regimental Adjutant rushed into the tent of the commandant of the third battalion, and almost instantaneously stout little Major A. ran out of his tent nearly naked, having divested himself of most of his clothing owing to the heat, and gave the order:

"Third battalion, strike tents! Leave knapsacks behind." He then disappeared into his tent, which was immediately struck, revealing the Major sitting on a folding-chair and being assisted into various necessary articles of clothing by his servant. At the same time there was an immediate change in the appearance of the third battalion. Men came crawling out of every tent like ants, hurriedly putting on their uniforms. Tents disappeared and were folded up, and great-coats were rolled. Within five minutes of the Major's command, the variegated, quiet bivouac had become transformed into regular sombre-coloured ranks of men. Here and there the sunlight played on the bayonets and rifle-barrels. Officers came running towards the battalion fastening on their sword-belts as they ran. The Major himself appeared before the battalion, mounted his horse with outside assistance, and gave a command, which was taken up by the company commanders. The mass of humanity stirred, and began, snakelike to draw out into column of route. Where was it going? The Major, having led the way on to the road, turned to the left and took the column towards Papkio. The battalion had not had time to get on to the road before our own orderly appeared.

"Kuzma Zakharich, call up the company; we are advancing."

"Without knapsacks?" asked a number of voices at once.

The question was one of the premier importance. Nearly one-third of all a soldier's discomforts during a campaign arise from the " calf," as the soldiers nicknamed their clumsy knapsack. Others called it a " chest of drawers." This " chest of drawers " hurts the shoulders, presses on the chest, tires out the feet, and lessens the stability of the body. Even in cool, fresh weather it makes the back under it wet with perspiration after five minutes' marching. It is not, therefore, astonishing that the order to leave knapsacks behind was met with general satisfaction.

The company ran to its bivouac. Everyone had already assembled. Knapsacks were thrown into a heap and tents struck. We hurriedly dressed. However much the Russian may like to make a noise on every convenient occasion and when he is in a crowd, there was absolute silence. I have always been struck with this quietness during the mustering of the men whenever the " alarm " sounded.

In a quarter of an hour's time we moved off. The total distance from Kovachitsa to Papkio is from nine to ten versts, but although we marched " light," without knapsacks and only with our great-coats slung bandolier-fashion across our shoulders with our tent-sheets wrapped up in them, these ten versts absolutely knocked us out. The heat was deadly, over 35° Reamur in the shade, and not the slightest vestige of a breeze. Everything seemed to have died. The maize did not move its dark-green leaves. The boughs and leaves of the pear-trees which we passed were motionless. Not a solitary bird did we see during the whole of this march. The men were done even after the first four versts. When half way a halt was called at a well, they were scarcely able to pile arms, and literally fell on to the ground.

" Have you got out of the way of marching, Gabriel Vassilivich ?" I said to my neighbour, as he lay with half-closed eyes breathing heavily.

"Yes, if one doesn't walk for a fortnight it spoils one," he answered dully. "Let us go for a drink."

We rose, and went to push our way to the well, or, more correctly speaking, to the spring. From an iron pipe placed in the wall of stone at about the height of a man a clear transparent stream ran into a stone trough. The men pressed each other as they got the water, and soaked each other as they passed their canteens full of water over the heads of their neighbours. We had a good drink and filled our water-bottles.

"Well, that's a bit better. I can manage another march now," said Gabriel Vassilivich, wiping his fair moustaches and beard with his sleeve.

He was an extraordinarily good-looking fellow, sturdy, active, with big blue eyes. He now lies on the Aislar heights and nothing is left of his blue eyes and handsome face.

Having given us a half-hour's spell, Major F. led us further. The nearer we approached Papkio the more and more difficult it became. The sun baked us with such fury that it seemed as if it was hurrying to complete the job before we reached our destination and could take refuge from its heat in our tents. Some of us succumbed. Scarcely moving along, with my head lowered, I almost tripped over an officer who had fallen. He was lying, scarlet in the face and was breathing convulsively and heavily. They placed him in an ambulance-waggon.

The one and a half verst climb out of the valley along which we had marched up its right slope seemed to us the worst part of the whole road. The smells which always notified us of any approaching camp added still further to the suffocating heat. How I "stuck" it I absolutely don't remember, but nevertheless I did. Others were less fortunate. Scarcely able to drag one foot after another we got into the order in which we were to camp, and, barely able to stand up, awaited the longed-for command from Major F.—"Pile arms!" That is, pile arms and do what you like afterwards.

II

The men were so worn out that even the insufferable heat could not make them go for water. Only after half an hour's rest did the orderlies assemble with their canteens and set off for the village. On that slope of the valley, on the summit of which we were encamped, was the Mussulman quarter of Papkio—literally deserted since the plague. On the opposite side crowded the Bulgarian kishtas, precisely similar to the Turkish houses, with exactly the same squat tiled roofs. There could be heard the barking of dogs. People could be seen, also sheep and buffaloes, or " bufflös," as our men called them. To the right was the valley along which we had just come, with a stream in the middle and endless fields of maize, barley, and wheat along its slopes. To the left, at right angles to our valley, was the valley of Lom, fading away on either side into a misty bluish distance, out of which the mountains on the right bank of the river could be seen with decreasing clearness.

Opposite us these heights rose to a great elevation. At one point on them there appeared at intervals a puff of white smoke which, slowly and slowly drifting, melted and disappeared, fused in the air. Half a minute later there would come a dull roar resembling the growl of distant thunder. This was the Morshansk Regiment carrying out a reconnaissance.

We found the springs, got some water, and returned in no particular order to our bivouac. The soldiers, having rested a little, were already more lively. The distant firing undoubtedly helped in this matter.

" Listen ! What firing !"

" What do you think, chums ? Are they ours or the Turks ?" asked someone.

Somebody else replied that the Morshansk Regiment had taken no guns with them, and certainly, judging from the situation and direction of the smoke, they could not be shots from our guns.

THE ACTION AT AISLAR

More to the right of the village, much nearer than the shell-fire, not on the heights, but below it in the Valley of Lom, began the sound of rifle-fire, at first desultory, as if several axes were hewing down trees, then more and more often. Sometimes the sound united in a prolonged crackle.

I went up to the officers of our company. Our company commander was talking to another officer—S.—telling him that he had just been informed that similar " brushes " took place here almost every day.

" Well, it seems we have got into action at last," said S.

" But what sort of action is this ? . . . Surely you cannot call this an action ? Some of the local inhabitants have squatted down with their blunderbusses in the woods and are sniping us. All the same, stray bullets may come this way, and I should not like to be killed in such a way."

" Why, Ivan Nicolaievitch ? " I asked.

" Because what sort of action is this ? "

Ivan Nicolaievitch was an expert on military matters and a tremendous admirer of strategy and tactics. He frequently expressed the opinion that if he was to be killed it ought to be done in the proper manner in a proper battle, or, better still, in a general action. The present skirmishing was evidently not to his liking. He tugged uneasily at a few straggling hairs on his chin, then suddenly with a good-humoured and serious smile exclaimed :

" Better to come along and have some tea ; the samovar is ready."

We crawled into the tent, and settled down to drink tea. Little by little the firing died down, and we spent the remainder of the day and night in absolute quietness.

By the way, I dreamt all night long of white puffs of smoke and of the rattle of musketry.

When I awoke the sun was already high up. The heat was like yesterday's. A battalion of the Nevsky Regiment which had passed us going in the direction of yesterday's cannonading marched along, however, quite spiritedly. The men were infected with the closeness of battle.

However, they soon returned, and, skirting the village, probably made for the scene of the previous day's rifle-firing. To-day it was less distinct, the shots were further from us. The guns, too, roared at first from our side, but soon white puffs of smoke showed themselves on the heights of the opposite bank. The Turks had brought up some artillery.

I proposed to S. going into the village to climb on to some roof and follow the fight. One could see better from this position. Although the minaret was untouched, and of course stood high above any roof, the mosque itself stood low down, almost in the valley, so we clambered on to the gallery of the first Cherkess house we came to which happened to face towards the scene of the action. But although it lay before us, we could see no troops or even any rifles-moke. There was simply nothing to be seen. We slid down from the gallery into a little garden of white acacias and apricot trees. Everything was in perfect order, as if it was only yesterday the owners had watered the flower-beds. Pumpkins were winding their clinging stalks along the hedge, whilst a few stalks of maize and high " rat's-tails " with red ears gave colour to the garden. We entered the house. The walls were smoothly and clearly plastered with a grey clay. All was in perfect repair. Only the hearth, made of pieces of tile, was broken. On the floor were scattered a few leaves of some Mussulman book with decorated headings in gold and paint.

There was nothing more to see, and climbing over the labyrinth of hedges we got out into the street. Here we met S.'s servant, who came running towards us, red as a lobster.

" Please, sir, please ! They have already stood to arms !"

THE ACTION AT AISLAR

We ran to the battalion, and in two minutes' time I, too, was marching along with my rifle shouldered.

We went towards the scene of yesterday's rifle skirmish. The soldiers began to cross themselves. A long string of ambulance waggons halted on the road to let us pass and followed on behind us.

III

We skirted round the village, descended, and passed over a small bridge thrown across the stream. The road led lightly to the mountain through a small thicket. Little medlar-trees, all red from the quantity of fruit, mingled with blackthorn. It was a narrow road, and not more than four men could march abreast. To the right of it gun and rifle pits had been dug out amongst the bushes, preparations in case of an attack by the Turks on Papkio.

We halted and allowed some regiment to pass us. It was the Nevsky Regiment, which had been under fire all day and was now returning to camp, as it had expended all its ammunition. So far as I can remember, its casualties that day had not been great. They marched as if worn out and tired, but with an air of gaiety and good spirits.

"What are you coming back for, mates?" we asked them. Some of them said nothing, but merely opened their empty cartridge pouches. Others replied that there were no more cartridges, that the Sofia Regiment, which was in front, had relieved them, and that the Turks had fallen back.

"Oh you!"

"Why 'Oh you'? You go yourself two days without food. Besides, there are no cartridges. A soldier without cartridges is like a pipe without tobacco," said one of the Nevsky's, knocking out his pipe. "Turn back? Yes if they came at us, but when it is a case of they firing and we firing, there's nothing in it. Chum, give me a draw."

He had a puff or two, and then ran to catch up his company.

A battery came trotting past, and we followed behind it. The sun was setting and was gilding everything. We went down into a ravine where a small stream was flowing. Ten gigantic black poplars hid the spot like a roof where we again halted. The ambulance waggons were drawn up in several rows. The doctors, dressers, and hospital orderlies were hurrying about and making preparations for bandaging. The guns were booming not far away, and became ever increasingly frequent.

Two more battalions passed us. Evidently we had been left in reserve. We were led to one side, piled arms, and laid down on ground which was covered with soft, fragrant smelling mint.

I lay on my back and gazed through the branches at the darkening sky. The giant trunks, which would have required some half-dozen men to span their girth, had shot up and thrown out branches which had interlaced with each other. Only here and there could there be seen a little star in the now blue-black sky, and far, far away they seemed, as if in the depth of some abyss from which they were peacefully grazing. The booming of guns continued, and the tops of the trees momentarily reflected the red glare which appeared immediately before each report, making them look even more terrible and dismal. There was no sound of rifle-fire. Probably it was what is known in military parlance as an artillery preparation for an attack.

I lay there half dozing; around me the men were talking quietly and with restraint. I remember now a curious circumstance which at the time did not occur to me. No one, by so much as a word, hinted at or recalled the fact that there was another world for him, with home, relatives, and friends. All appeared to have forgotten their former life. They talked about this menacing boom of cannon, why the Nevsky Regiment had gone back, and

THE ACTION AT AISLAR

why they had not had ammunition brought them. They conjectured on the strength of the Turks, and what of our force was engaged. Was it only the three regiments (Nevsky, Sofia, and Bolkhovs), or both divisions ?

"But perhaps the Eleventh Brigade will be in time also. We'll give it hot to them."

"Don't say that. Who can tell? Perhaps they have brought all their strength. If only we can hold them it will be all right. They will not ask more from us."

"Yes, that's right. Besides, they say we are not allowed to attack."

"Who told you that?"

"Ivanoff, the staff-clerk. He is a countryman of mine."

"How can your Ivanoff know?" said the man doubtfully.

The tops of the poplars commenced to pale and the leaves took on a silvery hue as they softly reflected the moonlight. The moon had risen, but we could not see it, as we were lying at the bottom of the ravine. Nevertheless, it became a little lighter. A mounted officer showed up on the brink of the ravine and shouted despairingly: "Send forward the cartridge boxes of the Sofia Regiment." But the boxes were on the opposite side of the ravine, and in spite of all his shouting his voice did not carry to the ammunition carts. One of our officers called out, "Pass the word along." Whereupon there commenced something in the nature of what musicians call a fugue. Somebody shouted "Cartridges boxes forward!" another began the same phrase as the first called out "boxes," and a third took it up when the second finished "cartridges." At any rate the slumbering ammunition carriers woke up, and, putting their horses at the gallop, crossed over the ravine.

In ten minutes' time musketry fire commenced. The ear, which at first had listened painfully to each shot, grew tired. Moreover, sleep was calling. Soon the shots became one confused roar, somewhat resembling the noise of a waterfall; then it, too, died down. I dropped asleep.

" Rise !"

The voice of our battalion commander awoke me. All got up, stretched themselves, and threw their greatcoats, which had but just served as pillows, over their shoulders.

" Take up arms !" The guns had not ceased firing. We clambered out of the ravine, and went along a wide road made by the artillery. The flashes of the shots were already nearer, and their sounds became unpleasantly loud. Immediately following the flash, which pierced the air like a needle, came a thunderous roar, after which something rang as it cut its way through the air. These were our shells, which were flying towards the gloomy precipitous heights occupied by the Turks. The gunners worked their guns silently, keeping up a continuous fire. Sometimes two guns united their roar, and two shells flew simultaneously, bursting on the slope of the mountain, right in the Turkish firing-line.

We continued to advance. It was two versts to the summit. The even and wide road had come to an end, and we entered a straggling wood all overgrown with bushes. It was difficult work, especially in the darkness, making our way through the gorse and bushes, but the men conscientiously kept their dressing. Some large stone slabs placed end up came into view. It was a Mussulman cemetery, in which were real Mahometan monuments—stones roughly hewn at the top in the form of a turban. Here we halted.

The moon lit up strongly the mountain behind which the battle was raging. At the foot of the mountain was a line of flashes—our firing-line—and above it another and thicker line—the Turkish firing-line. These lines kept intermingling. The Sofia Regiment was attacking. The upper flashes kept showing up higher and higher and farther and farther away. But we could not follow the

THE ACTION AT AISLAR

fight very long because they led us off somewhere to the flank and posted each company separately. From these points we could once more see the little flashes of flame, and the sound of these shots, as of something blunt and wooden, fell without ceasing on our ears. But soon it was more than sounds which reached us.

"S-s-s . . . s-s-s . . . s-s-s . . ." resounded in the air above us, left and right.

"Bullets!" cried someone.

"All right! Lie down. . . . They have come to die here."

It was quite true, the bullets were already spent, as can always be told by their sound. A bullet when fired at close range squeals and whistles, but when it "comes to die" merely hisses like a snake.

The bullets continued to fly around us. The company kept silent. The tense feeling which involuntarily showed itself at the sound of these heralds of death relaxed. All began to imagine that the bullets were merely flying over us or dropping harmlessly to earth. Some of the men, having taken off their great-coats, settled themselves down to sleep more comfortably, if it is possible to sleep comfortably under a shower of bullets, on ruts of dried mud, and holding a rifle in one's hands. I, too, dozed. It was a heavy, torturing slumber. Not far from us—I think in the 7th company—there was a sudden commotion. "Take him away," I heard. "Where can we take him? . . ." broke in someone. I did not hear the end of the remark. Ivan Nicolaievitch sent to find out what had happened. It appeared that a bullet which had "come to die" did not wish to die alone, and had actually buried itself in the heart of a soldier. This death caused a painful depressing impression. To be killed without seeing the enemy by a bullet which has travelled three thousand paces (two versts) seemed to all as something fateful, awful. However, little by little all became quiet, the men calmed down again, and began to doze. A not loud, harsh sound awoke everyone. A bullet had gone clean through the side of the big drum. Somebody was found even to make a joke about it, which met, however, with general disapproval. " This is no time to play the fool," growled the men.

Everyone was rather on the alert, everyone was waiting for something. A bullet found its way into the cartridge pouch of one of the men, who, pale and trembling, carried it off to show the company commander. Ivan Nicolaievitch examined the bullet attentively, and noting from its calibre that it had been fired from a Peabody and Martini rifle, moved the company into a kind of bend in the road.

Here we, notwithstanding the whistling and hissing, became calmer. Shouts of " Hurrah !" resounded on the mountain. It was the Sofia Regiment storming the position.

IV

I awoke when it was still almost dark. My sides ached unendurably. The bullets were flying as before, but now very high in the air above us. There were no flashes to be seen on the mountain, but a frequent cannonade could be heard. " It means that the mountain has been taken and the Sofia Regiment is holding the crest," I reflected.

The sun had scarcely risen when they roused us. The men got up, yawning and stretching themselves. It was cold. The majority of us were shivering and shaking as if in a fever. The companies mustered at the spring, and both our battalions (2nd and 3rd) moved off towards the mountain.

Immediately after crossing the Lom by a small bridge the road led up the mountain. At first the ascent, although all covered with bushes, was bearable, but the higher we got the steeper became the slope and the narrower the road. Finally we were compelled to clamber up one by one, sometimes helping ourselves up

THE ACTION AT AISLAR

with our rifles. The companies got mixed together with officers of another battalion; our Colonel appeared amongst us, having clambered with difficulty on to the heights. "What a brute of a mountain!" he exclaimed to his Adjutant. "How did the Sofia Regiment manage to take it?"

"It was difficult, sir," said some tiny little soldier of the 8th company.

The Sofia Regiment came down as we went forward to relieve them. Worn out by a sleepless night, by thirst and nervous excitement, they were somewhat unstrung, and made no reply to our questions as to whether there were many Turks and whether the fire was hot. Only a few said quietly, "God help you!"

At length we got to the summit of the mountain. At the last the ascent lay up an absolutely overhanging crag. Beneath it was a small ledge where the companies could reform without danger from the fire. Although the difficult ascent, the bushes, and the narrow track had absolutely mixed us up, the men re-formed and fell into their proper places extraordinarily quickly. The bullets as they flew past the ledge caterwauled above us in a piercing and extremely unpleasant manner. Here beneath the crag it was safe, but what was it like on it? Branches of the bushes growing on the crest cracked as they were smashed by the bullets, sometimes a few leaves came twirling down. We moved to the right, at first under the ledge, then little by little began to clamber up one by one from boulder to boulder. Having got round the crag, we crawled out on to the extreme summit and moved between the dense high bushes. I don't know who was leading us. All moved in the direction of the firing, pushing along with difficulty between the bushes. At last we came upon a narrow track. "Forward! Double!" Here there were lying fresh corpses, both of ours and of Turks. The wounded were already being carried along toward us. The little man of the 8th company who had so boldly entered into conversation with the regimental Colonel was now half delirious, wailing pitifully, and with one hand supporting the other, from which a stream of blood was flowing. We continued to rush forward, and at length arrived at an open space.ernt llti e Major F. was already there, walking unconcedly up and down the firing-line. "Where shall I go, Major?" I asked. He made no reply, but pointed to the left with his sword. I ran forward, throwing myself once to the ground to avoid a bursting shell. Ivan Nicolaievitch was slowly pacing up and down. tugging at his straggly hairs.

"Ivan Nicolaievitch," I called out. "I don't know where our half section is. May I join the first?"

"Go along, go along quickly!" he said, looking beyond at the Turkish line.

However, it was impossible to find either the first or second half section. Everyone had become mixed up in the wood, and it was too late to re-form under rifle and shell fire. I laid down behind the first hillock I came across and began to fire. On one side of me I found our corporal and on the other side a man of the Sofia Regiment. "You should have gone, chum," I said to him. "Your lot have gone—left this."

"Yes, but never mind, I shall stay until the end," he replied. I do not know what his name was. I do not even know whether he is still alive, but I shall always remember the enthusiastic tone of his voice.

The Turkish sharpshooters were about eight hundred paces from us, so that our rifles scarcely did them much harm. Moreover, a whole row of Turkish guns were in position from twelve hundred to fifteen hundred paces from us, and raining shell on our weak firing-line. Although bullets cause many more deaths and wounds, yet shells have a far greater moral effect. I lay, firing at intervals, and every now and then consulting Paul Ignatich (our corporal) as to the sights and whether it would not be better to fire

THE ACTION AT AISLAR

on chance at the artillery. The bullets began to whistle amongst us oftener and oftener. At last it became impossible to distinguish individual shots. It became one continuous hum. Shells came flying along screaming from afar. As they neared us they no longer screamed, but crashed and bounded along the ground, bursting and smothering us with splinters and earth. I raised myself to see what was happening in our firing-line. From time to time there arose a wild cry from amongst those lying down. Those standing behind trees would fall on to their knees sometimes with a cry, sometimes without a sound. Gabriel Vassilich, who had only just arrived, and was loading his rifle, fell headlong. A shell splinter had struck him in the stomach, tearing out his vitals. Such of the wounded as were able crawled away, for the most part silently, or perhaps it was that their groans could not be heard above the din of battle.

I began to shoot again. The Turks had collected below the deep valley, on the other edge of which was their artillery, and were advancing to attack our firing-line. The range became closer. Paul Ignatiovich kept methodically loading and firing. I, too, did not spare my cartridges, because it was easy to take aim. Dark figures with red heads coming towards us kept falling, but they still advanced. Suddenly the red heads disappeared. I do not know if it was the unevenness of the ground or the bushes which hid the columns. Having lost the near object at which to aim, I commenced once more to fire at long range into the masses standing at the bottom of the valley, and scarcely noticed that both Paul Ignatich and the soldier of the Sofia Regiment and our firing-line had disappeared. I turned round. The men had collected in groups, and were pouring a hot fire into the advancing Turks. I was alone between our men and the Turkish column.

What was I to do? This thought had scarcely flashed into my head when I heard my name called out near me.

I looked down. At my feet lay Feodoroff, the young soldier of our company who, having resided in St. Petersburg, had seized "civilization," and could express himself in an almost educated manner. Now he was lying white as this sheet of paper. A torrent of blood was flowing from his shoulder. " V. M., old man, give me a drink, carry me off, take me away," he begged piteously. I forgot everything—both Turks and bullets. For me to lift sturdy Feodoroff unaided was out of the question, and of ours there was no one, in spite of my despairing cries, who could make up his mind to race even those thirty paces to help.

Seeing an officer, the young subaltern S., I began to call out to him: " Ivan Nicolaievitch, help ! No one will come ! Help me !" Perhaps S. would have come, but a bullet laid him low. I was almost crying. . . . Finally two soldiers—I think of our company—rushed towards me. We seized hold of Feodoroff, who continued ceaselessly to cry out piteously, " Take me away, old man, for Christ's sake !" I took hold of his legs and the other two his shoulders. At the same moment they dropped him on to the ground. " The Turks, the Turks !" they yelled, bolting. Feodoroff was dead. I turned round. Twenty paces distant from me the Turkish column had halted, surprised, and frightened of our bayonets. . . .

* * * * *

A minute later something like a huge stone struck me. I fell. Blood was flowing like a stream from my leg. I remember that I suddenly recalled everything—home, relatives, and friends, and with joy reflected that I·should once more see them. . . .

THE END